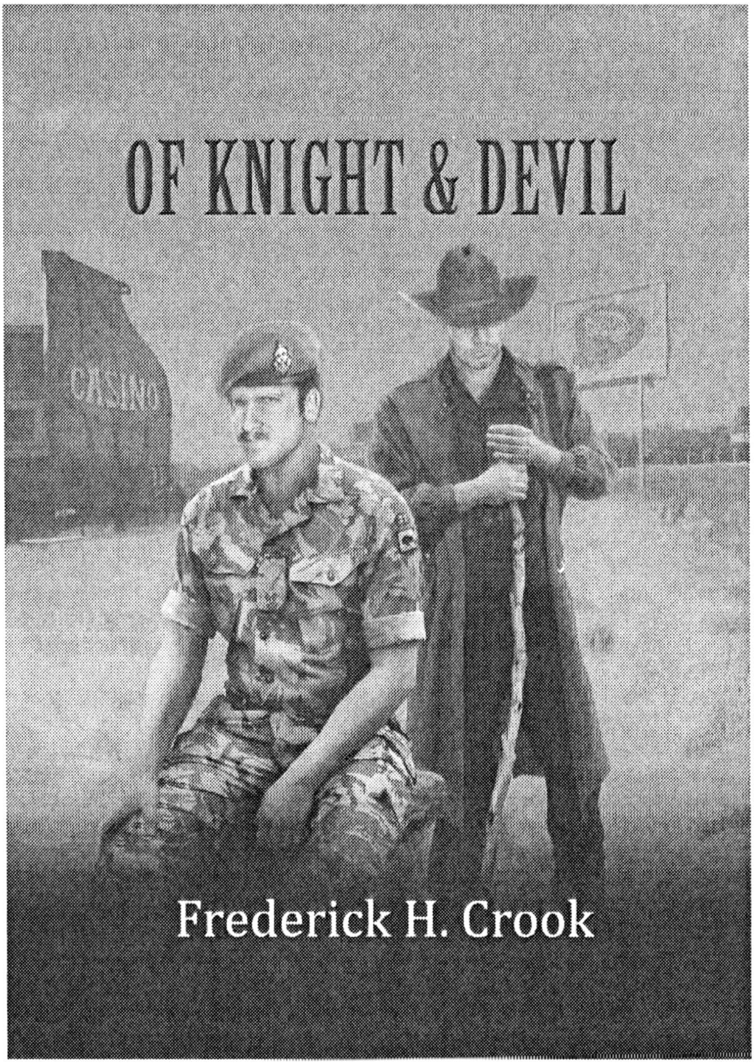
OF KNIGHT & DEVIL
CASINO
Frederick H. Crook

Cover Art:
Arvin Candelaria & Velvet Lyght of Stories By CL

http://www.storiesbycl.com/

Publisher's Note:

This is a work of fiction. All names, characters, places, and events are the work of the author's imagination.

Any resemblance to real persons, places, or events is coincidental.

Solstice Publishing - www.solsticepublishing.com

Of Knight and Devil
By
Frederick H. Crook

Dedication & Acknowledgments

I'd like to say thank you to the people of Villa Park, Illinois that have supported me over the years, and the wonderful staffs of the various establishments throughout town, especially those of the Villa Park Public Library and Cornerstone Used Books. I'd also like to thank the gents of LunaR Brewing Co. for having such a friendly place to be when I tear myself away from my computer long enough to leave the house. Cheers!

Chapter One

The long stretch of curvy road was bracketed by high rolling hills, which, at points, grew into far reaching mountains. From years of disuse and no maintenance whatsoever, the pavement was cracked, crumbled, and in places had been weathered back down to the fine sand that it once ruled over.

The wagon rolled along at its regular slow pace, which accentuated the bouncing of the vehicle as it was dragged over the uneven surface. A lone stallion, a white beauty with brown and black swathes draped over its hindquarters, midsection, and neck, was hitched at the front. It stepped along gracefully despite the summer heat and gravelly surface.

Nestled upon a seat removed from an abandoned automobile, the driver of the wagon remained in the shade afforded him by his vehicle's arched roof. He watched the road and the land beyond it with quiet diligence, passing his eyes from one side of the highway to the other. He had come to learn while traveling the roads that it paid to be observant and cautious. Many times, he would leave his movements to the night, but the necessity of water and this area's dangerous wildlife had pressed him along and dared him to venture under the hot sun.

The driver, the wagon, and the horse had been on this narrow stretch for several days. The hills had appeared the day before, adding to the human's wariness. The vigilance that the man had to show during the night as he protected his horse from the wolves and mountain lions had robbed him of valuable sleep.

Low on food and water, Reginald Mattersly hoped his good luck would return soon. The feeling in his gut was telling him that his situation was going to become worse before improving. The ridge that his wagon was approaching was not helping to put him at ease. He eyed it closely, increasing the magnification on his bio-electronic lenses for a better look. Ahead and from his right, a sandy trail joined the road. Leaning his head forward and out of the opening of his wagon's covering, he could see that the trail led north. Reginald considered taking the trail for a moment, but decided against it. Pavement, in most cases, led to the remnants of civilization, where he hoped to find what he needed. He gambled on the pavement and continued to follow it.

His trained and augmented eyes caught movement behind a small bluff in front of the foreboding ridge. He was sure of it. Mattersly unsnapped the holster of the semi-automatic handgun on his hip and locked his gaze on the area.

A head popped up over the bluff and another joined it within seconds. The first wore a cap that shared the color of the land, while the second, to the first one's left, displayed only dark and certainly dirty hair.

Reginald saw this as an ambush and jerked the reins to steer his horse to the left. Just as he did, something struck the pavement with a loud and familiar report following it. A rifle round had hit the road, having just missed the horse.

The second shot did not. His unfortunate animal took that round in the forehead and dropped dead without so much as a pained whinny.

With his military training, Mattersly wasted not a second in nostalgia or grief. He rolled backward and out of the car seat, realizing that he had turned his wagon toward someone with a sniper rifle some distance away. That person was providing cover for the bandits he had spotted at his right.

The two men opened up with small arms, filling the

air with gunfire that echoed among the steep rock formations. Many rounds struck his wagon, ringing off the thick steel framework while other shots hit the carbon fiber and Kevlar covering which made up the wagon's roof. Mattersly's electronic audio receptors dampened the reports of the shots, but not enough for him to be unable to track their direction. He unwillingly threw his trust behind the adapted body armor and retrieved his Dragunov. The sniper would have to be dealt with first as the high-powered rounds had the greatest chance of passing through the cover.

"Bloody Nora," Reginald mumbled as the balls of lead struck the cover while he readied his rifle. He dropped to his knees and gazed through the opening at the front of his wagon for signs of the sniper. The cover flailed and wavered at his right as the material absorbed the assault from his ambushers. Quickly magnifying his optics, he caught a glimpse of the man that had killed his horse. Seeing that the barrel of his weapon was now trained on the opening of his wagon, Mattersly dove to his left and landed awkwardly upon his containers of ammunition and foodstuffs.

No sooner had he done so than the sniper's bullet did tear into his wagon, filling the space where he had just been with a buzz and a lead upon steel '*thwack*!' The crack of the rifle followed in less than a heartbeat. The round struck the metal floor, poking a jagged hole through it.

Mattersly's military training dictated that action must be taken quickly. The sniper had seen Reginald's direction of travel and would most likely fire through the wagon's cover. With the Dragunov in hand, he got into a crouched position, and went to the back of the wagon. He peeled the aged Kevlar curtain open and hurriedly scanned for more ambushers behind him. Seeing nothing but the road over which he had traveled, he jumped out. The sound of his booted feet hitting the pavement was covered by the incessant and random gunfire by his ambushers. He crouched just as the anticipated follow-up shot from the sniper struck the curtain and passed through. To keep the two from the right side of the road from seeing him, Reginald stepped behind the left rear tire.

From his first glimpse of the sniper, Mattersly judged his height and distance. In his mind's eye, though his implant could have recorded it and played it back, something the military man had never quite gotten used to, he recalled his attacker's position near the top of the hill that lie on the left side of the road.

The guns of the two ambushers ceased firing. Reginald could hear them reloading and grumbling to each other. He took the opportunity and scooted to a position next to the left front tire, hoping they had taken their eyes from their target and had not seen his feet.

"Hey! You in the wagon!" one of the men shouted across the thirty-or-so meters between them and the vehicle. "Come out!"

Reginald ignored the order. It was elementary that he would do nothing that such a person would demand. It would be playing into their hands and he would simply lose his life more quickly. Instead, while the ambusher shouted ridiculous demands, Mattersly lifted the Dragunov and set it in his left hand. Though this was not his usual shooting hand, the need to conceal his position was paramount and overrode his natural shooting stance.

He leaned his wiry body against the wagon for stability and brought the Russian-made weapon to his face. One centimeter at a time, he slid the rifle into position. Through the scope, he searched for the head and shoulders of the sniper. One of the ambushers fired another round at his wagon, striking the metal frame and startling Mattersly only in the slightest bit. He accessed his implant, the

UnitCom, and reduced his hearing by the maximum his receptors could manage. He then commanded a reduction in adrenaline and a slight increase of serotonin. Taking a deep breath, he continued to look for the sniper, careful not to expose his legs to the view of the ambushers.

Movement caught Reginald's eye. The sniper was reasonably good at his job, though he really should have searched out a different position after being seen by his target. There was a reasonable wind heading to the east, so he compensated for it and released the safety. The target was just over one hundred meters away, according to the rangefinder embedded into the scope. Adjusting for that as well, Mattersly took another deep breath and held it. His target was still focused on the wagon, but it would not take long for him to notice the Dragunov peeking out from a place he did not expect.

***

The echoing gunfire made it difficult to pinpoint the direction from which it came, but the rider kept along the trail, carefully keeping his gray and white ride reigned in tight as he searched the hills for movement.

The rider considered turning around, but there was no water to be found behind him. The necessity of it carried him forward. The gunfire was fierce for a time, subsiding only long enough for the shooters to reload. It seemed one-sided, though the echoes could have been playing tricks. The trail ahead curved to the left, so the rider commanded his steed to hug the hill on that side. He edged forward until he could see a pair of men crouched behind a four-foot tall rise next to a paved road. These two men were the ones firing, but the weapons in their hands did not account for the loudest of the three distinctly different sounds. The situation seemed to be that of two men versus one, with the one being hidden up a hill and armed with a high-powered rifle.

After another few steps, however, the rider realized that his assumption was incorrect. The two men behind the bluff had their attention on a wagon that had come into his view. Just then, the powerful rifle fired again, and the launched bullet struck the rear flap on the wagon's thick hide, just above the owner of the vehicle, who had just jumped out of the back.

This man was being attacked by three men and one of them had shot the wagon owner's horse. *Bastards*, he thought and gritted his teeth.

For a few moments, he sat upon his horse, undecided on what to do, but definitely having chosen a side. He watched as the two men behind the bluff reloaded their handguns. With their eyes taken from their intended victim, they did not see their target move toward the front of the wagon along the opposite side.

The two scoundrels jabbered at each other, dismayed that their rounds were not penetrating the wagon's hide. The rider looked upon it in puzzlement, noticing the dirty black, dull skin of the thing, draped over a metal wagon painted in a green camouflage pattern.

A fourth weapon fired, disrupting the dust that had settled upon the disabled vehicle. It was another high-powered rifle and this one belonged to the would-be victim.

The horse upon which the observer sat reared and whinnied in irritation of the sound, making him grasp the horn of the saddle to remain aboard.

"Shhh! Damn it," he cussed.

When the horse came down, the rider saw that he had been noticed by the two men at the bluff. For a brief moment, all three men suffered from indecision, simply staring in disbelief and confusion. The stillness was shattered by gunfire erupting from the wagon. This weapon was different, however. The report was that of a smaller caliber and its rate of fire more rapid. The rider knew at that moment that the sniper had been taken out and the wagon man had done so with one shot. The rounds struck the rise in front of the ambushers and they took cover. Great clouds of dirt spewed through the air, but the rider could see that he had now become the easy mark. The ambushers turned their attentions and their firearms upon him.

Without further hesitation, the rider tapped his heels into the animal's side and it surged into motion. Fortunately for the man on top of it, the stallion tracked forward but to the right, sidestepping in its urgent need to move away from trouble, in direct conflict to what its smaller master was telling it to do. The ambusher closer to the man and horse took a shot and, due to this unintended maneuver, missed the target and struck the rock face behind, sending pieces of splintered pebbles everywhere.

The rider pulled his own weapon from his holster. It was a giant of a handgun with an immensely rare and powerful round, both designed for much greater distances than the barely twenty meters separating the two parties. He struggled with the reigns in his weaker right hand as his heels insisted that the horse continue forward in a gallop. His left thumb drew the heavy hammer back on the weapon and he took crude aim. Without the assistance of his military-issue bio-electronic implant, which he dared not use due to its tendency to malfunction, the shooting of these two hooligans would be difficult. Therefore, he knew that closing the distance with speed was to his advantage. This he knew also to be a double-edged sword.

Before the first shooter had a chance to try again, the rider squeezed the trigger on the miniature cannon. The explosion frightened his horse all the more, yanking his sights from the second target while the animal tracked to the right as it bucked and kicked its rear legs. It took every effort for the rider to remain in the saddle.

The shooter's first target had been found, however. The closest ambusher lay in the dirt with a ruined semblance of what used to be his cranium. The second man, shocked by the horror that lay before him, froze yet again, giving the rider time to correct his stallion with a clockwise spin, which settled in his direction.

The rider howled wildly and heeled his animal into a gallop.

***

The eruption of yet another weapon on the battlefield gave Mattersly pause. The unexpected outcome of which had virtually removed the head from the target on the right, sending a cloud of red to cover the area and the ambusher on the left. Unable to fathom his partner's violent demise, the remaining ambusher stared upon what was certain to be the body of the man. Mattersly took aim upon this third attacker when he heard a heart-stopping screech, followed by the unmistakable sound of horse hooves approaching at a mad pace.

Reginald held his fire, convinced that the area was now under attack by some members of a Native American tribe. He quickly looked about him for signs of others, but there was none. As his eyes returned to the bluff, he took in the sight of a beautiful gray horse bearing a white face and spots all about its slender body. Upon its back was a disheveled and dirty madman wearing a torn black overcoat, which flailed behind him in tails. The speed at which the horse galloped flattened the forward edge of the rider's hat against the crown. A long-barreled handgun was in the man's left hand and was leveled upon the staring ambusher, who was just now snapping out of his shock to raise his rifle.

The experienced British soldier could see that the ambusher had been too slow to react. The rider was upon him and bringing the horse to a hard stop, which lifted the dirt into the air. The ambusher had dropped out of Reginald's view, but the rider took aim and fired into the ground, not giving the man a chance to surrender. The gray and white protested at the immense sound, rising up onto its hind legs and giving a sharp, frightened whinny. The rider could not hold onto the reigns and was toppled to the ground, out of sight behind the bluff.

Reginald could not help but smile at the comical, yet horrific scene. Still, he did not drop his guard, for he knew not the intentions of the newcomer. He kept his handgun trained on the place where the man had fallen, fully expecting him to take up the attack that these three dead men had started.

At that moment, Major Mattersly's *UnitCom* chirped in his ears. He was receiving a mottled broadcast of a message from a nearby implant, delivering the "Friend or Foe" identification that one would expect to receive from a military-grade implant. The readout appeared on his lenses:

Bartel, Daniel, E-4/cpl

O/F: USAA- 82nd A/B, 504th P/PID

Reginald fought the impulse to relax upon the discovery that his would-be rescuer was of the United States Army's 82nd Airborne Division. In this post-Great Exodus world, one's being a soldier did not guarantee that one was also a gentleman. The next string of information came across as bad data:

no sync – bi/trace=.0000

vl<1.0001

no sig – datlnksrv=null

runt pulse – mlsclock trig=.000872

Mattersly shook his head in disappointment and sympathy. The term "runt pulse" indicated that his savior's bio-electronic implant was prone to malfunctions due to a bad clock on the unit's main processor. He shuddered to think of what hell the man before him suffered through.

Still, the soldier must have been of strong stuff to kill two armed ambushers through it all.

"I say!" Mattersly called. "Good show, old man! What say you show yourself, eh?"

He finished his greeting and quickly looked about him for more gunmen. There were none, though he kept his pistol trained on where his helper had fallen. The gray stallion stood by, clearly relieved over the shed weight, though it nosed the ground and the surrounding area for food or water.

"I'd love to!" the unseen rider shouted back. His voice echoed slightly against the rock formations surrounding them. "Give me a sec!"

"Are you injured, Corporal Bartel?!"

"Not exactly… and don't call me that!"

Mattersly's eyebrows popped up at that directive. *What sort of bloke would not wish to be called by his given name and rank?* "Very well! Take your time."

"Thank you!" Bartel answered.

Reginald remained quiet and vigilant as he waited for the corporal to gather himself. After a few moments, he saw a hand reach up and grasp the stirrup of his animal's saddle. The horse, in reaction to the weight on his left, began to track away to the right, dragging the rider with him. With a heavy thud, the corporal fell back to the earth.

"Are you *sure* you're all right over there?!" the Major inquired over the distance.

"Yeah! Fine!" The man grumbled and crawled to the disobedient stallion, again taking hold of the saddle and pulling himself up. "Stand still! Stupid horse!"

Major Mattersly received the impression that the man harbored no hostile intent beyond the disdain he held for his ride. He stood and replaced his handgun to his holster after setting the safety. As he waited for Bartel to recover his feet, he reloaded the Dragunov's magazine while it was securely hung from his right shoulder by its strap.

Bartel stood and limped after his animal, giving Mattersly a cursory glance over his shoulder. The corporal retrieved a walking stick from its place in the saddle and took hold of the reigns. He led the horse around the bluff and ambled toward Mattersly and his wagon while leaning heavily upon the cane at his right.

"I see they got your horse," David Bartel said and jerked his chin toward the carcass.

"Quite," Reginald agreed. "It was with one shot, so I don't believe the poor bugger suffered."

"And you returned the favor, I heard," the corporal said as he scanned the hillside from where he had heard the sniper firing. "One shot."

"Yes, well," Reginald agreed, not allowing his eyes to follow where Bartel was looking, "he was not particularly adept at hiding himself."

Bartel nodded as he approached, slack-jawed and curious. He studied Mattersly's face as he switched the large stick he was using as a cane to his left hand and struck out his right for it to be shaken. It was met with Reginald's smaller, but much stronger hand.

"You're not from around here, are ya?" David asked as he studied the wagoner's smooth features.

The man had taken care to remain clean-shaven, save for a well-groomed mustache. His cheeks were strong and his chin prominent. His eyes were a steady and penetrating blue. Upon the man's head was a military-style boonie hat, which featured a small curtain that hung to cover the back of the man's neck. Mattersly wore an army tunic, buttoned not all the way to the top and with the sleeves folded up, rather than simply rolled. His trousers matched the camouflaged pattern of the tunic and were tucked into his dusty black military boots. The only thing that didn't appear to belong on the man was the boonie, only because it was of a slightly different camouflage pattern.

"I am not." The man smiled reservedly as he shook the offered hand. "I am Major Reginald Mattersly, British Army, Special Reconnaissance Regiment."

"Really?" Bartel replied as his eyebrows disappeared into the crown of his dirty black cowboy hat. He could not help but be impressed. His own unit had been considered elite, but the SRR division of the British Army, an extenuation of the Special Air Service was even more so. "I'm Elias. Elias Mulhaney."

The mismatching names took Mattersly aback and his hand halted the shake though it arrested Bartel's. He studied the supposed soldier's uneven face suspiciously.

"I don't understand. Your 'link' indicated the name was David…"

"Yeah, I don't use that name. The rank, neither," Bartel/Mulhaney spoke indignantly. He was at a disadvantage. His weakened right hand was not strong enough to break free of the Brit's grip if he fought him, so he made it a point not to try. "They kicked me off Fort Bragg 'cause I stole a little food. I was hungry."

"I see," the major said with a hint of distaste. "You've come quite a distance since then. Have you suffered a stroke?"

"Yes, I have," Elias/David shrugged, happily disengaged from the handshake. "I lost much of the feeling on my right side a long time ago. I don't remember when it was, 'cause this thing forgot how to keep track of time." He tapped his temple to indicate the implant. "I'm fairly sure this thing caused it."

"Ah, well, that's quite possible," Reginald agreed. "In what way is it malfunctioning?"

"It turns itself on and off, which is why you were

able to read my ID and then it was gone again. Sometimes it sends loud noises to my audio receptors and sometimes it plays back bits of a satellite show on my optics."

"Let me venture a guess as to which one. *Mulhaney*?"

"Oh, you know that one, huh?"

"I dare say I do."

"Oh, well I still like that name better, so I'm using it."

"By all means, Corporal. If you wish…"

"And I don't like bein' called *that,* either!" the man formerly known as David announced.

"Very well, *Mister* Mulhaney," the major pronounced distinctly. He changed the subject, keeping the strange newcomer's hands in sight as he stepped around him to have a closer look at the horse. "I have some grass and water in the wagon. Let me refresh this creature," he said as he patted the animal's white face. "What is his name?"

"Name? I didn't name him," Mulhaney said with an air of incredulity.

"Really? Hmm," Reginald mumbled as he stepped to the back of the wagon.

"Don't tell me *you* had a name for *him*?" Elias said as he pointed to the deceased equine.

"I did."

Elias tugged the reigns of his gray stallion and tied them to a loop at the rear of the wagon. He watched as his new acquaintance brought out thick handfuls of wild grass from a burlap sack. Mattersly hand-fed the starving animal until it caught on, then dropped the rest near his feet. The horse ravenously devoured the pile.

"Do I dare ask what you named it?" Mulhaney asked as he stood back and leaned heavily onto the cane.

Reginald dipped a pail into a barrel and brought out

some water. He jumped down from the wagon and carried it to the horse, placing it on the ground and holding it in both hands. "Do you honestly care to know?"

"Sure."

"Very well. I called *him*, Ernest Lumley the Third," the major said once he turned to look up at Elias.

Mulhaney smiled toothily. "Cute. He was your third horse?"

"Actually, no," Mattersly answered as he returned to the water barrel. He noticed that David/Elias was eying the barrel intensely. "This one was only my second. The original Ernest Lumley was a childhood friend back home in England. You may help yourself to water, of course."

"Thanks," Mulhaney granted and hoisted himself inside the wagon. After a quick search, he found a metal cup hanging from the barrel by a string. He gave the cup a quick glance to make sure it looked relatively clean, saw that it was, and dipped it into the barrel. It was a far reach to the bottom, but he managed to fill the cup. Elias closely scrutinized the water, giving it a sniff, a visual inspection, and a tiny sip before upturning the contents into his mouth without his lips touching the cup. It had been two days since he had taken in water, so he knew not to take much more than that one cup for the time being. It was too dark to see into the barrel for the thickness of the wagon's cover, but one shake of the container told him it was close to empty.

"Yes," Reginald spoke abruptly, startling the man inside his wagon, "I am quite low, Mister Mulhaney, so do please drink sparingly."

"Yes, sir," he answered, "I see that." Elias replaced the barrel's cover, hopped out and sauntered to his somewhat happier horse. He realized that he was under close scrutiny by the Brit. He stood for a moment, silently leaning on his cane as he pat his horse along the snout.

"What?" he asked of the SRR soldier.

"I'm just contemplating, Mister Mulhaney," the major said as his brilliant blue eyes locked with Elias's muddy browns. "I can't help but wonder about your motivations when you decided to join the fight against these blaggards."

The question was serious, but the major's manner of rolling his 'r's at every opportunity put a crooked smile on Mulhaney's face. It was the only type he could muster since the stroke, even though his condition had been improving over a period of what seemed to him as many months.

"What's amusing you, Corporal?" Major Mattersly snapped.

The smile disappeared. "I told you not to call me that."

"Well, then tell me why you interfered. Did you have designs on stealing my wagon for yourself?"

"Oh… no," Elias stammered, derailed by the unexpected question. He imagined having to pull his revolver on this man and prepared himself. Not a natural left-hander, Bartel/Mulhaney figured that the British officer had the advantage.

"Then what? Tell me!"

"I was just ridin' by, Major. I could see what was happnin' 'n' I didn't like the odds."

"What?"

"Three against one, jus' don't seem right."

Mattersly shuffled his feet and squinted in thought. "Do you mean to tell me that you involved yourself in a gun battle without considering the circumstances?"

"Well, they kind of forced me into it."

"Ah. I see," Reginald conceded. He could understand being caught between two fighting factions. It was the story of his life, had he spoken of it. He had noted that one of the ambushers had fired in the direction that the former soldier had come from, which had naturally drawn the man to return hostilities. “So, now what, Mister Mulhaney?”

Elias thought for a moment and allowed himself to relax. His horse nuzzled him in the shoulder, still looking for more food, water, or perhaps merely attention. “Well, you’re in need of a horse… and this one’s in need of a name,” he replied and chuckled.

Mattersly allowed himself to crack a smile. “Indeed.”

***

The bodies of the ambushers were inspected for useful things and left where they lay, as was the carcass of Ernest Lumley III. There was no practicality for proper burials. The two men were short of water and food, and the dead flesh would serve to distract predators from the wagon.

It was decided that the men would continue their travel in the direction that they both had been heading. Mulhaney assured Mattersly that there was no food or water to be found in the direction from which he had come. Considering the slightly emaciated state of both the man and his gray horse, Reginald found no reason to disbelieve him. Further, since he knew the trail that he had left behind, the major found no alternative other than to press forward.

Mulhaney’s stallion tugged the wagon as best he could, but the going was slow, much slower than the late Ernest Lumley III had been capable. The major blamed neither man nor animal, for it was simply the condition that prevailed.

For a time, Elias rode at the back of the wagon, covering their sluggish escape with his newly acquired weaponry, peeking past the drawn curtain of body armor like a teenager spying on a neighbor girl. He inspected the bolt-action rifle closely as he rode and watched, working to familiarize himself with the weapon. It was in very good condition, considering its age. The stocks were of plastics that were bleached gray from the sun. The receiver was well-oiled and had a newer look to it than the rest of the rifle. He cycled the action several times and found that it functioned smoothly. The scope mounted to its top was not particularly powerful, but it was rugged.

Additionally, the pair had recovered a lever-action rifle of pistol caliber and a semi-automatic handgun from the two ambushers from the bluff. None of the three dead men had much beyond that other than some canteens of water, which Mattersly had allowed the horse to drink.

Hills lay on either side of the weathered roadway. After a few curves had been traversed, neither man could see anything in the distance other than the hills. As one gently passed out of sight, several more took its place. There was almost no breeze and the sky was bereft of merciful cloud cover. The heat of the day settled into the wagon and thusly, into the men themselves.

Mattersly drove on, contemplating his new acquaintance. Reginald understood that the man's horse was required to see himself and the wagon out of these wretched hills and mountains and he was, therefore, grateful. The major also contemplated the danger of having an armed stranger behind him and for a time had kept tabs on the man, turning around every couple of minutes to make sure he was not up to anything. Elias had appeared vigilant at the rear, not appearing to take his eyes from the hills they were slowly leaving behind.

After a time, both men became drowsy. The slow pace and meter of the horse's clopping hooves, the heat and the dwindling effects of adrenaline were taking their toll. Reginald noted countless places where other ambushes could be set up and where a sniper could take a position to get a clear shot into the front of the wagon, but he noted not a living soul. Despite the danger, their drowsiness continued.

"Say, Major," Elias addressed, shattering the near silence. "Your 'plant works, right?"

Mattersly recovered quickly from being startled and had hoped he had not shown that it had occurred. "My implant? Yes, it's fully functional."

"What time is it?"

Reginald thought the command for the *UnitCom* to display the time on his lenses. "It is nearly thirteen-thirty hours."

"What day? What's the date, I mean?"

"Wednesday, July the fifth."

"Wow. The day after Independence Day," Mulhaney muttered.

"Ah, yes. Quite so," Reginald remarked. "I'm surprised any of you Yanks still remember that insurrection and its meaning."

Elias chuckled. "Cute. Hey, I know this next question may sound funny…"

"It is twenty-one thirty, Mister Mulhaney," Mattersly offered.

"Oh, wow," Elias mumbled and gave another long gaze into the sunny hills from the back of the wagon.

"What year did you think it was?"

"I wasn't sure. My implant can't keep track anymore," he said with a trace of melancholy. "It's been a couple years at least."

The heat within the wagon had risen over time. Mulhaney removed his thin duster, revealing his torn, sweat-stained t-shirt. He noted the look of mild mistrust from the Brit, who had detected unexpected movement.

"Don't worry, Major," the man calling himself Elias Mulhaney said as he sat down. "I wouldn't have stopped those men from killing you if all I wanted was your wagon."

"I'm beginning to believe that, Mister Mulhaney."

"You can call me Elias."

"Indeed," Reginald returned through a sardonic smile that his passenger could not see.

In time, the hills that had tightly hugged the right side of the road receded into the distance. On the left was a ridgeline that appeared to Mattersly as if it terminated not too far ahead. Beyond that, directly in front of them, lay what appeared to be a mountain range, though he could not determine the true size of the land feature, never mind the distance.

The ridge on their left also fell away behind, and the wagon emerged into a plain, bracketed by hills that could very well have been mountains. Without satellites to support his implant's GPS system, their location was merely guesswork unless street signs or landmarks became apparent. Reginald leaned forward in his seat and peered in both directions, augmenting his vision for distance as far as the lenses could stretch.

The cracked blacktop bent to a continuous, gentle curve to the left and the land dipped into a slight decline, thus, their pace quickened. After some long minutes, the road straightened and the land flattened out. All the while, Reginald kept his eyes passing over the land for any signs of trouble. A noise from behind him took his attention.

It was Corporal Bartel, slumped in the corner with his head lying at an uncomfortable angle against the water barrel. His newly found rifle lay on the floor next to him. The sound was the man snoring. Mattersly thought to wake him and chide the man, but he could not bring himself to do it. He was in far worse shape than himself, physically. Reginald knew they needed to find water quickly.

***

Reginald brought the wagon to a stop at the remnants of a "T" intersection. Reaching back and to his left for his open backpack, he removed a small black box. He unsnapped it and pulled a pair of binoculars from inside. Though his military grade bio-electronic lenses could magnify up to five times, the binoculars were superior and could save his implant power. Reginald sat with his elbows on his knees and scanned the road to their left, which stretched into infinity to the south. There was nothing to be seen other than the plain and the bracketing hills which the strip of blacktop cut through. Looking ahead, Reginald could see little difference, though it was clear that the road continued on a mild decline.

"Be water, my friend," Mattersly mumbled to himself and smiled.

"What was that?" his now awakened passenger said from behind and alongside him.

Reginald did not start in the least, for he had detected the man's movement well before his arrival at the front of the wagon. He chuckled and urged the horse straight on. "It was something I picked up years ago from a martial artist that was once world famous."

Elias poked his head into the open and looked about, assessing the situation for himself. "What does it mean?"

Reginald looked to his new passenger and recited from the archives of his implant, "'Be like water making its way through cracks. Do not be assertive, but adjust to the object, and you shall find a way around or through it. If nothing within you stays rigid, outward things will disclose themselves.' Bruce Lee said that."

"Uh-huh," Elias nodded and relaxed. "Well, if that means follow the path of least resistance, I'm all for it."

"Splendid."

The wagon rolled on and Mulhaney shifted to the

rear of it, using the scope on the rifle to scan the land they were leaving behind. Despite their thirst and discomfort, both men agreed in their shared quiet, that the land was brilliantly beautiful. The sun had become partially obscured by streaks of white and gray clouds, easing the intensity of the summer heat. After a short distance, the major halted the wagon again.

"I'll be damned," he mumbled and gazed upon the land ahead through his binoculars.

"What is it, now?" Elias inquired as he buffaloed his way to the front, sending the wagon rocking back and forth.

"I say, old man. Do step lightly," Mattersly admonished. He had taken the frame of the antique scope to the bridge of the nose.

"Sorry," Mulhaney offered.

"There are some buildings ahead," the major narrated. "Light industrial by the look of it. Warehouses, perhaps." He let the binoculars hang around his neck and urged the gray and white stallion forward again. The animal complied, but protested with an elongated grunt. "I will proceed slowly, as if we have not already been doing so, but I dare say you should remain vigilant. We could be approaching the ambushers' place of origin."

"Got it."

They pressed on at such a slow pace that the horse barley needed to apply much effort. The decline of the road was enough to keep the wagon rolling. Mattersly watched the buildings closely, intent on searching for movement. It soon became clear that the series of buildings lay on the right side of the road, which now began to widen beneath them. A faded double-yellow line could be seen, delineating the path of traffic that no longer existed. Further on, the road flattened, putting the horse in complete charge of the vehicle's momentum.

"Another intersection," Mattersly muttered, not taking his eyes from behind the binoculars.

A few minutes later, Elias could see it for himself. Crumbling concrete guardrails delineated the farthest side of the intersection. Clearly, they were intended to keep larger vehicles from falling into the ditches at either side. After the intersection, the white guardrails continued to bracket the road. It soon became evident, once the wagon came within a few meters of the crossroad, that a highway ran underneath the road upon which they traveled. The buildings Mattersly had spotted were on the other side. Faceless road signs met them there. Not a letter or a number remained discernible.

As they began to cross, the men peered both ways. The highway below was three lanes wide in each direction. To the south, the pavement stretched out as true as an arrow until it passed out of sight. To the north, the pavement did the same, though it angled gently leftward some miles on. Beyond the place where even assisted eyes could make out lay a mountain range. It was certain that the roadway must yield to it at some point.

"Look there," the man calling himself Mulhaney indicated ahead with a pointing finger. "Cargo containers for trucks."

"Indeed," agreed the SRR soldier. "Lots of places for men to hide. Please remain sharp, Mister Mulhaney."

"Yes, Major," Elias agreed and brought the rifle to bear. He scanned the facility ahead for movement of any kind, but only the trees gathered his attention as the breeze had its way.

The gray and white stallion tugged the wagon past the next intersection. Mulhaney counted more than a dozen of the trailers in a lot. They had once been a different color from the others, but all had faded and rusted, making them appear identical from a distance.

As they approached the facility, it became clear that it, like countless places that both men had encountered previously, was long abandoned and most likely good for nothing but a brief stay out of bad weather. Mattersly kept the wagon on the road once they arrived at the entrance to the lot, though it was here that he stopped. He removed his boonie, ran his hand through his blondish-white hair, and scratched at his mustache in thought.

"Some sort of processing plant," the major opined lowly then pointed toward a structure that struck out above the others in the distance to the north. "That building processed and off loaded whatever it was into these trucks. The material was brought in by train," Reginald concluded as he pointed toward the tracks ahead of them.

"Mmmhmm," Elias agreed, "I doubt that there's anything in there we need."

"I agree," Reginald said and scanned the street ahead. "There appears to be a road sign." With that, he urged the horse onward. They crossed the long-unused tracks. It was tricky for the gray equine, for the pavement had buckled and crumbled around the warped iron. The wagon shifted and bounded across. The nearly empty water barrel threatened to tip over, but did not.

The sign stood upon a singular post, which was bent nearly twenty degrees to the north. Mulhaney tilted his head to read the word along the top, but he could not.

"Love…lock," the major said before they reached the "T" intersection. "In that direction," he indicated the south with his left hand.

"Uh-huh," Elias grunted. The rest of the sign was mostly obliterated by time and weathering. The name of the street was 'Something' Valley Rd. The name of the town that an arrow indicated was to their north was wiped from the sign's surface.

"Well, then Cor…er, Mister Mulhaney," Mattersly

spoke up with an air of optimism, "I dare say we should travel to this Lovelock and see what there is to see."

"Sounds good, Major," Elias agreed.

Mattersly urged the horse onward, left around the corner and down the road. This path was wider, but no less wrecked by time and erosion than any other. The wagon bounced sporadically as it passed over the edgy surface. The 'Something' Valley Road paralleled the train tracks on their left. Elias eyed them as they went along, mesmerized by the snaky twisting and bending the rusted rails had taken on over time. They passed a street that led to a rather expansive and broken down structure. Mulhaney eyed the building, which appeared to have been one floor high and pondered its purpose. There was no discussion between the men about whether or not they would inspect it. The wagon rolled on southward.

The ancient two-lane road was decorated with the remnants of man's past. The occasional telephone pole struck out into the sky, each one challenging the others that had not yet fallen, despite their long-lost cause. They passed a small relay station, nothing more than a few large boxes at the side of the road. One of which was barely taller than a man and had once been painted white. It was now broken and filthy with age. It was just beyond here that Mattersly stopped the wagon and gave the horse the balance of their remaining water and more grass to eat.

Reginald met Elias's eyes after he set the empty barrel back inside the wagon. Mulhaney nodded and lifted an eyebrow. The pair spoke not a word as the gray and white stallion swallowed everything it could get from the bucket.

The road took on a rightward bend and the late afternoon sun beamed into their faces. Elias leaned back into the seat and tilted the brim of his hat downward, as did Mattersly, though the Brit had the added benefit of lenses that could filter out much of the light. Also adjusting for distance, Reginald thought he could see railings on either side of the road ahead, indicating a bridge. As they went along and the railings drew nearer, it became certain that the land was too shallow to pass another roadway underneath the bridge.

Mattersly stopped the wagon. It was an abrupt halt, nearly upsetting Mulhaney's balance.

"What the hell?" Elias protested.

"Quiet. Listen," the major directed and fell silent.

In a moment, the former American soldier picked up on it. "Water!"

The wagon was again thrown into motion and halted upon the small bridge. Both men took in the sight of the gloriously green water. It flowed gently underneath them and off to the south where it passed underneath the small railroad trestle about seventy meters from where they stopped.

"What do you think, Major?" Elias Mulhaney asked as he hopped down to the road's surface. He leaned on his staff and looked up at the SRR man expectantly. He had left his rifle in the wagon.

"We must not abandon all caution, Mister Mulhaney," Reginald said as he pointed into the distance ahead of them. "There are buildings just ahead. We have no idea whether or not there are hostiles."

Elias followed Reginald's finger. In the distance were blurs of objects beyond some scattered trees. Without activating his unpredictable bio-electronic implant, Mulhaney was unable to make it out clearly. He did not belabor the point. It had been well made. Before he could reach back into the wagon for his rifle, Mattersly had retrieved his Dragunov and was scanning the buildings through its scope.

Mulhaney waited silently and patiently. Reginald

slowly traversed his torso to his left. After more than a minute, the Brit slung the rifle over his shoulder and retreated within the shade of the wagon. He exited from the rear, dragging a pair of empty buckets with him.

"Mister Mulhaney, if you would guard the wagon, I will replenish our water supply."

"Yes, sir," Elias agreed and reached inside for his rifle. He stood alongside his tired horse and petted it as he stood watch.

Reginald took three trips to fill the barrel halfway. He had fashioned a filtration system out of sand, rocks, and a pan with holes in the bottom. He poured each bucket through this pan, thereby removing many impurities. The process was quite slow, but in less than thirty minutes, the water was processed.

"The water looks well enough," Mattersly announced, "but we shall have to boil it to be sure. There are fish in the river. Trout, I believe."

"I was hoping you'd say that," Elias said cheerily and descended to the riverbank, where Mattersly had drawn the water. Mulhaney shed his battered, dirty boots. The major noticed that the man possessed no socks and wondered how healthy his feet could have been, unprotected as they were to the tortures of the thick leather. Elias then disrobed down to his threadbare boxer shorts and, retrieving a large, matte black blade from a trouser pocket, waded into the green water, relying heavily on his walking stick. He stepped further into the water and went still, waiting for one to wander close.

It did not take very long for Elias to catch two fish. He had struck quickly, despite his weakened right side. He speared them with the combat knife and plucked them from the water. Both of the trout struggled terribly but briefly and did not take long to die once they had been tossed to the shore. After that, Mulhaney bathed himself, dousing his head under the surface while holding his hat above it.

Mattersly scanned the land around them, keeping watch over his vulnerable new friend. Elias retrieved his clothing, but instead of dressing, he washed the items in the water, save for the boots. He returned to the wagon, draped his clothes over his saddle, and retrieved another set from his bags.

"Here!" Reginald called from inside. In his hand, he held a bundled pair of olive drab socks. He tossed them to Elias.

"Hey! Thanks!" Mulhaney returned and sat on the guardrail to put them on. "You should take the opportunity, Major. I haven't had a bath for… well, I'm not sure."

"I think I shall," the major answered. He hopped from the wagon and headed down to the water. Unlike the American, the SRR soldier toted his rifle to the water's edge with him along with a small bag. He returned some minutes later with his hair still wet, carrying the two trout with him. He had changed into nearly identical clothing.

"So, where are you from?" Elias asked out of the blue. "I know you're British, but… you know."

"I was born in Westminster. That's in London. You?"

"Indiana. Just outside of Indianapolis."

"Ah. I've not traveled that far north since I've been here in the States," Reginald explained as he eyed the structures up the road. "I've reckoned a general idea of our location from the rather dated map service on my device," he tapped his finger on his temple.

Elias nodded in understanding. "With mine being on the fritz, I don't even wanna try turning the damn thing on."

"I don't blame you," Mattersly said. "Well, I've found we are on 'Upper Valley Road'." The major turned to his left and swept a pointing finger from east to southeast. "The interstate that we crossed is 'I-80'."

"And up ahead is Lovelock?"

"Correct," confirmed the major. "Finding that sign was fortuitous."

"Ow!" Mulhaney shouted and his hands flew to his temple. His eyes were shut hard as if reacting from pain.

"What the devil? I say, old man," Reginald was alarmed but his voice portrayed utter calm.

Corporal Bartel's *CTL-Link* had activated without being summoned. Abruptly, loudly, and from both audio implants, a high-pitched tone emanated, keeping his ears from hearing anything else. David/Elias recognized the sound as being a piece of music that he had uploaded to the device more than a decade before. The malfunctioning implant had initiated and immediately slipped into playback mode, randomly choosing the piece to play, the volume at which to play it, and then promptly froze and repeated a short, second-long loop.

"Oh! Oooow! Shut down… shut down!" the corporal seethed. Though the implants were not designed to take verbal commands, speaking the demand had grown to be a habit with the man.

"Are you all right, Corporal Bartel? *Bartel*!" the major demanded more urgently. He feared the man was having another stroke. His complexion had turned a deep red and he was clearly in distress.

Bartel/Mulhaney turned from Mattersly in embarrassment and stepped to the middle of the road. As he looked up to the sky, the tone mercifully silenced. The faulty implant did not shut down as commanded, however. Instead, a rectangular view opened in his sightline and a file began to play. It was an episode of the holovision western, *Mulhaney*. David shut his eyes tightly against the sun to bring his childhood hero to solidity. There was no way to rid his view unless the implant would acquiesce to the shutdown command. It seemed that it would not. Bartel put his face to the armored fabric cover of the wagon and waited it out, hoping that it would be over quickly.

The scene unfolding before him was a wilderness at night. The wind howled and the sky flashed to a brightness that rivaled the sun. Thunder immediately followed each flash. The sound covered the voice of Reginald who spoke to him from his side.

"Corporal?" Mattersly pressed then changed his tack. "*Mister* Mulhaney. I say, can you hear me?"

David heard only the clopping of Elias Mulhaney's horse, named Chips, the wind, and the thunder. From the right of the screen his hero emerged, riding the white and gray horse. They had yet to be rained upon, but the wind was tormenting the both of them. A guest character rode along with him. David could not remember the name.

"*We've got to get outta this!*" the guest character shouted as he tried to control his startled horse.

"*Yup! It's gonna come down on us any second!*" Elias answered in kind. The camera angle changed to view the two riders from the front. Both men were struggling against the wind, holding their hats tight upon their heads to keep them on. "*There! Up ahead! That barn! Let's go!*"

The two riders galloped toward the barn in the distance as they dodged wind-thrown branches and leaves. The rain began to fall in torrents, drenching the men and horses as they twisted through the trees on either side of the narrow trail. Mulhaney arrived at the barn door first and tore it open, allowing the younger man through before quickly leading his horse inside. It was here that the playback ended. The implant had finally acknowledged the command to shut down.

Bartel/Mulhaney blinked hard and stood straight as he leaned fully on his walking stick. He took a deep breath and let it out slowly. His ears rang from the assault.

"Are you all right?" Mattersly inquired lowly from his right side, a meter or so away.

"Whew. Yes, Major," Elias answered as he regained his composure. "Season one, episode two. *The Driven Storm.*"

"What was that?"

Elias smiled as he breathed through his mouth. His lightly drooping eyelid twitched as he explained. "Implant malfunction, sir. At first, there was a screeching tone, then a scene from a holovision show. I know *Mulhaney* well. The series, that is."

"I see." Mattersly tried to sound sympathetic, but the incident had created much doubt within the SRR soldier. Reginald decided that, despite the corporal's actions earlier, his physical condition and the incapacitating implant bugs made Bartel a liability rather than an asset.

"Well, I know that you don't, Major," the ailing man began as he met the Brit's gaze, "but we've got to find shelter."

"Indeed," scoffed Mattersly. "Always a good idea, Corporal. There's no revelation there."

"I told you, *don't call me that*!" David shouted and pointed to his temple. "There's a bad storm coming, I've seen it. I know!"

"Now, see *here*, *Corporal* Bartel!" the major thundered. "I've had damned enough of this bloody 'Mulhaney' nonsense! I've seen your military registration and your name is David Bartel! Rank, Corporal!"

Bartel turned abruptly, spinning away from the SRR officer and striking off heavily toward his horse. "I'm not a soldier anymore, Major," he called over his shoulder. "I was dishonorably discharged, so I can call myself whatever the hell I want, and you are not my CO in any case!"

"That may very well be, Bartel or Mulhaney or whomever you bloody well wish to call yourself, but I have no intention of allowing you to dictate my actions based on some randomly generated vision created by your dodgy implant!"

"Fine! Then unhitch my horse!"

"We need it for the wagon!"

"It's not my wagon!" Bartel fired back.

"How will you carry food and water without it?" Mattersly insisted on finding out as he followed the corporal around the horse's nose.

"I've done pretty well this far!"

"You haven't! Look at this poor animal," the major directed and patted the horse's neck. "The bloody thing's emaciated. He won't be able to pull this wagon for much longer."

"Right! So, let's get shelter!"

"I'm not charging into an unscouted town simply because you received some ridiculous vision of disaster." The major stood his ground. "We will proceed with caution and by the numbers under my guidance."

"Really?" Mulhaney spat hotly and turned his eyes to the sky in frustration. He saw something and froze.

"Yes, really," Mattersly droned on. "I've not made it this far into my life by associating with… why the bloody hell are you laughing?"

Elias continued his harsh chuckle and merely pointed to the southwest. The irritated Brit followed the finger and found a darkened sky had encroached upon the horizon and settled between two distant mountain ranges. As they watched, flickers of lightning lit the patch of darkness and the two men felt the first gusts of wind upon their faces. There was no doubt that the storm was heading for them.

"Damn," Mattersly calmly pronounced.

"See? Can we move on now?"

"It would seem wise, Bartel."

"Mulhaney," he let the word drip from his mouth.

"Oh, very well, *Mister* Mulhaney," the major returned with a sardonic tone. "Under the circumstances, I think we should turn back and seek shelter within that processing plant we passed."

"No, Major," Elias disagreed, "we go on. There's shelter up ahead."

Reginald grunted in disbelief. "You're not going to tell me that you're going to believe an illusion brought forth by a faulty implant."

"I am, sir," Mulhaney said as the climbed up to the wagon. The feat was not easy, considering his weakened right side, but he accomplished it and settled upon the driver's seat. He set his walking stick down at his side and slid the rifle from his shoulder. "You drive and I'll keep watch."

"Now see here!"

"Hurry, Major!" he interrupted. "There's little time to argue. That lightning looks bad."

With one last look over his shoulder, Mattersly could see that his companion was correct. The wind was cool and intensifying by the minute and already, the dark clouds had become larger. "We will be driving into it," he called over his shoulder even as he walked around the gray and white speckled horse.

"It's not far," Mulhaney answered absently as his attention was funneled through the rifle's scope. "We need to get going, Major."

Mattersly settled upon the driver's seat next to the American and took up the reigns. "Indeed," he muttered.

The wagon rolled onward, being towed along by the partly refreshed stallion. They soon came to another "T" intersection. This road joined Upper Valley Road from their right. Elias leaned forward and stared as they rolled on. The adjoining road stretched on into infinity, disappearing long before the mountain range beyond it.

"So, what do we do if we encounter hostiles?" Elias thought to ask as the buildings ahead became clearer.

"It has always been my intent to avoid encounters entirely," Reginald quipped.

"Really?" the ex-army soldier spoke as if it were more of a statement than a question. He followed it up with another. "You have no interest in finding a friendly settlement?"

"I've only known one settlement to be friendly," Mattersly returned flatly. "It couldn't sustain itself."

"I see," Mulhaney mumbled. "By the way, I've decided to name my horse, 'Chips'."

"Ah. A bit undignified, but I understand the reference."

The road angled slightly to the southwest and it was soon obvious that the storm was intense. The trees on either side of the road swayed as the wind slapped at their trunks and branches. The air carried many of the leaves away, some of them into the faces of the travelers. The smell of rain filled their noses.

The home that they had focused upon was smaller than it had appeared. It lay within a small grove of trees just around twenty meters from the road. As they approached, however, it became certain that it would be of little use due to damage incurred from previous storms. At least two of the trees had been brought down upon the structure, collapsing the western side of the house. The single garage alongside the home had been similarly destroyed. The wind continued to batter the loose fragments of roofs and shutters.

Mulhaney noticed the look of intense irritation upon the wagon driver's face, but he gave the major no time to speak. "Up ahead there! Off the main road! A barn!"

Mattersly urged the horse to go faster, saying

nothing about the possibility that the homes just beyond the barn could very well have been inhabited and that someone might not take well to their sudden arrival. The worsening conditions helped convince the Brit to bring this up at a later time.

The wagon rolled forward and more quickly than it had all day, despite or perhaps due to, the increased pressures from the storm. Mulhaney said nothing, being too busy looking over the homes he could see through his scope, but he knew his stallion was skittish in bad weather.

Without hesitation, Mattersly guided the horse into a tight right turn at the next opportunity. This pavement was in much worse condition than Upper Valley Road, but it led to the white and rust colored structure that Mulhaney had pointed out. The wagon bounded and shook to the point where Elias could no longer use the scope to watch the buildings ahead of them for signs of movement. As the rain began to fall, the horse stumbled on the loose ground, recovered, and went on. Items in the wagon rumbled and rattled, but the rain striking the wagon cover and the ground drowned out the sound.

The sky flashed through the curtain of rain and the thunder strike immediately followed, startling the two men and the horse, which at the moment was in the middle of a slight right turn onto a gravel driveway. From what Mattersly and Mulhaney could determine, the aluminum or perhaps fiberglass structure was in good shape. As Reginald brought the horse and wagon to a stop, not without effort as the animal found great energy through panic, Elias hopped from the wagon and ran to the barn door. He unlatched it, gave a quick scan of the interior, and pushed the great wooden doors out of the way.

Reginald stood out of the way as the horse scampered inside, stopping once it reached the middle of the floor. Lightning flashed, revealing to Mattersly that the place was more of a shed than a barn and that it was empty, save for a dirty concrete floor and a small collection of hand tools set against the wall. Another round of thunder struck nearby, shaking everything about them. The roar of the rain made it impossible for either man to hear the other. Reginald set the brake as Elias shut and barred the doors, encasing them in noisy darkness.

Mattersly had predicted this and had activated his *UnitCom* and set his lenses for darkness. He jumped down as he patted the frightened horse and made smooth calming noises in an attempt to take the animal's mind off what was happening outside.

Mulhaney moved from the door as he was still getting wet by the driven rain, which seemed to drill its way through the poorly fitting wooden panels. The lightning was rapidly successive as was the thunder. The blue-white light that found its way through the cracks lit his way to finding the wagon.

"There's nothing in here to stumble upon, Mister Mulhaney," Reginald said in between thunderclaps.

Elias stepped toward the voice. With another successive flurry of lightning, he could make out the major's calm face. The air had cooled at least twenty-five degrees and with the cold rain, Mulhaney replaced his duster and hat. He sidled past Mattersly, keeping a hand on the wagon to help guide him on his way to his frightened steed.

"Come on now, Chips," he spoke loud enough to be heard over the drumming rain and rumbling thunder as he patted the stallion's face and neck. Still attached to the wagon, the weakened but still powerful animal bucked against the tethers and hitch. "It's okay," he murmured over and over.

Mattersly wandered about the shed. There was no hay, no lofts, and no workbenches. There was built-up dirt in the corners, suggesting that it had been a long time since anyone had cleaned the mess made by bad weather. He could make out a gap along the bottom of the doors that allowed the hard-driven rain inside. He flinched when another flash of lightning permeated the room. His implant compensated quickly for the disparity in light levels, but it lagged behind, only able to react to the flash, not predict it.

The tools along the wall were a mixture of shovels, spades, and rakes, all rusty enough to give the impression that they had not budged from their resting place in many years. Moving along the wall, he found a man-sized back door set into the north-facing aluminum wall. He checked it for accessibility and found that it opened freely. The clouds were as dark as night when they were not alight with lightning, which was rare. It was nearly six in the evening and hours from sundown, but this storm might as well have occurred at midnight, so blotted was the sun. Reginald closed the door on the weather, found the bolt, and locked it shut.

The major went back to the horse and began separating him from the cart. It was time to make the poor animal as comfortable as possible. The violent lightning storm had the potential to bring self-inflicted harm to the undernourished stallion. Mattersly could not have that.

Between the efforts of the two men, the gray and white equine did calm over time, though it may have been utter exhaustion rather than the slight lessening of the thunder and lightning. The tired stallion began to react adversely only to the loudest of the disturbances.

Mattersly decided to dump the water he had accumulated from the river earlier that afternoon. He explained that, even though he had passed the water through a filter, there was still a good possibility of contamination and boiling the water one kettle at a time was time consuming and, due to the heavy storm, not possible. The rain, on the other hand, was pure. With the help of Mulhaney, the two men took the heavy barrel outside through the back door and dumped it. They then set it and two buckets outside to collect more. In minutes, both men and the horse were enjoying fresh water. When the main barrel was half-full, Mattersly replaced it in the wagon and filled it, bucket by bucket. In less than an hour, the water supply was fully restored, though the two of them were soaked.

The evening slipped along as the sky rained down upon the region. The water that ran inside through the gap underneath the main doors knew right where to go. It flowed dutifully to a drain in the middle of the floor, underneath the wagon. Mattersly cleaned the fish in the dark, which was no problem given his night vision. He placed the meat of the fish in old military issue meal bags that he had saved and kept clean just for this purpose. Both men took a taste of the fish and decided it would be better cooked over an open flame. Reginald shared what he had with Mulhaney; some dried fruits and meat that he kept in small wooden barrels. There was not much, but it helped fend off their hunger for the night.

The night pressed on and the storm kept up its hard rain and sporadic thunder into the early hours of the morning. Elias helped his horse to lie down upon the thin padding of several blankets in a dry corner of the building. He slept nearby in his bedroll on the floor, though it would prove to be an intermittent and uncomfortable slumber on the concrete. The major prepared to spend the night in his wagon, stretched out upon an old thin cot. Despite being slightly more at home within the relative comfort of his space, Mattersly slept lightly. It was a matter of training and not fully trusting his new companion. He had rigged the front and rear curtains of body armor to rattle empty metal cans suspended by strings in case the wagon was boarded.

The night crept along, filled with the roar of heavy rain striking the aluminum roof and the occasional ground-shaking thunder.

Chapter Two

Mattersly awoke in the morning to the sense, rather than the knowledge that it was morning. He listened hard while his implant booted up, trying to determine whether or not he was alone in the shed. The thought had occurred to him that Bartel might move on in the night. Furthermore, he decided that it would have been for the best, even though the man would take his horse with him, abandoning the wagon to the shed.

Reginald enhanced the hearing in both ears, but discovered nothing but light winds rattling the doors at the front and rear of the building. He could hear no rainfall. The time indicated that it was nearly six in the morning. He raised the amplification of his audio receptors to full and remained still. The major thought he could hear the breathing of the horse, but he was not sure. He reset his hearing and lifted his body to a crouch to remove the tin cans from the curtains, then peered past the one at the front of the wagon. The man and his horse could be seen in the dim light, which bled through the seams of the big doors, both of them sleeping. Mattersly felt a mixture of relief and disappointment and was not able to tell which feeling was winning out over the other.

The major tied his boots upon his feet and exited the wagon through the front, carrying some firewood that he kept stocked in case of rain. His footsteps drew the attention of the resting horse, still prone on his right side as he had been when they all had gone to bed. The animal lifted his heavy head to see who had dared move so early in the morning, huffed a heavy breath through its nose in apparent disgust, and lay back down.

Mattersly had not bothered with his boonie hat and met the damp and sunny morning shirtless. The sunlight immediately burned upon his skin through the cool morning air and his implant-monitored eyesight dimmed to compensate for the glare. There was no sign whatsoever of the dark, lightning-spitting clouds from the previous evening, only a blue sky accentuated with fluffy streaks of white which bore no threat of covering the intense light beaming down upon the land.

Reginald stepped a few meters away from the door and set the wood on the still-damp ground. Using a bow and some hay for kindling, he was able to build a fire. With that on its way, he went back inside to retrieve his cookware. There would be fish for breakfast.

When he stepped inside, he found that Bartel had awakened and the horse was on his feet.

"Good morning, Cor… Mister Mulhaney," the major stammered over his instinct to use the man's correct rank and name.

"Good morning, Mattersly," he returned through a yawn. He either did not notice or it was too early for him to care.

As the major prepared breakfast, Mulhaney fed and watered his stallion. Reginald pondered his decision of the previous day to suggest that they go their separate ways. He had begun having second thoughts in the night and, having awakened to no surprises like missing food or weaponry, he began to feel that David Bartel was, at least, an honest man.

For his part, David/Elias had been thinking about something similar, though he had absolutely no intentions of leaving the Brit without means of conveyance. He felt the logical step would be to reach Lovelock before entertaining the possibility of ending their partnership.

"So, what brought you to the States, Major?" Mulhaney decided to ask as he sat near the fire and ate his fileted fish.

"Things in England weren't any better than here. At

the time, I thought perhaps it would be," Reginald began thoughtfully. "A navy man I knew decided that he had a proper following of men, so we liberated a ship."

This stopped Mulhaney cold. He eyed his companion, hunting for a smile that indicated humor, but he found none. "You stole a ship? A military ship?"

Reginald let out a short chuckle. "Well, truth be told, it was only a destroyer."

"Still, that's amazingly daring."

"Not particularly difficult if one looks at the circumstances. There wasn't much else left to us." The major paused and saw the questioning look on his companion's face. "Well, Parliament no longer existed, military personnel were no longer receiving their payroll, and when the Royal family took control of the country, nothing improved."

"So, you and a bunch of sailors stole a destroyer and came here," Elias concluded.

"Not until after the Royal family was publicly and brutally disposed of by some rabble, I didn't see much point in remaining," Mattersly answered nonchalantly and took another bite of trout.

"Where did you land?"

"Your Cape Canaveral, in Florida," Reginald revealed. "A rather hot and miserable place, if I'm honest."

"That's where they have the spaceport."

"Ah, well, not anymore," Reginald stated with a bemused smile and a knowing stare into Mulhaney's face. "There was a bit of a revolt by the populace. Civilians seized the station from my compatriots and destroyed it. With that gone, the whole band fell apart. I packed my things, whatever I could carry and took to the road."

Elias remained quiet for some minutes as he thought and ate. A question that would have at one time been considered routine entered his mind. "So, where are you headed, Major?"

"California. I want to find some vacated beach house and just... well, live." He shrugged and smiled.

"I'll bet all the big ones have some pretty powerful squatters," Mulhaney mused. "They may not like that."

"Oh, I don't need a mansion. A small house shall do nicely."

Elias had grown full with the morning meal. He had taken in more food in ten minutes than he would normally eat over the course of two days. He knew he would have a stomachache, but he cared not. The fish had been prepared perfectly.

Mattersly kicked out the flames once he had cleaned his cookware. He stepped inside the shack with Mulhaney closely behind him.

"So, what's our next step?" he asked of the Brit.

Reginald hopped inside the wagon and put his items away. "Well, I dare say we should continue on. If you would allow me the use of your horse for the time being, Mister Mulhaney, we shall determine whether this Lovelock is inhabited and by whom."

Elias smiled and tapped his walking stick upon the concrete, "I'm all for that, sir."

"Very well," the major said as he hopped down. "Assist me in turning the wagon around and we shall depart."

***

Chips found Upper Valley Road and Mattersly turned the wagon to the southwest, urging the animal to go along at a pace it found comfortable. The equine was still on the mend, as far as Reginald was concerned, and he would take no more from the animal than it would give freely.

The railroad tracks followed the road on their left and were not far from it, so only a thin line of trees lie on that side. On the right, however, many an empty home lay rotting from disuse behind their broken white fences. Both men eyed them warily as they rolled by.

Many other homes sat further from the road, and they were larger and built upon a greater patch of land. Some yards were littered with the hulks of abandoned cars, trucks, and farming equipment. All of it appeared to have sat for many years and were weathered beyond any appearance that hinted toward functionality.

The only sounds the travelers heard were the footfalls of the stallion and the occasional shifting of items in the wagon as they passed over imperfections in the pavement. Mulhaney watched the land ahead as best as he could with the major's binoculars, which he set at its full, eight times magnification. There was no sign of another human being anywhere and he was beginning to wonder if the town they were heading for would be any different.

They rolled past many intersections where once automobile traffic could cross the railroad track. Still other roads terminated into Upper Valley Road and stretched into oblivion to the north or south.

A few moments after they had passed yet another intersection, Elias found movement ahead.

"Hey! I've got something!" he shouted and steadied himself once the wagon halted. He set the binoculars down and reacquired the source of the movement through his rifle's less powerful scope. "Cows!"

Reginald took up his binoculars and guided his sight in the direction Mulhaney's rifle was pointed. "Yes, I see," he said.

The animals were not simply existing randomly on some grazing plain, Reginald determined quite quickly. They were penned in by a well-maintained wooden fence. Beyond them was a barn and just beyond that, a farmhouse. Both structures appeared to be functional and even bore recent paint upon their surfaces.

Mattersly pressed the horse onward. Slowly, they ventured past the ranch, its fences receded from the road nearly a hundred meters, he so reckoned. They were nearly beyond it when a man emerged from within the barn. His eyes immediately went to the source of movement on the road.

Mulhaney, who had been watching the cows as they drove along, waved at the man. The rancher, though he had come to a complete stop in apparent surprise, waved back and smiled.

"Well, we're committed now," the major muttered as he joined in the wave.

"Yep," Elias grunted through a forced smile. "It wouldn't look very good if we were to turn around or try to run."

"Seems friendly enough," Mattersly commented once the rancher disappeared from view. "Be a sport and watch him from the back of the wagon, would you? There's a good chap."

Elias nodded, slipped gently from the seat and headed to the rear of the wagon in a crouch. With rifle in hand, he gave the rear curtain a tug and peeked through the opening. The rancher had gone about his business and was walking to his home in a leisurely pace with his eyes turned to the sky as if looking for signs of further bad weather. He seemed to have put the strangers in the wagon behind him.

Mulhaney returned to the front and sat with a confident smile. "It looks like we're headin' to a nice friendly place."

"Perhaps," Mattersly said, clearly unconvinced.

"Oh, come on now, Major," Elias protested plainly. "We didn't scare him off. He didn't go running away. We waved to each other."

Mattersly appeared calm but thoughtful. His eyes

concentrated ahead of them and swung from one side of the road to the other in slow passes. "Did you happen to notice the antenna on top of the barn, Mister Mulhaney?"

Elias sighed heavily as his smile faded. "No."

"That is not much to worry about in and of itself, of course. However, it is quite possible our approach has been announced."

Mulhaney began to raise the rifle to search ahead of them through his scope.

"Put that thing down," the major interrupted and passed the binoculars to his companion. "Continue using this, but do keep the weapon handy. One does not offer an olive branch through the barrel of a rifle."

Elias took the lenses and set the weapon down to his side. "You think we're being watched?"

"I would bet on it."

Mulhaney grunted and intently scanned the road ahead through the binoculars. After several long minutes of travel, he could make out a shape. "There's an overpass ahead, Major."

"Very well. Ah, yes. I see it."

Reginald looked for a route of escape in case one was needed. There was a deep ditch to their left, rising to meet the railroad tracks. Another ditch lay on the other side. To their right was a field of tall wheat.

"There's…someone on the overpass," Elias announced as he squinted into the binoculars.

Mattersly slowed the wagon. "Is this person armed?"

Elias concentrated, thankful that the wagon had slowed enough to steady his view. "Umm, no. It looks like a kid."

"Don't let that dissuade you from watching him closely, Mister Mulhaney," the major warned. The wheat field looked none too far across; perhaps sixty meters or a little more. The problem was that there was no cover beyond that. There were houses beyond the field, but Reginald knew it would be foolhardy to assume that the people there, if any, would be any less hostile than the sentry ahead of them if the adolescent did indeed open fire.

"Well, he's not armed," Elias concluded. "In fact, he just left."

"I see," Reginald agreed. The shape of the child was now absent from the bridge. "Keep an eye out and that weapon close," he ordered as he checked for the availability of his Dragunov. As always, it was lying on his left. He pulled his pistol from his holster, pulled the slide to ready the first round, set the safety and then returned it. "I hope you have that hand cannon ready."

Elias instead prepared the semi-automatic that he had taken from the ambusher. Its appearance was a bit rough, but it was in good working order when it had spat a round at him the previous day.

"I take it since you are considering the use of that unfamiliar weapon that your supply of ammunition for the revolver has dwindled," Mattersly opined.

"You have a way of taking a long time to say stuff."

"Perhaps. Well?"

"You're right, Major. I have eight rounds left. The cannon takes five at a time."

"Very well, then. Do be conservative, Mister Mulhaney," Reginald directed. "By-the-by. I do appreciate your stepping in yesterday, considering your supply situation."

"Like I told you, Major, I didn't like the odds," Elias said as he inspected the sights on the pistol.

"I understand. Many others would have fled the scene."

Elias eyed the SRR soldier thoroughly, drawing a return gaze from the Brit. "Are you saying that you wouldn't have stepped if I had been in your shoes?"

"It's not in my nature to choose sides when I am not familiar with either," Reginald answered levelly.

"Wow," Mulhaney uttered and leaned away from the driver. His eyes evaluated the man from head to feet then back.

"What?"

"That's messed up, dude," Elias said and shook his head. He turned his attention back to the world in front of them. He no longer needed the binoculars to see that no one occupied the overpass.

"Mister Mulhaney, you must admit that you're not in the keenest physical condition, nor were you, at the time, in a very good position with regards to supplies to put up an extended exchange of gunfire."

"There you go again," the former soldier mused through a crooked smile.

"What?"

"Taking all day to say those long sentences. We may be in a situation here."

"Very well," Mattersly agreed and scrutinized the overpass and the land beyond. "I do not see anyone else, nor do I see any traps in the road."

"I don't, either."

"Just try not to be too quick to open fire if we are approached."

"Not to worry, Major," Elias provided. "I've no wish to shoot a child."

The wagon slipped into the shadows of the disheveled overpass. The supports ran red with rust and the concrete was deteriorating and cracked. The same red ran from the gaping wounds, a sign that the rebar reinforcement was decaying as well.

Once on the other side, Mulhaney could see that a large wooden ladder had been built and attached to the bridge. Elias told his reluctant partner of his discovery.

"Look," the major directed. Elias followed the finger to a shack with a thick wire coming out of it and running to a wooden pole. The wire stretched on from that pole to another, then another and still another until it disappeared into the mass of trees. "A telephone line."

"I see."

"We have not yet been accosted. Keep your weapons out of sight for the moment. For God's sake, look friendly," Mattersly ordered as he appropriated his own pleasant lip bend.

Mulhaney smirked in amusement over the Brit's manner of speaking rather than from the attempt at friendliness. As they came closer to the small structure, he could see that it was not a shack but a trailer home set upon a concrete foundation. The walls of the home were patched with scrap sheet metal and a couple of broken panes were covered with the same. A curtain hanging over the one window that faced the road moved. Elias thought he could see a face, perhaps more than one. Instinctively, he waved and smiled as best as he could, given the partially immobile right side of his lip.

As they passed the structure, no one greeted them, though the eyes following them went on doing so as they rolled on. Certainly, one of the people inside was on the phone or whatever it was that the wires were supporting.

Without being asked, Elias slipped to the rear of the wagon and discreetly watched the mobile home and the land they left behind.

"No one's following, Major," he grunted when he returned.

"Very well."

They approached and passed more homes along the side of the road. These appeared livable and some even showed signs of current habitation. Their yards were more or less well kempt and free of broken down vehicles. Their roofs were well maintained, and their windows whole. A few of them had stables complete with horses and other animals.

They crossed a short bridge, which covered the expanse of a dry creek bed. Beyond that, the signs of a town came into view. The road widened, curved to their right, and transformed into a multi-lane main artery. Commercial buildings in various states of usable integrity lined both sides of the street. There were more, larger stables, motels, and a few restaurants. The motels may very well have not been open for business, but some were obviously being lived in.

In moments, they came to an oddly arranged intersection. Reginald stopped the wagon. To continue west, they would have to jink to their left as they crossed. The road that stretched south curved to the southwest and out of sight behind trees and homes. Mattersly glanced to their right and found the pavement snaked northward into nothingness.

Mulhaney peered out of the shadows of the wagon covering and saw the same. "What do you think?" he said lowly.

"I'm inclined to continue westward, Mister Mulhaney," Reginald said but remained still.

Elias watched his fellow traveler expectantly for a long moment. "What are you waitin' on?"

"Shhh," Mattersly admonished not unkindly. "I hear something."

Mulhaney could see the concentration on Mattersly's face and knew that he had augmented his implants. Despite the temptation to do the same, Elias knew the odds of his own devices coming online without a failure were low, so he did not risk it. He listened keenly with his natural hearing, but could detect nothing beyond the wind and the horse's breathing. The gray stallion as well as Mattersly must have heard something, for the both of them appeared startled at once. It took only another second for Mulhaney to hear the high-pitched, warbling cry in the air.

"What is *that*?" Elias asked as the horse whinnied and stomped.

"Heeyah!" Reginald shouted and shook the reigns. The horse yanked the wagon hard in a burst of acceleration that neither man expected. The major steered the wagon slightly to the left in an attempt to get across the road. Elias held on, trying not to fall out of the seat and perhaps out of the wagon entirely.

Before the wagon could get more than a few meters, an automobile appeared, coming from the west at a high rate of speed. The machine was vibrantly lit with flashing lights of red and blue. Its tires and motor whistled airily as it came. The siren had ebbed from its wailing cry, but the driver gave it a few shorts bursts as the machine approached them.

Neither man in the wagon could utter a word. They stared in disbelief as the gray equine's forward momentum halted. The animal was panicking, having not seen or heard such a machine in its life.

"Damn!" Mattersly shouted as he wrestled with the reigns.

In a desperate effort to get the horse calmed enough to get running again, Mulhaney launched himself from his seat and landed on the horse's back. He tried to utter words in calming tones to the animal, but another rude, piercing, warbling screech erupted from the approaching vehicle.

Both Mattersly and Mulhaney began to pull their weapons at the same time, but froze when they heard a voice emanate from somewhere within the automobile's grillwork as it came to a harsh stop directly in front of them.

"Don't do that! Raise your hands!"

"You'd better do what he says, gents!" another voice called out from behind them. Someone had boarded the wagon from the rear.

Elias turned back to see a very large double-barreled shotgun pointing in their direction. Behind it was an old man, small in stature and bald. His eyes, though laughing, meant business.

The doors of the vehicle in front of them flew open simultaneously and two men emerged in a heartbeat. A dirty and scratched up decal could be seen on both doors identifying them as Lovelock Police. Neither individual wore a uniform, nor did the man behind them, but all three were armed and had the advantage.

"Damn," Reginald grunted as he raised his hands. Mulhaney followed his lead.

"Come on out!" shouted the driver of the police cruiser. His pistol was trained on Mulhaney while the partner's was on Mattersly. "Out here now!"

Both "officers" gestured with their hands in the direction they expected Reginald and Elias to move and move they did. Neither Reginald nor Elias saw the advantage of defying their captors for the moment. They dropped to the pavement with their hands in the air.

"All clear in there, Thumps?" the cruiser driver called to the third man in the wagon. Tall, light-skinned, and bald, this man appeared to be in charge. His brown eyes concentrated on Mulhaney but shifted occasionally to Mattersly.

"Hold yer horses!" the old man shouted back then cackled obnoxiously over his own joke. He could be heard rummaging around through the barrels and crates in the wagon. "Well, I gots me two rifles... holy! Holy sheeit!!"

"What is it, Thumps?!" the driver shouted. Both policemen tensed at the sound of their compatriot's voice.

"*Thumps!*"

"All right, all right! I hears ya!" the elderly raider returned. "I got the usual food 'n' water stores, some hand grenades, and coupla' pounds a' C-4 *with detonators!*"

"No shit," the partner grumbled. He was not as confident as the driver of the cruiser nor was he quite as tall. His blond hair was short and spikey and his facial features plain but stern. His lean body shook with nervous tension, but not outright fear.

Mattersly noted all of this and decided that he was the weakest of the three. Staring down the barrel of the nine-millimeter pistol, he activated his *UnitCom*'s communication system and ordered it to search for other systems in the area. It found two immediately, though no identification was allowed by either. Reginald assumed that the implants he found were those of the two "policemen." He immediately shut down the program, stopping the device from trying to gather more information. The effect of this tactic was generally called, "pinging" and was used in the battlefield to quickly ascertain whether or not enemy combatants were in the area. Their implants would not communicate together, of course, but the number of failed "handshakes" between devices would at least put a number on the enemy within a soldier's implant range, generally around one hundred meters. The downside to that, of course, is that it announced the presence of a pinger.

"Hey!" the blond-haired passenger snarled.

"Knock that off!" the boss barked. "If I get pinged again, we're taking the both of you down! I don't care which one of you did it."

As if nothing had occurred, the old man they called, Thumper, went on. "I got a Dragunov! Hot damn!" the old man shouted gleefully, drawing out the pronunciation of the Russian name.

Reginald was somewhat impressed that anyone but

himself knew enough about the items in his wagon to identify them on sight. He arched an eyebrow unconsciously and decided that the old man was either former military or a well-versed gunsmith.

"Holy sheeit!!" Thumper screeched again, making Mulhaney cringe. "Looky what I foun'!" he called, plainly having leaned out of the front of the wagon. Elias did not have to turn to know that the weapon the old man was shaking in his grip was the rifle he had taken from the ambushing sniper. While the weapon itself was built to narrow tolerances for accuracy, the rattle he heard over his shoulder was that of the shoulder strap rings.

"Is that Momo's?" the blond man marveled, shifting his eyes from Reginald to the rifle in Thumper's hand.

The driver sidestepped around the cruiser's door and moved with great speed toward Mulhaney. With one meaty hand, he knocked the black Stetson from his head, sending it tumbling to the street. The knuckles connected with Elias's face and sounded off with a slap, but he uttered not one sound of pain, merely blinking at the strike.

"It's not him, I don't think," the driver discovered. "Where'd you get that?"

"I took it off a dead man," Elias admitted freely.

The driver took a second to ponder that. "Take off the coat!" he ordered and pointed the pistol to Elias's head. The duster hit the ground with a clatter from everything in its pockets. The Lovelock cop's eyes grew wide once he discovered the giant revolver in Mulhaney's belt. "With your right hand, tug the revolver out. If you touch the trigger, you're done! Good. Hand it out to me!" Elias did so, but because his right side was weakened, he had to use most of his fingers to handle the heavy handgun. "Put your damn hands on the horse!" he ordered then yanked upon Mulhaney's right arm to turn him. Elias complied, stumbling with the shifted weight as he turned.

"What's wrong with him?" the second 'policeman' demanded.

As the leader of the three frisked Mulhaney for weapons, he drilled him with the direction to answer the question.

"I had a stroke a couple years back. Right side's not very good," Elias answered.

"That checks out," Thumper spoke up from the wagon. "He's got hisself a walkin' stick in here."

The boss removed Elias's combat knife, which was clipped to his belt and dropped it upon the discarded duster. "Two handguns and a knife on this one," he announced once he crouched and felt the semi-automatic in the pocket of the coat. The bulky authoritarian warned Mulhaney not to move and stepped over to Mattersly. He stripped the SRR soldier of his gun belt and patted him down.

"Brass knuckles!" he exclaimed and pocketed the weapon. "More knives…well, you guys are here to cause some trouble, huh?"

"On the contrary, constable," Reginald spoke up. "I'm actually on my way to California."

The boss chuckled and looked to his partner, who did the same and sprouted a sarcastic grin. "Yeah, Cali… sure. So, why are you carrying C-4 and grenades and all this shit?"

"A man has to protect himself," Mattersly said mildly.

"You talk funny," said the blond through a smirk.

"I could say the same, sir."

"Okay, you can shut up, now," the boss grunted.

"He's British," Thumper chirped. "This is his, then," he tossed a flexible greenish-gray item to the boss.

"What's this?" the big man demanded of Reginald as he twirled it in his hand.

"That's his beret," Thumper answered for him.

"That there insignia is SAS. British Army!" he concluded and cackled shrilly.

"Is that so?"

"Not entirely correct, I'm afraid," the major differed and passed his eyes over the blue sky in apparent boredom. "I am Major Reginald Mattersly of the *SRR*. Special Reconnaissance Regiment."

"Oooo... big shit!" the one on the passenger side exclaimed mockingly and beamed perfectly white teeth. His gun never wavered from Reginald's chest area. The man's light blue eyes laughed just as heartily.

"Okay, *Major*," the man in charge oozed with sarcasm, "we'll see about that. We're taking you both in to see the boss," he explained as he took Reginald's left wrist and cuffed it to the other behind his back. "Denny, load him up," he ordered his partner and gave his prisoner a light shove.

Reginald saw no alternative at the moment, though he had pondered the possibility of resistance. With one gun trained on him and the shotgunner behind him in his wagon, he decided to bide his time. At the shove from behind, Mattersly stepped toward the cruiser.

He was roughly guided into the back seat and was joined by a glum Elias Mulhaney who was ushered in through the other door by the burly driver. The doors were closed on them and they watched through the windshield as their captors gathered in front of it.

"Well, now what, *genius*?" Elias griped.

"We meet with their employer, just as the constable said," Reginald answered, ignoring the accusatory tone.

"Constable my rumpled ass," Mulhaney fired. "They're nothing but thieves! They better not hurt my horse. Jesus, it stinks in this car. They must transport livestock in it or somethin'."

Reginald could see the faces of all three men. The

large one, the driver, spoke as he wiped the sweat from his bald head and patted the stallion along its nose. It appeared to the Brit that the man had no intention of harming the animal. The bald man looked over at them as he continued to talk, allowing the major to read his lips.

"...her place and see what she thinks," he said before he turned back to face the old man sitting on the bench of his wagon.

"You want me to drive shit over share?" Thumper seemed to say with a mouth that had suffered from some amount of tooth loss. Reginald translated that into, "You want me to drive this over there?"

Finally, the one called Denny looked over at the two men in the car and Mattersly read: "Do you think he is who he says, or what?" To which, the big goateed man in charge just shrugged.

The policemen picked up the weapons and other objects removed from their prisoners and dropped them into the sedan's trunk. They boarded the vehicle and turned it around without a word being spoken.

With a burst of acceleration, the police cruiser tore off in the southerly direction. Neither he nor Elias had been in a vehicle capable of such speed in a long time and were planted roughly into the back of the seat. Mulhaney grunted uncomfortably as he braced his legs into the floor.

The reluctant traveling companions watched the town fly by through the side windows. This section of the small town had been reasonably well-maintained. The street was lined with a few homes that appeared lived in and commercial structures that were certainly, at the very least, intact. Mattersly tried to count the number of people standing alongside the street, but could not. The town was inhabited all right and, if the people on the street were any indicator, the population could well be in the hundreds. The major had not encountered such a concentration of people since his time in Cape Canaveral.

The siren blared for a few blocks and then was switched off as the car began to slow. The two visitors could see a few vehicles of various designs and modes of propulsion lining the streets. Mixed in with these were horse-drawn wagons, parked in the same manner. A couple of city blocks went by before the driver pressed the brake and gave the steering yoke a turn to the left. The car bounded up a low curb and onto a gravel parking lot next to a white, two-story building.

The two policemen exited the car, flung open the rear doors, and guided their prisoners to their feet. Mattersly looked about him with curiosity. The sidewalks beheld gatherings of people that regarded him and his companion with curious expressions. Some spoke together while others were outwardly silent, clearly engaged in implant-to-implant conversations.

"Anti-aircraft guns? Really?" Mulhaney marveled and gave a sharp bark of disbelieving laughter. "What the hell are those for?"

"We've got a nasty vulture population," the barrel-chested driver returned sardonically. This drew a chuckle from Denny, who was busy escorting the SRR man out and away from the cruiser.

Reginald followed where Elias was looking and confirmed it for himself. Upon the roof of the building on the northwest corner was a quad-barreled contraption with ammunition canisters and a seat attached to it. The barrel width suggested something of mid-caliber, but Mattersly could not be certain. The two men apparently assigned to operate the gun watched them silently with neutral expressions on their faces.

As he was brought toward the front of the white building, Reginald passed his eyes to the gravel upon which he walked and caught the shadow of a similar gun cast there. Lovelock appeared to be at war and with something airborne. The citizens manning the weapons seemed well-prepared and alert.

The bald man swung a heavy door of glass and steel out of his way and led Elias through it, not pressing the limping man too hurriedly. Denny and Reginald went inside next.

Elias blinked, trying to adjust to the low light inside. Reginald simply thought a command and the sight of the large room came to him. The walls vibrated with the sound of music coming from an adjacent room. There was a soft percussion of a slow beat, the strumming and picking of electric guitars and a trumpet providing the overall melody. The bassline of one guitar flowed with the drummer, while the lead electric guitar sang out in gentle runs, chasing the commanding trumpeter. The interior of the bar area was done mostly in a deep red theme. Red carpeting was underneath their feet and stretched beyond the floors, covering much of the walls until it met with a red leather or perhaps vinyl-lined padded bar. Above that was deep mahogany paneling. The stools set all around them were of dark wood and red vinyl padding. Framed pictures and electric lights with decorative glass fixtures were mounted throughout. None of these details appeared new, however. The carpet had turned to an unappealing brown near the door and worn to a dirty pink under the barstools. The stuffed padding of the bar was cut or torn in places as were some of the stools and some of the ceiling tiles were stained from leakage.

The bald constable mumbled to Denny, who nodded and stepped back outside.

Behind the bar were glass shelves set against a mirror that took up most of the wall. Upon the shelves was a collection of bottles of alcohol, many of which were empty. Elias stared at the vision of himself looking back.

He shuffled his feet and cast his eyes away, feeling embarrassment over his appearance. Not only was he lightly disfigured by the stroke which had left his right eyelid drooping slightly and the corner of his mouth turned downward, his face was sweaty and his hair greasy and matted. In comparison to the two that had brought him and the Brit into the air-conditioned tavern, he was the very picture of a derelict.

Reginald felt similarly as he gazed at his reflection. He found himself longing for a change of clothes and a bath of hot water and soap. Clearly, their captors were so supplied. The bald constable and his partner, Denny, suffered from no such depravities. Even their clothes, while not being uniforms, were clean, if not a bit plain in design.

The moment of quiet thoughts was broken by the entrance of another man, rather tall and muscular as his suit-adorned frame suggested. Like the constable, this one wore a goatee, though it was complete with a mustache and as black as the hair upon his head. The man's vanity shone through the emerald green eyes that stared into the face of Mattersly then that of Mulhaney. They were most likely the civilian models of bio-electronic lenses as the military-grade types avoided extreme, unnatural coloring.

The air inside the bar or club was clean and cool, with a flowery scent enveloping the place. That scent became prevalent when the woman walked into the bar, entering where the suited man had come from. Both Elias and Reginald involuntarily let their eyes wander over her. Not only had neither man seen a woman in a great amount of time, neither had ever seen one quite so exotically appealing.

She was not tall, just over a meter and a half, though the high heeled shoes certainly added to her stature. Her black hair was arranged in a sort of braided bun that was centered upon the upper back of her head. Her facial features were striking in their elegance. The light of the room rolled from her gently curved cheekbones and the slope of her nose. Her mouth appeared on the small side, but her lips seemed pursed in thought as she scrutinized the prisoners before her. Her chin was strong and so was her gaze and poise.

Upon her voluptuous body, she wore an electric blue dress that sparkled under the light. It was sleeveless and dove into a shallow 'v' at her chest and the vented skirt came to an end just above her knees. Her shapely legs were sheathed in dark sheer nylons, bearing an embroidered shape of a winged dragon on each outer calf. Three strings of pearls decorated her neck and her fingers and wrists were covered with rings and bracelets that played with the light as she moved. Delicate golden hoop earrings hung from her thin lobes.

Reginald found himself staring into her eyes after taking in her alluring shape and ensemble. Unable to determine their color, he magnified his view with a thought. As the orbs studied him in return, he decided that they were so dark brown they appeared black as he had a very difficult time pinpointing her irises.

"Who do we have here, Antonio?" she inquired crisply. Her voice was every bit as confident as her elegant yet demure stature proclaimed.

"This one says his name's Elias," the bald man spoke up and indicated Mulhaney with his thumb. "That one there says his name's Reginald Mattersly and claims to be a major in the British Army."

"Really," the woman returned with a flat hint of doubt. She looked over Mattersly from face to foot and back up. Her gaze shifted to the door. Denny had returned with their rifles and Mulhaney's walking stick, which he dropped to the floor. "Oooo… toys," she muttered in a creamy smooth tone of mild amusement.

Denny strode right up to the woman and held out the rifle that Mulhaney had been carrying. "Denny, don't come any closer to me with that damn greasy, filthy gun," she said sternly, boring her blackish eyes into the taller man's face.

"Sorry, Jazz," Denny offered as the weapon was taken out of his hands by the man in the gray suit.

"Hey, this is Momo's gun!" he exclaimed. He turned it over in both meaty hands and scrutinized it closely. "I'm right, Jazz. Here's his name scratched in it." He pointed it out.

"Well, I'll be damned," the woman said and lit the room with her smile. Her teeth were well-cared for and white as snow. "Neither of you two is Momo." Her smile remained as she passed her eyes from Elias to Reginald. "Which one was carrying it?" she asked the room.

"This one. Elias," Antonio, the bald constable, indicated again with his thumb.

Jazz stepped over to Mulhaney, but came no closer than an arm's length despite him being cuffed. Marco followed her as if he was attached by a cord. She scrutinized Elias's face through narrowed eyelids. "What happened to you?"

"A stroke, ma'am," Elias said. "Pretty sure the cause was my implant. It's not working right. I keep it off if I can." Jazz continued to stare at him, apparently wanting more of an explanation. "Well, it paralyzed my right side, but it's been getting better."

Jazz gave Elias's legs a glance, noticed how he was standing, and then saw the walking stick on the floor. "Do you need to sit?"

"I'm fine, Ma'am," Mulhaney said with finality, though he smiled.

Jazz nodded. "Suppose you tell me how you got Momo's gun."

"Well, actually, *he* did." Elias jerked his chin toward Reginald. "Three men were ambushing him and I just stepped in. The Major here took out the sniper… this Momo guy, I guess, with the Dragunov on your man's shoulder."

"Did he, now?" Jazz said as she looked over to Reginald and sidestepped to him slowly. Her eyes met his. "Well, you've got no reason to know this, but Momo's been a real pain in our asses lately."

"Perhaps." Mattersly stared into her face and smiled, "I hope that means I have done you a service, rather than a slight."

"Oooo!" Jazz brightened. "Listen to that accent!" She fanned herself in a faux swoon, eliciting a chuckle from Antonio, and a smile from Marco. "What's a major from the British Army doin' out here?" she inquired with her hands on her rounded hips.

"I'm afraid that's a rather long and complicated story," Reginald explained. "Suffice it to say that I came to Cape Canaveral with some hope of escaping troubles in England only to find more of the same over here."

"Mmm… mmm!" Jazz's black eyes flashed in the electric lights of the barroom. "I could listen to you talk all day. But see, we have a problem."

"Oh? Do tell," Mattersly said.

"See, I don't know if you're full of shit or not," she stated. The smile and any trace of infatuation with the Brit disappeared in a hot flash. "How the hell do I know that you're not one of Gillespie's men? Maybe you didn't kill Momo at all. Maybe you two are just scouts sent here to pinpoint where *I* am."

"Pardon me, miss… Jazz, was it?"

"That's me, Jazz Hernandez. Nice to make your acquaintance, now tell me a friggin' story," she demanded curtly. Her demeanor set her black eyes afire.

"Very well," Reginald started off. "I hate to fall to the temptations of cliché, but I can think of no other way to put this: I was riding along in my wagon, minding my own business, when I was fired upon by rabble."

Jazz shifted her hips and crossed her arms, but could not keep a trace of a smile from the very corner of her lips. "Go on," she pressed and tilted her head as she narrowed her eyes.

"This Momo fellow killed my horse…" Reginald was cut off.

"Ask him what its name was," Mulhaney put in and chuckled.

"Oh, shut up, Corporal!"

Elias's smile disappeared. "I told you not to call me that!"

"*Enough*!" Jazz shouted and held up a hand. Getting its signals crossed, the band in the other room halted mid-tune. The woman of the house sighed and dropped her hot gaze to the carpet. The raised hand slapped her thigh and, in frustration, she turned her head to the archway into the band's room and called, "Not you, Murph!"

"All-righty," a disembodied voice returned. The music resumed.

"You're military, too?" Jazz demanded of Mulhaney as she pointed at him.

Elias grunted and sighed as Mattersly searched the ceiling. "Yes, ma'am. Eighty-second Airborne. Five hundred 'n' fourth," he said in a tone of utter boredom.

"Interesting." Jazz dropped her hand to her side. "Go on," she commanded Reginald.

"With my horse killed, I then received fire from two ambushers to my right. Well, I gathered my rifle and hopped out of the back, located the sniper, who had taken a place upon a hill to my left, and killed him."

"Just like that?" Jazz asked with heavy doubt.

"Just like that, ma'am. I saw it myself," Elias put in.

"Uh-huh," she commented and studied Reginald's face with her hands on her hips.

"I must say that at this point, my companion here came to my rescue," the major provided. "He distracted and immediately engaged the two ambushers that were firing from behind a rise. He killed them both."

Jazz nodded then stepped to a bar stool to take a seat. She scrutinized both men for a long moment while all were silent. The upbeat music filled the room, though did little to alter the mood set by her contemplations. Thumper then came through the front door. The lever-action rifle that Mattersly and Mulhaney had taken from one of the dead ambushers was in his hand and he appeared rather pleased with himself. Noting the lack of a smile on Jazz's face, Thumper tipped his hat, sauntered off to one side of the room, and sat quietly.

Jazz motioned the bald constable to come closer. He joined her on her right and sat facing the captives. "What do you think, Antonio?"

"I think I believe them."

The woman nodded in thought then pointed to Mattersly. "Link with me. I want to see your military ID."

Reginald bobbed his head once and booted up his implant. He found that her device was available to chat with, so he selected it. As a result, his name, rank, unit, and service were transmitted to her civilian model. She asked the same of Mulhaney. Without protest, he did the same.

"Okay, this stinks." Jazz strode over to Elias. "Why does your implant tell me your name is David Bartel?"

"I don't like that name," he muttered.

The petite woman stepped into Elias's personal space and lifted herself up to her toes to put her nose just inches from his. "You don't like your own damn name?" she grilled him. "Got somethin' to hide, *Corporal Bartel*?"

"Not exactly."

"Then what's the deal? Explain."

"I was discharged and kicked off the base for stealing food! All right?!" Bartel shouted. Jazz did not so much as flinch, but Marco's lips curled into a snarl as he stepped forward. Antonio, the bald constable, stood up from the barstool.

"Is that all?" the woman chuckled and flashed a wicked smile, holding the man's eyes with her own.

"Yes," he said with certainty. "Our base was short on rations for a long time. I had no other place to go. Neither did anyone else. I messed up and got thrown out of the only home I ever knew. Okay?!"

Jazz watched his face for many long seconds. Even through the slackened muscles along the right side of his face, she sensed truthfulness. "You really paid a big price for that little mistake, haven't you?"

David/Elias said nothing. He blinked and continued to watch the dark orbs reading his.

"Thrown away like garbage," she murmured to him. Her voice became so low that it was obscured by the music in the air, unheard by anyone beyond the man to whom she spoke. "Genetically altered, trained, used, then discarded as if you didn't matter... after an incident so trivial it *shouldn't* have mattered. Then, this," she reached out to David's right arm and grasped it firmly at the bicep, "injury on top of insult. You've wandered ever since?"

"Yes," he replied in whisper.

"The glitches haunt you?"

"Every day." He nodded shakily.

"Makes you see things," she stated as if he were transmitting his thoughts. He nodded again. "So much pain...and yet you're still here."

Neither said anything for a time. Beyond the grime, the beard, and the filthy greasy hair that shadowed his brow, she could see his heart. His brown eyes blinked and glistened. Jazz let his arm free and stepped back while she nodded in understanding.

"Antonio," she called behind her.

"Yes, Jazz?" he replied and appeared at her side.

"Unhook this man and give him his cane," she ordered. "Marco, get Gigi and tell her to get Mister Elias Mulhaney here a room upstairs."

Marco nodded and stepped forward. Antonio removed the cuffs from Elias's wrists and handed the man the gnarled tree-branch, but remained vigilant, waiting for an adverse reaction from the road-worn stranger. He may have proven himself somehow to the lady of the house, but not to him.

"Thank you," Elias whispered as he rubbed his irritated wrists.

"Go with him," Jazz directed gently, indicating the large bodyguard with a hand.

Mulhaney nodded gratefully and cast a glance to Mattersly as he walked past. His eyes were unreadable to Reginald, who remained restrained and standing at ease. The two men exited the room through the archway.

Jazz sidestepped to look once again upon Major Mattersly, coming close to his face just as she did with Elias. "That's a very brave soul right there," she said of the departed Mulhaney, indicating him with a jerk of her head. Reginald arched an eyebrow and nodded, not taking his eyes from hers. "He wants to die, you know," she whispered as the song in the other room ended and another began.

"Oh?"

"Uh-huh." She nodded. "Like yourself, he's been trained to kill, but the military never removed his heart. He's very brave, but he suffers."

"I know," Reginald replied.

"Do you? I don't see much suffering in your eyes," Jazz said accusingly. "I see a hardness in them. You've done things you're not proud of."

"As I've already told you, Miss Hernandez..." He clamped his lips together when she interrupted.

"There's something else there. There always is, you know. The world's full of talentless drifters with nothing to offer. Then you two gems show up," she said with a guarded smile. "No matter what, they always have their secrets."

Mattersly understood what Jazz meant and a flash of memory came to him. Upon the orders of another, he had killed. Coming to America, it had not changed. His talents had been called upon by men whom he had accepted as his commander, though in truth, they were no more than pirates. With trained efficiency, he did kill and did so from any distance.

One little, two little, three little Indians, he recalled himself singing maniacally as he fired his Dragunov at the pursuing Choctaw warriors, killing or maiming one with every shot as they paddled their way up the river toward him. The memory was not yet a year old, but it replayed in his mind with as much clarity as any implant was capable of providing. *Four little, five little, six little Indians!*

Jazz's dark eyes searched his face for traces of regret or guilt, this he was certain, but her purpose in doing so was lost on him. Mattersly set his jaw and kept his eyes on those of the demure female who seemed to be in charge of this town of Lovelock. He remembered something else. In any losing battle, there comes a time where a soldier discards any thought of victory and the will to survive takes over. His band of pirates was defeated that day, but he chose to live on. Had he not fled Cape Canaveral, the Choctaws would have killed him.

To his surprise, Jazz Hernandez smiled. "Yeah, it's

there. It's buried, but it's there."

Reginald remained silent. The mysterious and exotic woman had seen behind his eyes, certainly not in detail, but the fact that he was a killer was quite clear.

He was released as well by her order and ushered out to the right of the barroom. On the far wall was a stage and upon it, the band that had been playing since they arrived. Not one of them gave him notice as Marco accompanied him to the foot of the stairs, where a pleasant young lady awaited him. While very attractive in her own right, the chestnut-haired twenty-ish paled in comparison to the mistress of the club. She showed him to a well-appointed room with a bed, dressers, and a bathroom.

"Do you need anything right now?" she asked as she stepped between him and the door.

"I don't suppose you can tell me what happens next?"

"I'm sure Miss Hernandez wishes you to be comfortable," she said with a brilliant smile.

"But it would be unwise of me to try to leave," the major concluded with a hinted question.

The young lady thought this over a moment and tilted her head in confusion. "But where would you go?"

Mattersly chuckled. "Of course. Thank you, Miss."

"My name's Beth. If you need anything, just ask the gentleman outside the door for me. Miss Jazz expects you to get all cleaned up for dinner. We'll be launderin' the clothes from your wagon and I'll be back for those." She indicated his tunic and trousers and then left.

Reginald inspected the room, looking for cameras or bugs. He launched his *UnitCom*'s bug search program and stood closely to one wall after the other. There were none detected by the device. He stepped into the bathroom and was elated to see a bar of soap at the sink and clean white towels, so clean that they glowed in the sunlight coming in through the window behind him.

He picked up the creamy white bar and lifted it to his nose. Though it lacked a flowery scent that he often associated with civilian products, it had a gentle clean and airy scent. Excitedly, he began removing his clothes, aware of how ineffective the rainwater had been that morning when he had bathed himself. A thought occurred to him and he froze, staring at the faucet in the bath. He reached over and gave the 'hot' handle a turn and was instantly gratified to witness a flow of water explode from the downturned pipe.

Mattersly could not take his eyes from the sight as he continued to undress. In a few moments, steam began rising into the air. He stepped into the tub, bringing the bar of soap with him and happily made use of it.

***

Elias, though partially hindered by his weaker half, enjoyed the bath just as his partner was beginning to in the next room. Having given the bar of soap a thorough wear-down, he clumsily stepped over the tub, holding onto the rail tightly. As he dried himself off, he noticed that his discarded set of clothes had gone, replaced by a clean set that hung on the door. He inspected them and found that they were certainly his clothes, though he barely recognized them. The wrinkles had disappeared and they smelled of fresh air and some sort of citrus fruit. The job had been recently completed, as every item shared a faint dampness.

Mulhaney looked at his reflection in the steamed-up mirror. He blinked and wiped the fog from the glass surface and stared for a time. He was shocked over how rough he appeared. The wrinkles had deepened, as had his eyes. The sagging eyelid, slack cheek, and downturned corner of his mouth only made it worse. He gave a heavy sigh and began to make use of the electric shaver he had found on the sink.

Many minutes later, Elias stared at himself in the mirror. He had not been clean-shaven in so long, he could not remember. He practiced his smile, happily noting that the defects caused by his stroke could be diminished with the effort.

He dressed, took up his walking stick, and made his way slowly to the window. His bare feet padded along silently while his stick thumped along the wood floor. Elias parted the thin curtain and winced when the sunlight assaulted his eyes. There were men on the roof of the building across the street. One sat casually on the seat attached to the anti-aircraft gun while the other stood near him. They were clearly having a conversation and were pretty well at ease. He looked to the street and found that Mattersly's wagon had been brought to the front of Jazz's club or hotel or whatever she wished to call it. Chips was nowhere to be seen. The streets were bare of cars and people at that moment, and the town seemed asleep except for the men on the rooftops.

Feeling adventurous, Elias walked to his front door and opened it. He was greeted by Antonio, the man Reginald had addressed as 'constable'.

"Need something?" Antonio asked in a guarded voice. He had risen from the wooden chair he had been lounging upon and made as if to block Elias from entering the hallway.

"No, not really," Mulhaney answered. "Just sort of wondering what comes next around here."

"Miss Hernandez will probably extend an invitation to dinner to you and your friend. When she's ready, that is," he finished, unmoving and watching Elias's eyes and stance.

Mulhaney could see that the man expected trouble, so he leaned upon his walking stick, exaggerating his need for it. "Ah, so I'm not free to walk around and explore the place, eh?"

"Not at this time, Mister Mulhaney," the big bald man said.

Elias smiled over the acceptance of his adopted moniker. "Oh, uh, where's the Major?"

"Major Mattersly is next door," Antonio indicated Elias's right with a tilt of the head.

"Okay, cool. Er, thanks." Elias stepped back inside. Antonio wordlessly closed the door for him.

For a few moments, he paced the room. Even though he was thrilled to have found an apparent oasis of civilization, there was a deep uncertainty within him. He did not care for being held prisoner, no matter how comfortable the room was. He went to the window again and pondered an escape. Mulhaney gazed down upon the sidewalk and street. He estimated that he could very well lower himself a good distance toward the ground by dangling from the windowsill. He dismissed it quickly, realizing there was no apparent means of conveyance once he landed. The men on the rooftops could pick him off or bear witness to his escape.

Mulhaney stepped away from the window and eyed the bed. He had not slept on one for a good long time. He sat upon it first, giving it a test with his hands. With nothing for the moment to do but wait, Elias laid down upon the mattress, setting his walking stick next to him. It was quite comfortable and once his head sank into the soft but firm pillow, he relaxed. In moments, he was asleep.

Chapter Three

In the room next to Elias's, Reginald lay in bed but did not sleep. While he wondered what exactly was in store for the both of them, he had a strong feeling that they were not to be harmed. Of course, he had no real worries about that. In his estimation, he could take on Marco and Antonio in a physical confrontation and win. He doubted that they possessed any military training. Their positions as bodyguard and constable were most likely given to them because of their size, not ability. Still, he could not discount the possibility that he was wrong, therefore, he would have to dismiss his assumptions if he were to attempt an escape.

But then, there was this Elias fellow to think about. The former paratrooper should possess similar training to his own and, being taller and with a greater reach than himself, would be quite formidable. The problem was, of course, his partial paralysis. He had seen the man fire his gun with his left hand while controlling the horse with his weakened right, but it had led to the man falling from his mount when it reared on him.

Reginald remained grateful to the man that had intervened during the ambush and he decided that he would not abandon him now. With that resolution, his eyes closed and he drifted into a light sleep.

Time passed and he was awakened by a knocking on the door. Reginald opened his eyes to find the room lit by the orange light of the falling sun. The bodyguard, Marco, had entered after knocking and stood looking at Mattersly with an unreadable, blank expression.

"By all means, do come in," Reginald said as he sat up.

"Follow me," Jazz's protector ordered and backed out of the room.

"Certainly. Mind if I put on my boots first, or is this a short stroll on the beach?"

"Listen, smartass," Marco exuded as he stormed forward, "I don't like you. So put yourself together and follow me before I throw you through the window and claim self-defense."

"Well, I say," Reginald replied as his hands tugged the first boot onto his foot, "there's no reason to be testy, my young friend. I was merely making conversation." He returned Marco's hot angry stare with a mild gaze. Reginald smiled slightly as their artificial lenses studied each other.

The bodyguard was quick to goad into physicality. He strode toward the seated Brit and pointed a fat finger into the man's face. "Listen to me, you little..." Marco began but could not finish.

The major's bare right foot slashed across his jaw in a blur, turning the world many shades darker for the big man. From far away, Marco heard himself ask, "Did you just *kick* me?"

Another powerful blow to the upper chest sent the stunned bodyguard reeling backward. His right hip struck the open door and his body turned gracelessly. His face met the hallway carpet and the entire floor sounded as if a hippopotamus had dropped down from the attic.

Heavy footfalls approached at running speed. The constable shouted Marco's name as he came. Reginald sat on the handgun that he had taken from the fallen man and proceeded to put on his other boot in a leisurely fashion.

Marco groaned and tried to lift himself up. Antonio's eyes were wide with shock that quickly turned to anger. His gun was drawn and the barrel turned to Mattersly, still seated on the bed and tying his laces.

"What the hell happened?" Antonio boomed.

"Your friend appears to have clumsily bonked his

head on the door," the major replied with informative innocence. "Is he always that unsteady?"

Reginald's calm demeanor fooled the constable into holstering his weapon. He stepped back, not turning from the SRR officer for more than a second to check on his friend. Antonio was about to bend down to help Marco from the floor when he felt a disturbance in the air near him. Glancing up, Marco's handgun was in his face.

"Ho!" Antonio screamed and backed into the open door. He blinked as he reached for his own weapon only to find that Reginald was holding Marco's semi-automatic by the barrel.

"He dropped this," the Brit said mildly.

Antonio blinked again. He was sure he had seen the barrel of Marco's gun pointing in his face, but now here it was, surrendered butt-first by the man that had just been sitting on the bed several meters away. He had not felt a tremor in the floor or heard the man move. Reginald Mattersly had appeared next to him as if teleported.

"Secure this for him, won't you? There's a good chap."

Antonio took the offered handgun and dumbly stared at the man in front of him.

Reginald nodded, squatted next to Marco, and hooked his arm underneath the prone man's armpit. As he stood, he brought the dizzied bodyguard up with him. "I say, old man, you all right?"

"I think so," Marco breathed. A bit unsteadily, he reached for the doorjamb for balance.

"You should really watch out for this door. I don't think it's hung correctly." Mattersly demonstrated by tugging the door away from the wall and giving it a push. It remained fully open with its knob resting on the rubber pad. "Well, I suppose it could have been the wind."

"Your window's closed," Antonio protested, though

not strongly.

"Ah. So it is," Reginald agreed. "Shall we be off, then?"

Marco merely nodded and stepped back into the hall. Antonio could tell that the man's head had not cleared, but not knowing what had truly transpired, he was prepared to let it go. He led the way to the next door and knocked upon it. He turned behind him to see a neutral expression on the Brit's face while his friend and partner brought up the rear. Marco had his jaw in his hand as he checked it for movement and winced in discomfort. Antonio shook his head in wonder and decided to ask about it later.

The door to Mulhaney's room opened and he appeared. "Somebody wrestlin' elephants out here? What happened to him?" he asked this last with a jerked thumb toward Marco.

"Just a little accident. Let's go," Antonio ordered, wanting no more nonsense.

The four men walked toward the staircase, led by Antonio and bookended by Marco. As they approached the head of the stairs, Elias leaned over to his new friend and whispered, "Are you the little accident?"

"So it would seem," Mattersly answered.

The four men descended the stairs in silence. Elias took care as he stepped, relying heavily on his walking stick.

"What fell up there?" Jazz met them at the foot of the stairs.

"Marco, did," Antonio said. He shifted his eyes away from hers.

"Really?" she stated more than asked. She searched Mulhaney's face for a better answer or perhaps just proof that there was something else to that. She found that trace of doubt in the smug grin of Reginald Mattersly. "Uh-huh."

"He looks a bit concussed if you ask me," Elias

offered as he followed the directions of Antonio, who gestured for them to enter a room off to their immediate left.

"Yeah, well, I didn't," she fired back and shooed him inside.

The room was wood paneled and a bit narrow, just wide enough to accommodate the long dining table, chairs, and some walking space. The table was set for three, with one at the far end and the other two places across from each other and more than a meter away. It was well lit and cool, like the rest of the building.

Reginald went to the right as he was motioned to do by Antonio. By default, Elias went left. Both men sat. Hernandez stepped past them on the way to the head of the table. She continued to scrutinize Mattersly's face, certain that there was more to the incident. He met her gaze and smiled while trying to maintain an innocent exterior. She smiled back and took her seat. Reginald made an attempt to rise, apparently to push her chair in for her. Jazz held up her hand abruptly and with authority. She wagged a finger at him and wordlessly, he retook his seat.

When she was settled, she opened her mouth to speak but movement at the other end of the room distracted her. Antonio had stepped over to Marco and turned his back to her. A look of surprise and a deep red blush appeared on her bodyguard's face and, as Antonio went back to his place, she caught sight of Marco replacing his handgun to the shoulder holster under his sport coat.

Her mouth dropped open. Marco understood that the exchange had been seen and turned an even deeper red as he studied the wall behind her. Jazz shook her head and rolled her eyes. Whatever had happened, she refused to ask about it.

"So," Hernandez said through clenched teeth, "I take it you found the accommodations comfortable?"

"Absolutely, thank you," Reginald returned and Elias agreed.

"The both of you clean up pretty well," she commented and took a deep breath. "It's nice to have guests for dinner."

"Guests, Miss Hernandez?" Mattersly spoke up. "We've gone beyond being prisoners, I take it?"

"You'll have to forgive the initial contact, Reggie." Jazz smiled. She could tell that he did not particularly care for his name being shortened. "You have to understand, Lovelock is a town more or less under siege."

"Oh? Is that the reason for the triple-'A' all over the place?" Mulhaney asked.

"You're correct, Elias. We are fighting for our very existence."

"Who and what is attacking your town?" Reginald inquired as Gigi stepped in to pour the wine.

"Our neighbors in Reno don't like us very much. Well, one in particular does not like *me*. We used to be... let's say 'friendly'. Our two towns traded with one another and then we had a falling out."

"So, they are able to harass you by air?" Mattersly pressed with a raised eyebrow. He had not seen a functioning aircraft since well before leaving England and even then the machine was a low-tech recreation of a museum piece.

"My counterpart is pretty well supplied," Jazz admitted, "and they have the benefit of some manufacturing equipment. All pretty antiquated, of course, but functional."

"Just what exactly are they attacking your town *with*, Miss Hernandez?" Elias asked once he downed the red wine. He reached for the carafe and poured another.

Reginald took a sip from his glass as he watched her face.

"They have built a Cobra helicopter," Jazz explained then sipped her wine.

"Surely not," Reginald protested.

"I'm crapping you negative, Major." She smiled briefly. "It's not an authentic museum piece. It was built from scratch from rudimentary blueprints that were interpreted by the machinery. I've been over there and I've seen the layout of the equipment. It's a traditional fabrication station kept up by a few technicians, I assume. I never met them."

"But they must have some supply of munitions as well. A fabricator can't produce fuel or propellant," Reginald stated.

"They do, but I don't know where he's getting it."

"What's his name, anyway?" Elias asked.

"He goes by one name. Gillespie. Like myself, he's their mayor, their president, their everything," Hernandez explained.

"You've got some connections, too, it appears," Mulhaney went on as the food was brought in by Gigi and Beth.

"Well, the anti-aircraft guns were traded for and we're still paying for them with produce."

Mattersly thought this over as he dug into the steak on his plate. The cut of the meat was of high quality. Like his partner across from him, he had not eaten beef for a long time. The mixture of carrots, broccoli, and cauliflower made for a tasty side dish. It was simple, but in comparison to living off the land and eating aged processed foods, it was a feast.

Gigi poured more wine. Elias smiled at her as she walked away and a question occurred to him. "Say, where does the wine come from?"

"More trades, Mister Mulhaney. I have a couple wagons not unlike Reggie's that make trips for me." She gave Mattersly a wink, which melted the grimace that had appeared upon hearing the short version of his name. "We give them food, they give us wine and beer."

"Well, it sure is good stuff," Elias proclaimed. "I wonder what the beer's like."

"Beth," Jasmin called to the girl standing by the door. "Would you get these gentlemen a couple of pints?"

Beth acknowledged with a grin and slipped out.

"Why, thank you, Miss Hernandez," Mulhaney said cheerfully. He raised the wine glass to her and swallowed what remained.

"Call me Jazz, please."

"I must say that your hospitality is exemplary, Jazz." Reginald received a nod of gratitude from his hostess. "But, it leaves me to wonder a few things about our…well, captivity."

"Oh, you mustn't call it that, Reggie," Jazz protested.

"Yeah, Reggie," Elias chimed in and chuckled. He received a glare from his British friend, but he smiled back at him.

"Well, my dear, I just don't know what else *to* call it," the major went on. "I mean to say, we have been treated rather well, all told, but as to our status with you and the town of Lovelock, I'm afraid I'm at a loss to categorize it."

Hernandez rested her head on the palm of her left hand and begun to stare. The wine glass in her other hand was left to lazily swirl the red liquid. "Oh, I could listen to you all night. How are your reading skills?"

"Miss Hernandez…"

"Call me Jazz, darn you, Reggie," she insisted, feigning hurt as she sat back and emptied her wine glass.

Reginald sighed as Beth returned with two glasses of amber-colored brew. She set them down in front of both men and silently returned to her place near the door. Elias scooped up the glass, gave the fluid a quick sniff, and tasted it with a slurping inhale.

"Oh my God, that *is* beer," he declared and took a gulp.

To this, Jazz laughed heartily and slapped the table.

Reginald sampled his glass as well and found it to be a palatable pale ale with a generous helping of hops. This told him that the brewer had quite the spread of land if he were able to grow most of what he needed to make beer and wine.

"Yes, well," he began and interrupted himself with another swig of the beverage, "I'm afraid my question stands, Jazz."

Another burst of laughter erupted from Jazz Hernandez as she regarded her serious guest. "Oh, Reggie, you must relax *sometime*."

"Oh, I assure you, I will. All I'd like to know is what I am to regard the room in which I shall sleep tonight? A suite or a cell?" Reginald pressed and stared hard at the leader of Lovelock.

Jazz stared back, her humor lost in a heartbeat. "Very well, *Mister* Mattersly! I had hoped that our relationship would have a bit of a transitional period, *from* prisoner *to* guest, but I see that you need to be spoon-fed that information instead of having it happen organically."

Reginald blinked and sat up straight. He had not intended to insult the woman. He had simply not seen their predicament from her perspective.

"You must understand. We are a small town at war," Hernandez told them in a calmer tone. "We have no real army, no federal government to turn to for help, and limited resources."

"I understand that…" Mattersly began but was cut off.

"*Tsk, tsk, tsk.*" She wagged a finger back and forth.

"I'm not done. We often have strangers come into town from every direction. Some are just passing through or are curious about us and mean us no harm and they move on. And, *I* allow them to, *because* they mean no harm. Others come by because they have nowhere to turn to. *I* allow them to stay if they have something to offer Lovelock. And there are those few that Gillespie sends here to try to infiltrate our town and gain our trust, only to sabotage us, or perhaps blow up some of my people."

Jazz stood from the table, bumping it with her leg. The heavy table shook, but she gave no notice. The leader of Lovelock began to pace behind Mulhaney while Marco and Antonio stilled as if made of marble. The server girls looked to their leader with nervous eyes.

"It's happened, gentlemen!" Jazz took up and struck her right arm out toward Gigi, who came to her side quickly to refill the wine glass in her hand. Hernandez resumed pacing as her black eyes focused intently on Mattersly's face. "My own sister was killed just last month! My niece…*taken*!" She downed the precious red wine in a single gulp and dropped herself into her chair. The empty glass tumbled onto the table, saved from shattering by the thick tablecloth. "And you have the *balls* to insist on something from me!" she nearly howled.

The room was deadly silent for several long seconds. Reginald and Elias both looked about the room, watching the eyes of the men and women who were subservient to the demure black-haired woman at the foot of the table. Jazz herself stared at the turned over glass, her lips pursed with anger and grief. Beth stepped in, righted and refilled it.

"I do apologize, Miss Hernandez," Mattersly said lowly as he watched her face. "My only defense is that I have been on my own for a great amount of time, concerned only with the daily tasks of my own survival."

"Ditto," offered Mulhaney, who then downed his pint.

"That's the only thing you could have said that makes it all right, Reggie," Jazz murmured and gave a hint of a smile.

"Who was it that murdered your sister?" he dared to ask.

She shook her head sadly and sipped more wine. "She was knifed to death by her boyfriend, a man that came through town a few years ago and proved himself to be an asset to the town. Sanitation department, street department, whatever else."

"Why did he kill her?" Elias asked.

"Who the hell knows?" Jazz grumbled. "He just went crazy."

"Where has he taken your niece?" Reginald inquired and took a drink from his glass.

"Witnesses say he took off in his car that night," Antonio spoke up. "He's a Renoite now."

"Could they have bypassed Reno?" Mulhaney pondered.

"They didn't," Hernandez said with finality. "The Cobra dropped a mess of flyers along the north end of town. It had a picture of my niece on it. The only way they could have known her identity is if the bastard that killed my sister told them."

"Is your niece his child?" the major inquired.

Jazz shifted in her seat and straightened up. "No. My sister's husband died a few years ago."

"So he has no real attachment to her. No reason to keep her alive," he surmised.

"Not really, other than to deliver her into the hands of the enemy for spite," Jazz said. "Gillespie and I were to be married many years ago, gentlemen. It didn't work out and he left Lovelock for Reno. He was a genius with electronics and must have repaired or figured out how to use their fabrication device. He put that helicopter together, climbed up the totem pole, and is now the Mayor-guru of Reno."

"But what is he after? What does he mean by all this?" Reginald wondered.

"He wants me, Reggie," Jazz revealed with a heavy sigh. "If he can't have me, he'll kill me and some of my people have died keeping me from either option."

"Indeed," Mattersly grunted and finished his beer.

"Yes, indeed, Reggie," Hernandez emphasized then leaned further forward as she looked from one guest to the other. "So, tell me again why I should believe you when you say you aren't with Gillespie?"

Mattersly and Mulhaney looked to each other for a moment. It was Reginald that said what they both were thinking. "Well, I suppose the only thing we can do is take you to the bodies of our ambushers... if they haven't been carted off piece by piece by the wildlife, that is."

"That sounds messy, but I suppose that should do it," Jazz agreed with a scrunched up nose.

"Oh, one stipulation if you please, Miss Hernandez," Reginald added.

"And what's that, Reggie?" she asked sweetly.

The major passed his eyes over Marco, Antonio and then back to Jazz. "I would like you to accompany us when we go. I'd hate for my friend or I to become... er... victims of an incident."

Jazz laughed and looked to Marco. "I *knew* something happened upstairs!" she shouted gleefully and clapped her hands. "Now, Marco, don't you pout," she warned, though the man had done no such thing. "You're a good man, but you tend to underestimate people." She turned to Mattersly and patted his right forearm. "That's agreed, Major Reggie." She winked. "Shall we go in the morning?"

***

Until the morning, the men remained in their rooms, more or less as prisoners, but now with refreshed understanding. Their rooms were guarded by other men overnight and in the morning they were retrieved by both Marco and Antonio and escorted outside. Reginald and Elias were cuffed once again, despite mild protest. Jazz Hernandez stood smiling alongside a somewhat large sedan of German design parked behind the squad car. She wore a pair of form-fitting gold slacks, walking shoes, and a red button-front blouse that shone in the sun like satin or silk.

"Good morning," she greeted.

"It *was*," Mulhaney snapped. The handcuffs were uncomfortable and he made sure she knew it.

"Not to worry, gentlemen," she said. "If your story checks out, those will come off."

Mattersly spoke not a word as he held her dark eyes for a few heartbeats. He was stuffed into the back seat of the police cruiser. Antonio sat in the front while Marco chauffeured Hernandez in the other.

Under the guidance of the two visitors, Antonio retraced their path, rolling along Upper Valley Road until they met the street that led to the strange processing plant and deep into the hills. In a relatively short period of time, they arrived at the spot where pavement met path.

The carcass of the horse was spotted first as it was on the road. It had been mauled by animals and a small gathering of vultures were perched upon the exposed ribs and hind quarters, barely taking notice of the vehicles that had rolled up on them. The two vehicles parked. Elias and Reginald were left to lead them over the remnants of the gun battle. The smell of death was thick on the warm air. The lack of breeze made it all the worse.

The bodies of the two ambushers behind the bluff

had been picked over as well. The upper body of one of them had been dragged away, leaving a blood trail in the dirt.

Jazz seemed not to mind the gory scene at all, as she remained close to the men as they went over the scene. The only place she did not venture was up the hill. For that, she let Antonio lead Mattersly to the place where the sniper had laid waiting.

"Yup! It's Momo all right!" Antonio called down to her.

Hernandez smiled. "Very well! Unhook them!" she shouted then turned to her bodyguard and nodded.

"So, we're free to go?" Mulhaney asked after Marco released the cuffs from Elias's wrists.

"If you have to," Jazz granted. "There's no reason to rush off just yet."

Antonio and Mattersly returned to the ground from the hill. "It was Momo, Jazz. Half his head was gone, taken off by the Major's bullet, but it was him."

"Best news I've heard all month," she oozed through a tight grin as her eyes roamed Reginald's face. "Can you drive a car, Reggie?"

"Of course," he said with a smile while he rubbed his wrists.

"Marco, Antonio," Jazz addressed, "go patrol something. These two will be with me in my car."

Marco was about to protest verbally, but she looked up to him and gave a slight nod. Antonio did not say a word though he was clearly apprehensive as he strode toward the cruiser.

"Elias, get in the back," she directed as she walked to the passenger side of her car. "Follow the police car back to town," she told Reginald once he had taken a seat behind the wheel.

He touched the button to activate the motor and

turned the sedan around. He brought the car to a good speed and was relieved to note that the machine could absorb the ruined pavement in better fashion than the police car. It was also quieter in spite of its more advanced age.

"So, I take it that we are to be spared," Reginald said as he steered the car around a hole.

Hernandez laughed. "Oh, Reggie! You can be so dramatic!"

"It's not every day that I am a prisoner one moment and a chauffeur the next," Mattersly went on. "You have me wondering about your agenda."

"My agenda?"

"Yeah," Mulhaney spoke up from the back. "You told me we could leave but to not be in a hurry."

"I have something to show you two," she said. "Just follow my direction, Reggie."

Mattersly sighed, displaying his dismay over the continued shortening of his name. "Very well."

Hernandez directed the major to make several turns once within the city limits of Lovelock. As they traveled to the northwest, some homes and commercial buildings showed damage while others were burned to the ground.

"Is this some of the helo's handiwork?" Mattersly asked as he came to a stop in front of a two-story brick building. The entire front half had been blown away, revealing a blackened interior.

"Uh-huh," Jazz confirmed. "That's my old club. Bastards blew it up almost two years ago. We didn't have the best protection at the time."

"How often are these helo attacks?" Mulhaney asked.

"There's no pattern." Hernandez tossed her hands up. They landed with slaps to her thighs. "We won't see one for weeks, sometimes months. He just shows up and trashes the place and then leaves. It's almost like they build up enough ammo for a hit, do it, then go back home to make more for another run. One week last year, they hit us twice, then nothing for six weeks."

"They seem to miss you every time," Mattersly noted.

"I used to move around a lot." She leaned against her door so she could see both men's faces. "With the addition of the guns around my current hangout, he's a lot more careful. He flies fast and low, and holds his fire until he sees someone on the street."

"Is this Gillespie chap the pilot?"

"I have no idea, but I doubt it," Jazz chuckled and smirked darkly. "I don't think my ex-bee-eff has it in him."

Reginald pressed the accelerator gently and rolled the car down the residential street. Hernandez directed him to make a right turn and then another. The car soon gathered the attention of the populace. Children called out her first name and came running to the curb. Very few actually ran into the street, but Reginald slowed the sedan in case they did.

Hernandez pressed a button to drop the window and struck her hands out, waving and shouting back. "Hello everyone! Hello!" Mattersly slowed the car further. Jazz turned to him in the midst of receiving her adulations. "Keep going for a couple blocks."

The major did as directed, though the people of Lovelock crowded the sedan's path. The citizens were left behind once the car rolled through the next intersection. He accelerated and guided the vehicle back to the middle of the street.

Hernandez put her window back up. "What can I say? People here love me."

"It shows," Mulhaney said from the back seat.

"Where are we going?" asked Reginald.

"Just up ahead here." Her smile faded. In the

distance of two blocks, the neighborhood again changed from upbeat and lively to desolate and depressing. Homes on either side of the block had been attacked by the helo. Some were nothing more than scorched cinder blocks, while the lucky ones merely showed large holes in the walls and roofs. “Right here, Reggie. Stop here.”

Mattersly complied. Before the car even came to a complete halt, her door was open and she was getting out. As if in a trance, Jazz walked across the sidewalk and toward the house in front of her.

Mulhaney watched her for a moment then turned to Reginald. “What do you think’s going on?”

“Apparently, she has something she wishes us to see,” he answered and exited the car. He looked up and down the street before continuing on. It was nearly silent and devoid of life, though his ears could pick up the sound of vehicles rolling along a paved road some distance away.

Mulhaney stepped up alongside him and watched the town’s matriarch glide up the front steps. The building was a bi-level single family home, as were almost all the structures on the block. This one stood out as it seemed to have been taken care of quite nicely before it was shot to hell. Holes from a large caliber machine gun peppered the stucco walls and wooden fascia. Almost all of the glass had been shattered as well.

“Can you make it, Elias?” Jazz asked as she turned back to them. It was clear she wanted to show the both of them something inside.

“I sure can, Miss Hernandez.” He stepped in behind Mattersly. In good time, he joined the both of them on the porch, some eight steps above ground level.

She pushed the front door out of her way and entered. The two men followed. Mulhaney cussed under his breath and stepped to a spot in the center of what had been the living room. The place had been well-furnished at one time and recently, but the attacks on the home had destroyed much of the furniture, which lay splintered and shredded. There were stairs to their left and great wooden sliding doors to their right. They, too, had been struck by the aircraft's cannon-fire, appearing to have been chewed from the inside out by a predator long gone.

"This was my sister's house," Hernandez announced as she approached the doors. "This place was pretty nice when she and my niece lived in it."

"It was beautiful," Elias mumbled and shook his head.

"All of this happened after she was killed?" Reginald indicated the shell-tattered walls.

"Yeah." Her black eyes shone in the curtain-filtered sunlight as she inspected the damage. "I guess Miguel gave Gillespie the location of the house and the helo was sent to level the place. They shot it up the day they dropped those leaflets I mentioned."

"It's a good thing there was no one here," Mulhaney commented in a near whisper.

"Well, if Miguel hadn't trashed the place the day he killed my sister," she narrated as she threw open the destroyed sliding doors, "we would have had the wake here."

Mattersly and Mulhaney both grimaced. The dining room floor and table were covered with dried blood. The walls near the doorway to the kitchen had been smeared with it, apparently by hand. More blood covered the kitchen floor and the sink, all of which could be seen from where the men stood.

"It was pretty obvious that we couldn't use this house for it." Hernandez stepped into the dining room. "So, we had it at my place. Three days after Miguel Costa killed her, that's when the Cobra attacked it."

"That tells me that your sister's murderer made

friends with Gillespie pretty fast," Elias figured.

"It's easy to do with the presence of the niece," Reginald went further, "whom he has met before. Am I not correct?"

"Yeah, you're right, Reggie." Jazz smiled. "My niece, Nora, is eight. Gillespie and I were an item for a few years. He last saw her when she was five, maybe six."

"She was used by Costa as a ticket to escape," Mulhaney said and shifted his weight onto his walking stick.

"Yes, Elias." Jazz nodded and cast her eyes upon him. "She must have been. See, all the roads going into Reno are guarded. Gillespie and his people don't like strangers unless they have something to offer. I've sent scouts there on occasion and the ones that come back say it's hard to get past them."

"How many have been caught?" Elias wondered.

"It's impossible to know for sure," Jazz answered vacantly. "Some may have stayed because they liked it better. Some may have been killed, others may have just not gone there at all. Who can say?"

At that moment, Reginald received a request on his implant from Hernandez. Her eyes scanned him quickly as the SRR soldier accepted the link. She looked to Mulhaney with a blank expression as she sent: "*How far do you think we can trust your friend?*"

Mattersly stepped leisurely along the living room carpet with his hands behind his back as he crushed glass shards underneath his boot and composed a reply. "*Trust him for what?*"

"*Cut the crap, Reggie. I need to ask you both for a favor and I think you know what it might be.*"

"*In which case, present your favor to the both of us plainly and your question will be answered,*" he sent back as he turned to her.

"Fine," she said aloud. "I'll come to the point." She slammed the sliding doors shut and stepped up to both men to watch their faces for a reaction as she crossed her arms. "Our situation here in Lovelock is looking pretty damn grim. Our suppliers are out of ammunition for the anti-aircraft guns. We have just over two thousand rounds, *total.*"

"After that, you are defenseless," the major declared. "You've no energy weapons?"

"That's right," Hernandez said hotly, "and once we're out of ammo, I don't know what the hell we're gonna do."

"So, what are you asking of *us*?" Mulhaney spoke up.

"You two are the only people I know with any military background other than Marco. People will notice if he leaves."

"Do you have reason to believe there are spies in your midst?" asked Reggie with a raised brow.

"I can't prove it, either way." She shrugged. "But it stands to reason. If I just let you two go, you can infiltrate Reno with less of a risk."

"Whoa there, young lady," Elias said. "*Infiltrate* Reno? You've got to be kidding me. It sounds like a place that's just begging to be avoided."

"What are you expecting from us?" Mattersly demanded. "A rescue mission? The destruction of the Cobra and the fabrication plant? The assassination of this Mister Gillespie perhaps?"

"Honestly? Hell yes!" Jazz came close to the Brit and stared up into his face. "Look, I know you have no stake in this town and you have no reason to help us. I figure that some guy carrying C-4 in his horse-drawn wagon must know how to use the stuff. It's just an idea I'm kicking around, okay?"

Reginald broke his gaze from Jazz's eyes with great effort and looked to Mulhaney for a reaction. The man had an amused expression upon his face. He shook his head slightly.

"You have to appreciate my position here, guys." Hernandez began to pace, kicking debris out of her way as she went. "Lovelock is dying and it's because of me. Gillespie can keep this shit up all he wants and what can I *do*?!"

"Jazz, listen…" Elias started but was shut down.

"You listen! I know it's been hard for you two out there," Hernandez hissed. "But appreciate this place for a moment. It might be the civilized haven you've been looking for…except for the fact that some madman likes to unload rockets on us," Jazz took a deep breath and calmed before continuing. "A few years ago, we had no problems. Reno and Lovelock traded and got along fine. We had a glimmer of civilization. It wasn't perfect, but it was better than wandering out there." She swung an arm into the air at the rest of the world.

Elias rubbed the back of his head in thought. His eyes passed over the broken items in the home and then to the holes in the walls. The thought of taking down some bothersome armed helicopter was intriguing. *If we could just manage that part, it might be enough. But, then no. They could just build another if what she said was true.*

"How many people live in Reno, Jazz?" Reginald inquired as he rubbed the stubble on his chin.

"A few thousand," she answered, "which might as well be a damned metropolis in this day and age."

"How many people in Lovelock?"

"About four hundred, including the ranchers and farmers on the outskirts."

"So, he's not attacking them, just strafing the town, trying to kill you specifically?" asked Elias.

Hernandez nodded. "The Cobra has never opened fire on them. He just attacks the town."

"But a lot less since the triple-'A' was added," he surmised.

Again, she nodded. "We've hit the thing a couple of times, but not badly enough to bring it down.

The three stood quietly for a long moment. Reginald turned and looked through the space where the front window used to be. Jazz broke the silence, sensing she had lost her audience.

"All I can ask is that you two think about it," she said as she shuffled to the door. "I've got nothing to offer you but a home when… if… you return. Beyond that, I don't know what to do. God knows, I'm open to ideas." She yanked the door out of her way and stalked to her car.

Elias stepped up to the window alongside Reginald and watched her go. "You think she's crazy?"

"Not at all, Mister Mulhaney," he answered and moved to the open door. "She's a woman backed into a corner and knows there's nothing left to do but fight."

***

The trio returned to Jazz's club and for a long time, Elias and Reginald sat at the bar as liberated men of Lovelock and exchanged stories about a great many things: Their home life before the military, the genetic alterations during their adolescence, their training as adults, and finally, a few campaign tales. The conversation naturally gravitated back to their current situation, which was essentially Lovelock's situation. The club was quiet, as it was only late afternoon and the band was not rehearsing. It was hours until nightfall and the two soldiers came up with an alternative to a covert invasion of Reno.

Hernandez had retreated to her suite on the third floor, which was blocked off for all except herself and her bodyguards. Since they had returned from her sister's abandoned and destroyed home, they had been left to the first floor, unsure of what to do other than talk. Together, they left the bar and casually walked about the neighborhood, taking note of the anti-air defense coverage and layout of the center of town. They returned after some time, deep in discussion over what could be done.

That evening, citizens began to enter the club in singles and pairs. A few sat at the bar where the brunette, Gigi, served them drinks. Elias and Reginald were given cursory glances by the patrons, who seemed interested in anything but new people in town. Many of these customers were oddly dressed in ornate and exaggerated cuts of clothing. Some of the men wore suit jackets that were too big in the shoulders, further decorated with fedoras with brims that cast their entire faces in shadow. There were variations on the theme between a dozen men. The women who accompanied them were outfitted with dresses similar to those that Hernandez seemed to prefer. Sparkly decorations covered the outfits of shiny fabric, capped off by fanciful hats sporting colorful feathers. Necklaces of pearls, gold and silver bracelets, anklets with high-heeled shoes painted a picture of another time and place within the reality of desolation that the two soldiers had experienced beyond the establishment's doors.

The people now matched the décor. Extravagant and gaudy, the mood of the club was that of happiness bordering on gleeful debauchery. As the sun began to fall, some of the more ornately dressed men moved from the bar area, taking the women that were sharing their space into the larger hall. Soon after, the music began.

Curious, Mattersly wove his way through the gathering of relatively opulent humanity and saw that these men made up the band. Having moved to a prominent position in the doorway, the major had begun to gather attention. From the men, he received dismissive glances while many of the women gave him curious assessments from top to bottom before most of them seemed to label him as not of their ilk. Despite his handsome features, his military tunic and trousers made him stand out, denoting him as little more than perhaps one of the help.

Reginald was nonetheless enjoying the music when he realized that he stood alone in the archway. The disapproving faces had receded from him as if they sensed his inner strength. He gave a crooked smile of satisfaction and turned to see that Mulhaney had joined him. The taller man had taken a place just behind and to his left, standing straight but relying on his walking stick. He had kept his big black Stetson upon his head and cinched low, so it obscured most of his uneven face. It had grown warm in the club, so the man had removed his duster, revealing a freshly washed olive drab sleeveless shirt that displayed his tattoo of the five-hundred and fourth parachute regiment on his upper right arm. The red devil set before a pair of blue wings under a banner of gold which read, 'Airborne' had the effect of a stink bomb on the civilians. Mattersly chuckled at his own arrogance and smiled widely.

"What?" Elias growled over the music, wanting in on the joke.

Reginald was relieved of the duty to answer when the lady of the house walked up to them. She wore a burgundy dress that glowed in the yellow electric light of the increasingly smoky room. The white elbow-length gloves were only outshone by the string of irregularly-sized pearls around her neck. In one hand, she carried a martini glass full of a clear liquid and an olive. Her patrons bid for her attention with their greetings, which she met in cursory fashion. She would not be kept from her destination. Marco walked behind her from a distance, blocking any who would wish to fall into her wake.

"Good evening!" she called to them.

"Good evening," the major returned.

"Hello!" Elias called as the band leader's horn reached a crescendo, which received applause and whistles from the audience.

"Where are your drinks?" she asked.

"I did not wish to assume that we had the run of the bar," Reginald explained.

Hernandez made a dismissive sound with her lips and motioned for them to follow her. With most of the patrons watching and listening to the band, the bar stools the two men had been sitting upon earlier were still open. She went behind the bar, stepping around Gigi, who was busy mixing a drink.

Jazz poured beers for them and remained there while they drank. They could tell that the martini she was working on had not been her first. Her dark eyes were glassy and pink where once there was a brilliant whiteness.

Mattersly took a deep gulp of his ale and looked to Elias, who nodded. "Listen, Jazz," he started out. Immediately, he had her attention. She locked eyes with his and stared expectantly, appearing almost playful with her hair gracing her shoulders and embracing her neck. "Elias and I were speaking of your town's predicament."

"Uh-huh." Her faint smile disappeared and a business-like expression replaced it.

"Well, it seems to me that perhaps you haven't been able to bring down that menace because your troops lack some training," he explained.

"Possible," she admitted.

"We'd like to meet with your gunners and evaluate their methods. Perhaps give some pointers. At the very least, we could prevent them from wasting ammunition."

"Sounds good to me." Jazz took another sip of her martini. "We can at least annoy Gillespie by bringing the thing down once. Who knows? Maybe that'll give us a few weeks before they build another one," she finished with a hint of frustration and downed the drink. Before Mattersly could explain further, Hernandez stalked off to tell Gigi to mix her another.

Mulhaney leaned over to be heard. "I'm sensing she's underwhelmed with our solution."

"It does lack of permanence, Elias," Reginald returned. "It's also highly unlikely that the pilot is this Gillespie fellow. If it were, it would solve a great many things."

Elias nodded and drank.

In a few moments, Jazz returned with a fresh martini and regarded her new friends. Her gaze was not of anger, but of wonder with a trace of melancholy. In her eyes, Reginald could define the weight of responsibility within her. The knowledge that citizens of Lovelock had died under her watch was causing the woman deep conflict and she wanted nothing more than to have it end, one way or another.

"Jazz," Reginald said as he leaned closer, "let us start there. We can always think of something else."

Hernandez smiled with her lips pressed together before tilting her head to one side. "Okay, Reggie. Let's start there."

The evening went on around them with some interruptions. Jazz was a popular public figure and as such, received some calls on her attention. After some hours and a few pints, Reginald and Elias said their good nights and retired. The music had ended around midnight and the club emptied of its guests.

For almost an hour after lying in the comfortable bed, Mattersly thought over Lovelock's situation and wondered if they were being told everything. In every conflict, there were two sides of the story.

Chapter Four

The morning came all too soon. Though he had enjoyed just three pints of the local brew, Reginald's head pounded and the sunlight sent streams of ache penetrating deeply into his eyeballs. He shut them tight and rolled out of the bed. His implant had not yet completed its startup sequence, so there was nothing else he could do but shut the shades to the offending sunlight.

Mattersly shuffled to the bathroom and took down a couple tumblers of water. He had not had beer in a long time and the brew of Lovelock was high in alcohol, so its effect on his body was similar to the very first time he had overdone it. He had been a young man then and about to head off to the army. His friends had liberated a small cache of English ales in cans. It had not taken many of them to create a similar aftereffect.

The major showered, shaved, and dressed in his freshened uniform. It was the only set he had left with matched camouflage patterns, though the colors had faded somewhat over the years. The black pixels had turned to gray and the tones of the deep forest had changed to wintergreen. As an afterthought, he placed his SRR beret on his head and checked his appearance in the mirror before he ventured out of his room.

The second floor was quiet and there was no one watching their rooms. Mattersly's booted and carefree steps upon the bare wood thrummed through the narrow hallway as he headed for the stairs. The main room was in a disheveled state from the previous evening's bombardment, though many of the tables had been cleared. Reginald heard the clinking of glass in the direction of the bar area, so he sauntered over. To his surprise, he found not Gigi or Beth, but the lady of the house herself.

"Well, good morning," he called.

Jazz startled and nearly dropped the wine glass she was washing. "Shit, Reggie!" she squeaked. She stared at him angrily for a fleeting moment before taking a deep breath and letting it go.

"Apologies." Mattersly smiled. He stood at the side of the bar where he could see all of her. Instead of a fancy evening dress, she wore form fitting gray slacks and a white t-shirt. Her hair was up and appeared perfect in its non-perfection. For a pair of heartbeats, they stared upon one another.

"Good morning," she finally said and smiled. "Love the hat."

"It's a beret," he corrected and received a smirk for his efforts. "But, thank you. I thought it fitting since we were to meet some of your defense volunteers today."

Jazz nodded and continued washing her glassware. Reginald became aware that his gaze had turned into a stare. He moved to the other side of the bar and took a stool across from her.

"I take it Mister Mulhaney has yet to show his face this morning," he thought to say as he watched the light cascade across her features. Her head was enshrouded by the silvery reflections of the morning sun from the mirror and bottles behind her.

"Haven't seen him," she murmured pleasantly.

"Well, I must say, I do appreciate that we have been set free, as it were, but I am wondering something."

"Do tell," she replied as she dried a glass with a towel. Her head was cocked to one side and her dark eyes traced his narrow face.

"What exactly has happened to my wagon and my… er… belongings?"

"They're safe," Jazz allowed. "So's Elias's horse. In

fact, he's looking much better since Thumper's been takin' care of him."

"I guess what I mean is: will I get my belongings returned to me?" he tried again.

"I'm not holding them for ransom, you know," Hernandez explained over the rushing water. "A wagon full of explosives is not something I wanted parked in front of my place."

"Understandable," Reginald replied. He smiled crookedly as he watched her wash another glass. He did not feel it appropriate to mention that it was not he that parked his bomb-on-wheels on the street, but Thumper himself.

"You'll get it back. All of it," she said as her eyes met his again. Her smile slipped away as she tilted her head to one side.

"I say, have you had any sleep?"

"Nope." She popped an eyebrow.

"Terribly sorry."

"It happens," she said as she put the cleaned and dried pint glass on the shelf.

There was much Reginald Mattersly wanted to say in that moment. He wanted to tell Jazz Hernandez that he, alone, would storm the walls of Reno, take down the fire-breathing dragon, kill the evil king, and rescue the young princess. He wanted to tell her that all things were possible and that all things would be well. He opened his mouth to speak before his next, more rational thought was fully formed. She turned toward him and picked up the next dirty glass, and noted his dropped jaw and thoughtful eyes. She smiled and lit up the room beyond the capabilities of the sun alone.

She uttered a young girl's laugh. "What? What is it, Reggie?"

The step-step-thump rhythm that he learned to be that of Mulhaney was heard as the man descended the stairs. "It shall wait."

"Good morning!" Elias boomed as he rounded the corner. A beaming smile lit up his face. He was wearing his best outfit: a pair of army trousers with a plain white t-shirt. His hair was carefully combed and still wet from his shower. "What's for breakfast?"

***

Over a small morning meal of eggs, fish, and coffee in the small private room next to the club's main room, Hernandez, Mattersly, and Mulhaney spoke of the town's situation. Marco, the bodyguard, was stationed outside the door for privacy. He had not taken the order to remain out of the room very well. Had Mulhaney's implant not been a factor, such a precaution would not have been necessary. The three could have conversed in silence.

"Am I to understand that you have no access to any type of energy weapons? No sonic disruptors? No EMP weaponry?" Elias started off as he poked his fish with a fork.

"What you saw is what we got," Hernandez replied with an insistent shake of her head. "A mixture of pieced-together throwbacks to the twenty-first century. We're damned lucky to have them."

"Who is in charge of your anti-aircraft group?" Mattersly asked after a bite of food.

"Well, no one, specifically," Jazz answered. "All six emplacements are linked together by handheld radio."

Reginald was surprised by this revelation. He glanced at Elias, who blinked back at him with his eyebrows raised. "You mean to say that they are free to engage firing at any time?"

"Not at all, Reggie." She waved off with the fork in her hand. "They are only cleared to fire at the Cobra when they have a clear shot."

"I'm thinkin' a 'clear shot' is too much a matter of

opinion to be left up to an untrained gunner," Elias said.

"So what am I supposed to do about that, Elias?" Hernandez asked testily.

"I think suggestions will come up when we interview your people," he replied.

"I certainly hope so," she agreed. "I'd just like for one of them to damage it enough that it doesn't come back for a while."

"Are any of your gunners ex-military?" Reginald followed up as he sat back in the chair. He had polished off the meal quickly in his eagerness to get on with his day.

"Not really, but the man I have in charge of ordnance was a sergeant in the marines. Jerry Horn is his name."

"Really? Why is he not in charge of a gun or perhaps, training?" Mattersly asked.

"He only has one functioning arm, Reggie," Jazz explained. "He lost both in combat and they were replaced by artificial limbs. Unfortunately, he lost one of *those* to some sort of failure and he had to remove it. He also happens to be pretty damn old. Maybe eighty."

"I see." The major nodded and set his empty coffee cup onto the table. "And where is Sergeant Horn typically stationed?"

"He likes to be called 'Gunny'. I don't really know where he is on any given day," Hernandez admitted. "He makes sure every gun is supplied and oversees the disassembly and reassembly of a gun when it comes time to move them. During an attack, he'll run to the closest one and get up on the roof to see what he can do. He's sort of a moral supporter for the volunteers. He also happens to be our good luck charm. Both times that we've hit the Cobra, he's been present at the emplacement that's hit it."

"Nice," Mulhaney commented.

"I look forward to meeting with him," the major

declared. "By the by, I'd like to know when we may have our weapons returned to us. If for no other reason, they may add to our credibility with your volunteers. I've noticed that they are all armed."

"Terribly sorry, Reggie," Jazz answered with a genuine expression of recollection. "I completely forgot. I will have Marco or Denny bring those to you both before we head out."

***

True to her word, their handguns were returned to them while they waited in the small concert hall.

"Thank you, sir," Reginald said to the youngest of Jazz's bodyguards, "and our rifles?"

"I placed them in your rooms," Denny replied. "I didn't think you'd need them for anything today."

"Very well," Mattersly agreed and strapped his gun belt around his waist. He thanked the bodyguard, who nodded in return and left the room.

Mulhaney adjusted his belt to let the giant revolver hang over his right hip. The smaller caliber semi-automatic was stuffed into the small of his back. "Well, I feel a little better about this whole thing, don't you?"

"Indeed," Reginald murmured. "It's good to be trusted."

The two men milled about for another few moments until Jazz beckoned to them from the top of the stairs. "You gentlemen ready?"

Marco stood by her side with his arms folded and not looking too happy. Mattersly was certain in that moment that the bodyguard was not one to forgive and forget. The two men, now equally armed, stared at each other briefly. Reginald was the one to look away, not out of fear, but of tact. He looked instead to where he was to go and began walking.

"We are," Mulhaney called up to them and followed

the major up the stairs. The access to the club's roof was on the third floor, accessible by a ladder and an open hatchway located in front of the door to her personal quarters.

Mattersly went up first, striding into the morning sun ahead of the other three. The SRR officer looked about the area, taking in the view of Lovelock and the lands beyond. The tops of trees could be seen in every direction, with mountain ranges much further away. The sun was warm, hinting to what could be expected later in the day. Reginald saw two men standing on the western end of the roof, just past the olive green machine settled upon the middle of the roof. One was obviously this Horn fellow, as he was missing his left arm from just above the elbow. He stood alongside a shorter man, though it might have been a child, considering the difference in height. This younger individual scanned the area to the west through a pair of binoculars.

Mulhaney was the last one up to the roof. It was not a particularly difficult climb for the man, but he was certainly less expedient. He arrived in time to join in on the introductions.

"Jerry Horn, this is Major Reggie Mattersly, British Army," Jazz said with a hint of pride that seemed out of place to the SRR soldier. "Reggie, this is Sergeant Jerry Horn, U.S. Marines."

"How do you do, Sergeant?" Reginald greeted.

"Pleased ta' meetcha," Horn returned with a gritty smile. The old man suffered from tooth decay and loss, but his smile was winning, anyway. His white hair gleamed in the sunlight as it was tossed by the wind. He shook Mattersly's hand in his mechanical one.

"Reggie here is from the Special Reconnaissance Regiment," Hernandez added and indicated his beret with a hand gesture.

"Really? I'll be damned," Jerry grunted through the

grin.

"And this is Elias Mulhaney," Hernandez went on. She respected the man's wishes to downplay his military experience. The two men shook hands and greeted each other.

Mattersly stepped closer to the gun emplacement and began looking it over. At that moment, the younger, shorter man joined him on the left. He was either in his late teens or early twenties. His black hair was matted and slick with sweat and his white t-shirt was grease and pit-stained. The look in the boy's dark brown eyes seemed to come from a much older person.

"Hello there," Reginald said and stretched his hand out to him. "I'm Major Mattersly. What's your name?"

The young man hesitated and took a moment to wipe his hand on his dirty dungarees before touching the offered hand. "Zorba."

"His real name is Anthony Karakakis," Horn interjected. "I just call him 'Zorba the Greek'."

"Ah," Reginald replied and shook his hand. "Very nice to meet you. Looks like you've been busy."

"Yes, I was," Zorba agreed and looked himself over. "I was greasin' and cleanin' this thing like ol' Jerry showed me," he finished with a wide grin.

"Zorba here is one of two gunners who tagged the Cobra," Jazz added once she sauntered close. "How you doin', Hon?"

The boy beamed and blushed. Even through his deep tan, Reginald could see the redness in his cheeks.

"Fine," he answered sheepishly.

"I see we have only the two guns on top loaded," Reginald commented. Hernandez grasped his right bicep immediately. He perceived a look of mild alarm on her face.

"Yes, sir," Zorba answered. "That's just 'cause

we're trying to conserve the barrels for the fifty-cal. Jerry wanted us to keep 'em lookin' like all four work."

"Ah, I see," he answered the boy then sent a message to Hernandez with his implant. "*So, I take it no one knows about the ammo shortage*."

"*That's right, Reggie-dear. No one beyond Jerry, that is*," she sent back. She held his gaze for a moment as she gave his arm a sharp squeeze before releasing him.

"Tell us how you scored that hit, Zorba," Elias chimed in.

"It was a couple weeks ago," the teenager started off, "and he did something different from normal. Most of the time he flies around us, picking off people along the edge a' town. That time he came right at us."

"He was firing at this building?" Mattersly asked.

"Yeah," the youngster said proudly, "guess I was pissin' him off."

"He's a good shot, this one," the sergeant said of his protégé.

"So, you've been taught how to lead the target?" the major continued.

"Yes, sir."

"Tell me, Zorba," Reginald pressed a little further, "what is this weapon's effective range?"

"Couple thousand yards," Karakakis answered crisply, glancing at Horn. "But, the shots'll go a lot further than that if I lift the barrel. See, Sarge tol' me to be careful when the Cobra's really far out there, ya know, like small." Zorba held his thumb and forefinger a couple of inches apart. "We don't want to be shootin' our own folks in their homes or nothin'."

"Quite," agreed Reginald. "A stellar job, Zorba." The boy thanked him and shook the Brit's hand. Mattersly stepped to Horn's side and spoke lowly. "Who is the other brave lad that's laid lead on the Cobra?"

"Actually, it's a girl," Jerry Horn revealed with a smile. "She was the first of us to put a hole in that flying menace."

"Smashing," the major replied. "Where may we find her, then?"

With Horn leading, the quintet worked their way to the ground floor and went to Hernandez's car. The three former soldiers crowded into the rear to let Jazz have the front seat next to her driver, Marco.

The automobile snaked through the streets of Lovelock, heading roughly north until Marco pulled up to a single-floor commercial structure. The group exited the car and, as Mattersly and Mulhaney looked about, they realized that the trees were minimal here and the structure was surrounded by high capacity parking lots and other single-level buildings. Looking up as they headed to the front door, Mattersly could see the outline of the anti-aircraft gun in the shadows cast unto the ground. Next to it was the shadow of a head. Reginald knew not if he was the only one to have seen it, but he kept quiet. It was a good sign that the volunteers were vigilant.

Jazz knocked on the blackened glass door and was immediately answered. She spoke lowly and stepped through the doorway.

"This gun has been here for a while," Mulhaney said and gestured to the shot-up fascia above the door and the boarded up window at the corner.

"So it would seem," Mattersly replied and followed the other three inside.

The inside of the former office building or whatever it had once been was about bare save for a reception desk that was free of any piece of office equipment. The walls had been painted white many decades before and were now decorated with obscene cartoons, marks of wear, and holes from gun fights and air strikes.

Jazz introduced the two strangers to the woman that had let them inside. She was much older than the rest of them, perhaps around sixty years of age. She was thin and a little taller than Hernandez. She did not make any move toward Mattersly or Mulhaney and merely nodded to them when Jazz spoke their names.

"Nice to meet you, Milly," Mattersly said and nodded in greeting. He did not go against her wishes and force a handshake and neither did his American counterpart.

"Hello," Elias added.

"Is Angel up top?" Jazz asked. Receiving a nod in the affirmative, she stepped toward the waiting hallway. Marco fell into step behind her, followed by Jerry Horn who turned to Elias and Reginald.

"Don't mind Milly, she's had a rough life," Horn said, as if they had not all seen their share of hard times. Reginald nodded in response. There was nothing he could think to say.

Jazz led the group through the hall and a short maze of dimly lit rooms until she rounded one last corner. The room was nothing more than a broom closet, but was more brilliantly lit than any other room they had yet seen. A great square of sunlight filled the tiny room, cascading down the metallic steps of the unfolded staircase like water. It was so bright that Reginald's optics compensated, shading the view to a comfortable level. Hernandez scampered up the steps and disappeared into the yellow light. The rest of the group followed.

Reginald and Elias found an identical gun emplacement to what was on top of Jazz's club. Upon close inspection, he noted that it, too, was rigged to only fire the two guns on top. As the major looked around the blacktopped roof, he noted several large caliber bullet holes in the surface, more than he had seen atop the club.

"Major Reginald Mattersly of the British Army's SRR," announced Jazz Hernandez. "Reggie, this is Angel."

He turned and stepped toward the woman stationed there. She was slightly taller than Jazz and a little younger. Her blond hair appeared ablaze in the mid-morning sunlight. It was cut short, almost like a male's would be. Her eyes were an attractive hazel.

"How do you do?" Reginald inquired and shook her hand.

"Very well, thanks," she replied in a bubbly manner. "Nice to meet you!"

"And this is Elias Mulhaney." Hernandez gestured toward the taller man in the black Stetson.

"H-hi," Angel stammered as she looked into Mulhaney's face. "Nice to meet you."

Elias shook her hand and let her hold onto it while she searched his face. He could tell that she had noticed the slackened muscles and his cane, but it seemed not to bother the young woman in the least. Mulhaney smiled in return. After another moment, she let go.

Reginald had not noted the exchange, instead he rounded the front of the antique weapon and found a gnarly hole in the armor plate. "I say!" he exclaimed, which drew the attention of the retired marine.

"Oh, yes," Horn said. "That happened during the same attack when Angel hit that bastard."

"She's damned fortunate that she wasn't injured," Reginald declared.

Everyone, Marco included, joined him at the front of the gun emplacement and stared. Angel just smiled and hooked her thumbs into the pocket of her faded and torn jeans.

"Let me guess," Elias said as he caught Angel's eye once again. "You were shooting at him and then suddenly he came straight at you, peppered you and you hit him."

"That's right," she replied. "Thought I was gonna bring down that sucker, too."

"How many times did you hit him and where?" asked Mattersly.

"Undercarriage, by the nose and on back as he turned," she explained. "He dove away, *real* low… off that way." Angel gestured southward and swept her arm to the west. "I couldn't get another shot off. I swear he must have scraped the pavement."

"Sounds like a pretty competent pilot, Reg," Mulhaney commented.

"Perhaps, but not infallible," the major judged. "He gets annoyed by the ground fire and makes poor decisions. He relies on his skill to get him out of a jam. I dare say he's awfully lucky not to have bought it thus far."

"Why is he not attacking with rockets at that point?" Mulhaney asked the talented gunner girl.

She shrugged. "He tends to strafe the homes on the outskirts with those," she said with her eyes squinted in thought. "He never fires all that many. A handful, really."

"It's possible that their ordnance supply is dwindling or," Reginald said thoughtfully as he scratched his chin, "perhaps their ability to manufacture them is not particularly efficient."

"Or," Elias added, "perhaps this Gillespie guy really wants Jazz back."

"And doesn't want to take the chance of harming her," Mattersly finished.

Jazz folded her arms across her chest. Her eyes glassed over with the hint of frustrated tears. It appeared as if she were going to speak, but could not bring herself to utter a sound.

"*Let's discuss more of these details privately,*" Mattersly sent in text. Hernandez replied only with a curt nod. To Angel, he said, "Can you describe the helicopter for me?"

"Sure," she said and crossed her arms. "It's black. Not reflective, but like a flat black. It has two people in it. You can see them through the window."

"How are they arranged?" Mulhaney interrupted.

"Uh," she faltered, unsure of what he meant. "Oh! One sits in front of the other. And it has the rocket launchers on these wings that stick out from the body and the main gun is on the nose. It can swivel."

"How many guns are on the nose, Angel?" Reginald asked.

"Um, two. I remember seeing two barrels sticking out with both of 'em spittin' fire at me." She laughed uncomfortably.

"You're doing a wonderful job, baby. Thank you!" Hernandez said and gave her volunteer a tight embrace.

After some further conversation, the group left the brave young woman on her rooftop and returned to the club. Jazz led them into the side room once again and instructed Marco to leave and close the door. With a grimace, he complied.

"What are your thoughts, Reggie? Elias?" Hernandez started them off eagerly. Jerry Horn sat to her right, relaxed and appearing confident.

"Firstly, get the gun off this roof," Mattersly replied and pointed to the ceiling. "Move it to another site. Do the same for Angel's emplacement."

"Why?" Jerry blurted as his face took on an insulted expression.

"The pilot is zeroing in on the two best gunners in your group," the major explained, then turned to Hernandez. "It is my belief that, even though this Gillespie fellow wants you to return to him, his patience is thinning. He will soon order the Cobra to level this town, which it is entirely capable of doing."

"Bullshit!" Horn shouted. His reddish complexion turned an even darker shade. "We're getting closer to taking that thing down!"

"Perhaps so," Mattersly admitted. "But, soon you will see the Cobra unleash its full potential. Zorba and Angel told us that the helo rarely fires its unguided rockets. It's been toying with the citizens of Lovelock."

"Burying fourteen of my people is hardly toying!" Hernandez exclaimed. Her expression was that of injury, not insult.

"I understand, Miss Hernandez," Reginald said more loudly. "My point is that, until now, your town has been attacked by *one* machine, using *one* of its weapons, for the most part. Things will ramp up."

"Okay, so what the hell am I supposed to do, Reggie?" she asked in an only slightly calmer tone. Her dark eyes penetrated him, pleading for an answer to the woes of her people while maintaining her inner strength.

Mattersly looked across the table to his companion, Elias, who sat with fingers interlaced in front of him. He shared an expression of genuine concern, but no answer seemed to be present in his eyes. Reginald stood and unconsciously patted his breast pockets for his tobacco and pipe, which were not there, but upstairs in his room.

"Let's go over what we know, before I present my thoughts on how to proceed," he said as he removed his beret and set it upon the table. He paced in a slow, leisurely gate as his eyes swept the walls in thought. "Firstly, how sure are you, Jazz and Mister Horn, that there has only been the one helicopter?" The two looked to each other, clearly not having an answer.

"Does the thing have any symbols painted on it?" Elias added to the query.

"Not that I've seen," Horn murmured.

"It appears to be the same one each time," Jazz said.

"Matte black, no markings."

"How much time went between the first confirmed hit on the Cobra and its next attack?" the major followed.

"Hmm," she grunted in thought, "I remember it being not quite two weeks. But there's nothing unusual in that spacing. We've gone as long as seven… eight weeks."

"No help there, Reg," Mulhaney opined.

Mattersly nodded. He knew that the lack of pattern pointed to other things, perhaps even the whim of the leader of Reno. "I maintain that these attacks are carried out by one crew with one aircraft. I think what we need to do is bring it down on its next attack."

"The only thing that's consistent is that the Cobra attacks during the day in clear conditions," Hernandez thought to add.

"Indeed," Reggie uttered and arched his brow. "That indicates a reluctance to fly in adverse conditions. There have been no night attacks, but do you have people up on those roofs at night?"

"Yes, we do," Horn answered. "I've got people on at three shifts, eight hours each. Night time tends to be boring, so I rotate them."

"Good man," Mattersly granted. "Now, is every emplacement outfit with only two barrels?"

Horn nodded. "We've got around thirty-two hundred rounds left in inventory with no possibility of replenishment. We go through anywhere between three and four hundred rounds each time that Cobra pays a visit."

"We've got to cut that in half and removing another barrel from these guns is not the answer," Mulhaney asserted.

"Your gunners need better discipline and better training," Mattersly said. "We can help with that. With improved skills, your chances of scoring hits increases and wasted ammunition should decrease."

"I've got some people on the line that are not good shots," Horn said with strong hints of regret.

"Let's see if we can't improve on them," Reginald said. "If they don't improve, we'll have to release them."

"Wait a minute, Reggie!" Jazz blurted. "With such a low supply of ammunition, just how the hell are we supposed to train these people?"

"Does anyone in town shoot skeet?"

Jerry slapped the table. "God damn it! Why didn't I think of that?"

"You mean with shotguns?" Jazz asked and left her mouth agape.

"Certainly," Elias said with a grin. "That's a great way to teach people how to lead the target and project its path."

"Do we have the weapons and ammo for that, Jerry?" Hernandez asked with renewed hope.

"We sure do, but I don't know where we'd get clay pigeons," he answered.

"I'm sure there must be an excess of plates in town," Mulhaney suggested. "I've been through a lot of abandoned or mostly abandoned towns and I tell ya, not a lot of people packed their dishes for the trip to Alethea."

"Well, that sounds rather rudimentary, but it's a place to start," the major judged.

"Should I get some volunteers to start gathering things?" Horn asked with a glimmer of enthusiasm.

"Do it, Jerry," Hernandez commanded. He rose from the chair and turned for the door. "Oh, and have Zorba's and Angel's guns relocated. Think about where they can go and have it done by the end of the day."

"Yes, ma'am," the old marine returned and made his way out of the room. Reginald and Elias could see that Horn did not agree with that part of the plan, but complained not.

"Can he get enough people to help him with all that?" Elias asked.

Jazz answered the question with a mild nod as her eyelids blinked slowly. "So, all this seems to me to be a temporary measure."

"Well, truth be told," Reginald said as he looked to Elias for the reaction to his words. "I'm afraid that what you suggested yesterday might very well be the best course of action."

"The hell you say!" Mulhaney exuded heavily.

"Tell me a story, Reggie," Jazz directed and rested her head on her palm as she studied him.

Mattersly retook his seat and laced his fingers upon the table. "Lovelock's situation is dire if more ammunition cannot be found. It is my opinion that even if we are able to bring down that Cobra that another may simply be built and thrown against you. In fact, it should not be assumed that the same one has been used in these attacks. Gillespie might have several and is hiding his numbers."

"Uh-huh," Jazz smiled. "Go on."

"You said yesterday that you had sent spies into Reno."

"I did."

"I'd like to interview them. Can that be arranged?"

Hernandez sat back and gave it some thought. "I'm sure. You've met one of them already. Angel. The other I can send for right away."

"Do you have a map of Reno?" the major asked.

Jazz hesitated before answering. "Of course."

"An intelligence map? One that you've made notes on after debriefing your spies?" he smiled.

Hernandez chuckled. "You know I do, Reggie."

"Excellent," he announced. "I should like to know what they know."

"I'll arrange it," Jazz proclaimed with confidence.

***

It was early afternoon before the two brave individuals could be gathered and brought to the club's dining/meeting room. As Jazz had mentioned, one was Angel and the other was a young man, demure in stature and wiry in build. His hair was a wild collection of confused brown curls that swirled every which way, appearing as if it were the ocean during a heavy storm as it prepared to form a whirlpool upon his smallish head. His facial features were sharp and gaunt while his starkly blue eyes were perpetually widened in either thought or dryness. He blinked intermittently and often.

Jazz Hernandez introduced the man as Eric Hemmel, an air defense volunteer and plumber. His eyes danced from Mattersly to Mulhaney and back, reflecting both curiosity and nervousness as they shook hands.

"Nice to meet you both," Hemmel said as he took the seat offered. "Ah, Reno!" he blurted upon noticing the map unfolded upon the dining table.

"Indeed," Reginald began, "we understand that the both of you paid a visit to this place at some point. When exactly?" he asked.

"Four months ago," Angel answered.

"My visit was almost ten months ago," Eric said.

"Very well." Mattersly nodded. "So, I'd like you to look upon this roadmap and pay special attention to Miss Hernandez's notations, which are drawn in blue ink. They were created from the facts you brought to light during your debriefing when you returned."

Angel and Eric leaned over the map and scrutinized it closely for nearly a minute before Hemmel commented. "Looks right to me."

"Yeah, she's got everything right, here," Angel agreed.

"Very good," Mattersly said as he leaned over the

map with them. “So, which one of you can locate the fabrication plant?”

“Oh, that’s easy,” Angel spoke up, but it was clear from Eric’s nodding that he did, too. “It’s right here.” She pointed after only a moment of searching. “It’s this building on the corner of McCarren and Nugget.”

“How close were you able to come?” Mulhaney asked, fascinated. The plant was depicted on the map as a rectangle, drawn in ink.

“Not very close, sorry to say,” Hemmel admitted. “It’s right within an old commercial district where there used to be a lot of shops. No one lives around this part of town. It’s all military-like.”

“You’re both too young to have implants, am I correct?” Reginald straightened up and paced in the small area. The young adults both nodded. “I don’t suppose there are pictures of the building.”

“Not from me.” Angel looked to Eric.

“I wish,” he answered with a nostalgic smile. “But, I was hassled by so many of their militia that I’m glad I didn’t have one.”

“Oh?” Mattersly halted and studied Hemmel’s face closely.

“They would have killed me.” The young man nodded. “Especially if I had been caught right there.”

“How do you know this?” Elias asked.

“Townspeople told me,” he replied.

“Wait,” Jazz interjected with annoyance. “You’re not saying that you told anyone in Reno that you were there to spy for me, are you?”

“Oh, no, ma’am,” Hemmel returned excitedly with a hint of fear. “I was just passing through a marketplace not far from there and got to talking with some folks. I happen to make a comment on a merchant’s antique cameras and he warned me not to get caught with it if I bought it.”

"What would happen if you approached that building, Mister Hemmel?" Mattersly asked, already having suspected the answer.

"The penalty for espionage is death," he answered as he sat down. "Anyone caught with a camera in the controlled areas would be immediately killed right there in the street."

"Did you witness any of this?" Mulhaney put to them as he scratched at his freshly shaven chin.

"No," the young man answered.

"I did," Angel said. "Well, I didn't see it when it happened, but I heard it and saw the aftermath. Someone near the area was shot by their police one of the days I was there. People in the crowd told me it was because he had a camera."

"Very well." Reginald nodded. "Tell me about these buildings here," he directed with his finger, pressing it upon the hand-drawn rectangles to the south of the fabrication building.

"That's the airport," Angel explained. "These are all hangars. I saw the Cobra take off and land here on the last day. I got the hell out of there after that."

"Do they have any other aircraft?" Elias inquired and leaned over the map to see.

"Not that I saw."

Elias and Reginald looked to Hemmel expectantly.

"I stuck around especially to see aircraft and one is *all* I saw," he said.

"How long were you both in town?" the major asked.

"Four days," said Eric.

"Eight," answered Angel without a hint of pride.

"Why only four, Eric?" Mattersly put directly.

"I got too close to the airport," Hemmel answered as he shook his head. "I wound through this commercial area here." He pointed at an area east of the airport with his finger, which then settled upon a rectangle to the northeast. "Did pretty well until I got close to this one."

"What happened there?" Elias asked.

"One of their men stationed on the roof of one of these forward buildings spotted me through his rifle scope and took a few shots. I crawled to the roof access door and hid in there for most of the day. I moved at night and eventually got out of there."

"Was this before or after you saw the Cobra?" Reginald pressed.

"Before." Eric Hemmel inhaled sharply and puffed his cheeks as he exhaled. "They used it for a search the next day. I couldn't get out of there the whole time. I hid in this building, I think it was this one, anyway," he amended as he pointed to an "L" shaped depiction of a structure next to a wide street. "I just stayed there all day. I think it used to be some sort of hospital. Single floor with some attic spaces that were just large enough for me to squeeze in."

Mattersly, Mulhaney, and Hernandez could see that the man was becoming upset as he relived his ordeal. Jazz patted Eric's hand and he smiled.

"God damned place was so hot, I retched at one point. I heard people walking through below me many times. That damned Cobra just kept flying overhead," Hemmel described as he ran his hand over his gaunt face. "I've never been so scared."

"It's all right, Eric," Jazz murmured.

"So, you see," he continued as his eyes hopped from Elias to Reginald and back, "I messed up and got myself noticed. I *had* to get out of there."

"I understand, Mister Hemmel," Mattersly acknowledged. "I would have done the same if I had kicked over the wasps' nest. You proceeded correctly."

Elias nodded in agreement and smiled at the

younger man.

"Let me tell you somethin' else," Eric blurted as he dropped himself into a chair. "They've got some armored vehicles, too."

"Tanks?" a surprised Mulhaney ejected with his eyebrows pinned high on his forehead.

"What type of armored vehicle, Mister Hemmel?" the major asked. Hemmel shrugged. He noted Angel's nodding and turned his attention to her. "You've seen it as well, Miss…?"

"Yes, I have, Major Mattersly," she answered. "And it's just Angel. No 'miss'."

"Very well." He nodded. "Can you describe this vehicle?"

"There's more than one," she said, "but they appear to be modeled after one another. They have eight big wheels and a couple of guns in a turret."

"What caliber of guns?"

"They look a bit like our fifty-cals," she said as she stood to her full height and arched her back in a stretch. "They can carry troops in the back, too. Fully armored and enclosed."

"Sounds like a version of the Stryker," Mulhaney stated.

"They're used to patrol the streets and keep people away from Gillespie's home, which is somewhere in this group of interconnected hotels here," she described and pointed to a group of squares drawn to the west. "There's no telling where Gillespie's living quarters actually are, but the townspeople I spoke to agree that he lives somewhere in these buildings."

"The streets surrounding the complex are blocked off by concrete barriers and heavily guarded," added Hemmel. "You'll encounter a few of those armored cars there."

"Let me ask the both of you something," Mattersly went on and took a seat. He crossed his arms over his chest and searched the ceiling in thought. "How many people does Gillespie employ as his police force, and in what manner are they compensated?"

"No one knows the number, Major," Angel answered. "I spoke to a few regular citizens about how to become part of the militia, which is what they call it, and no one knew the answer. They all look well-trained and mean as hell, the men and the women."

"But what is their motivation?" Reginald restated.

"A good safe place to live," Hemmel speculated, "power trips, a chance to be big fish in a tiny pond. Who knows for sure?"

Mattersly looked to Hernandez and then to Mulhaney. Jazz appeared to be at a loss and Elias wore a carefully guarded expression. "Very well, Angel, Mister Hemmel," he granted as he addressed the two brave spies, "well done. I hope if we have any further questions, that you won't mind speaking to us again."

"Sure," they said nearly at the same time.

"Thank you for coming," Hernandez concluded with a generous smile and stood. "See Marco outside and tell him I said to drive you anywhere you need to be."

Both spies thanked her and left the room.

"Who needs a drink?" Elias asked playfully, but sincerely.

"Indeed," confirmed Reginald.

"Well, what *do* you think, Reggie?" asked Jazz as she sat back in her chair.

"I think those are two very brave people."

"I agree," said Hernandez, "but what now?"

Mattersly stood and ran his hand over his short blond and white hair. His eyes were planted on the map as he reached out and turned it so that north pointed away from him. He read the notes on the buildings that had been drawn onto it and sighed heavily.

"What I don't understand is, if they have this armed militia, why doesn't Gillespie just invade Lovelock and just take you?" Mulhaney asked of Hernandez.

"That might very well be in our future, Elias." Jazz nodded grimly.

Mattersly remained in deep contemplation over the map at his fingertips.

"What do you think about that, Major?" Mulhaney pressed.

"Hmm?" Reginald answered absently. "Oh! Yes. Yes, indeed. That may very well be, I agree. We must consider that the loss of this Momo fellow may spur that very reaction. Jazz, how many citizens of Lovelock have been wounded or killed by Gillespie's people?"

"Well, let me think." Jazz sat back with hers eyes searching the ceiling. "Momo's harassment with that damned sniper rifle of his accounts for…five killed, three wounded, so badly they won't be the same again."

"And by the Cobra?"

"Umm…eight dead," she went on as she sat forward and searched Reginald's face. "I'm not even sure at this moment about the wounded. Why are you asking, Reggie?"

"Well, I'm thinking that it may soon be time to go on the offensive," the major said and gave the lightest of grins.

"You've got to be kidding me!" Elias blurted, dumbfounded. "We have a minimal amount of information to go on! All we know is that Gillespie has a loyal fighting force in numbers unknown, complete with a handful of armored vehicles… oh yeah, and at *least* one attack helicopter with a strong possibility that they're building more. You *cannot* be serious about an offensive against

Reno."

Mattersly casually left his chair and kept the slight grin as he looked to his friend and said, "Well, as you Yanks are often fond of saying, 'I shit you not'."

"Wonderful," Elias grunted as Hernandez laughed like a schoolgirl.

Chapter Five

In the following days, Mattersly and Mulhaney inspected and instructed the anti-air defense volunteers. As they had the full trust of Hernandez, they were allowed to do so without supervision or interference.

It was Tuesday, July 10th, and the pair had spent the late morning and early afternoon taking part in the training of some volunteers that were not on duty. Some had terrible discipline with firearms, having rarely, if ever, handled a weapon outside the fifty-caliber machine gun they handled routinely. Still, it had gone well, so Reginald and Elias left the session to continue in the capable hands of Jerry Horn and Thumper.

The reports from the firearms behind them echoed off the walls of the buildings on either side as they casually walked along the street. Elias half-expected to have buckshot rain down on them, sent by an inexperienced gunner tracking a plate thrown in an unsafe direction. There were a few times that the session had nearly gone horribly wrong, but now he could allow himself to smile about it.

"What?" asked Reginald.

Elias chuckled before answering. "I'm just thinking about the kid that almost took your beret off the hard way."

"Hmm, yes," returned the major. "I was fortunate. I'm rather shocked by the lack of skill we have been finding amongst these people."

"Aw, give 'em a break," urged Mulhaney. "They're just young kids."

"That's what worries me. I fear I shall no longer sleep when the night shift is on."

The sounds of shotgun rounds behind them, Mulhaney's cane tapping on the pavement, and the boisterous laughter were joined by something else.

Reginald halted and listened to the air.

"What is it?" Elias asked once he realized that he was walking alone.

"Shh."

The two military men stood like statues in the middle of a once busy street. Mattersly augmented his hearing and turned his head. The rhythmic thumping sounds danced down the street as it bounced from building to building. The shotguns had stopped firing, replaced by shouting voices. The glass windows in the abandoned shop Reginald and Elias stood in front of began to vibrate.

Though it had been years since either man had heard one, they knew what it was even before the air raid siren began its heart-hammering wail.

"Come on!" Mattersly shouted as he bolted up the street. He knew that he would outdistance his companion quite quickly, but he needed to get to the closest defensive installation, which was a block away, across from Jazz's club.

"Go! I'll catch up!" Mulhaney howled over the siren.

Mattersly's run accelerated into a sprint when he heard one of the defenders open fire. The short bursts of fifty-caliber rounds seemed to be originating from the western-most gun, just a block west and one north from where Zorba's weapon had been relocated. Beyond the gunfire and the siren, the thumping blades of the Cobra could be heard viciously chopping at the air. He did not have to see it to know that it was moving fast and quite low. The reverberating report seemed to come from the west, from the north in the next second and then everywhere at once.

Reginald registered the fact that Jazz's car was not in front of the club as he burst through the door of the building across from it. The volunteer upon this building had not yet opened fire, though it sounded as if the helicopter was close enough. He withheld judgment as he flew up the stairs to the second floor.

He quickly located the ladder that led to the roof and climbed it, halting briefly as he poked his head back into the afternoon sun. A teenaged boy and girl team were manning the site. Reginald halted before bounding out onto the pebble-strewn roof for fear of taking the crew by surprise. The girl was Maddie, a quirky young lady with ginger hair and a thick southern accent that Reginald could barely decipher. The boy, Franky, sat in the gunner's seat and was busily tracking the helicopter. The light brown haired lad stared into the distance north with wide eyes and dry lips. At the moment, no one in Lovelock was shooting.

"Ho, there!" Mattersly called and pulled himself up.

"Major!" called Franky. He had not been on duty during an attack before and had just taken over for the morning shift.

"Where is that helo?" the major shouted over the dying siren. He turned to look in the direction that Franky had the guns trained but saw nothing but trees and buildings. The beating blades could be heard clearly from the rooftop, having lost some of the echo effect from his place on the ground.

"Follow me, Franky!" the girl commanded. With one outstretched arm, she was tracking the Cobra's movement, though it had dipped below their line of sight.

"I am!" shouted the boy as he traversed the gun to his right.

Reginald fell into step with Maddie, who moved as the gun moved.

"He's circling the edge of town, Major!" she called to him.

"I see," he said with an air of calm.

As the helicopter cleared the buildings of northern

Lovelock, it became visible. Reginald could see that Jazz had been correct. The machine did resemble an early version of an AH-1 Cobra and the pilot was obviously very skilled in flying it low and fast. It was banked hard to the right, turning to the south. Mattersly opened his implant's targeting and range finding application, and saw that it was well within range of fire, just beyond five hundred meters.

"Get ahead of it, Franky!"

"Almost there!" Franky replied excitedly.

The major could see that the Cobra was mere meters above the ground and straightening out, apparently to continue on a southerly heading.

"Come on, come on! That's it, lad!" he encouraged. The boy followed the machine as quickly as the turret's motor allowed. Now, he had caught up and the barrels were now ahead of the quick aircraft.

At the same moment, however, the twin-gunned turret on the nose of the Cobra found them. It fired first, sending rounds their way. Dozens of them struck the building all around them just as Franky depressed the triggers on his weapon. Reginald grabbed Maddie and held her near him as he kept on the move. Franky's twin fifties spat their fire, but the framework of the weapon rang out from hits delivered by the Cobra. Mattersly shielded his eyes at that point, for the air was filled with bullet fragments and bits of the roof's pebbles and dirt.

As the helicopter proceeded southward, Franky no longer needed to make great strides to lead the target, but the gunship was quickly out of range. Reginald locked his gaze upon the Cobra and called for the boy to cease fire as the range approached sixteen hundred meters.

Franky let go of the triggers and turned to the both of them. "Are you guys okay?!" he shouted beyond the ringing in his ears.

"I am," answered the major. "How about you two?"

Maddie nodded and shrugged her way out of his arms. She was shaking and breathing heavily from the rush of adrenaline and anger mixed with fear. Franky nodded and slipped out of the gun's perch to inspect the damage. Apparently, he could not hear that the Cobra had not left the area. Though he could not see the helicopter through the trees and buildings to the west, it sounded as if it were returning.

"Get out of here! Now!" Mattersly shouted and tugged Franky away from the weapon by his t-shirt. "Elias, clear the way!" he screamed at his compatriot, whom he noticed had just arrived at the top of the ladder.

"Hey!" Franky squealed in protest as he was flung toward the access hatch.

"Go! Now!" the major bellowed and hopped into the gunnery seat. Having become familiar with the controls in the days past, he quickly swung the gun to the right. "Get them out of here, Elias!" he shouted over his shoulder.

The machine gun emplacement to the north, Zorba's location, opened fire at that instant. Mattersly commanded his eyes to magnify his view in time to see streaks of fire and smoke erupt from the Cobra's rocket pods. The air was filled with the screeching of unguided, but carefully aimed rocket fire. The rooftop where brave Zorba and his helper were stationed exploded in fire, dust, and debris. The entire building beneath Mattersly and Mulhaney shook as if it were going to collapse, even though the stricken building was almost two blocks away.

The air became thick with dust as Reginald located the target. The Cobra shot through a passage of trees and began turning toward his position, evading fire from the remaining western-most machine gun. The helicopter's machine guns were pointed away from Mattersly's emplacement, having exchanged fire with the other. Mattersly squeezed the triggers and held them, elated that the elusive Cobra had flown right into his guns' path.

Fifty-caliber rounds struck and ripped into the helicopter's body. Reginald could see the two occupants quite clearly as they passed in front of him at just over two hundred meters away. He watched as the bullets he launched shattered the canopy. The gunner, sitting in front, shrank away under the onslaught. The engine housing, located just under the twin blades, disintegrated into a cloud of fragments as a burst of flame and black smoke swept underneath the flying machine. The mortally wounded Cobra wobbled and shuddered, visibly slowing as the pilot battled gravity. It was out of his hands, however. The helicopter engine silenced and powerless, dropped out of sight. A moment later, it crashed to the ground with an earth-shaking roar of metal and concrete. A thick black cloud coiled into the sky, blanketing a fiery red core.

Mattersly climbed out of the mounting and rushed to the edge of the roof. Despite this, he could see nothing but the smoke and flame.

"Nice shooting, Major!" called Elias who joined him at his left side.

"Come on!" Reginald exclaimed as he turned and rushed to the access hatch. "There may be injuries!"

"Augh," Mulhaney grunted as he followed at his more casual pace. "More running," he complained, but now he was alone. The major had long gone. "Of course there are injuries!" Elias yelled down the hole after his British friend. "Who shoots down a helicopter and doesn't think there are injuries?" he muttered as he awkwardly stepped down to the lower level.

Reginald ran to the intersection and turned left, maintaining as much speed as he could. His military training had taken over and he let it. His legs pumped and his feet pounded the pavement, propelling him to a sprinting speed that he had rarely achieved. Even his tightly fit emerald gray beret threatened to leave him. Ahead, about three blocks away was the burning Cobra. It had crashed upon the embankment of the highway's overpass and was burning. The black smoke, which continued to ooze upward, seemed as tactile as the street underneath him.

Over the sounds of his heavy breathing and the distant cries and screams of the town's populace, he heard a siren, though it was not that of Antonio's squad car. It was a deeper, elongated cry and he soon understood it was that of a fire truck. It was replaced by a second siren, higher and at a faster tempo.

The major slowed enough to turn and see the police vehicle rushing up to him. Behind that, several blocks further away, he could see the fire truck. It had stopped in front of the stricken building. He hoped that Zorba had survived, but it did not look good.

Antonio had built the cruiser up to a high speed, but upon recognizing Mattersly, he hit the brakes hard, grinding the rubber orbs into the rough-hewn and weathered street.

"Get in!" the constable shouted.

Mattersly yanked open the door behind the driver and flung himself inside. It slammed shut as the car launched forward, screeching the tires as the engine whined and the siren resumed. Reginald struggled against the G-forces to pull himself forward. He magnified his vision and found the stricken aircraft in time to see someone fall from its burning carcass. It was a small figure in black, almost too small to be human. The injured occupant trailed smoke as he dragged his burning body along the ground away from the Cobra.

"The pilot!" Reginald shouted and pointed.

"I see," Antonio returned just as small objects began to pelt the area. The citizenry of Lovelock were determined to finish what the crash had not accomplished. "Damn!"

The cruiser bounded recklessly over a set of long-unused railroad tracks. Reginald banged his head on the roof, but barely felt it. The car crossed the distance to the fallen aircraft in seconds as Antonio laid on the horn and set the siren to a high warble. Three men armed with various types of clubs were approaching the aircraft and its wounded pilot cautiously. At least two women had ventured close enough to throw rocks.

"Get away from there, now!" Antonio bellowed through the vehicle's public address system.

This received the attention from everyone and was heeded, though with great mirth. The tallest of the club-wielding men backed off not an inch, but watched the speeding police car through widened and insanely angry eyes.

Antonio stomped on the brakes once again, sending the tires into another aria of woe. The experienced driver placed the car between the largest civilian, who wisely decided to take a couple of steps back, and the wounded pilot. Both men exited from the left side before the car had shed its momentum. The body roiled upon its suspension.

While the constable dealt with the tall lingerer, Reginald bolted to the pilot. He knew that a flare up could happen anytime once the flames reached the destroyed machine's fuel tanks, which he believed to be at the center of the airframe, behind and below the cockpit. The heat of the flames did little to dissuade the man from his approach, though he was quite aware of them.

The major crouched as he came closer to the wounded flyer. He grabbed the fabric of the flying suit at the collarbone and pulled, registering in his mind the awful site of the absence of legs below the knees and copious amounts of blood upon the ground. The pilot was mortally wounded.

Still, he pulled the body away quickly. It was sickeningly light. Over the crackling flames, he heard a high moan escape the lips of the dying flyer as he rounded the front of the squad car. Reginald knew even before he removed the helmet that the pilot was female. Her facial features were strikingly attractive despite the incredible paleness of her skin. She did not have long.

"Oh, my God," she said as she searched Mattersly's face and the emblem on his beret. "What the hell are you?"

"British Army," he answered.

"Why are…?" Out of breath, she gripped his offered hand and simply stared in confusion.

"Never mind that now," he quipped. "I'm Major Mattersly. I need to know why you're attacking these people."

"I…" she trailed into a howl of pain. Reginald gathered her upper body into his arms and held her face close.

"Why?" he repeated.

"Boss… wa… wants his woman," she grunted with much effort. She panted for breath and writhed in pain.

"Why try to kill her then? It makes no sense."

"He don't care," the fair-skinned young female blurted. "Done… waitin'. He wants us to level this place."

"Us?" Mattersly returned. "There are more helicopters?"

She nodded and smiled darkly. The woman was angered by the waves of pain she was feeling, and she seemed to know that she was through. The smile disappeared when the air filled with intense heat. One of the Cobra's tanks erupted, spitting a thick ball of flame into the air. The world brightened to a hellish yellow. The dying pilot screamed and began to sob. Her gloved grip upon Reginald's hand tightened and tears spilled from the corners of her eyes.

"It's all right," Reginald spoke quickly as soon as the roaring flames subsided. "What is your name?"

"Kara," she replied.

"Kara." He smiled and held her face gently. "What would it take to make Gillespie stop the attacks? All these people want is peace."

"You can fu… forget," she finished with the shake of her head.

"He won't stop? There's nothing we can do?"

She held his gaze as she shook her head. He was uncertain if she comprehended his words. Her chest heaved with the effort to breathe, but each exchange felt weaker.

"Kara," he said to her in his most soothing tone. "Will he send more Cobras?"

The pilot swallowed hard, unable to speak, choosing to gasp and nod instead. Another tank erupted, sending light and heat to wash over them. Kara flinched, but no longer had the energy to scream.

"Does Gillespie have Jazz Hernandez's niece?"

Kara nodded weakly. The light in her eyes was fading.

"How many helicopters does he have?"

"Ma… making more," she whispered then cleared her throat. "Shooting us down is only gonna piss him off, Major. Get out of this shithole while you…" She coughed harshly, obliterating the rest of the sentence.

"Kara, how long until they complete another helo?" the major pressed. He had not yet finished the question when he realized her grip on his hand had gone limp. "Kara!" he shouted as her head dropped back. With care, though she would never feel it, he set her body upon the warm pavement and stood up. Over the roof of the police car, he watched the Cobra burn. The flames ate the paint from the machine's hardpoint and licked the surface of the rocket pod.

"Bloody hell," he muttered and turned to Antonio, who had convinced the gathered citizens to recede and had watched the major interrogate the deceased pilot. "We have to get the hell out of here!" He dove into the back seat. "Drive, man! Drive!" he shouted as he slammed the door.

Antonio questioned nothing. He dropped into the driver's seat and put the transmission into reverse, not bothering with the door. Reginald held on to the seats, but was thrown across to the other side as the driver spun the wheel to the left. The car slipped into a one hundred and eighty degree turn in a cloud of tire smoke. The driver's door slammed hard, propelled by the centrifugal force. While the car was still moving, Antonio shifted the transmission to drive and floored the accelerator. The car quickly left the dangerous scene behind.

Elias had been keeping up a pretty good pace, though he could not run. He watched Reginald pull the pilot away from the aircraft and speak for a few moments as the constable convinced the citizenry to leave the area. Mulhaney understood the danger Reginald and Antonio were in and decided to halt his forward progress. He was a block away, but he knew that was still too close if the aircraft's unspent ordinance cooked off in response to the immense heat of the fire.

"Oh, shit," he muttered each time the Cobra flared up from a fuel tank eruption. He yelled to a few onlookers to keep their distance. A few men armed with clubs ignored him, though refused to get closer.

Elias decided to seek shelter and walked toward the abandoned gas station to his left. Despite the dangers of triggering an implant malfunction, he tried to access the device to warn Mattersly away. He cussed harshly when the unit refused his commands. A sudden screeching of tires caught Mulhaney's attention and he turned to see the squad car reversing from the scene. Only the pilot remained behind and he was absolutely still. Elias could see that the person must have expired. The squad car spun around and accelerated like a shot, leaving white tire smoke everywhere. Though relieved to see his friend getting away from the danger, he was still not sure that he was, exposed in the middle of an empty lot. He picked up his pace and headed for the open door to the unused establishment. In the doorway, he could see a teenaged boy. Looking out from the dirtied and yellowed windows were two adults.

"Everyone get back! Get down!" he shouted to them as the tires of the police cruiser shrieked. Elias turned to see that Antonio had turned the car hard right, toward the refueling station. The car was decelerating hard, with the driver intending to place the building between the car and the burning bomb.

As Mulhaney stepped through the open door, he straight-armed the mesmerized teenager, shoving him back inside. As he did, an unseen force knocked Elias's hat from his head and carried it inside the disheveled structure. Behind that rush of air came a roaring wave of heat that pressed the unsteady man from his feet. Windows shattered and the world became a bright, wavering orange.

When the thunderous explosion subsided, he heard the ringing in his unprotected ears and the cries of the people that had been standing at the window. Elias could not make himself get up. He lay there on the dirty and cracked tile floor, very well aware of how uncomfortable he was laying. Moderately strong arms pressed small hands against his ribs. He realized that he was lying on the teenaged boy. He pressed his left arm into action and rolled away, setting his captive free.

Elias lay still for a few moments, aware of a pounding in his head and not much else. Other than the cries and nearby talking, he could hear nothing. Now on his back, he opened his eyes. The world was white with traces of flickering yellow and orange. He lifted his head toward a field of blue, which he recognized as the sky beyond the door he had been pushed through. Mulhaney propped his upper body upon his elbows and looked about him. The windows had all been broken and the man he had seen in the window was crouching over the woman that had been standing next to him. She appeared to be bleeding from the face but she was patting the man's hand. The teenager was kneeling at her right side.

Elias smiled. They did not seem to be badly hurt. As he tried to regain his feet, Mattersly appeared in the doorway with Antonio right behind. Seeing his recently-made friend strewn on the floor, he bent to help him. The bald bodyguard spoke into a handheld radio and rushed to the three civilians by the window.

"Bloody hell!" Reginald spouted. "I say, old man! You all right?!"

Mulhaney's ears were still much compromised by the shock of the explosion, but he read his British friend's lips. He nodded, but his spoken answer contradicted him. "No!"

Reginald checked the ex-paratrooper over and dusted him off. Seeing the Stetson on the debris-ridden floor in the corner, he picked it up and handed it to Elias.

"So, what in the hell was *that*?!" Mulhaney shouted over his own ringing ears and the approaching fire truck.

Mattersly stepped to the glassless opening before answering. Elias joined him to get a view of the destruction. A wall of flame engulfed the overpass on which the Cobra had just moments before laid broken. Pieces of the aircraft were strewn about the empty lot surrounding the area. Of the deceased pilot, nothing remained. The fire truck shot past and halted well short of the decimated airframe. The two-man crew jumped from it and attacked the fire with a pack-mounted sonic-emitter that disrupted the air around the flames while the other bracketed the area with a chemical foam.

"I was expecting the rockets to cook off, one, maybe a couple at a time," the major explained, "but it appears that they are rather unstable!"

"Well, you know what that means!" Elias exuded as he managed a weak smile.

"What?!"

"It means that he's probably using vintage munitions that should be disposed of *and* the place where Gillespie keeps that ordnance should go up really easily! But, do we even have to worry anymore?" he asked with an outstretched arm pointing to the burning wreckage.

"I'm afraid we do!" Reginald answered.

The conversation ended there when Antonio asked for help in taking the woman to the car. She and her male companion required medical attention for burns and cuts.

Chapter Six

The two warriors let Antonio take the three people from the abandoned refueling station to the doctor. Both men were surprised to learn that Lovelock even had a doctor, but neither questioned it. They had learned to accept the slow trickle of facts about the town and its people.

For a long while, they stood near the destroyed Cobra, watching the decimated remains of the airframe leach white smoke into the air. The fire truck had long since departed. There was not much of the airframe left and not a piece of it had survived unscathed. Not one dial from its control panels was recognizable and not one physical feature of the machine remained. It literally could have been anything once built from metal or carbon fiber. The major spoke of his conversation with the deceased and now, efficiently cremated, pilot.

Mattersly shook his head in disappointment. "I wish there was something here to study," he said almost to himself. He was surprised that Mulhaney's ears had recovered enough for his words to be heard.

"Well, you can bet the thing was built from any material they could put their hands on," Elias supplied as he pointed to the destruction with his walking stick. "I can't imagine that an original airframe would have come apart like this. There could not have been any armor here. It was a copied design, based on something that they knew would fly."

"I agree."

Elias adjusted his Stetson and regarded his British companion with feigned surprise. "You do?"

Reginald chuckled. "Yes, I actually do, Mister Mulhaney."

"Cool," Elias returned and gazed upon the destroyed aircraft once again.

A few moments later, Jazz's vehicle arrived at the scene. Marco exited and stood staring at the two men for several heartbeats before opening the driver's side rear door for his boss. The mayor of Lovelock took her chief bodyguard's offered hand and stepped onto the pavement wearing high heels, though this time it was with dark slacks. Once she stepped away from the car and approached them, they could see that she had adopted an appropriate look for the circumstances. She wore a deep blue pantsuit complete with a simple ribbon tie upon a white blouse. Her black hair was set back in a clip. Her eyes were serious, but she could not hold back a smile.

"Congratulations!" she shouted as she covered the distance to them in a strut. She smiled widely as her eyes passed over the wreckage. It slipped away quickly, however. Mattersly suspected some bad news was forthcoming and he was pretty sure he knew what it would be. "I hear you were the one that took it down, Major."

"Truth be told, Miss, I think it had been hit before the fatal blow was struck," Reginald answered as he clasped his hands behind his back and regarded the remnants of the Cobra.

She stepped to him and pulled hard upon the collar of his tunic, forcing him to turn to her. As he did, she took hold of his neck and forced his lips to hers. She released him with an orated, "Muuah!"

He straightened and, utterly stunned, stared into her face, speechless.

"Humility is sexy, Major," she declared and smacked him on a buttock. "I've got witnesses that say you cleared the roof across the street from my club and shot this fucker down. I can't say 'thank you' enough."

"Well… er… rather…" Reginald stuttered and

looked to the smoldering wreckage.

"Yeah, um... by the way," Mulhaney spoke up, "I'm fine, too. And... you might want to let the Major take a breath and tell you somethin'."

"Oh?" Hernandez smiled. She looked to Elias then back to Reginald. Mulhaney's statement had stirred the major from his subdued state and he quickly picked up the conversation from that point.

"Ah, yes, well," he began, "I pulled the pilot away from the Cobra before it went up in flames."

"He's *alive*?!" she exclaimed and began to look about.

"No and no," Mattersly managed, which wiped the smile from Jazz's face. "*She* lived only for a short time, I'm afraid."

Hernandez was quiet for a few seconds, having just discovered the blood that was splattered upon his trousers. "So, did *she say* anything?"

"Yes, Jazz, she did," Reginald answered. He pushed on just as she was about to shout at him to continue. "She indicated that other such aircraft were being assembled, that she was not the only pilot, and that as soon as her Cobra was found to be overdue this Mister Gillespie would most likely... well... unleash the hounds, so to speak."

"Damn," she breathed and dropped her eyes to the pavement.

"Quite," he responded thoughtfully.

Hernandez began to pace slowly. A cloud of the white smoke from the aircraft drifted her way, initiating a harsh cough, which she waved away. "So! That's it then!" she declared angrily to the men surrounding her. "I've got to surrender myself to him to save this town!"

"Well, Kara, that was her name," the major said. He saw not a trace of recognition upon Jazz's face. "Kara said that Gillespie is way beyond that point. He just wants the town leveled."

"But why?!" she shouted to the sky. "These people have done *nothing*!"

"Excuse me, Jazz," Elias chimed in, "but, you're expectin' reason when there's none to be found."

Hernandez stepped to the big man leaning on the walking stick and pressed her forehead upon his right arm. "I believe you. The both of you," she said then stood back, "but now what do *we* do?" she finished and swept her right arm to encompass not only the citizens that had emerged to see their destroyed tormentor, but the town itself.

"Well, my first suggestion, of course, is to evacuate," answered the major.

Jazz nodded, where before, to have said a thing would have started an argument. She resumed pacing, shooting short looks to Marco, who was of no help at all. Had he not been following her movements with his eyes, he may as well have been granite.

"I must point out that he has not directed the rocket attacks on anything but the town center, where his intelligence places you," Reginald explained.

"So?" she spat, still pacing.

"It is my belief, Jazz, that Gillespie is not out to kill those who you have conducted business with. In fact, is there any reason to think that some of your connections are not his connections as well?"

To this, she stopped and stared into his face. She folded her arms across her chest in thought. "No," she admitted, "I've never asked any supplier for exclusive trade. Even the local ranchers and farmers are not restricted from doing business with anyone else."

"And he's never attacked them, has he?" Mulhaney inquired.

"No."

"So, we must assume that what you have heard and

what Kara, the pilot told me is true," Mattersly spoke softly, "that he may well be satisfied with the destruction of Lovelock itself."

Jazz buried her face in her hands. Her throat emitted a sob, then another. Marco stepped forward, as did Elias.

"'Course, we could always sneak in there real quiet-like and burn that shithole down," Mulhaney spoke in a slow sing-song.

"Indeed." Mattersly gave Jazz a smile.

"Huh? I wasn't sure you wanted to..." she said when she looked up again. Her black eyes danced from one man to the other.

Reginald gently grasped Hernandez's shoulders and gave Elias a kind gaze. "I just don't like the odds."

***

The elevator doors slid open to the penthouse suite's foyer. The lone occupant stepped out briskly and rapped on the thick metal, white-painted door. Knocking was not necessary, as the security monitors would have alerted the full-time security guard as soon as the elevator car arrived, but there was urgency.

The door swung inward silently and quickly, dumping cool air and music into the small space. A short, heavily armed man stood behind it. He eyed the visitor through round-rimmed glasses with an arrogant gaze that overrode his physical stature.

"What's happening, man?" the doorman demanded more than asked.

The visitor, a taller man, had no use for Gillespie's personal bodyguard. The reason why the leader of Reno allowed such a critter to remain so close to him was lost on the man. He walked past the doorman, bumping his shoulder slightly.

"Hey," the little man protested angrily, "I'll knock you right over, man." He shoved the door closed and adjusted his shoulder holsters, which had been sent askew.

"Blow it out your ass, Harry," he shot back. "Don't speak to me directly or I'll take one of those forty-fives and feed it to you."

The older, thinner man drew himself to his full, but unimpressive height and stared up into the larger man's face, keeping his distance just to be sure.

"I'd like to see you try that, General Ricky," he threatened. His voice had jumped up an octave unconsciously.

"Keep talkin' and I will," Ricky returned with a smile that only touched his lips, though his feet barely halted during the minor confrontation.

He turned his back on Harry and strode toward the music at the far end of the penthouse. In the back of his mind, he could see the little bodyguard reach his limit and pull one or both of the weapons. Harry Clima was a creep and a coward, not above shooting a man in the back. The man knew one day that he would have the ultimate confrontation with him.

Ricky Desmond did not look the part of a military man, certainly not one holding a rank of general. He detested the title, but did the job because he had been appointed. With his more casual attire, blue polyester pants, matching button-front shirt with an angular collar, tan tweed sport coat and shiny black leather shoes, he looked more like a pit boss that belonged on the ground floor of the Reno hotel's casino. His black hair was well-brushed in a mild pompadour and his face was meticulously clean-shaven.

Desmond was aware of Harry's proximity to him as he strode toward Gillespie's grandiose chair. The seat was elevated upon a carpeted stage, which had once been a dining table. Reno's leader had his full attention on the entertainment monitor set against a drapery-adorned window. He was watching a film from the mid-twentieth century, Ricky guessed, considering the grainy quality of the picture and the low definition of the soundtrack. The actor upon the screen was a bearded version of the one that sat in the throne, watching and clapping his hands against his thighs, in time with the music. The man on the screen was singing about a place called, 'Camelot' to an attractive woman in the snow.

"Ah! General Desmond!" Gillespie shouted over the music and reached for a glass jar that sat upon a table to the left of the throne. He retrieved a white cylinder of paper from within the container and handed it to Desmond. "Another new shipment from our northern friends that just arrived this morning," Gillespie smiled widely.

"Um… thank you, sir," Ricky responded as he took the delicate tube of packed tobacco. He placed the filterless cigarette between his lips and retrieved his lighter from an inside jacket pocket. He let out a few puffs as he watched the film on the monitor. "Sir, there's an urgent matter that you need to know about."

Gillespie's iron gray eyes slipped from the monitor as the joy bled from his face. He met the dark brown orbs of his most trusted man and marked his urgency. With his implant, he ordered the film's playback to pause. The music silenced and the image froze. The leader of Reno pulled his red velvet robe more closely to his breast and leaned back in his great chair. He said nothing, leaving silence begging to be shattered.

Desmond knew no other way to tackle a problem like delivering bad news to a sociopath other than to get it over with quickly.

"The Cobra's two…" he began, but halted to check his watch, "…almost three hours overdue from its last mission over Lovelock," he said and puffed on the cigarette. He could see the storm clouds forming on

Gillespie's face. "There's been nothing on radar, no radio communication, nothing."

"Damn it, *all*!" Gillespie shrieked and stood with such ferocity that the chair wobbled on its stand. The leader of Reno stepped down onto the red carpet with a floor-shaking thud. Gillespie was a big man and taller than Desmond's six-foot-two stature, even more so with his thickly-heeled, tan leather boots. The golden chains around his chest rang out briefly before being stifled by the ornate robe. "My Cobra... *shot down*?!" he bellowed incredulously.

Ricky Desmond saw more than simple anger in Gillespie's watering eyes. The emotion stirring in their gray depths was far from sadness, but much closer to madness. Despite being a rather big man, Desmond felt fear. He knew that the leader of Reno carried various weapons under his robe as he had witnessed spur-of-the-moment murders by his hand. With a madman in front of him and a dim-witted little weasel behind him, Ricky wished he had brought a couple of his loyal adjutants with him.

Desmond swallowed hard and took a puff of the cigarette, exhaling through his nostrils as he spoke. "Sir, we have no proof of that for the moment," he said as calmly as he could, trying desperately not to let his voice waver. "All we know is that the Cobra has not returned. Kara is an excellent pilot, our best. It's very possible that there were mechanical problems and she had to set it down somewhere."

Gillespie tilted his head back and placed his bejeweled hands upon his hips as he looked down his angular nose upon his appointed subordinate. The madness in the eyes abated slightly, though not enough to make Desmond less wary.

"I've sent search teams out along I-80," Ricky went on. "The flight plan has always called for her to keep that highway in sight and in the event of an emergency she knows that's where to land."

Gillespie took in a deep breath and lowered his head, though he did not look away from Desmond's face. His lips pursed in thought as his shoulders relaxed perceptively.

"How long until that other contraption is completed, General?" his voice rumbled.

"The shop is very close to completing the second Cobra," Ricky went on, "and we're waiting on more aluminum for that Ranger helicopter project."

Gillespie stomped a heavy foot, gritted his teeth and shook his head. "Damn it," he grumbled as he paced casually. "Where the hell is Momo when I need him?" he asked the air as his eyes searched the ceiling.

"If Momo or one of his team witnessed anything, sir, they're probably on their way to help or headed for the high ground for a clear signal to call home," Ricky said.

It was not uncommon for their premier sniper/scout to be out of communication for a couple of days. Ricky glanced over his right shoulder to see Harry Clima smirking with one hand on the butt of one of his pistols, as if waiting for the command to snuff the man next to him. Desmond blew smoke in his face, turning the smug grin into a grimace and a cough.

"He'd better be," Gillespie grumbled darkly.

The mayor of Reno stared upon the screen, scrutinizing the immortalized image of a once internationally famous actor, frozen in time, and appearing deliriously happy. Gillespie wanted that for himself and there was only one way he could think of to achieve that.

"General, I want you to order Momo and friends to infiltrate Lovelock and do away with our Miss Hernandez," Gillespie murmured just loudly enough to be heard.

"Yes, sir," Desmond agreed as he tapped cigarette

ash onto Clima's shoe. The seriousness of Gillespie's command kept him from having to chomp on his cheek to keep from laughing. "I'll leave written orders at the station to be relayed."

"Good," Gillespie granted. "Was there anything else, General Desmond?"

"No, sir."

"Very well," Reno's boss exuded as he returned to his throne. "One last thing: I want that Cobra finished and flying by the weekend. *AND...!*" he shrieked so unexpectedly that both Clima and Desmond were startled, "...whoever is holding up our supply of aluminum needs to understand how upset that makes me. Make a call."

"Understood," Desmond returned.

"Leave me," Gillespie concluded and resumed the playback of his movie.

Ricky Desmond nodded and turned from the leader of Reno, wanting nothing more than to be off the penthouse level and onto other duties. He strode toward the door with the cigarette dangling from his lips and Clima desperately trying to be the dutiful bodyguard and seeing the irritating visitor to the door. It pleased Desmond to hear the shorter man's gait quickened to an uncomfortable pace.

Without a word between them, Ricky exited the penthouse. The musical silenced once Harry slammed the door behind him. Desmond smiled to himself as he slipped into the elevator and tapped a button for a lower floor.

***

Marco carefully drove the car from the smoking wreckage, through the gathering of happy citizens. Some cheered as Jazz waved through the open window while others whistled and chanted either, "Major!", or "Reggie!" as he was known to them. Word had already spread about who had brought down the Cobra and it surprised the Brit that anyone had known his name at all, outside of the air defense volunteers he and Mulhaney had coached.

"You're famous," Jazz said from the front seat as she smiled upon Mattersly, who sat in the rear behind the driver.

"Apparently," he agreed, but found no glory in accepting the fact.

Marco drove the car past Jazz's club at a leisurely pace. There was no hurry to get to their next destination. Soon, it became clear. The building that the Cobra had stricken with its unguided rockets was just ahead and to their right.

Elias removed his hat, put his window down, and stuck his head out. He could see the burned out structure, still smoking like the remnants of the Cobra were at that very moment. There were a scattering of citizens here, too, but none appeared jubilant.

"Oh, my God," he said as the car came to a stop at the curb, one building before it.

The car emptied and Mattersly made his way quickly to the front of the rubble. The two-story building had been struck with a few of the rockets, decimating the storefront so badly that the roof that had supported the anti-aircraft gun had collapsed.

Reginald realized that Jazz had stepped to his right side. "Zorba?" he whispered.

She shook her head and wrapped her arm around his. "He was only seventeen," she whispered with tears barely restrained.

"Was he alone?" Mulhaney asked from her other side.

"No," she said. "But, that young man said that Zorba told him to get off the roof when he realized the Cobra was targeting him. He's hurt, but not badly."

"Are there any other casualties?" asked Reginald as he looked over the handful of citizens that milled about.

Some of the women sobbed as two men, on the verge of tears themselves, consoled them.

"Zorba's mother," Jazz said quietly and gestured to an attractive Mediterranean woman. Slightly older than Hernandez and taller, she wept like a child as a man at least ten years her senior held her shoulders and whispered words that failed to console.

Reginald sighed and turned his eyes to Elias who was stalwart in his gaze upon the smoking, broken building. "Well, my friend," the major addressed him, "I think we have some war planning to do."

"You bet your ass we do," Mulhaney answered.

"Jazz," said Reginald, "we must move quickly. I believe to make this mission successful, we require the input of your spy, Angel, once again."

"Let's go," Hernandez quipped to the group and led the men to her car.

***

Mattersly paced the floor of the dining room-turned-planning room. He had removed his beret and set it upon the table next to the roadmap. Elias sat in his usual place, stoic. His hat lay upon his aged duster, which he had casually discarded upon the floor in the corner.

Once Angel arrived, Reginald started them off. "I've been mulling this over since our last debriefing and I believe that I'm correct in thinking that to destroy the next helicopter may not be enough. I feel that destroying the fabrication machinery is also a must-do," he tapped the space on the map with his finger. "This is in addition to the recovery of Nora Hernandez and Miguel Costa, of course. If these objectives are carried out, I believe that Gillespie may halt his campaign against Lovelock."

The room was quiet. Angel nodded as she watched his face expectantly.

"I believe our best approach is via I-80," the SRR

officer went on as he traced the road with his finger. “At what point, Angel, did you depart from the road to avoid detection?”

She stood up, leaned over the map, and ran a hand through her spikey blond hair in thought. “Here,” she declared, picking a spot nearly a kilometer from the overpass at a town labeled ‘Fernley’. “Then I went over the hills here, wound through the abandoned homes at night until I arrived at the center of town where I sort of…you know…blended in.”

“Outstanding,” muttered Elias, who had left his chair to watch her point out her route.

“Daring. Straight to the objective with only the night to protect you,” Mattersly marveled. “Very brave, young lady.”

“Not really,” she smiled and straightened. “Gillespie’s guys are more interested in snoozing and drinking than doing their job at night. As long as they ain’t lookin’ for us, they should be a snap to get past.”

“My dear,” Reginald said gravely as he straightened and placed his hands behind his back, “I believe that after bringing down the Cobra today, they will be on high alert. We must take that into account.”

“If they really get after us, Major, and they have an idea of what neighborhood we’re in, all they have to do is set some houses on fire to trap us. The trick is not to let them know which way we’re headed,” Angel advised. “There’s more than one way to sneak up on downtown Reno,” she demonstrated by pointing out the spaces on the map that were marked as ‘Residential’. “The problem is downtown Reno itself. That’s tight as a drum with militiamen.”

“Yes, about that,” Mattersly took up, “how close did you actually get to downtown? Were you able to lay eyes on the hotel complex where he is said to take residence?"

"Yeah, but from blocks away," she said. "I was afraid to get too close."

"Well, my dear," the Major pressed, "we intend to get close enough to kill this man, either with sniper rifle or with explosives."

"I see," Angel said as she glanced to Jazz, who had been deadly silent with a serious expression on her face the entire meeting. "Okay, I'm in."

"Beg your pardon, miss?" Reginald blinked.

"I'm in," Angel repeated with a wicked grin. "You need a guide that's been there, Major, and I'm her."

Mattersly smiled back upon the young woman and looked to Mulhaney to find one of similar grit. Jazz had one, too, but hers was accompanied by a small tear in her eye that she wiped away so quickly it might as well not have existed.

"Tell me, Angel," Reginald bid, "how are you with handguns, rifles, that sort of thing?"

"Good enough to cover your asses," she proclaimed with confidence and winked one of her alluringly hazel eyes.

Mulhaney broke out into hearty laughter and ran his hands through his thinning grays upon his suntanned skull. "I believe her, Major!"

"I do, too!" Hernandez chimed in as she shook her head.

"Very well!" Mattersly declared over the raucous, quieting it. "You may accompany us, Angel, upon one condition, and you listen to this as well, Mister Mulhaney," he indicated both with a steady finger. "*I* am in charge of this operation," he finished with raised eyebrows, which demanded acquiescence.

Angel nodded willingly. Elias took a moment of thought then nodded curtly.

"Also, young lady," he said as he steadily pointed at her face. "I may, at some point, order you to return home upon your own recognizance and you will do so without argument."

It was Angel's turn to hesitate. She looked to Hernandez and saw that Mattersly's demands were not hers to debate. "Yes, Major," the spy agreed.

"I have your word, then," the SRR officer pushed, stating it rather than posing it as a question.

"Yes, Major, *sir*," she affirmed with a trace of annoyance though it only showed in her eyes, the smile was unaffected.

"I will hold you to that," he grinned then quickly moved on to the next topic. "Jazz, I'm afraid I require a visit to my wagon. I trust that its contents have not been disturbed."

"I guarantee that what you came to Lovelock with is still there," she nodded.

"Excellent," he granted. "I will need access to my explosives and other items. Now, it is certain that I cannot take my wagon along on this journey. I was hoping, if our enemy is so accommodating, that we can get a ride in the constable's police car as far as he dares to take us."

Hernandez thought for a moment then stood and regarded the map closely. "The last time any of my people went up this road was to about this point," she said as she placed the tip of her finger upon a place that appeared to be around twenty kilometers from where Angel had indicated her point of departure.

"That's quite a hike," Mulhaney said flatly.

"This was not that long ago and the pavement is in decent shape," Hernandez affirmed. "A vehicle can hold a pretty steady forty miles an hour over the worst part of it. If things haven't changed, Antonio may be able to get you a little bit closer."

"Understood." Mattersly nodded thoughtfully.

"One thing, Major," Elias spoke up. "We've no idea if Reno's launched some sort of rescue mission for their Cobra."

"True," Mattersly granted.

"Looking at the map, it seems to me that the Cobra never had to wander too far off the interstate. She might even have used it as a guide," Mulhaney opined. "They could be sending ground units up the highway as we speak."

"Very possible," the major agreed and quieted as he rested his arms across his chest, rubbing his chin with a thumb and forefinger in thought. After a moment, he paced.

Angel retook her seat and watched the man, desperately wishing she had something to contribute, but she was silenced by Elias Mulhaney's suggestion. She understood that it was a real possibility and she envisioned a squadron of the armored vehicles she had seen, thundering up the interstate, and squashing them before their planned infiltration had even begun. She wished she had not been so brazen to volunteer for another visit to Reno.

After some moments of contemplation, Mattersly stopped and regarded all three people with thoughtful gazes. "I think that we have no choice but to move forward," he spoke with reverence that held a trace of regret as he smiled and stared upon Jazz's face. "I think that we have a solid plan here, but if it all goes to hell, the people of Lovelock need to rely on your good judgment when you say it's time to leave."

Jazz Hernandez said not a word, but held the major's eyes with sincere hope that such an event would not occur.

***

After the gear was retrieved from Mattersly's

wagon and packed for transport, dinner was held that evening within the same dining room while music filled the rest of the club. Mattersly and Mulhaney spent some time watching the show afterward, interrupted many times by patrons that wanted to shake their hands and offer their sincere gratitude. After several incidents of false identity, Mulhaney stopped correcting people when they addressed him as 'The Major' or 'the man that shot down that awful machine'. He accepted their kindness and their gifts of drink with much gratitude.

Once the night was done, upon Reginald Mattersly's strong advice, he and Elias retired to their rooms. The band on the ground floor would not end their set for several hours, but the SRR officer insisted, fearing that the imbibing of much more alcohol would impair the morning's mission.

The music ended sometime in the dead of night. Reginald no longer kept the time as he once did. He shut his implant down to relax and let the darkness take command. He lay in bed on his side as he watched the stars host the strips of fleeting clouds through the open window, faced to the northwest. The air had lost the heat of day and, though its flow was restrained by his closed front door, insisted its cooling will upon the suite.

For a short time, Mattersly remained awake and contemplative. If he were to speak the absolute truth, such a mission as they were about to take on had little chance of success. As his military training had ingrained upon his psyche, it had become natural for him to think his way out of an untenable situation. As his eyes closed, he envisioned his body rising from the bed, taking the backpack from the floor and slipping out the window. He watched as he lowered the backpack with the help of the rope that he had packed within. Remaining as flat against the building as he could manage it, he followed. Quickly and silently, he gathered the heavy pack and rounded the corner, scampering out of sight of the volunteers manning the gun that he had used earlier that day. He stepped lightly from shadow to shadow, for even in the night the stars and partial moon could reveal him to someone whose eyes had accustomed to the darkness or one of the night patrol, older citizens of Lovelock that kept watch over the town with their bio-electronics. Even civilian models had decent night vision that could pick him out as easily as if it were daytime.

Just as he dismissed his imagination's traitorous scenario as ludicrous folly, a gentle knock sent it away with greater dispatch. His heart pounded in response and he quickly located his pistol as he sat up. Routinely, he booted his *UnitCom* and waited.

The knock came again. No louder and no more urgently.

"I say, who's that?" he replied in a voice barely above a whisper. A shadow of feet showed at the gap between the door and the floor. He augmented his hearing and sat completely still.

"Reggie, open up," he heard someone answer. The whisper rendered the voice unrecognizable, but only one person called him Reggie.

He padded along the floor quickly, but quietly. Mattersly had memorized the places in the wood floor that creaked and avoided them. He jerked the door open only an inch and peered out. Jazz startled at the man's sudden appearance and covered her mouth to stifle a cry of surprise. She pushed her way inside and closed the door behind them.

"What the devil…?"

"Shhh!" she returned and silenced him by pulling his head down to her level with an unyielding arm. Her lips mashed more than met his.

Impulsively, he bent and placed his arms around her, feeling the satiny and thin nightgown that held the warmth of her body. He picked her from the floor and, stealth mostly forgotten, set the wood creaking along his return to the bed.

***

Major Mattersly awoke at some point in the darkness and noted Jazz's departure. He slipped back into his light sleep and arose sometime later to the sun reflecting from the windows of the shop across the street. The sky was light blue and perfect.

He reveled in the last shower he would have, at least for the next unknowable number of days, shaved, and sculpted his mustache before gathering his belongings onto the bed for a final inspection. He loaded the Dragunov and packed the extra magazines into his tunic pockets. Reginald strapped on his sidearm and went to the mirror to place his SRR beret upon his head. He turned away, and stepped to his pack and adjusted the straps so that it fit tightly. With a heavy sigh, he gave the comfortable little room to which he had quickly become accustomed a long look. Reginald draped his rifle over his right shoulder and slipped out the door.

As he descended the stairs, he could hear voices from the bar area. The rest of the club was empty of people, but very ready to entertain that evening. The little round tables, adorned with their red table clothes were spotless and perfectly surrounded by the darkly lacquered wooden chairs. The stage was bare, save for the band's drum kit and amplifiers. Reginald wished that his chosen course of action were not necessary. He could simply not imagine wanting to destroy the cozy club, nor could he understand wanting someone so bad that one could be driven to kill.

Major Mattersly rounded the corner to find Mulhaney seated at the bar next to Angel. Both were eating breakfast and conversing with Hernandez, who absolutely glowed with her black hair up in a bun. The body that he held so closely in the night was now elegantly covered with one of her finest business suits. He stood at the end of the bar and could not help but stare for a brief moment.

Jazz turned and saw him there. She locked eyes with him and smiled. "Good morning, Reggie."

"Good morning," he returned and joined his mission mates.

"Good morning," Mulhaney and Angel murmured. Neither of them seemed to be quite awake.

Reginald set his pack and rifle next to his chosen seat. Jazz set a cup of coffee in front of him and remained, smiling.

"Ah, thank you," he breathed and took the cup in hand.

The beverage was not quite steaming hot, so he was able to sip freely. He watched Hernandez watch him and set the cup down. There was so much he wanted to say, but the worry and fear behind her gaze kept him from speaking.

As Mattersly ate his eggs and toast, Thumper, Marco, and Antonio entered through the front door. The three men stood for a long moment, looking somewhat uncomfortable. Marco's arrogant, slanting grin was gone, as was the constable's hardened authoritarian scowl. Thumper's smile had lost most of its craziness in favor of what appeared to be respect and appreciation.

"Are we about ready, Antonio?" Hernandez called to her policeman.

"Car's all set, Jazz," he answered.

Elias left his seat and placed his Stetson upon his head. "Thank you for breakfast, Jazz. I'm going to put my things in the car."

"Let me help," Marco piped up, which took Mulhaney aback for a second or two. He watched the big bodyguard hoist the pack from the floor and set it upon one shoulder. Without another word, he carried it through the door.

Elias could not help but smile with appreciation as he stepped to his rifle with the help of his walking stick. He slipped the weapon onto his left shoulder and turned toward the door.

"Say, young feller," Thumper spoke up as he blocked his way and fished through a satchel that was hung from his shoulder. "I want you to have these. I rec'gnized your handgun's ammo and found some in our armory," the old man explained as he gave over handful after handful of the large caliber rounds.

"Wow, thank you, Thumper," Mulhaney uttered as he frantically scooped up the offerings and dropped them into the pockets of his duster. Instantly, his heart lightened over the act of kindness. Until that moment, the fact that his finest weapon was down to its last few rounds had weighed on him.

Having given all he had, Thumper reached out his hand to the tall man. "You be careful, young man," he wished with a crooked smile.

"I will," Mulhaney promised as he shook the old man's hand. He tipped his hat and walked outside.

Marco returned, picked up Angel's smaller, lighter pack, and headed through the door. The young lady, knowing that their departure was moments away, left the bar and followed her luggage without a word.

Reginald turned in his chair and found that he and Jazz were alone. Before he could say a word, she rounded the bar and seized his face with both hands. A kiss immediately followed.

"I don't know what to say," the major said once the kiss was broken.

"Say you'll come back to me when this is done…if

it gets done," Jazz spoke frantically but quietly.

Mattersly thought about the implications of that. His dream of a house on the beach somewhere in California would be compromised. He had not spoken of this, he realized.

"If you get into trouble… real trouble, just go on," she added, sensing his reservation. "But, just know that I want you to come back."

Reginald nodded and accepted a follow up kiss. The two separated just as Marco returned for the last backpack. Before he bent to pick it up, he approached the major and struck out his hand. "Wanted to wish you luck," he said.

Mattersly sensed no subterfuge, so he took the offered hand. "Thank you, my good man."

With that, Marco nodded, picked up the heaviest backpack of the three, and carried it outside.

"Well then," Reginald announced and stood after having emptied his coffee cup and plate, "I think it's time."

"Yeah," Jazz whispered as she watched him from the end of the bar. Her eyes were becoming wet.

The major could think of nothing to say to comfort her. In all his years in the military and wandering the post-Great Exodus world, such rare, tender moments rendered him speechless. He hoisted his Dragunov upon his shoulder and walked outside.

The squad car sat at the curb. Angel and Mulhaney both leaned up against it, waiting. The morning air was crisp and cool, but the summer heat would put an end to that soon. It was nearly 06:30 hours from his implant's clock.

"Well, then, Constable Antonio, are we ready to depart?"

"We are, sir," the bald lawman answered. He stood next to his vehicle upon the driver's side. Marco stood alongside the man with his arms crossed over his chest.

Thumper watched from the sidewalk, silent for a change as he scratched an itch somewhere under his dirty white shirt.

"Very well. Let's mount up," the major commanded.

Antonio shook hands with Marco, exchanged words of farewell, and dropped into the driver's seat. Elias took the front passenger seat and Angel, armed with the lever-action rifle that Elias loaned her, took a place behind him. Mattersly stepped off the curb when Hernandez's call caused him to pause. He turned to her in time to be grabbed by the lapel and kissed once again. It was a kiss of haste, but also of great passion.

"Come back to me," she all but pleaded as her black eyes searched his.

"I cannot promise that," Reginald said plainly. It was the truth and they both knew it.

"Well, promise me *something*, goddamn you," Hernandez spat. "Promise me that if you can't pull this off that you… all of you!" she spoke loudly enough for those in the car to hear her. "Promise me that if everything goes to hell, scatter and get out of there. If you can't come back here," she went on very lowly as she once again stared at the major, "go somewhere safe. Survival first, do you understand me?"

"I do," Mattersly affirmed.

"Okay," Jazz agreed with a forced smile. "Get the hell out of here so you can get this over with and come home," she said gruffly and took a few steps back from the car.

Mattersly took a seat behind the driver and they were off. Antonio turned the car toward the highway and soon they were upon it, heading for Reno.

At some point, Reginald realized that he had not given a look back at Jazz before the car turned and left the club out of sight behind them. He wished he had. He thought of her dark, earnest eyes and, though the future for the four people in the car was uncertain, he imagined everything working out as planned and returning to Lovelock. He dropped his head back onto the seat hard enough to gather attention.

"You okay?" Angel asked as she ran her small hand through her short, spikey blond hair.

"Yes," Reginald said and turned his attention to the land flying by his window. The car was traveling faster than he had anticipated. The road was in better shape than Jazz had indicated and he said so to Antonio.

"Oh, just wait," the driver answered. "We're at about sixty miles-an-hour here and it's not too bad, but in a few miles it's practically gravel."

"I see," replied the major. "Tell me something, Antonio."

"Sure, sir." The driver eyed the SRR officer in the mirror.

"How far are you actually comfortable with taking us?"

"I'd like to get you to Fernley. It's about fifty miles from Lovelock… about thirty to Reno.

"That's the abandoned town with some farmers on the outskirts, correct?"

"Yes, Major," the constable affirmed.

"From what I remember on the map," Elias chimed in, "there's not a lot of options if we get ambushed, that is, no real place to hide."

"Well, there are a few places to turn off, and this thing's pretty quick," Antonio explained.

Mulhaney and Mattersly shared a knowing look that Angel picked up on. They had all discussed the possibility that Gillespie would unleash hell once he realized his precious Cobra was not returning.

"All we can do is hope we don't run into a

procession of military vehicles headed the other way," Reginald said dryly.

"Or another damned helo," Mulhaney amended.

For a long time, no one spoke. Each person's attention was either on the road ahead or in the skies above as they searched for Gillespie's reprisals.

Chapter Seven

The cruiser made good progress along the cracked and weather-beaten pavement for much of the first hour. Antonio was forced to slow the car due to the eroding surface. The cool desert morning air was succumbing to the sun's influence, moving everyone to open the windows near them.

Mattersly felt vulnerable in the wide open space along the old interstate. The hilly lands surrounding the roadway were beautiful, but their comforting concealment was too far away for his taste, considering their mission. He stuck his head out of his window often, magnifying his vision to look ahead along the opposing lanes of traffic, separated from their southwesterly lanes by a thickly grown swath of brown brush that seemed as infinite as the road.

Mulhaney appeared to be very calm from Reginald's perspective, despite the rifle he held across his chest. The barrel of which struck out the open window a few inches. Overall, the tall man seemed to be taking the ride in stride. He had removed his black hat once the heat of the day became present, but showed no signs of fatigue from the mesmerizing view of the world they passed through.

At an hour and twenty-five minutes into the drive, everyone in the vehicle could see an overpass ahead of them. Antonio began to slow the car.

"On the other side of that is Fernley," Angel provided. During planning, she had mentioned passing through the small town, the site of an abandoned truck depot and several large marketplaces. Numerous residential tracks of land lay near the interstate to the west of the shops. According to both Angela and Eric Hemmel, Lovelock's other spy, there had been no sign of life there when they had passed through.

Satisfied, the constable accelerated to a cautious forty-five miles per hour. The Lovelock Police vehicle passed underneath the overpass without incident, though Mattersly could tell that the driver was under stress. The man fidgeted in his seat and his bald head was dotted with beads of sweat.

As they drove on, several plain and immense markets or warehouses lay to their left and, much more closely placed to the interstate, a large refueling station appeared on their right. Mulhaney pressed his head through the open window and thought to scan ahead using the scope, but the vehicle was shuddering and shaking too much from the disheveled roadway for him to steady the weapon. He gave up, though he eyed the building closely. They soon passed the ruined, dusted-covered structure. Elias could see from the missing windows and collapsed roof that it had been untouched for a great amount of time.

The interstate rose into an overpass itself to allow an access road to run beneath them. The street joined the truck stop to the rest of the town, which they could see had been built mostly on the south side of the highway.

Mattersly marked their progress on his implant's unsupported map program, noting that they were soon to leave the empty town behind them. They were making good time and Antonio was getting them closer to Reno than the major had dared hope. He would cut the constable loose at the Truckee River, just over two miles ahead.

It was just minutes to 0800 hours.

***

"I've got to get the hell out of this thing," the commander of the armored vehicle said as he sat back from the viewfinder and popped the hatch open. Standing, he linked his implant's optics to the eight-wheeled machine's periscope, shaped the view into a small rectangle, and placed it onto his dominant right eye. "Hey, Tim! Wake up!" he called down into the crew area.

"What?!" an irritated voice shouted from below.

"It's almost eight," the commander pressed.

"Okay, Pop," Tim grumbled. The younger recruit knew that the sooner they completed the search for the missing Cobra, the sooner he could get back home to his bed. "Rabbit, get up," he ordered the man stretched out on the seats parallel to his.

"Yeah, yeah," the even younger and thinner teenager replied. He was called Rabbit because of his nervous glances to every noise he heard and could not identify. He was also a fast runner, despite being the shortest in the crew. "Where's Spud?"

"Dunno," Tim answered as he stepped onto the ramp and into the morning sun. "Probably somewhere taking a shit."

"Somebody call me?" the fourth man in the crew hailed from just down the embankment as he emerged from the line of fences that separated them from a row of run-down homes.

"See?" Tim said to Rabbit over his shoulder and laughed. He grabbed his boots from their place under the seats and began to tug them onto his feet.

"All right, guys. Get it together," Pop said as he joined them outside. "We've got a little bit of a drive to go before we can go home."

"Aw, come on, Pop," Spud spoke up as he pulled his desert-camouflaged shirt over his shoulders. He was called 'Spud' by his peers because of his round, pock-marked face. Together with his short hair and eyes that appeared to be too small for his head, the name fit. "Can't we just say we went the rest of the search pattern and just go home?"

Tim groaned. He knew what was coming.

"Spud, if you want to go home, go!" Pop shouted as

he went nose-to-spud with his least favorite person in his vehicle. "We are looking for fellow Renoites! Not just *any* Renoites, either! Fellow soldiers!"

"Okay! Sorry," Spud surrendered and took two steps back.

Eager to get away from the confrontation, Rabbit hopped inside the armored vehicle and sat at the commander's seat to put on his boots. In doing so, he glanced at the periscope's monitor.

"Holy shit," he grunted. "Pop!"

***

"Pull over! Quick!" Reginald shouted when he realized that the glint of sunlight he had caught had been reflected by the vehicle parked at the side of the road ahead. "Everyone out! *Now*!" he roared as he threw himself through the open door and rolled onto the ground.

Elias did the same, but his weaker right leg made it difficult for him to recover his feet. He had seen the direction that the major had been looking before he ordered the evacuation of the cruiser and peered around the front of it as he tried to find the problem.

The problem found them first.

Angel slithered more than launched herself from the police car, dropping her lithe body behind the right rear wheel. As she cycled the lever to put a round in the chamber of the rifle, the vehicle shook as if a miniature earthquake had surrounded it. The air was full of the buzzing of rounds from whatever it was that the major had seen and the shrapnel of the disintegrating vehicle. Unaware of it, she had begun to utter cries of terror when she found that trying to make her body flat actually made her more of a target for the flying debris. Angel felt tiny sharp objects strike her face, arms and back until she curled her body up into a ball behind the wheel.

At that moment, an arm wrapped around her lower

abdomen and she was hauled away from the car and dropped rudely into soft dirt. The shrapnel content of the air lessened and she dared to open an eye to find out who had grabbed her.

"Stay down!" Elias Mulhaney shouted into her face. His eyes were wide, though with awareness, not fear. She blinked and he was gone.

***

Pop noticed the car's movement as soon as Rabbit shouted his name. "Car!" he shouted to his young crew.

Stupidly, they froze, leaving the man in charge to assess the situation. Pop brought the vehicle's periscope camera to the forefront of his lenses and accessed the vehicle's main weapon, twin fifty-caliber machine guns on a motorized mount.

"Where?" someone from behind him called out.

"Right where I'm lookin', damn it!" Pop shouted as he aimed the crosshairs on the vehicle.

There were strict orders from General Desmond that anything coming from the direction of Lovelock was to be engaged, considering the possibility of a counterattack after they had found a way to bring down the Cobra. The car was rolling toward them at a steady speed, but decelerated hard as he watched. Somehow, his vehicle had been seen, despite the lower profile of being off the roadway and partially shaded by a nearby tree. Accessing the firing controls, he let the machine guns rip, mentally commanding the crosshairs to track along the car's front end.

Just as three of the four doors sprang open, the front end of the car was torn apart, throwing dust and debris into the air and partially obstructing his vision. Pop thought he saw a man dive into the brush dividing the highway, but he was not sure. Leaning against his armored eight-wheeler, he made his way to the front of it for a better look as he let the main guns hammer away at the car.

***

Mattersly crawled through the overgrowth in the center of the highway and glanced back at the police car. He wished he had not, for it was being torn to pieces by the wilting power of the enemy vehicle's guns. Constable Antonio had not moved quickly enough to escape the attack.

The major cussed and stayed low and on the move, swimming through the brown but sturdy desert brush. The assault of the underlying rocks upon his flesh went by unnoticed. He manually overrode the hearing protection of his audio-receptors, adjusting them slightly to pinpoint the location of the incoming fire. Bending his prone body to face it directly, he brought the Dragunov forward and lifted his upper body upon his elbows. Grasping the weapon tightly, he disengaged the safety and found the armored car.

He could see the vehicle's upper body through the brush and the gun, which he could now see was unmanned, controlled from inside or remotely.

"Bloody hell!" he grunted.

Understanding that the gunner was well-protected, he targeted the small sliver of glass that had given the machine away in the first place.

Mattersly took a deep breath and muted his hearing as far as the implant would allow. The world beyond his became narrow and finite, nothing more than could be perceived within his riflescope. He estimated the range to be a bit under four hundred meters and the wind was minimal. He squeezed the trigger and the tiny window spider-webbed.

The machine gun fire halted immediately. An enemy combatant, who had placed himself alongside the wheeled beast's left-front corner, stood up in response. Reginald placed the scope's reticle on that target and fired again.

***

Rabbit knew not what to do other than to watch Pop work with the Stryker's main guns. He had raked the car with rounds and had virtually taken the front end off when the monitor went dark, accompanied by a metallic ringing sound and he felt something strike his shoulder.

"Ow," he said lamely.

The world outside became quiet and as he placed his right hand on the suddenly painful spot on his shoulder, that was now hot and wet. The sound of a rifle shot was barely audible within the armored vehicle, but the shock of seeing blood on his palm put the importance of it out of his mind.

"*Holy shit! Help*!"

He turned from the tank commander's seat to get his friends' attention, but he could see that something else had happened. Spud ran past the opening at the rear of the vehicle with a panicked expression and his rifle up. Rabbit thought he could hear shouting outside, but the voices were muffled by the ringing in his ears from the chattering fifty-calibers on the roof, which had strangely gone silent. He stood from the seat and staggered through a sudden dizzy spell that required him to remove his hand from the wound that had come from nowhere. He held onto the machine's inner wall for a moment, tried to call for help again, but nothing came out of his mouth.

Rabbit winced in pain and confusion as he decided to let his body drop to the thinly cushioned seats.

***

The head of the second target disappeared in a dark mist. Mattersly set the Dragunov's safety and slithered to his left, knowing not to stay still for very long.

Nearly forty meters away, Elias crawled frantically until the armored personnel carrier stopped firing, then he froze. The next sound he heard was a familiar report from behind and to his left. *Mattersly's Dragunov?* He popped his head up and brought Momo's rifle up for a look across the road just as the weapon fired again and brought down a man who had been standing next to the machine.

"Ha," he allowed himself, though he kept it quiet.

There was no time to celebrate anything however, as two companions of the major's victim ran to the prone body, both armed. The first one to the scene crouched as he moved and Elias could see from the man's expression that Reginald had made a mess of his friend. The one behind him, a bit of a pudgy round-headed man, stopped well short, but as he was inexperienced, he did not even bother looking downrange with his semi-automatic rifle at the ready. Instead, the slacking soldier's eyes never left the body felled before him, even when the second Renoite soldier opened fire. Apparently, he had caught sight of the major.

"Shit," Mulhaney grunted and hurriedly searched for the shooter.

During practice, he had found that firing the weapon left-handed was problematic, but preferable as the fingers of his right hand could barely feel the trigger. He could fire the weapon that way, but not for accuracy. Elias knew that he had to settle his nerves, though he worried that Reginald had been hit. As the enemy crouched and appeared to draw a bead, Mulhaney pulled the trigger. The thirty-caliber thundered away as its energy lifted the dust around him and adding to his already aching ears. It was a sloppy shot, but it felled the shooter before he had a second chance. The round struck his target in the rib cage on the man's left side, which dropped him like a sack of rice.

The remaining round-faced man shrieked in horror, but did not retreat. Instead, the poorly trained soldier panicked and tried to return suppressing fire in Mulhaney's direction, but had left the safety on.

Elias worked the lever, expelled the spent shell, and sent the next one into the receiver. Immediately, he acquired the next target in his sights. Before the young and inexperienced blunderer had a chance, Elias took him down with the next shot. Quickly, he cycled the action again and searched for another target through his scope. Movement from downrange and from the left caught his attention.

"What the...?" he murmured as he watched Reginald Mattersly run toward the vehicle in a crouch, "...hell are you *doing*?" he finished, seething.

Mulhaney could feel his heart pounding even faster than before. He threw his caution away and thought the command to activate his *CTL-Link*. He had to communicate with the major to at least find out what the madman was up to.

***

Reginald heard Elias's assault and acknowledged the puffs of dust. He was elated to see that the American soldier had thought to move away from the ruined cruiser and had the wits about him to return fire. From the cries of terror and groans of bewilderment and pain, he concluded that the former paratrooper had taken down at least one target.

Mattersly had no idea how many Renoite soldiers were with the Stryker, but he had seen only one and heard the gunfire from a second. The vehicle itself remained with its engine silent and the machine gun still. He arrived at the front right corner of the machine and halted. Getting his body low, he looked underneath the eight-wheeled machine and noted that Mulhaney had indeed done outstanding work. There were three bodies lying in the dirt on the other side of the Stryker, only one of which was his kill. He shouldered his Dragunov and made his nine-millimeter ready.

Reginald silently stepped toward the back of the

vehicle, well aware of the possibility that some of the crew could be inside the disheveled homes at his left. His implant's communication device warned him of another implant attempting a handshake. At first, he thought it to be the enemy soldier that he had taken down, but as he had witnessed his seven-point-six-two round remove the man's face, he found it to be all but impossible.

As the major arrived at the right rear wheel, the other device held a lock with his own long enough for identification. It was Corporal Bartel. There was no time to address him, however, as Reginald felt the vehicle rock with movement from the inside. A whimper of pain or despair came from the rear. It was then that Mattersly noticed the open rear ramp.

He checked around the corner with a quick look from a low crouch and found no one. He placed the semi-automatic handgun in his left hand and went further, peering inside the Stryker's crew hold.

Lying along the driver's side row of seats was a fourth crewman. To Reginald, he appeared to be no more than eighteen years old. The boy was covered in blood from a shoulder or upper chest wound. There was no weapon near the prone Renoite, so Mattersly decided to move forward.

"*One wounded inside. Remain where you are for cover*," the major sent in text to the corporal. He received a short acknowledgment and took a seat opposite the dying teenager. Reginald could see that there was not much to the lad. He was perhaps five and a half feet tall and very thin. He kept the pistol trained on the Renoite just the same.

"I say, what is your name, son?" Mattersly said gently.

The semi-conscious boy startled at the sound and let out a cry of agony. Upon seeing the speaker across from him, he realized that it was no one he knew. "Pop?!" he shouted in a cracked and screechy voice. His light brown eyes, already widened with fear, grew bulbous once he discovered that his call only received silence.

"I'm afraid they've gone," Reginald said, "I'm Major Mattersly, commanding the invasion force and, I'm sorry to inform you that it appears you will be joining your comrades, soon."

"Wh... what?" Rabbit whispered. His body shivered from the cold he felt throughout his being. "Just a shoulder wound," he insisted.

"Oh, I'm afraid not," Mattersly disagreed as he looked about the vehicle's interior. He quickly deduced how effective his first shot had truly been from the hole in the periscope window and the computer monitor. "You are quite obviously bleeding out and I'm terribly regretful in saying that I am utterly powerless to do anything for you."

"Water?"

"Oh! I stand corrected," Mattersly smiled sympathetically and rose from his seat. The vehicle's roof was too low for him to stand erect, but he slid over to the teenager and took a knee. "Now, then," he went on as he replaced his pistol and unclipped his canteen from his belt and held it out, "I take it that there were four of you?"

The boy took several gulps of the offered water, spilling some due to his endless shivering. "Ye... yes."

"I see. Very good," the major granted as he set the canteen down. "Right, and how many of these Strykers... am I correct in assuming that this is a Stryker? How many of them are there in Gillespie's possession?" he asked as he loaded his amber bowl pipe with his dry and aged tobacco.

Mattersly watched the Renoite's eyes follow the process with interest, though his eyelids were apparently heavy.

"Eight," he answered weakly.

The major struck a match and lit his pipe. "Eight,

you say. Indeed," he muttered as he let out a few puffs of smoke. "You are this far from home in search of the Cobra helicopter, are you not?"

Amidst the wounded teenager's shivering, he detected a nod in the affirmative.

"Very good, my lad," Mattersly said lowly as he helped the young man with another gulp of water.

Reginald had more questions, but kept them to himself. He remained nearby as he smoked his pipe and patted the boy's sweaty head until the shivering stopped.

"*All clear. Check on Angel, won't you?*" he sent to Mulhaney.

A few minutes went by and Mattersly turned to see his remaining companions had joined him. They stood upon the ramp, looking none the worse for wear, but definitely agitated. Angel stared at the dead body of the teen lying next to the major with disgust and mild shock while Elias looked about the vehicle, clearly wondering about its condition.

"Ah, there you are," Reginald addressed. "As it turns out, my first shot was rather well placed. It took out the Stryker's computer interface with the weapons' systems and this boy, who happened to be sitting here," he described and patted the commander's seat.

Angel swiped the tobacco smoke from her proximity. "Jeez! I thought the thing was on fire with you in it!"

Mattersly forged on as if he had not heard. "According to our friend here," he gestured to the dead teenager with his pipe, "this is one of eight such machines in Gillespie's forces." He lifted himself to a crouch and headed toward the ramp. Angel and Elias backed away to let him exit. "Furthermore, he confirmed that they are looking for the Cobra."

"Alone? That doesn't make sense," Mulhaney

commented with an expression of confusion and doubt.

"Exactly," the major agreed as his feet dropped to the dirt. "I say, good shooting, Mister Mulhaney," he said as he looked over the bodies of the other three Renoites.

"Okay, count me lost," Angel spoke up from Mattersly's left, "but I don't understand why that doesn't make sense."

"I believe this squad was a scout," the major supplied as he began walking toward their ruined squad car as he puffed away. "Considering these men were so casually lying about and the Stryker itself was cool to the touch, I believe they camped at this spot overnight. They were either expecting reinforcements or signs of a counterattack."

"Okay, and?" Angel pressed as she strode briskly alongside the major as he kicked through the brush separating the lanes of traffic.

"Well, quite obviously, we need to move. Immediately," he stressed as he stopped to tap out the ash from his pipe onto his heel and allow for Elias to catch up. "They are probably in contact with whatever passes for their command in Reno and most likely, there are additional forces inbound."

"Wait!" called Elias as he rushed to the major's side. "Let's take that damn thing and get going!" he insisted as he pointed back at the Stryker.

"That won't be possible, I'm afraid," replied the major as he stepped past the shot-up constable and his car. "I've already attempted to gain access to the computer, but my first shot damaged it and I do not believe we have the time to bypass the system."

All three were quiet for a moment as they came within proximity of their dead compatriot. Mattersly opened the rear driver's side door and pulled down the rear seats to access the trunk. He pulled out one pack after the other and emerged from the car. The morning sun was already working on the dead constable. The aroma of blood and death were just beginning to be noticeable.

"Shouldn't we bury him?" Angel asked.

"Problem number one," replied the major as he removed a small gray package from his gear, "we have no shovels. Number two: we may not even have the time."

Mattersly slung his pack upon his back and replaced his Dragunov to one shoulder. He strode toward the crewless armored vehicle with only Angel behind him. Mulhaney went to the passenger's side of the cruiser to retrieve his walking stick and Stetson.

"Well, *shit*," he grumbled. The hat was torn to shreds and the large tree branch snapped in two and splintered, both done by the Stryker's machine guns. He dropped his ruined affects to the ground and put the cruiser behind him.

Reginald opened a classified file within his implant and stared upon the gray parcel in the palm of his hand. In a moment, it responded with a quick flash of a muted red light. He chose the 'Stand By' option upon his display and boarded the Stryker from the open rear ramp. He set the explosive onto the engine cowling in the center of the beast. The major removed a satchel of magazines and another of sealed food packets from the storage compartments on either side of the crew area. The major slid them onto the ramp and took the young soldier's semi-automatic assault weapon.

"As much as I'd hate to carry anything more than we already have, these may come in handy," the major said of the lightweight weapons.

His implant identified them as being made by an Austrian company that had folded in the mid twenty-first century. The rounds were American-made and extremely common to that time period.

"Hell, yeah," Angel smiled and promptly dropped the old lever-action to the floor of the Stryker.

She quickly expelled the extra rounds she had kept in her pack along with it. Grabbing an M27, she hefted it and made sure she knew where the safety and fire selection switches were.

Mulhaney did the same, though he would not abandon Momo's sniper rifle. Instead, he strapped one of the Austrian models to the side of his pack and took as many magazines as he could bear.

The major disarmed the corpses of the Renoites, closed the Stryker's ramp and led Mulhaney and Angel away from it. Not far from where he stood, he could see a break in the fence in between two of the homes.

"Bloody hell!" he called out in disgust. "Filthy blighters didn't even bother learning how to prepare a proper latrine! Watch your step, here," he pointed and carefully stepped through the opening in the fence.

"Oh, great," Angel muttered and made a retching sound. On the other side of the fence, she jogged ahead of the major, in between two decrepit homes.

"Come now, Mister Mulhaney," Mattersly chided as he walked ahead of the man. "I'm afraid you'll have to move on the double-quick for a bit."

"Coming, Major," Elias promised.

He already regretted taking on the extra weight. Beyond Mattersly, he could see a tree with a great amount of branches. He headed toward it, hoping he could find a replacement walking stick.

"All right, everyone take cover here!" Reginald ordered once he and Angel had walked several houses down the line.

He removed his emerald gray beret, folded it, and sent it to a pocket on his trouser leg. From the opposite one, he retrieved his boonie hat and placed it upon his head.

"Is that little gray square supposed to do some damage, Major?" the young guide asked as she placed her back against the wall.

"We shall see," he answered. "Get down and cover your ears," he recommended to the both of them when Mulhaney joined. He removed his backpack and held it over his head as he slid down the cracked stucco.

Noting Elias's precaution, Angel's eyes grew wider despite her expression of doubt. She thought it over and decided to do the same.

Mattersly selected the military program to return to his view. He was still in contact with the small charge inside the Stryker. He crouched beside Mulhaney and gave the both of them a wink as he selected 'detonate'.

For barely a heartbeat, there was nothing. Then, a muffled sort of gong noise filled the major's ears, tripping the audio implants to negate the assault. The ground and the wall behind them shook briefly. In an instant, it was done.

The major peeked around the corner the way they had come and he saw black smoke rising from where the Stryker had been parked. As he was about to turn toward the others and announce that it was all clear, a mighty clang erupted from Mattersly's right, sending the man to instinctively spring backward and crouch to his knees. The first metal-upon-pavement ringing was followed by one not so mighty. It was then that the major saw the piece of the armored personnel carrier as it tumbled back to the sun-worn street. As it came to a stop, he could see that the detached item was the vehicle's commander's hatch, which was located directly above where he had placed the C-4.

Mattersly took a deep breath and let it out. "We are clear," he declared as he took up his backpack and rifle.

"Holy crap," Angel marveled as her eyes went from the black smoke beyond the fence to the torn hatch and back.

"That looks a lot lighter than the original to me, Major," Elias commented as he discarded his duster and stuffed it in his pack. Underneath was only a plain olive drab sleeveless shirt, already sweat-stained at the armpits. "I think they've reproduced them, but did it on the cheap."

Reginald stepped to the smoldering metal door and gave it a tap with his boot. It moved with some effort, but he thought his companion was onto something.

"If it isn't the armor itself, Mister Mulhaney, it's the supporting hardware," he finished with a point of a finger toward the twisted hinges. "For instance, I sincerely doubt that my first shot would have penetrated the glass of a true Stryker. At any rate, we need to move along. Angel, this is familiar territory to you, is that not correct?"

"Yup," she smiled as she hefted the freshly stolen assault weapon.

"By all means, lead on," the major ordered.

Without another word, the petite young lady slipped into a medium stride. Mattersly watched as the taller Mulhaney reached up to a thick, low-hanging tree branch and, after a brief struggle, snapped it off. He fought to keep Angel's pace as he shaped the knob of his new cane with a combat knife.

Reginald could see that the young lady was leading them directly south, so he caught up to her and asked her for a reason.

"We turn west just up ahead," she explained. "There's a road lined with trees that will give us some cover."

"Ah, very well, then," the major smiled. "Carry on."

The two men followed their guide around the next corner, off the decaying pavement and onto a dirt road. Mattersly regarded his implant's compass and noted that they were heading west. Though the land was surrounded by homes, all appeared as if they had been abandoned for decades. Their exterior colors faded to pastels by the relentless sun and covered in cakes of dust. The sight of them was no deterrent for their ensuing thirst.

The dirt path bent to the southwest, where the sun's efforts were reduced by the graces of the trees that had been growing untrimmed and unrestricted for a great long time. The heat of the day seemed barely abated, however, and soon their water supplies were tapped into, one member after another. Under normal circumstances, the major would have warned his companions of being conservative, but he knew from the maps and intelligence gathered from Angel and Eric Hemmel, that fresh water would not be hard to discover.

The scatterings of low-cost homes and overgrown trees gave way to another path. This one was cut for the railway and Reginald wondered if this was the same set of tracks he and Elias had discovered northeast of Lovelock just days before.

The major smiled at that thought as they crossed the aged tracks one after the other. Just a matter of days before today, he had been all by himself in his wagon. The ambush had brought about a complete change to his life. A new friend, a new allegiance, possibly even, a new love. Unconsciously, his smile grew ever wider as he thought of Jazz.

"What's the joke, Major?" Elias said from his right side.

Apparently, the man was capable of shorts bursts in his stride, for the hypnotic thumping of the walking stick had subsided just before Reginald found his American army friend at his side.

"Ah," Mattersly uttered to cover for his being lightly startled. "Sadly, I've no joke to share, Mister Mulhaney."

"I hope that your lightheartedness points toward optimism for this mission of ours," the taller man said in a lower tone.

Angel was ahead of the both of them by nearly twenty meters. Despite the weight she carried and her slight frame, she was moving along much more quickly than either man had suspected she had been capable.

To this, Reginald found no need for deception. "I believe that we have little chance of succeeding in every aspect of our mission."

"Really?" blurted a stunned Elias Mulhaney.

Mattersly nodded and grunted in the affirmative.

"Really," the American repeated flatly. His smile, which had mirrored Mattersly's since his having discovered it, disappeared.

"Oh, now, don't let that bother you," Mattersly was quick to amend. "I simply believe that there are odds against us and that we may very well be diverted from the heart of Reno and any of our objectives."

"Is this change of heart because we lost a man this morning?"

"Not at all, Mister Mulhaney," the major explained. "I am simply speaking from experience. I'm sure your five-oh-fourth was never pressed into service under such circumstances or certainly, against such odds."

"Well, no," Elias said, "but we've done okay so far."

"Indeed," Mattersly agreed as he wiped the sweat from his eyes and readjusted his boonie hat. "Don't mistake my misgivings as a lack of intent. If there is any way we can destroy the Renoite fabrication devices, rescue Miss Hernandez's niece, *and* remove this Gillespie fellow from power, than I most assuredly will have us do so."

"Okay, good."

Further conversation was halted by the fact that

Angel had stopped in the shade of a tree to take water. She let her backpack slide to the dirt, but kept the recently liberated weapon to hang levelly by its strap over one shoulder.

"Please make sure the safety is engaged if that's the way you're going to carry that," Mattersly said. "If something catches that trigger, you very well could shoot one of us."

"There's not even a round in the chamber, Major," she replied and took another drink. "I checked."

"Good girl," Reginald returned in a gentle tone that he hoped would come across as fatherly rather than condescending.

"Man, are *we* out on the open," Mulhaney said as his eyes passed over the street they had picked up after the tracks. They were in the middle of a commercial district that appeared very similar to the buildings of Lovelock, though they had gone unused much longer. "I don't like this."

"We won't make the same mistake I did on my first trip," Angel promised as she stretched her back. "I kept on this road, mostly at night because I wasn't sure about the local populace, which I found out was about none. This place is quiet at night except for the wildlife. I slept in there," she pointed to the commercial building just meters from the trees under which the trio cooled themselves.

"So, what was your mistake?" Elias asked as he lowered his backpack to the ground and began to root around inside it.

"Well, up ahead is this manmade river. I crossed it, badly, and went on up and over that range of hills," she explained and pointed to the west. "What I should have done was follow the river around, which is what I think we should do."

Mulhaney found a large neckerchief within his pack

of a camouflage pattern of greens and tans. He stared into the distance as he draped it over his head and tied it into place.

"Nice tat," Angel granted as her eyes went to his right arm's bicep, exposed since he had removed his duster some time earlier. "What is it?"

"That's my old unit," Elias said with a trace of a grumble. "Five hundred 'n' fourth paratroopers of the eighty-second," he explained as he held still for the young lady to see.

"A red devil and blue wings," she murmured. "Cool."

Mulhaney just smiled and reached for his pack. He froze once he noticed the major's stance. The man was slightly hunched and held out both hands, apparently to quiet his companions.

"What is it?" Angel whispered and received a harsh glare from the major's blue eyes.

"A vehicle," he answered after a moment.

He turned his head so that his right ear was aimed toward the interstate, less than a half-mile to the north of their position.

Mulhaney snatched up the sniper rifle and used the scope to search the road in the distance. The risk for reflection from the lens was minimal as the sun was behind them.

"I got 'im," Elias said.

From this distance, he could only see the upper half of the machine, but the carrier's commander and machine guns were clearly visible.

"Stryker?" the major inquired lowly.

"Yup."

"Let's move," Mattersly ordered and snatched up his pack and Dragunov. He quickly set the pace, sticking close to the buildings as he led his people westward.

Angel jogged to catch up.

"Sir!" she addressed him as she came alongside. "If we turned to the south for a block or so, we'll be walking amongst more cover."

"Very well," he agreed and let her take the lead.

He watched Mulhaney's progress for a moment before turning the corner and briefly leaving the paratrooper's sight. Even on a cane, the man was maintaining a good pace.

Once in the middle of the block and back amongst residential structures, Angel turned from the street and strode between two homes. Mattersly halted in the front yard for a moment, just long enough to make sure that Mulhaney saw where the procession had turned.

From there on out, Angel wound her way in between the abandoned single-story homes, heading roughly to the southeast. The yards of the bland, featureless structures were littered with children's toys, outdoor furniture, grills, and the occasional animal carcass. Reginald noted that there were no lawns to speak of as the long-unattended patches of grass had most likely turned brown by the end of the first week after the owners had walked away. Some of the driveways featured vehicles as well, though it was more than obvious that they were no longer drivable. In Mattersly's experience, unless one was maintained and used somewhat often, a vehicle was useless for one reason or another. He had not bothered to even look at one if it appeared to have remained still for a time.

From behind her, Angel heard the sound of Mattersly's boots sliding to a stop in the loose dirt. She stopped and turned to see what had occurred. "Major?"

"I say, Angel," Reginald addressed her without looking up from the object he had found. "How far is that manmade river you were telling us about a few moments ago?"

He consulted his implant's map program, which he had set to 'roaming' mode. This tracked his movement from a point, which he had verified, and set, measuring his steps rather than relying on the now defunct satellite systems. It was not a very accurate system, but it worked reasonably enough to verify the information Angel would give him.

"Outstanding," Elias proclaimed as he sidled up next to Mattersly to see what the man had found.

***

Desmond paced the communications room at the top of the mostly empty apartment complex two blocks south of Gillespie's Platinum Reata hotel and governmental headquarters. The radio operator was unable to reach the lead Stryker and they were almost ninety minutes late checking in.

His radio operator leaned forward at his desk-full of equipment. A man close to Desmond's age, the extra weight around his middle and in his face added almost twenty years to his appearance. The communications expert had arrived early once the overnight relief man reported that the scouting Stryker had become unreachable. He had checked over the transmitter and tested it with complete success.

Nevertheless, *Ranger*, had gone silent. Desmond knew most of the men in the Stryker teams pretty well, so it was not like Pop, *Ranger*'s commander, to drop out of radio communication.

What was worse, Gillespie's sniper superstar had still not checked in. Momo and his flunkies had not been heard from for three days. He had been late to check in before, it was expected, given the man's mission, but he had never been more than forty-eight hours overdue.

General Desmond pulled another cigarette from his tweed sport coat and lit it. He fell back into his pacing pattern, silent on the neon-accented black carpet. He let the smoke ooze from his nostrils on his next exhale and checked the condition of his hair in the reflection of a picture's glass surface. He straightened the collar of his blue satin shirt and turned from the wall.

The urge to ask the obvious overcame the experienced gambler-turned-militia-commander. "Still nothing, Bill?"

Bill Atwood looked around and tugged a headphone speaker from his left ear. "Nothing but background noise, Ricky. Just like before."

For the thousandth time that morning, Ricky Desmond adjusted the rings on his fingers, carefully avoiding the burning cigarette between the fore and index fingers on his right hand. The worry on his face was palpable and Bill felt sorry for his friend. The both of them had been career gamblers back in Vegas and then Reno long before the nation's economic collapse. Atwood hated Gillespie for making Desmond such an important person in the organization. Like Desmond himself, he saw through the honorary military rank and thought it ridiculous.

Ricky checked his watch rather than use his implant. It was a habit of the lifelong gambler, as casinos were equipped with communications inhibitors to reduce cheating. As the accumulation of hours of gambling tallied into days, weeks and then months, his implanted devices were sometimes forgotten. It was past ten a.m. and well beyond the time he had expected the other two Strykers to rendezvous with his lost scout at the remains of the town of Fernley.

"I want an update," Desmond told his friend.

Bill nodded and keyed the microphone. "*Necromancer*, this is *Almighty Oz*. Do you read?" Atwood let a few heartbeats pass and called again before receiving a reply.

"*Almighty Oz*, this is *Necromancer*," Captain Sam Holsbeck returned. "Over."

Bill Atwood nodded to Ricky Desmond and turned on the loudspeaker. "*Necromancer*, where are you? Over."

"*Necromancer* here. I was about to give a call," he described. "We remained on the interstate and have arrived in Fernley. I see smoke ahead. Wait one."

"Shit," Ricky mumbled and took a drag from his cigarette. He stepped closer to the speaker on Atwood's desk.

"*Almighty Oz. Necromancer,*" the Stryker commander called less than a minute later, "I have one destroyed Stryker at the side of the road…" to his gunner he asked, "What's that out there?" There was a bit of low, indiscernible conversation, then an order for the driver to move up and stop. "Confirmed *Ranger* destroyed. Three crewmen dead outside vehicle."

"God damn it!" Desmond rumbled as he slapped the table.

"*Necromancer*, confirm three bodies of *Ranger* crew," Atwood spoke glumly into the microphone as he rubbed his temples. "Over."

"*Almighty Oz. Necromancer*. The vehicle is pouring out black smoke from openings at the hatches. It's *that* smell, Bill. I see Pop, Tim, and Spud. I don't have visual contact with Rabbit, but I'm willing to bet that he's inside burning. Over."

"Very well, Captain. Report on cause. Over."

"We're seeing…" he began and then broke off to order the driver to stop. "…we're seeing the remains of a second vehicle that appears to be Lovelock's police car. It's been shot to hell. Over."

"One car?" Desmond questioned with a frown aimed at the speaker. "Tell Captain Holsbeck to deploy and investigate. Where's their backup?"

"*Necromancer*, deploy and investigate. Over," Bill hastily ordered and received the acknowledgement. "*Almighty Oz* to *Lancelot*. Come in, *Lancelot*."

"*Lancelot* here, *Almighty*," returned the voice of the third Stryker's commander. A man in his fifties, like *Ranger*'s deceased commander, he had been friends with Pop for years. The loss was evident in the man's voice.

"*Lancelot*, please advise on the ETA of your rendezvous with *Necromancer*. Over."

"I'm full throttle. Uhh... five minutes to *Necromancer*'s locale. Over."

"Very well, *Lancelot*. Advise upon your arrival. I've ordered *Necromancer* to investigate scene. Prepare to deploy your squad as needed. Over."

"Roger. *Lancelot* out."

As the conversation ended, Desmond snatched up the wired telephone from the desk. There were only a handful of the devices in the city of Reno, so all Rick had to do was dial a three-digit number to get to whom he wished to speak.

"Yes?" the voice of Harry Clima replied.

"Get me Gillespie," was all Desmond said.

"Who's this?" the bodyguard demanded, though he knew who it was. He enjoyed giving Desmond hell at every turn.

"Clima, put Gillespie on, *now*! I've got a Stryker crew down and I'm in no mood for bullshit!"

Harry said not another word. Desmond was about to shout his name and cuss him out when he heard the mayor's voice.

"What is it, General?"

Desmond filled Gillespie in on the morning's developments. By the time he had finished, Ricky feared that the powerful leader of Reno was about to have him killed.

"Very well, General," Gillespie oozed flatly through grinding teeth. "I want Lovelock smashed."

"I know," Desmond replied.

"I want it to burn to the ground. I want a progress report on the new Cobra. We need it up and running, *today*!"

"Yes, sir," Desmond answered as he looked to Bill Atwood. Together, they rolled their eyes. "I'll call the shop in a moment and see what they need."

"Tell the two Strykers on the scene to hold their position at Fernley for the time being. Once that Cobra is ready and tested, I want the city of Lovelock to burn so that I can see it glow at night!"

"Yes, sir," Desmond replied, though the line went dead before the words had a chance to be heard.

"I take it 'Lord' Gillespie wants to unleash his wrath upon his enemies, such as they are," Bill said with a grim smile.

"Somethin' like that, yeah," Desmond answered as he replaced the receiver. "Let *Necro* and *Lance* know that they are to hold their ground and advise us of any other attempts on them," he said as he turned to leave the room.

"Sure thing," Bill answered and moved to key up his microphone.

"Oh, and Bill?" he halted with the doorknob in his hand. "Tell the guardhouse I want extra personnel added to the eastern checkpoints."

"You got it."

***

"Clima!" Gillespie shrieked once he had ended the call. He set the ancient relic upon his thick glass table hard enough to make the transparent surface thrum within its frame.

"Sir!" Harry answered as he jogged toward his master's throne.

"Get the young Hernandez girl up here," he said heavily. "Lovelock's military capabilities have been improved somewhat beyond our intelligence. She and I need to talk about that."

Chapter Eight

Jazz could not bring herself to leave the roof of the building across from her club. The anti-aircraft volunteers chatted her up for a while until the heat of the day sapped the excess energy from them. From this vantage point, the interstate was in sight, though she often augmented her vision in search of the only remaining Lovelock police car.

It was fifteen minutes to noon and the brave constable, as Reggie had called him, was long overdue. She wanted to scream, though she knew that she dared not exhibit panic or weakness. It was bad enough that she showed these two young volunteers the worry on her face. Very few people had noticed the police vehicle leave that morning with Mattersly, Mulhaney, and Angel, but no one outside of herself, Marco, Denny, and Thumper knew of the mission.

By now, surely someone had noticed the absence of the town's only police officer. It was a small town, after all, and not without its petty squabbles that Antonio was slated to deal with.

A few more minutes passed by before she decided she had need of a drink. She descended the ladder, carefully not missing a step in her high heels. On a day like today, she felt out of place wearing them and her maroon pantsuit, but she knew to do otherwise would be cause for suspicion. She wished to avoid questions of any kind, but she knew also that to hide from people and to change her routine would be a mistake.

Jazz stepped inside the club and forced a smile for Gigi and Beth, who were straightening up the lounge area. She exchanged pleasantries and slipped behind the bar to fix a simple, yet effective drink. Her hands grabbed a bottle of vodka and the vermouth next to it. Without bothering with a shaker, a step she had little patience for, she spun the caps from both and poured the vodka into a martini glass. Hernandez tipped the bottle of vermouth over the glass and allowed a few drops to escape.

She gave it a quick swirl of her finger and took a quick, healthy gulp.

"Everything okay, Miss Hernandez?" Gigi thought to ask.

Jazz stared at her levelly for a moment, insincerely wishing that the slightly taller woman's head would explode.

"Everything's fine, Gigi," she said as a thought occurred to her. It was rash, risky, and wrong, but it felt like something she must do. "Call Marco, would you? Have him bring my car to the front door."

"Sure will," Gigi agreed as she watched her employer and leader of Lovelock walk briskly to the stairs.

Jazz went into her living quarters and shut the door. She was done risking the lives of other people for Lovelock. It was time she followed up with something herself. From a drawer in her closet, she retrieved a pump shotgun and ammunition. She tossed both on the bed and fished out her nine-millimeter handgun and holster. Jazz watched herself from the mirror as she placed the rather tricky shoulder holster over her cream-colored satin top and replaced her thin jacket. She had set her hair up in a swirling knot, which went excellently with the professional-looking outfit and kept it out of her way. The concern she felt over Reggie, Antonio, and the others had formed a tight knot in her gut.

She loaded the pump shotgun with five shells and dropped the rest into her large purse. The extra magazines for the pistol went in there as well. Jazz went to her front door and opened it just a crack. She saw no sign of anyone, so she quickly and deftly descended the carpeted steps and cringed every time one of them creaked. Hernandez turned hard left at the bottom of the stairs and headed for the rear exit. From behind her, she heard the voice of Marco, asking Gigi where she, Jazz, was located.

Knowing Marco's height and walking stride, she knew he could bound up the steps to the third floor very quickly, so she wasted no time slipping outside through the heavy fire door. She scampered as best as she could in high heels, something that she immediately regretted not having removed.

Hernandez pressed herself into a jog, threatening a twisted heel and a fall as she went for her car. Marco had left it running but locked, so she was forced to activate her implant and access the computer to gain entry. The extra few seconds that she had to stand there in plain view made her cringe.

Once she had the door opened, she tossed the shotgun onto the passenger seat and dropped herself inside. Without unwarranted screeching of tires or the grumble or whine of the hydrogen and electrically powered beast, Jazz departed from the parking space in front of her club, drove to the end of the street, and turned left. In a few moments, she joined with I-80 and headed west.

Nearly fifteen minutes later, Marco discovered that the antique automobile was no longer in front of the club. Bursting into Hernandez's living quarters, he discovered she was missing as well. The man was no genius but was far from a moron. He realized immediately what she was up to. He cursed loudly and ran from the room as he hurled himself down the staircase and shouted in his giant, booming voice for Denny to join him.

***

Between Reginald and Angel, they were able to keep a pretty decent pace with their new find. Mulhaney was dealing with enough of a burden, considering his weak right leg. Though the major wished that the little trailer's wheels were quieter, the impromptu adaptation to their plan promised to at least be interesting. Along the streets of Fernley they did drag the fiberglass rowboat atop a trailer, which featured a pair of squeaking wheels. Upon the trailer hitch they had tied an aged, but sturdy rope and for blocks they did progress with Angel at the front and Reginald just behind. Both of them had draped the rope over a shoulder and trudged along.

The rowboat was just large enough for the three of them, they surmised, and Angel suggested that they take it along and use it in the manmade river, get some distance along it, then relocate it to the Truckee.

The three of them were quite ripe with sweat as they carried or towed their burdens. Reginald and Angel had set their backpacks inside the boat to make the going easier, but the boat was proving to be at least as difficult. Mattersly hoped that the gamble paid off.

They left the residential neighborhood behind them and for a time, there was nothing to take cover behind if the need arose. The sun assaulted them without restrictions. The two military men kept their heads on a swivel as they walked out in the open. The road they were on curved to the north, so Angel guided them to a side road, which joined it and continued westward. Soon, they were among the trees and empty homes again.

"Let's take a break at that tree, Angel," Mattersly directed as he pointed to a large, thick trunked beast that had clearly become master of its corner. She nodded and panted, saying nothing. In another dozen steps, she dropped the rope to the ground, slid the assault rifle from her shoulder, and then let herself sit with her back against the tree.

Mattersly removed his boonie hat and wiped his head with a handkerchief. Mulhaney gently set his pack upon the ground and shared the shade with Angel, sliding down the tree to meet the ground.

There was almost no wind, which gave the hot, dry air added weight. The major fished through his pack and found some food to go with his water. Jazz had given them each a large bag of dehydrated fruit chips to take along the journey. He thoughtfully munched on the bits of apple, apricot, peach, and little squares that tasted like cherries. He stared along the road that stretched westward and looked back the way they had come. To the west, he could see nothing but hills, though according to his map, the waterway that Angel described was just under a kilometer away. He explained this to Angel as he crouched next to his recuperating friends to offer them bits of fruit.

"That's because it's dug into the hill, Major," Angel explained. "It's an irrigation canal. I don't know the particulars, but it must have come in handy for farming."

"Indeed," said Mattersly. "I can't understand why this town has no one living in it. It seems more prolific than Lovelock, if I'm honest."

"Chances are, there are some people that live here," Angel went on. "They just keep to themselves like hermits."

"In this heat?" Mulhaney chimed in. "I don't know about that. These homes are nice and all, but to barricade oneself inside and try to live it out? Not likely. We'd hear air conditioning units running."

"Perhaps, Elias," Angel conceded. She cared not to argue. She was too tired, too hungry, and too thirsty.

"In any case, we are still in for a rather long haul in the heat of day," the major explained. "As much as we are in a hurry, we should not be so that we tempt fate. We shall rest here for an hour."

"Fine by me," Elias agreed and made himself comfortable against the tree. In less than a minute, he was asleep.

Angel downed gulp after gulp of water. If it were not for the fact that there was water nearby, Mattersly would have warned her. As for himself, Reginald was taking to the heat much easier than he thought he would. In the few years he had spent in the ridiculous humidity of Cape Canaveral, his body had become acclimated, but never did he grow comfortable. Here in Nevada, the heat was more pronounced, but its dryness did not hinder each and every breath taken.

"Do you think that group sent off a distress signal, Major?" Angel spoke up. "Izzat why the second Stryker rolled up?"

"Possibly," he considered as he sat between the young lady and the sleeping Mulhaney.

"Do you think they're going to attack Lovelock?"

"They very well may do just that."

"Wouldn't you if an enemy settlement took down your helicopter?" she asked sleepily.

"I can't say," replied the major.

"Why not?"

"I've never owned one," he said with a smile.

Angel chuckled lowly, not wishing to awaken Elias. "I'll be damned. You have a sense of humor."

"I do try to remember that it's there from time to time," Mattersly said and closed his eyes.

The two, which remained awake, rested in silence for a few minutes. Angel was next to fall asleep in the shade of the tree. Reginald checked the time on his implant's display. It was 12:40 hours. With the two others asleep, the major turned up the sensitivity to his hearing. As he closed his eyes and leaned his head back against the tree, he thought he caught a trace of something in the distance. A deep rumble that resembled an animal growling traveled faintly through the air. That was not particularly unexpected considering the packs of wild, feral dogs and wolves that he had seen during his travels.

Reginald took a deep breath and listened some more. The rumbling continued. The sound was rhythmic, droning, and quite obviously, mechanical. Whatever was making it was coming their way.

In a flash, the major was on his feet. "Come on, get up!" he demanded as he gave Mulhaney's and Angel's feet a kick each.

"What?!" Elias spat as he began to get up.

"Tank!" Reginald shouted. He turned to Angel and yanked her up from the ground. She gave a shrill, short cry of surprise. "Angel, Elias, take cover there!" he ordered and pointed at the corner house. "Angel! Your rifle!" he called after the young woman who had already taken several steps. He tossed the weapon to her and it was caught gracelessly.

The vehicle was definitely coming from the west and along the road the trio had been traveling upon. Reginald knew it was only a matter of seconds before it would come around the bend and discover the three of them running. He snatched up his Dragunov, shouldered it and reached for the rope. Taking it up in his two hands, Mattersly had no time to be careful. He moved at a jogging pace with the rope over his shoulder. The incline onto the corner lot was mild, only rising to a peak of perhaps a meter and a half from road level. The uninhabited home sat upon this peak, like a castle perched upon a mountain. The slack taken, Reginald now bore the full weight of the boat, trailer and two backpacks. The going became agonizingly slow until a yellow and white blur appeared from nowhere and took the excess rope from the major.

It was Angel. For several long seconds, she pulled right along with Mattersly as the sound of the armored vehicle became louder. For a moment, he was convinced that if he had taken a gander over his left shoulder, that he would have seen it approaching. Further, he felt certain that the driver or commander of the vehicle would notice the boat and trailer as it crawled up the embankment from the street.

Angel made a sudden juke to the right, away from the side of the house and the spot where Reginald felt was a good place to leave the boat. He was too involved with breathing and churning his legs through the loose, sandy soil to protest. In another second, he saw what she was trying to accomplish. Angel hooked to the left, taking the rope with her and angling it around a tree. She quickly turned her back and pulled with all her weight, using the tree as a fixed pulley.

Her idea was working, so Reginald let the rope go and sprinted to join her in the pull. Before he could get there, Elias Mulhaney reemerged from his hiding place, took hold of the loose rope behind Angel with his left hand and gave a mighty tug with his full weight in reverse.

Major Mattersly kept running, though this time he went past the girl, jumping over the rope and sliding in the dirt to drop out of sight. The trailer and boat were lifted to the top of the embankment and rolled harmlessly into the tree. Mulhaney's help had come at the perfect time, for the machine was almost certainly on top them.

"Get your heads down," Mattersly hissed as loud as he could.

Angel had landed flat on her back when Mulhaney had lent his hand. Her eyes were widened with fear as she acknowledged his order. She turned her head toward the street and realized that the armored vehicle was tall enough that most of its upper half was in view. The machine gun turret, identical to the one on the machine that Mattersly had destroyed earlier, swung in their direction as the Stryker came to a jerky stop.

"Oh, shit," Angel whimpered.

She was frozen in place, though she knew that she was fully exposed if a crewman were to pop out of the hatch. As it was, the guns seemed to be locked on the tree just a meter away from her.

A heavy hand came from somewhere behind her.

"Stay flat," Elias whispered, then began to crawl backward, dragging Angel along with him.

She did as she was told, but could not help but stare at the heavily armed vehicle. In a couple of seconds, she was out of sight of the machine, lying in the relative safety behind the house and out of sight.

Mattersly smiled to himself over Mulhaney's priceless assistance. Being that he was now in line of sight with the machine gun turret's camera, Reginald felt that a retreat into the brush behind him was prudent. Slowly, soundlessly, he crawled backward until enough of the brownish-green plants were now between himself and the halted vehicle.

***

"What the hell did that?" the gunner asked of his commander.

His optical gun sight was set in infrared mode and when a streak of reddish-purple suddenly appeared on his display like a burning slash, he asked his commander to stop. He just stared at the magically materializing gash in the tree's bark, dumbfounded. The gunner traversed the camera over the area around the tree and noted the heat signature of the rowboat on the trailer and the ground around it. The temperatures in the dirt and grasses were higher than normal considering the place's yard was in the shade.

"Hmm."

"Looks like it was a group of animals. Feral dogs, maybe," the commander said.

“I don’t know, Sarge,” the gunner shook his head and shifted his optics to low light.

It was just a yard next to another abandoned house with a rowboat on a trailer parked in the back. The place on the tree that bore the hot spot must have been on the other side of the tree from his vantage point as the bark that he could see was undisturbed. He switched the sight back to infrared and noted the hot spot’s reappearance.

“Looks like something shot through the bark on the other side of this tree.”

“The mics didn’t pick anything up,” the commander stated. “Look, we have to meet up with *Necromancer* or we’re going to get it. Come on, get going,” he instructed the driver.

***

Angel was near hyperventilation when Mulhaney set her against the house. She was sweating, but cold to the touch.

“Calm down,” Elias whispered and handed her a canteen. “Drink. You’re dehydrated.”

The roar of the armored vehicle’s motor drowned out her ‘thank you’. Daring a peek around the corner of the house, Elias could see that the Stryker was rolling away, apparently no longer interested in whatever had caught a crewman’s attention. He smiled and looked to the place where he had last seen the major, but there was no one. The smile faded a bit as he looked about the area.

“Major?” he whispered, then repeated it more loudly.

He held still, listening to the Stryker’s engine fade into the distance and for rustling in the surrounding area. What he did hear did not make sense. Angel was giggling through her hand.

“What’s funny?” he whispered to her.

She pointed to something over his right shoulder.

As he turned to look, a face seemed to dance just a couple of inches next to him at his extreme right.

"*Holy crap*!" he uttered and tumbled away.

"I say, old man, are you all right?" asked the major with a grand smile that seemed out of place, considering the potentially deadly encounter that had just occurred.

"How the hell did you do that?" Elias breathed as he returned his semi-automatic pistol to his belt.

"Sitting still just gets one killed, Mister Mulhaney," Mattersly said in a sing-song. "Excellent work with the boat and dragging Angel to safety, by the way."

"Yeah, thanks," Elias replied, rolled his eyes and smiled.

"Are you feeling poorly, young lady?" the major asked of the still giggling Angel.

"I think I just need water, Major," she smiled and emptied the canteen.

"Very well," granted Reginald as he stood up and offered her a hand. She grabbed it and got to her feet. "Shall we?"

The trio quietly dragged the boat and trailer back onto the pavement and continued on their way. The sun blasted them in between periods of tree-given shade. A question occurred to Elias as he walked alongside the major.

"Say, I half expected you to destroy that Stryker with one of your little gray toys."

"I considered that, Mister Mulhaney, but decided against it."

"Oh? Why?"

"Well, I considered several options, including attaching the C-4 to the Stryker with a timed explosion, but to have destroyed that machine anywhere along this trail would be to reveal our path of travel to the enemy," Mattersly answered.

"That's true," Mulhaney agreed.

"This way, they are left to speculate."

"I get it," Elias agreed.

"Right up here, guys," Angel called over her shoulder.

The street bent to the north, the same curve the last armored vehicle had driven along just minutes before. Angel's feet left the tattered pavement and trudged into the loose soil of a long-unused trail. Winding around a telephone pole, which probably had not born a wire upon it for a half a century, she led the small procession up an incline. Elias hung back for a moment, then placed a hand on the back of the trailer and pushed. He put his entire weight into the action, which did seem to help maintain the pace.

At the top, the trio discovered that the trail paralleled the green and nearly still waterway just on the other side of it.

"I'll be damned," Elias mumbled.

"Now, this canal gets narrow and turns due west," Angel explained as she and Reginald removed the rowboat from the trailer, "at that point, we need to get out and drag this thing down the hill to get it to the river."

"Understood," answered Mattersly.

They dropped the boat into the green water as Mulhaney held onto the rope to keep its bow against the sharp embankment. Angel led the way to the rowboat, stepping down onto it and quickly taking a seat to keep from tipping it. Mattersly followed and went to the rear of the boat. Mulhaney boarded last, and nearly tipped into the water when his weight shifted onto his weak right leg. He prevented this by falling onto his knees.

Once situated, Mattersly and Mulhaney took up the oars and pointed the bow to the northwest. Soon, the trio was floating along, completely out of sight from anything other than the buzzards overhead.

***

It was one-thirty in the afternoon and Jazz had seen no trace of the city's police car. She had been driving at around forty miles per hour the whole time, aware of the possibility of being discovered by advancing Renoites or damage to her tires. There were great stretches where the road was in pretty good shape and she was tempted to floor the accelerator, but she refrained. If Antonio had driven off the road for something, it was possible she would miss it if she went too fast.

As she approached an overpass that she remembered as having a sign that indicated one mile left to Fernley, her eyes picked up a trace of black smoke in the air beyond it and off to the right, where the interstate angled westward to accommodate Fernley.

"Oh, please, no," she moaned.

Her mind conjured the picture of a burning police car with all four people still aboard. Then the picture of the car exploding into a million pieces came to mind and she growled loudly and gripped the steering wheel tightly to force it away.

She slowed her big forest green sedan and decided that the black smoke was not too far off the highway, but she could be driving into a trap. Jazz recalled a rough knowledge of the town's layout. She could exit the interstate here, take a left to cross the overpass, and wind her way through the town to have a better look. She needed to know what was making that black smoke.

Once upon the sun-bleached overpass, Jazz brought the car to a stop and hopped out. She magnified her vision and focused on the black cloud, but she could not make out what was burning. Frustrated and beyond simple concern, she strode back to the car and drove along.

Jazz watched her implant's communication device

for the presence of Reggie's or Antonio's implants. If they were activated and if she came within range, she would see the option to connect to them appear on her display.

She steered the car onto the first street that came up. According to her map program, it was a frontage road that ran alongside the interstate for a time, but then curved southward, into a maze of abandoned commercial zones. From there, she would turn west and continue through the town of Fernley on her quest to find out what had happened to her people. She never thought to be driving so close to Reno ever again and was surprised that Antonio had ventured so far.

As Hernandez drove further and deeper into the abandoned town of Fernley, her heart pounded faster and her worry grew. She had an impending sense that something had gone horribly wrong and it had to do with whatever was burning near the interstate. She wiped away tears born of near-panic, but drove on.

***

Mattersly analyzed what Angel had said several minutes before. Consulting his map, he saw that the canal terminated at the river approximately thirteen kilometers further on.

"I say, Angel," he said as he and Elias paddled, "do you have any objections to staying on the canal until it meets the river?"

"Um, yeah," she replied as if his question had the most obvious of answers. "The canal tunnels through the hills at a few places. I'm not a fan."

"Oh, come now," Reginald pressed, "it cannot be all *that* bad. Where's your sense of adventure?"

"I'm already on one, Major," she answered, "I have no reason to want to make it harder than it already is."

"On that point, I dare say we are in agreement," Mattersly went on cheerfully, eager to make his pitch.

"While we are paddling through the tunnels, we are safe from the prying eyes of anything the Renoites might be able to rush into the air. Not to mention, staying on the canal would keep us out of visual range of the Strykers."

"I guess," she put in dubiously.

"It should be cooler in there, too," added Mulhaney. "I could stand a little shade."

The thought of riding in the boat in near darkness gave Angel the chills, even though it was nearly one hundred degrees.

"You guys are going to get me killed."

"I'm suggesting this to do exactly the opposite, I assure you," Mattersly added.

Angel made a small sound of defeat mixed with disgust in her throat. "Fine."

"That's the spirit!" the major exclaimed with a pat to her shoulder. "On to the end of the canal, then."

"Yay," Angel exuded with nothing near the emotion or sincerity of Mattersly. Elias laughed and kept paddling.

The waterway curved westward and narrowed. It was at this point that the current against them increased, but it remained easily manageable. Angel took over paddling from Elias for a short time so that the man could eat and take water. She did the same for Reginald afterward. In time, they came to the first tunnel.

"Let's rest before heading inside," the major called to his companions and guided them to a low embankment to their left.

Mulhaney stood and carefully hopped to the shore, tugging the boat by the rope until it ran aground. He sat heavily into the dirt and rubbed his arms.

"Are we planning on rowing all the way into Reno?" he asked.

"Well, the river does run right through it," Mattersly answered as he stretched and sat. "It's likely that we will have to abandon it once we get closer. The flow of the water may be against us."

"There's a lot of militia activity at the river," Angel added. "Once we get into the thinly populated neighborhoods on the outskirts of town, we can figure out which objective to handle first."

"Sounds like a plan," Elias agreed as he stood up to stretch his legs. He leaned heavily on his new walking stick, but Mattersly deduced that it was due mostly to being in a seated position for a time.

"Well, shall we?" the major invited after a few minutes of rest.

"Let's do this," Mulhaney said. "How about you taking the bow, Major? You've got the eyes."

"Excellent suggestion, Mister Mulhaney," Mattersly agreed and stood by to let the big American aboard first, followed by the diminutive, but tough young lady. Reginald hopped on last, just as he shoved the small boat from the shore.

The opening to the first tunnel lay ahead of them and to Angel, the aged white concrete structure did not portray confidence. The angled walls were streaked with cracks that ran into the tunnel, further into the darkness, stretching into the unknown in a threatening manner. She took little comfort in the confidence that the two men with her exuded. One of their number had died just hours before and now into the depths of some ancient structure they did paddle.

Angel took a deep breath and let the darkness swallow her.

Mattersly adjusted his eyes for darkness and paddled on. According to his map, this structure was nearly a half a kilometer. He looked about the walls and ceiling and noted their deep cracks. Had anyone remained in authority to keep track of such things and affect repairs, he was certain that this process of aging and stress would have been something they would want to address.

Reginald decided not to focus on the slowly decaying material surrounding them as he paddled a bit faster.

***

Desmond had finally begun to relax, not out of comfort, but from exhaustion. He had taken a seat in a padded office chair and within five minutes, his eyes had begun to close. A couple of minutes later, he was asleep.

Atwood remained at his desk, waiting for contact from *Necromancer* or *Lancelot*. The man was every bit as tired as his friend, but stress had a habit of keeping him awake. Insomnia was another byproduct of lifelong gambling. No matter what time it was, if Bill was on a hot streak, he remained awake and alert enough to ride it out. Sometimes, it even paid off. Ricky had been the same not long before, but as Bill watched his younger, smarter friend sleep, he realized the immense strain that Gillespie's employment was beginning to inflict. Atwood wished that Desmond would not have such a flippant attitude toward their employer. Great men need to be surrounded by other great men, and he was beginning to think that his longtime friend did not have the fortitude to serve such a man as Gillespie.

The communications expert had put up with enough discomfort from the headphones, so he took them off and engaged the external speaker. Like Ricky Desmond, Atwood leaned way back in his chair and closed his eyes. He would not sleep, but it was an attempt to rest his eyes.

Some minutes later, the radio received a signal and it shattered the silence of the small room.

"Lancelot, this is Necromancer. Over."

"Lancelot here. Over," came the reply.

Atwood opened his eyes and leaned forward. He

could hear the diesel engine groan as it held a speed close to its top end.

"What is your ETA? Over."

"Almost to you, Necromancer. We're rejoining the interstate from the south. Over."

"Roger," the commander of *Necromancer* said with an air of annoyance.

Atwood checked his watch. It was after one in the afternoon. *Lancelot* either had trouble along the way or had taken an alternate route.

"What the hell took him so long?" Desmond said from the chair. The man was awake, but made no move to get up.

"Wanna ask him?" Atwood offered the microphone.

Ricky checked his watch again and waved Bill away. "Screw it. I have to call Gillespie anyway to find out what he wants done."

"Oh, great," Bill replied and rolled his eyes sympathetically.

"Yeah," Desmond agreed and stood up with some effort. His body ached from the lack of sleep and slouching in the old creaky chair. He stepped over to the phone on Bill's desk and dialed Gillespie's suite.

"Get me Gillespie," he grumbled. Atwood knew that Harry Clima had picked up the phone.

"Yes, General?" erupted Gillespie's heavy voice, clearly audible by both men.

Ricky moved the speaker from his ear and winced slightly before his reply. "Hello, sir. Yes, well, *Lancelot* has rendezvoused with *Necromancer* in Fernley."

"Since you have not indicated so, General Desmond, I'm assuming they have had no contact with the enemy?" said Reno's leader in a boisterous and theatrical manner.

"They have not, sir."

"And what have you learned of the status of our new flying contraption?"

"I've got extra people on it," Ricky lied, as there were no others in town that had any helpful skills, "but they tell me it won't be ready for flight testing for about three days."

"Three days?! Three days, General?!" Gillespie howled madly into the phone. "That's utter nonsense! I decree that the Cobra is to be flying in two! Two! Do you hear?!"

"Yes, er…yes, sir," Ricky said as he held the received several inches away from his head. "They're working almost around the clock as it is, sir, but I'll tell them."

"Remove the word 'almost' from that sentence, Desmond," Gillespie went on in an ominous, seething tone. "If I don't see that Cobra in the air by Thursday afternoon, your engineering team will pay dearly!"

"Yes, sir," the old gambling man said, defeated. "I'll let them know right away." The call ended and Desmond replaced the receiver to its cradle.

"That man is going to get us all killed," Atwood said, repeating the very statement that Desmond had said more than once.

"Yeah," Ricky murmured as he lit another cigarette. "I'm starting to think he's lost his mind."

***

"Right," Gillespie declared as he handed the phone back to Clima, who hung it up and set it upon its table. "Where were we, Mister Costa?"

Miguel Costa mumbled sounds that formed no words. The severe concussion that he had been dealt by the hands of the little balding man had made it difficult to convert thought to speech. His broken jaw hindered him further. His tightly bound wrists had gone numb some unknown amount of time ago. The pain from his shoulders was maddening, as they bore the hindrance of his entire weight. He dangled from a metal hook in the ceiling, leaving his toes to scrape against the white canvass tarp that had been stretched over the suite's thick red carpet. His bruised and quite possibly bleeding brain could not recall Gillespie's question.

"Mister Clima," Gillespie addressed sharply, startling the smaller man. "Kindly restate my question to Mister Costa."

"Oh, right," Harry responded with a smile. "Mister Gillespie…"

"*King*!" the leader of Reno harshly reminded his servant yet again.

"Yes, Your Majesty," Clima bowed and continued. "His Majesty asked you about Lovelock's military strength… oh, and asked you about the experience of Hernandez's military commanders."

"Very good," Gillespie allowed and took a seat upon his throne. He stared at the captive and awaited an answer. Costa could do nothing, not even lift his pounding head. Another moment passed by without an apparent attempt to cooperate. "You know, I really hate to do this, but I've only now just realized that we haven't tried this tack before."

"Er… what tack is that, Sire?" Harry Clima inquired as he adjusted his spectacles.

King Gillespie said nothing, but he pointed to the young dark-haired girl seated comfortably upon his couch. Clima smiled crookedly, as he had been waiting for an opportunity to thrash the arrogant child. Nora Hernandez was an intelligent girl and she had both acknowledged the fact and flaunted it during many games of strategy and intellect that she had played with Clima to pass the time. She also understood that she and Miguel Costa were only alive to either antagonize her Aunt Jazz or provide Gillespie with information.

She had heard the expression, 'my heart leapt into my throat' from her mother and Aunt Jazz, but she never truly understood what it meant until her eyes locked onto Harry Clima's at that moment. The fear she felt mixed with her loathing and contempt for the unintelligent bully, keeping her miles from panic, but just as far from comfort.

Clima strode to her and yanked the little girl to her feet. She withheld any sound and at that moment, deciding that it was unwise to meet the man's gaze. It would be better if he felt that he won and she would not dignify the man by looking upon him.

Nora did her best to stay on her feet as Harry, barely twelves inches taller than she, did what he could to topple her, just short of taking her feet out from underneath. He was an easy read for Nora, who understood that he wanted to humiliate the girl in front of Gillespie by driving her to her knees.

She refused to kneel in front of the leader of Reno, the self-proclaimed king, though her left arm was screaming painfully in Clima's tight grip to the bicep. Instead, she looked up into Gillespie's face and tried to keep her expression as blank as possible.

"Leave her be," Miguel mumbled from behind her.

It was the first comprehensible sentence from the man in hours, but she felt nothing for her kidnapper. She knew better than to think Miguel had any sympathy for her. He had proven that when he had taped her arms and legs together and drove her to this hell called Reno, brandished her to the guards of the interstate like the sword Excalibur, born by a supposed faithful servant who wished to present it to the king. She had read a book about King Arthur and his Knights of the Round Table just weeks before, but understood that Reno was no Camelot and the Arthur in this reality was out of his mind.

Gillespie and Clima ignored Costa. They understood the girl's feelings toward the man, not that it would help her in the end, she figured. Gillespie was not the same man she had known as a younger girl. He had gone insane with power and delusional about his own worth. Nora feared the man deeply, but hoped that a glimmer of his former self would surface.

"So, how about *you* tell me, little Nora," Gillespie drawled as he looked down his nose upon her with eyes wide with fury, "what has changed over there in Lovelock? Who do they have that was good enough to shoot down my Cobra?"

Nora said nothing. She knew not what to say to the question and further, had not been aware that the flying menace had been taken down until that morning. Lovelock was a small town, but the little girl did not know everyone, especially the names of the town's defenders. All she knew was that she wanted to go home to her mother and aunt.

"Answer him," grunted the little bald man to her left.

His words seemed to annoy Gillespie, for he blinked slowly.

"I don't know what you mean," she said.

The sentence seemed to hang heavily in the air and she was certain that she would be beaten by Gillespie's bodyguard. Her eyes pleaded with the King of Reno, but she saw no mercy there. She had when she had been smaller, just a few years before when he and her Aunt Jazz were together. Now, he was a different person. Gillespie had transformed into a dangerous, insane stranger.

"Do you see what I've allowed my dear friend and bodyguard to do to your stepfather?" Gillespie oozed as he leaned toward her, so lowly that she wondered how his body was not tumbling from the chair and on top of her.

Nora leaned backward and placed her hands over her mouth, but she remained planted. She nodded in answer to the question, but did not turn around to look.

"Don't you *dare* think that you're special!" the leader of the Renoites howled. "I will have this man tan your hide!"

Nora had never heard the expression before, but she correctly guessed at its meaning.

"I wanna go home. I want my mommy," she managed to squeak.

Without a hint of mercy, humanity, or decency, King Gillespie smiled in the most unfriendly manner she had ever seen and said with great relish, "Your mommy's dead, child. Didn't you know? Stepdaddy here didn't just beat her, he stabbed her to death."

"Noooo!" Nora Hernandez screeched as she hid her eyes from the leering monster.

She cried without restraint, as a part of her had already known the truth. The night of her kidnapping was of blissful sleep until a loud argument between her mother and Costa had broken out. It was more violent than usual as furniture was tossed or knocked over, glass was broken, and her mother's cries for help ended in silence.

After moments of trepidation in the dark, Miguel had burst through her bedroom door and snatched her up without a word. He had stunk of liquor, sweat, and the metallic odor of what she since came to understand as the scent of blood. Costa carried her in the dark, ordering her to be quiet over and over until he located what he wanted. She was tossed into the back seat of his car and he drove quickly away from town. The morning sunlight revealed that they were in the hands of Renoite militiamen and were taken to the town of Reno, her aunt's adversaries.

Now, in the presence of Gillespie and his dim-witted sidekick, she came to recognize and accept his reason for fleeing. Miguel Costa had killed her mother. Rage broke her sadness and the little girl turned and began assaulting the captive man. She kicked and punched him wherever she could land a foot or fist, not caring for the blood she was now wearing upon her person. Miguel did nothing but groan as he hung there and it was more than a minute of this before Nora's mind registered that the sounds from behind her were that of heartless and cruel laughter. Her rage against the hanging murderer shifted into something she did not understand and, without thought, she snatched up a metal stool that had sat alongside Costa and swung it at the man within reach, Clima.

Harry's laughter transformed into a high-pitched screech of pain as the unpadded seat of the stool impacted with his right knee. Nora's assault was not finished, however, for she had been treated well as a prisoner and thus, had been fed and kept comfortable. With a child's frantic energy, she swung the stool again and it connected with Harry's head, destroying his spectacles and sending them tumbling through the air.

Gillespie stood at his throne and thundered with laughter at the sight of Clima being beaten up by an eight-year old. The pathetic state of his personal security had not yet occurred to him.

Clima reeled with the second swing of the stool. His vision had gone dark and he held onto the back of a couch to keep himself on his feet. The room came back into view but it was spinning. His mind acknowledged that the devil-child was coming at him for a third time, so he removed one of his handguns from his shoulder holster. He ducked the flying stool and in a fury of retaliation, struck Nora in the temple with the butt of the gun. She fell to the carpet like a broken doll.

Harry's right knee and temple screamed in pain and, for the moment, leaning against the couch with his weight off the leg was the only thing he could manage to do. All the while, Gillespie bellowed with amusement. For a fleeting moment, Harry considered shooting the man down. His anger and embarrassment over the child's assault was tripled by his employer's laughter. He envisioned himself emptying the magazine into the leader of Reno and then, to cover up what had occurred he would pull the other pistol and end the other two people in the room. In a moment, however, he realized that he was too scared of Gillespie to try it.

"You're pathetic, Clima," Gillespie spat out after his laughter died away. "I can't believe you let a little girl do that to you."

"I'm fine," Harry said as he replaced his gun to the holster, "I took her down, didn't I?"

"Watch your tone," the bigger man warned with no trace of amusement. "You'd better hope you haven't killed her or done her serious harm. Get her downstairs for medical attention and don't show your face up here for a while," Gillespie finished with a deadly tone.

Without a word, Clima gathered up the unconscious and bleeding child and limped to the elevator.

***

The other end of the tunnel came none too soon for Angel. The dark cavern filled her with dread and her imagination convinced her that she had heard additional splashes in the water beyond the rowing of the oars. In her mind's eye, she had conjured miniature sea monsters that followed the boat with hungry eyes that could see in the night. She dared not look at the water the entire time they were inside. Instead, she placed her eyes on Mattersly's back and, when things were at their darkest and she could not even make that out, she closed them entirely.

The heat-blasting sunlight assaulted the three of them as they emerged from the darkness, but all were grateful for it. They rowed on for a long time afterward, sweating heavily in the heat. Angel took over for both men when the need came for each to take on a bit of water.

The small boat wound through the canal's twists and turns until it reached the next tunnel. To Angel's relief, this one was impassable. The ceiling had collapsed at the entrance, taking with it part of the south wall. It was not enough of an obstruction to stop the water flow, but it was certainly enough to ward off would-be daredevils.

The trio was forced to remove the rowboat from the water, after letting the current take them back in the other direction for about one hundred and fifty meters, according to Mattersly's map. The concrete sides of the canal leading to the entrance were angled too steeply for them to climb.

The three of them were forced to march along the old trail in the hot mid-afternoon sun, each of them bearing the weight of the old rowboat that they dragged along the sandy trail. To make the going harder, the path was uphill for half the journey to the other side, where the canal resumed.

Once they approached the water on the other side, they were faced with more bad news. The canal was lined with the same angled concrete sides as they had encountered previously. There was no way to safely get the boat into the water then board it with their heavy packs. Mattersly consulted his implant's map program, but it did not address that detail of the canal. There was no way to determine how long this concrete 'lining', as Reginald described it, went on.

"Sorry, Major," Angel said as she stared into the not-so-accessible water. "I went along on foot the whole way. I never saw this part of the canal."

"Not to worry, my dear," Reginald reassured her. "This is definitely not your fault. It is merely a circumstance we need to overcome. You indicated that the river itself has too high a current in the opposite direction, did you not?"

"There are rapids further west. I'm not sure how far we could have gone before paddling became impossible," she affirmed. "There's no other way but on foot, I guess."

"So be it," Elias said and dropped his bit of the rope. "It was a nice ride while it lasted."

"Quite," Mattersly agreed. "I say we stick to this path to keep us out of view of any Renoite traffic."

"That should work," Angel agreed, "for now, at least."

After a short rest, the three of them gathered their belongings and proceeded to march westward in the summer heat.

***

Jazz kept the automobile on a slow crawl through the unmaintained streets of Fernley. The old vehicle whispered along on electric power as she was saving the hydrogen fuel for a quick escape, if need be. The commercial buildings were left behind as the car passed into a residential neighborhood. She guided the sedan down one street then another, keeping the black streak of smoke in her view as she came closer.

At an intersection with a fallen and faded 'Stop' sign, she obeyed it. With the windows down and the car running so silently, she thought she heard something in the distance. A groaning of something mechanical in nature filled the air, sounding as if it was only a block or so away. Remembering what Angel and Eric Hemmel had retrieved from Reno, she became certain that what she was hearing was the din of a Stryker engine.

Hernandez pressed the accelerator and passed through the intersection. At the next opportunity, she made a right turn into a cul-de-sac, then a quick left into an empty driveway. Jazz parked the old car behind an abandoned home and exited, making sure she was careful to close the driver's door quietly.

She kept the shotgun close to her as she skulked through the yard. Jazz caught a glimpse of herself in the reflection of a basement-level window and could not help but smile. The maroon outfit and thick-heeled pumps contrasted garishly with the shotgun that she grasped. She was glad she left the purse in the car for she may have laughed out loud.

As she moved closer to the black smoke, she could now smell a strong and familiar scent. It was pungent and would be quite capable of turning her stomach if it became much stronger. Hernandez moved toward the rhythmic sound of the diesel motor and stepped between two homes. Her shoes clacked over the debris that had fallen there from the roofs of both structures. Over time, the wind had its way with the houses, having torn tiles and bits of wood from them and dumping the refuse in the space between.

Jazz held the shotgun out in front of her and halted with her back to the wall of the western-most home. She peeked around the corner and found that she could see little beyond a tall wooden fence that ran parallel to the interstate. It was missing quite a number of panels, but Hernandez shied away from the temptation to approach one of these gaps to have a closer look.

Frustrated and quite frightened, she flattened herself against the wall.

What the hell am I doing?

As she asked herself this question, she gazed skyward and found a small square window on the second floor of the home across from the one she leaned against.

Hernandez turned and stepped quickly to the front of the two-family structure and found the front door. Quickly, she broke one of the small square windows in the door with the butt of the shotgun. Reaching in with small, deft fingers, she unlocked it and pushed it out of her way. The hinges sang loudly to announce her presence to no one.

Jazz walked quickly throughout the abandoned home, not allowing herself the luxury of her usual casual contemplation of the empty spaces left behind by people she would never know. This home was in decent shape, considering the external weather damage the place had suffered. The family had left behind much of their furniture. The hot sun had faded the colors of everything it touched and even now, made the air trapped inside the residence agonizingly difficult to breath.

Despite this, she soon found the access to the attic in the main hallway. Jazz realized immediately that she could not reach it, so she strode to the kitchen to retrieve a dust-covered kitchen chair. She dragged it into place and stood upon it. Jazz found the handle and pulled the access panel downward. As she expected, the panel bore a folding ladder on its inside. She kicked he chair out of the way and uncoiled the ladder, dumping dust and dirt upon herself.

"Shit," she spat as she wiped away what had fallen on her face and ascended the aged wooden ladder. It creaked and felt weak beneath her, but she went up anyway. The air was hotter in the attic and very stale, making her wish she had left her thin jacket in the car. The dust and mold made her sneeze almost immediately, so she wasted no time locating the small window. She had to wipe away the grime, but she finally found what she needed to see.

The burning machine was indeed a Stryker and not Antonio's police cruiser. Jazz smiled widely even though she still had no idea where her friends were. From her vantage point, she could see several Renoite mercenaries digging graves at the side of the road. The two remaining Stryker crews were milling about, seemingly unsure of their next move. Hernandez supposed that it would be an assault on Lovelock. She watched as a couple of Renoites dragged the body of a similarly dressed mercenary to the first grave and carefully set him within it. The dead man was very young and looked to have been shot in the chest area. The next one was also a mercenary, but this one had suffered a fatal head wound.

Hernandez looked away and decided it was time to go. She carefully went down the ladder step by step, hoping that it would hold together. She took a moment to swipe the dust from her pants and stepped toward the front door.

"Well, hot *damn*!" a male voice shouted from all too close to her.

It was a young Renoite militiaman with greasy hair, pimples, and a bad tooth. He was blocking her way to the door and looking her over.

"I thought I heard somethin', but I… wow, never expected ta' find someone like *you*."

Jazz noted that the young man was armed, but his weapon was not at the ready. As quick as she could get her body to move, she raised her shotgun and pointed at the young man's chest.

"Hey," he protested as his smile disappeared. What replaced it was utter disappointment, an expression that appeared well-practiced.

"Drop that gun," Jazz ordered. "Hand *away* from the trigger. Move *slow*."

"Whoa, I thought you were just a resident," the mercenary explained as he did what he was told. "It's okay. I'm not here to hurt you."

"Funny," Jazz chuckled and realized that if he had been an older man, she would have had to kill him on the spot out of fear that he would be sending for help over his implant. This one was too young to have one, but he most likely had something else to keep him in contact with the group. "Ever think I might be here to hurt *you*?"

The mercenary's eyes grew wide. "Are you with those guys that killed our people and blew up our APC?"

"You know of them? Were any of them hurt?" Jazz demanded as she reached out to take the young man's assault weapon.

As her fingers were about to grab it, the mercenary rushed her. His chest pressed against the shotgun barrel just as it fired. The boom sent Jazz's ear implants to activate and cancel much of the raw sound. She racked the second round into the chamber just as the teenager fell lifeless to the dirt-smeared floor. Hernandez paused only to pick up his weapon and a couple of items from his belt then sprinted through the door and out into the hot sun.

Jazz could hear shouting from the Renoites at the side of the interstate. There was a mixture of what sounded like orders and the calling of names. As she ran, she slipped the shotgun over her left shoulder and placed the newly acquired submachine gun in her left hand. In her mad dash, she lifted the stolen hand grenade to her mouth, pulled the pin in her teeth, and tugged it hard. It did not budge.

"Ouch, damn it!" she growled as she let the submachine slide down her left forearm by the strap. Near panic, she gave the grenade's pin another try. It popped free. Turning on her heels, she deftly walked backward as she let the lever fly off and hurled the round explosive in a high arc toward the space next to the house she had just left.

As she sprinted, she lost both shoes. In her thinly stockinged feet, she rounded the corner of another home when the grenade exploded. Beyond the muffled thud were the screams of at least two men. Once she reached her car, she threw the weapons on the seat and activated the electric motor. She reversed down the short driveway and impulsively decided to head directly to the interstate. She pointed the car south and made the next left with her precious tires squealing under the strain. Jazz activated the hydrogen drive of the car for more power and hung another left. She had spotted what appeared to be a school on her way there and she headed for it.

A right turn was followed by another left into the parking lot of the school-like building. Jazz aimed the car to the northwest and cut across the parking lot. She left the rough pavement for even rougher dirt and steered the vehicle parallel to the embankment she would have to force her way over to get to the road.

The old sedan rocked and swayed as its tires slipped and caught. Stones and dust were thrown high in the air as her speed bled. Nonetheless, the car did what it should not have been able to do. It climbed the embankment and found I-80. Jazz howled in delight until she saw a familiar shape on the other side of the road.

It was Lovelock's police cruiser. Hernandez yanked the steering wheel toward it, flying from the hard-fought-for pavement and into the dirt and brush that separated the lanes of traffic. As the sedan popped up on the other side, she slammed her foot to the brake pedal and stared at the ruined face of her long-time friend and law-enforcer, Antonio, still seated behind the wheel. The cruiser had been shot to pieces, apparently by the now-destroyed Stryker, and yet somehow Antonio appeared to be the only casualty.

Remembering the fact that there were two more of Reno's mechanical beasts behind her, she floored the accelerator and headed back for the dirt. She had begun sobbing when her eyes had found the constable's carcass, which compromised her vision. The end result was beneficial to her, however. With the raised cloud of dust, the gunner of *Necromancer* could not find the fleeing car on his monitor. The crew of *Lancelot* had boarded their vehicle, leaving their infantry squad behind, and had headed in the direction of the gunfire and grenade explosion. They had no target to acquire.

Necromancer's gunner switched his gun sight to infrared mode, where the shape of the old green sedan turned into bright yellows, oranges, and reds. The car was pretty quick, so he would need to get some rounds off quickly. Setting his crosshairs on the vehicle, he pressed the trigger and the fifty-caliber machine gun shook to life.

Jazz screamed when the back of her car was struck with what sounded like a thousand hammers. The rear window disintegrated and the trunk lid flew open. Flecks of metal, plastic, glass, and dirt flew through the air. The hydrogen fuel cell was struck a multitude of times, but thanks to it having barely twenty-five percent of its capacity remaining and the safety feature of a self-sealing blister, there was no fire or explosion, only the loss of the drive.

The car went along on its electric plant and was soon out of sight.

Chapter Nine

"A*lmighty Oz. Necromancer*," the voice on the radio called out with a calm, yet urgent inflection.

Desmond recognized the tone from the Stryker's commander, Sam Holsbeck. Ex-military all the way, he had his calm demeanor ingrained in him. Ricky nearly jumped out of the chair despite his having just wakened from a light nap.

"Let me talk to him," he said briskly.

Atwood pushed himself from the desk to let the man in charge have the microphone.

"*Necromancer*, this is *Straight Flush*," he called, using the new call sign that he despised. Gillespie made *Royal Flush* as his own and had ordered Ricky's changed. "Recognize and acknowledge."

"Roger, *Straight Flush.* Acknowledged. Over," Captain Holsbeck replied.

Whenever Ricky heard the new one spoken by someone else, he cringed. "Go ahead with your report, *Necromancer*. Over."

"We are holding at Fernley as ordered. We have been attacked by a small number. I have three men down. Attackers have fled in a green sedan proceeding northeast. Do we pursue? Over."

That explains Sam's level of subtle excitement. Desmond thought over the idea of pursuit for a brief few seconds before replying.

"*Necromancer*, that is a negative. No pursuit. Acknowledge. Over."

"*Straight Flush. Necromancer.* No pursuit is acknowledged. Over."

"Very good, Sam. Listen, I need both *Necromancer* and *Lancelot* to hold at Fernley for the time being,"

Desmond swallowed before continuing. "Do you need medical evac? Over."

Holsbeck took a moment to reply. "That's affirm, *Straight Flush*. Two of three are wounded. Over."

Ricky motioned for Bill to make the phone call. Atwood nodded and dialed away.

"On the way, *Necromancer*. Be vigilant out there. Sweep your immediate area for infiltrators and await orders. Over 'n' out."

"Acknowledged, *Straight Flush*. Over. Out."

"Ambulance is on the way to them. Forty-five minutes out," Atwood provided.

"Thanks, Bill," Ricky nodded and fell into a slow pace. He slipped out of his tweed sport coat, retrieved a cigarette from a pocket, and lit it. "I think it was a probe sent to go out after the patrol car," he said as smoke oozed from his nostrils and lips.

"Sounds like it," Atwood agreed. "The question I have is, 'why?'"

"Yeah, I know. I don't like it, either," Desmond went on as a thought occurred. "Sam said the attackers fled in a green sedan, right?"

"Yeah."

"The car that comes to mind is Hernandez's personal car," Desmond said lowly as he paced, thought, and smoked. "So, did someone steal her police car for a joyride? Hmmm…no. Maybe not a joyride. After shooting down our Cobra? No. It's no coincidence. *Then*, Hernandez's boys show up, as if they're chasing after the cruiser. No, not *chasing* it, but they came looking for it. Like it was supposed to return… and they knew *where* to look, too."

"Was the driver of the cop car on the way to us? Maybe to deliver something?" Atwood put forth.

"Hernandez has tried to talk to Gillespie before, but

the jerk had us demolish the phone line. You may be onto something, Bill," Ricky said and moved to the microphone.

Atwood chuckled, "I think *you* are, boss."

"*Necromancer*, this is *Straight Flush*," Desmond called into the microphone.

"*Necromancer*, here. Go ahead, *Straight Flush*," Sam Holsbeck replied immediately.

"I've got a job for you, Sam…"

***

Mattersly had decided that the best way to avoid contact with Renoite militia was to follow the railroad tracks sandwiched between the canal and the river. The three of them marched along in the loose soil alongside the rusted and rotted rails. They had been glad to see that the Truckee River came close to their chosen path and took a few minutes to run water through Reginald's purifying canister to replenish their canteens. While they waited for the water, they sat and watched the river.

All three went still and silent as the sounds of engines came to their ears from the interstate, just to the north of their location. Reginald boosted his hearing to maximum gain and placed a finger to his lips. He stood from his task and stared northward, listening to the sounds. There were two separate vehicles with internal combustion engines operating at different revolutions per minute. One was smaller than the other and both were moving rather quickly. After another passel of seconds, his eyes caught movement on the highway. He watched the rooflines of two vehicles rolling along the interstate. One appeared to be as large as a six-wheeled truck, rather than the expected Stryker, while the other was smaller. Reginald thought it perhaps some sort of sedan or military-style passenger vehicle.

In either case, the major reset his implants to normal function and went back to his task. "Not to worry," he said, "they're not coming for us, whatever they are."

"Man, I wouldn't mind a house right here," Mulhaney commented after a few tense minutes. He pointed to a building that could barely be seen through the trees on the other side of the river. "That would be perfect."

Angel made a sound of affirmation in her throat as she stretched her tired legs straight and leaned back on her hands. Her already short hair was matted to her skull with sweat. After Mattersly took care of replenishing their water supply, she intended to let her feet and head soak in the water before they moved on. She hoped they would be camping soon.

Elias was like-minded and removed his boots and socks to cool his feet. As he watched the land around them, he smiled. There were some birds in the air, though he knew not what kind, fish in the river that resembled trout, but he could not be sure, small reptiles he could not name, and squirrels of a variety unknown to him. There were always feral dogs and in rarer cases, cats, but the coyotes, wolves, and varieties of mountain lions were animals to be feared most, and could appear at any time.

Mulhaney daydreamed about finding a home and a pet dog. In this place, a land that was once named Nevada, he thought it could happen. All he would have to do is survive this matter in Reno and he felt pretty confident that he would.

Reginald stood from the river once he filled the water purifier for the final time. The device was not as efficient as a thorough boiling, but it would have to do. His eyes fell upon the structure across the water once again and thought he saw something moving upon what appeared to be the porch. He activated his implant and magnified his vision. The Dragunov on his shoulder had a scope capable of magnifying the view by six, but peering through a riflescope could be provocative if what he thought he saw was correct.

At just under two hundred meters was an old man, seated upon a chair on his home's back porch. His hair was fluffy white and long as was his beard. That hair was also light, for as the breeze was not strong, the whiteness fluttered along with it. As Mattersly stared, so he was stared upon. The old man's body steeled when his eyes found someone on the other side of the river, telling the Brit that the old man was equipped with similar lenses. For a few seconds, the two stared at each other until Angel interrupted.

"I'm cooling off my feet, Major," she declared happily as she splashed her way into the river.

Elias joined her promptly, though he waded in a bit more sluggishly as he leaned upon his walking stick. The tall man wore a childlike grin on his face. He was making the best of a possibly dreadful situation.

"Not too long, children," Mattersly teased as he stepped to his pack to replace his purifier.

Once done, he returned to the shore, nearly to the same place so that he might view the old man again. He had not moved and he remained watching them. Reginald saw no weapon near him.

Wishing not to alarm his companions, Reginald waited for an opportune moment. Angel dunked her head into the water while Elias turned his eyes to the skies in the other direction. Reginald decided to attempt a wave of his hand in greeting and peaceful intentions. He struck his left arm into the air and gave his hand a waggle.

The old man waved back.

The major dunked his feet and head into the river water like his two companions and dressed. A few minutes later, they were marching once again, keeping the railway in view, but adopting a path they had discovered near the river.

Mattersly looked back at the old man's house. There were no wires on poles leading to it, no antennae on the roof, and no vehicle anywhere near the place that he could see. As the trio passed by a group of trees, Reginald slowed and took up the rear. Once he saw that he was concealed from view by a crowd of branches and foliage, he strode to the nearest tree and found the old man with his much more effective binoculars. He could see him in greater detail, still seated on what Mattersly could see was a rocking chair. Next to the old man was a bolt-action rifle, complete with scope. Reginald copied the satisfied smile that the old man wore as he rocked and rested his eyes. It was clear that the man wished only for peaceful seclusion in his home by the river. Major Mattersly replaced the binoculars to his tunic pocket and quickly caught up with his team.

***

Jazz Hernandez was convinced that one or both of the personnel carriers were on her tail. As the hydrogen motor had failed the moment the car had been struck by the Renoite gunfire, the rest of the way had to be done on her battery. She pressed the sedan's remaining drive hard and bounced it heavily over the sections of ruined pavement as she tried to maintain a highway speed of sixty miles per hour. Any more than that was a certain method of destroying tire tread upon impact with a risen and sharp edge of road.

She watched her mirrors frantically, looking for signs of the pursuing military vehicles that were sure to be able to chase her down. After driving like a wild woman for nearly twenty miles, a light on her dashboard changed from amber to red.

The nano-lithium fuel cells' remaining power had dropped to below fifteen percent. In a matter of a few minutes, the sedan would be unable to keep up even a modest highway speed. The car would travel slower and slower until it crawled to a stop.

"No, no, no," she begged the shot-up and rattling antique.

Her eyes were trained on the road as she swerved around buckled pavement or potholes. Every time there was a stretch of smooth road, Hernandez took advantage of it by flooring the accelerator. The sedan responded, sometimes shooting up to one hundred miles per hour. This time, the battery life meter dropped to nine percent. It was to be her last burst of speed.

Jazz took her eyes from the road for a brief second to check the rearview mirror. As she did, a violent explosion rocked the car and sent it careening to the left. Hernandez let out a shout of horror as the wheel tried to tear itself from her grip. She refused to let it spin hopelessly to the left and kept it from doing so by lifting her leg to her left elbow, bracing it in place while her right foot mashed the brake pedal.

The remaining three tires screamed as they left behind long black streaks and let loose of their thick white smoke. The car ran out of pavement and crushed through many yards of brush before its momentum finally bled away to a stop.

Jazz did nothing but breathe for several minutes. The dust she had raised eventually succumbed to the Earth's gravity and she released her aching fingers from the steering wheel. She realized that it had become stiflingly hot in the cabin, so she opened her door. Hernandez moved to exit the car and found that her entire body ached sharply from bracing for a much harder impact. Slowly, she stood and stepped to the front left of the car. As she suspected, that tire was in shreds. It had either overheated or caught the edge of a sharp piece of the buckled road.

With a blown tire and an almost dead battery, she

was going nowhere without putting one bare foot in front of the other. She knew she had only halved the distance to her home and that the going would be tough in the summer heat. She felt that she already lost many pounds of water weight into her business suit and it looked like she was going to lose a lot more.

Hernandez went back into the car and picked up her purse, the shotgun, and the submachine gun. It was immediately evident that this was far too much cargo for the walk. Quickly, she decided to dump the shotgun and the shells. As she fished through her purse to remove them, a humming noise came to her ears. She froze as her heart began to pound violently. Not wanting to see, but needing to, she stood straight and cranked her head to the west, the direction she had come, expecting to see one of the metal monstrosities that had pursued her from Fernley.

There was nothing but the highway, the sand, and the waves of heat rising from both which distorted her vision. The humming persisted and grew louder. Disbelieving her eyes, Jazz lifted the submachine to her shoulder and pressed her finger to the safety. Still, nothing moved but the heat waves.

The sound of a truck horn snapped Jazz out of her fright-driven assumption that a Stryker was on its way to her. The double blast of tuned air also served as a direction finder. Swinging her head to the east, a vision of her rescue rolled toward her. One of two remaining towing vehicles in Lovelock approached along the interstate with two beloved citizens inside.

"Marco! Denny!" she screamed with relief and delight as she waved and hopped up and down in the sand like a little girl. When she was a child, Jazz had been warned about the heat of the desert. Her father always stressed the importance of water and today, she had forgotten the lesson and had not brought any with her. She was light-headed, weak, and frightfully thirsty. She prayed that the arrival of her two bodyguards was not a mirage.

***

A half a mile or so along the railroad tracks, Mattersly spotted more riverside homes. This time, they lay on their side of the river. As they marched closer, it was evident that there was little to worry about. There were three structures in total, built closely to the water and shaded heavily with a grove of trees. Two of the three had suffered a fire or perhaps several, while the third was partially collapsed from unknown means. As they passed, there was no sign of life outside of the little lizards that bounded about at their feet.

The late afternoon sun was in their eyes, but they marched on, not to be dissuaded from their objective. Elias had brought his handkerchief low over the top half of his eyes, while Angel walked just behind him in his much taller shadow. Mattersly had tugged his boonie hat lower, using the dimming effects of his bio-electronic lenses sparingly. The hills had begun to glow orange with the falling sun, casting deep blue shadows where the light could not reach. The Truckee curled northward away from the path of the railroad tracks, which added to the land's dry desolation. The psychological effect was an increased intake of water, which Mattersly noticed, but said nothing about as his map showed the Truckee swinging back into their path several times along the way.

Though he would not say so, he had noted the solid and consistent pace of Elias Mulhaney. The limping man was not slowing the march by very much at all and it very well might have been a good thing that he was setting such a pace. Only time would tell. Mulhaney's limp did not seem to worsen as they went along, though the man was clearly as fatigued as himself and Angel. Though they had some thirty kilometers yet to march before they arrived in

Reno, Reginald understood how exhausting the trauma of the brief skirmish in Fernley had been, especially on Angel, who had no combat training as far as he knew.

The major decided he would march them today only as far as they wished. The next couple of days, perhaps more, would likely be hell.

Within another kilometer, the trio approached a trestle that carried the tracks over the Truckee, which had angled south just as Reginald's map described. The trestle was bleached white concrete, weathered freely for decades to the point where any sharp edges were rounded out and the metal parts of the structure were stained orange and brown with rust. As the bridge was designed for trains only, there were no side railings to prevent a fall into the water.

"Watch your step, everyone," Mattersly warned, though he understood that it was not necessary.

The rails and ties were obviously in bad shape, making each step rather treacherous. Elias was kept in the lead as he would have the hardest time.

As a former paratrooper, Mulhaney was not intimidated by the distance to the water below. Nonetheless, he endeavored to keep his path to the very center of the trestle, even if a gnarled rail or a disintegrated tie caused him additional effort. Fortunately, the trestle itself remained sound and all were unconcerned about collapse.

Reginald had no sooner cleared the railroad bridge when the sounds of engines again approached, this time from behind. He stopped, turned, and augmented his hearing and vision. It took only a couple of seconds for him to determine that the approaching vehicles were the same ones that had been heading for Fernley just over an hour before.

"Everyone down! Trucks coming!" the major shouted and left the tracks, which were still elevated, suspended by an embankment of rock and soil. “Angel, get down!” he repeated to the young woman who appeared frozen in surprise, fatigue, and fear. The major grabbed her arm and led her to the edge of the embankment. Leading by example, he let himself slide down the loose dirt until his boots settled upon a large embedded rock. Clumsily, Angel and Elias followed suit and waited for the assumed Renoite vehicles to pass by them.

Allowing only the top of his head to show, camouflaged by the boonie, he watched the truck and what looked like a roughly thrown together carryall-type of vehicle roll along by and out of sight. After listening for another moment, Reginald decided they were safe, so he helped Angel to her feet and back up to the top of the embankment. Elias did so for himself.

“What do you think that was about, Major?” Mulhaney asked. “Resupply? Reinforcement?”

“Perhaps, Mister Mulhaney,” Mattersly answered thoughtfully. “In any case, it won’t do to remain still for long. Let’s continue, shall we?”

His two companions wasted no time in resuming their pace and soon, the railroad tracks became level with their surroundings. Mulhaney was aware that the three of them were in plain sight if more vehicles rolled by on the interstate, for his pace picked up to a level that Mattersly had not noticed before. The man appeared quite aware that this gait had become a liability, so he put up his maximum effort.

The river ran in a wide arch to their south as the railroad track, now their only possible path, lay alongside I-80. After a distance, some cover became available as the track rose up an embankment. At least if they had to, they could lay flat and hide. Once the highway curved away to their north, Mulhaney let his quick pace falter. The man had spent a great amount of energy to achieve a normal walking speed and the major could see that it was time for him to consider a place to camp for the night.

In the distance and to the right of the tracks, Reginald could see another set of structures built amongst a grove of tall, richly green trees. While the Truckee flowed noisily over banks of stone, another body of water appeared on their right, just ahead of the small neighborhood in the trees.

"Hold here, everyone," the major muttered as he went ahead of Angel and took a knee.

The other two followed suit, grateful for the rest. Viewing the area ahead through the binoculars, he determined that there was indeed only one house among the scattered buildings. It was not a neighborhood at all, but an estate complete with a decrepit and collapsing barn, a pair of garages that appeared intact, and an elongated equipment shed. The garages and shed were constructed of metal and showed much rust and attempts at repair. The home itself was set at the northern part of the lot, nearer to the comma-shaped pond. The property was strewn with antique vehicles, trailers, farm tractors, and other contraptions that the British soldier would have no hope in identifying from such a distance.

"What do you think, Major?" Angel asked quietly.

Reginald looked to her and saw fatigue, but not quite to the degree that Mulhaney tried to hide from his face.

"I think we may have found our resting place for the night," Mattersly said. "If no one's home, of course. Everyone on your feet. It's just three hundred and seventy meters ahead."

"Great," Elias said with a smile. "What's that in feet?"

"I suggest you count them as we go, Mister Mulhaney." The major smiled and began walking.

The shadows had grown longer throughout the afternoon, as it goes day in and day out, but neither Mattersly nor Mulhaney had ever experienced anything quite like sundown in Nevada. Under the focused orange glow from the setting sun in front of them, the hills had turned a mix of pinks and purples while the green trees showed glittering gold in the cooling breeze. Under their feet, the soil was light to medium-brown and clay-like, causing Mattersly to wonder how the land could grow such strong trees and lavishly green brush and grasses.

They crossed the tracks once they had put the property to their north. Mattersly took the assault weapon in hand and softened his step as he moved forward. Angel and Elias did the same. Reginald met the line of trees that were purposely planted, or perhaps spared, to line the southern end of the property. He crouched between a pair of these trees and remained deadly still. Angel looked at Elias after a few moments as if to ask what the delay was, but she found an equal amount of patience and vigilance upon his face.

Just as she was about to let out a sigh of boredom, Mattersly moved forward. Mulhaney urged her to follow while he took up the rear. Through the thick grove of trees they did weave, led by the SRR officer who did not allow them to come in view of one of the big house's windows. All of the objects scattered about the vast yard appeared to have been there for a long time. A few of the rusted and gutted automobiles were so old, that they could not identify them by either make or model.

The sheds appeared as if they had been through some strafing runs. They both bore ragged holes made by machine gun fire, most of which were obviously from above. In the thicker trees to their right were two garages of a dark green color, though both had been patched and repainted gray, possibly in repair from other such strikes or, perhaps, rust. Large tire tracks leading from them both indicated fresh activity.

The major caught Elias's gaze, so he pointed them out. The experienced soldier knew what their presence meant. The home they were sneaking up on was inhabited. Mattersly stared at Angel until she found his gaze. He placed a finger over his lips and she nodded.

Even after augmenting his hearing, Mattersly could hear nothing beyond the chirping birds and flowing water of the Truckee behind them. They moved forward as a unit until they were about to move into plain view of the large home's front windows, of which were many, though one on the second floor was boarded over. The building was quite large, so Mattersly had assumed that it was a multi-family residence. The single front entrance dispelled that thought. The door was very wide, intact, and its doorknob shiny. The front porch was swept free of dirt and debris from fallen foliage. He stared for a few minutes, taking in every detail.

Major Mattersly found no signs of booby-traps or pitfalls, so he indicated to his companions that they were to remain where they were. Mulhaney nodded right along with Angel in agreement. Mattersly made their jaws drop in unison when he left the cover of the trees and strode to the front door.

"What the…?" Angel whispered. She received a 'shush' from Mulhaney.

The major bounded up the four steps leading to the door, not making any attempt to silence his booted feet upon the wooden surface. Then, he knocked on the great door with the exuberant confidence of a pizza man.

"Holy shit," whispered Elias as he lifted his weapon.

Angel shushed him back, but prepared herself to provide cover fire for their mad leader's retreat.

After only a moment's wait, the door opened. It was not thrown wide, but carefully guided open enough to hold a conversation. Reginald was obviously speaking to someone inside and felt little threat. His mannerisms were that of patience, and his weapon was made safe and placed to his side, barrel pointed down.

The inside of the home was nothing but shadows. Only a vague shape of a human stood just a meter in front of Mattersly, that is, until a masculine hand emerged from the darkness and took the major's in greeting. Reginald turned to Angel and Elias and waved at them to stand down.

"Hold here," Mulhaney said to Angel as she began to stand up.

Elias rose up from his crouch with the help of his walking stick and stepped into the clear.

From inside, an old man shuffled more than walked into the orange light of the falling sun. Due to a humped upper back, he was much shorter than Mattersly, though in his younger years he must have been close to the major's height. The old man was well-dressed in a white button-front, short sleeved shirt. His pants were denim and not too heavily worn. Upon his feet was a pair of rugged-looking sandals. Mulhaney could tell the man was left-handed due to the large pistol he wore at his left side. The holster was meant to hang from a belt, but it hung from the denim pants' front pocket.

Suspicion must have been stamped all over Mulhaney's face, for the old man's slight smile withered and died as his hand slowly went to the pistol.

"Stand down, Elias!" Mattersly ordered and placed a hand to the old man's shoulder.

There was resolve in the old man's eyes, but there was peace as well.

"Hello," Elias said as he set the safety and let the

semi-automatic weapon dangle from its strap. The old man nodded, but said not a word. "Have we surrendered?" he asked jokingly of the major and adopted a smile.

"This is George Innes. The owner of the property," Mattersly announced. "We are welcome here as long as we behave ourselves. Angel, come on out."

The young lady did emerge from the thick brush and trees. Her weapons were not in hand. She wasn't sure what was happening, but she had a feeling that the old man was as she saw him. He appeared physically frail, but stout in spirit. His eyes showed him to be kind, but resolute and independent.

"Are you the reason my damn highway's been busy all mornin'?" George demanded of the trio. His voice was harsh, but his eyes smiled.

"I'm afraid that we are, Mister Innes," answered the major. "We're at odds with the Renoites for the moment."

"'At odds', eh?" Innes mocked. "At war, more damned likely. I heard a 'whump' a few hours back and saw a little smoke in the sky. That from you guys?"

"Yes, sir," Mulhaney answered.

"What was it you blew up?"

"An armored personnel carrier," the major answered.

"Ah, well, three of them damn things went by here. One last night, 'n' two this mornin'. I guess you got one," Innes surmised.

"We did," Reginald admitted.

"You better hope that chopper don't come after ya," George scolded with a bent and shaky finger. "That son-of-a-bitch is always flyin' over my place. You can see what it does around here, sometimes," he indicated his shot-up buildings and old vehicles.

"You won't have to worry about that, Mister Innes," said Elias, and pointed to the major. "You're looking at the man that shot it down, yesterday."

"Eh?" the old man beamed. "You did?"

"Yes, sir," Mattersly admitted.

"Well, I'll be damned!" Innes exclaimed and took the SRR soldier's hand in the both of his. "Thank God for that, son! Come on in, all 'a' ya!"

Despite the heat of the day, the large residence was much cooler. Mattersly relieved himself of the backpack and his two main weapons. Angel and Mulhaney did the same.

Innes stepped to his old, heavily stuffed recliner and dropped himself into it. He watched the three young people shed themselves of their burdens. Each of his visitors looked about the dimly-lit residence. The place was decorated with antique furniture and not the type that factories churned out on the cheap that would be replaced in a couple of years. Everything was wooden-framed and lavishly cushioned.

The walls were clean, though not freshly painted as it peeled at points high on the wall and ceiling. The curtains billowed with the fan-driven breeze. The west window of the living room hummed along as it dragged air from the outside. Another could be seen well off to their right, mounted in the kitchen window and blowing air outward.

"Tell me how you did it, um…Reginald, was it?" George pressed almost giddily.

"He prefers, Reggie," Elias quickly inserted with a wry smile as he leaned on his stick, grateful to be free of the pack.

"I most certainly…" the major began but was cut off.

"Tell me how, Reggie," the old man repeated. His face was alight with keen interest nearing glee. "Sit, everyone. Please sit. Looks like y'all been walkin' for days."

"It's been just the one," Angel spoke up.

"Hell of a day, though it was," Innes concluded. "Anyway, tell me about bringin' down the chopper."

Mattersly relaxed and told of the events in Lovelock, which led to the Cobra's demise, including the training of the rest of the defense force, how he had found himself at the controls of the machine gun and how the pilot survived for a long enough time after being brought down to warn them of the possibility of others. Innes listened silently and wide-eyed, eventually allowing himself to settle back in this chair to take in the tale.

The major's story changed to the morning's activities and the firefight with the Stryker and their lost friend. At the mention of Antonio's demise, George's eyes grew ever wider. Mattersly became quiet once the story led them to Innes's door.

"Well, you three are very fortunate," the old man declared. "So, why on God's green Earth would you be headed *into* Reno? Shouldn't you kids be runnin' t'opposite way?"

Mulhaney shared a hard look with Mattersly. Neither man knew for sure where Innes's loyalties lay, though it seemed he sympathized with the three of them.

"Well, Mister Innes, quite honestly, we are on a mission that takes us rather deeply into Reno itself," the major stated plainly. "We are out to destroy Reno's fabrication facilities, rescue the niece of Lovelock's mayor, and to assassinate Gillespie."

"Just the three of ya?" George said, wide-eyed yet again.

"As clandestinely as possible, of course," Mattersly provided. "Any of the three objectives we complete will be considered a success, but to rescue the child from this Gillespie is priority."

"I see," Innes said flatly.

"Do you have any objections to that, Mister Innes?" Elias said.

"Not at all," the old man returned immediately. "I do business in Reno for supplies all the time, but no one that lives there has love for the man, except perhaps his militiamen. Don't sound to me like you three want to harm the civvies none."

"We do not wish any of them harm," Mattersly promised.

"Sounds fine by me, then," Innes agreed. "Y'all are welcome to stay the night here. So, any of ya' hungry?"

***

Jazz's green sedan looked ruined, but Denny hooked the carcass up and brought it aboard the flatbed anyway. The few Lovelock mechanics that remained would have a blast trying to repair it, or perhaps, scrap it for parts. One did not simply let a vehicle sit to rot in the desert. The three of them crowded in the cabin of the big truck, with Hernandez turning to the rear window constantly, on the lookout for one of the Strykers.

"You can rest easy, Miss Jazz," Denny stated. "I'm watching in the mirror. There's no one back there."

"Maybe not at the moment, or even today, Denny," Hernandez said tiredly, "but if they wanted to crush Lovelock, they have the means of doing so."

Denny and Marco looked at each other over their leader's head. Neither had ever heard Jazz speak so doubtfully before. Marco decided it was the dehydration talking, so he handed her a full canteen of water.

"Thank you," she granted and drank from it.

"Mind telling me what this was all about?" Marco asked.

He had let go of any anger hours ago. Once the truck had gone past fifteen miles from Lovelock, fear for her life had joined it. When they had finally discovered her, joy dispelled all until he had several moments to think about it.

"I went to look for Antonio. He was overdue."

"Still is," her loyal bodyguard and longtime friend said flatly. "What did you find?"

"He's dead," Hernandez answered. Her eyes dropped to her legs as she tried to stifle tears. Had she not been so dehydrated, there would have been some to spare.

"What? What happened?" Denny piped up as his eyes jumped from the road to Jazz, Marco, and back. He had always thought his bald friend was invincible.

"He got shot up," Jazz choked then covered her mouth.

Denny slapped the steering wheel, but otherwise remained quiet.

"What about the others?" Marco queried after the truck had covered another mile or so.

Jazz shrugged and cleared her throat. "No sign other than a destroyed armored vehicle."

"But there were others," her longtime friend dragged on. "They shot up your car pretty good."

"I'll say," Denny interrupted. "Don't know if anybody can fix *that* mess."

"Two others showed up at some point," Jazz spoke in between swigs of water. "I drove into town to spy on them. They were burying a couple guys when I got close enough to see what they were doing."

Denny slowed the truck way down to avoid the heavier bumps and potholes in the road. Despite this, the beast rattled, clanked, and shook violently enough that all three people looked back at the car on the bed. It remained as it was well-secured, but it swayed threateningly.

"What is that? Blood?" Marco exclaimed as he pointed to a streak of dark red that stood out from the shiny cream silk of her blouse. "Are you hurt?"

"No, no," Jazz protested but checked anyway. "One of 'em sneaked into the house I was hiding in. I let him have it with this," she indicated the shotgun at her feet with a toe. "I guess I got some of him on me when I stole his grenades."

Denny and Marco both shared a knowing and appreciated chuckle. Their mayor was a badass and they loved her for it. Marco reached a heavy arm around her neck and planted a kiss to her temple as the truck rambled on.

"Welcome home," he said over the throaty drone of the big old diesel, "but don't ever fuckin' scare me like that again."

"Yeah, that outfit is ruined," Denny put in with a smile then the three of them broke out laughing.

Jazz Hernandez stopped laughing first. It was then she decided that if it came to it, she would attempt to surrender to Gillespie to save Lovelock. In her heart, she knew he was going to send everything he had after her. She imagined herself standing on I-80 with her arms in the air in defeat with Gillespie himself sticking out of the top of one of his vehicles as its machine gun rounds tore her to bits. She accepted it as an upcoming truth.

***

"So, what brings a limey to America?" Innes asked Mattersly with a sharp glint in his eye as he ate his trout.

All were seated around the man's dining room table and ate with him. The house was permeated with the scent of the wood-burning stove and fried fish.

Surprised at the question, Reginald nearly gagged on his food, but smiled. "I would call it a poor life decision at the time, sir. However, as time continues to go by, it may certainly prove to have been the correct path," he thought of Jazz when he said this.

"How'd you get here?" their host pushed on.

"Well, as my country's parliament was dissolved and then the king himself assassinated, along with the rest of the Royal Family, I realized that there was no reason to stay in Britain," Mattersly explained this as he sat back in the chair, sipping a glass of water. "I joined a band of sailors and a mixture of men from different branches of our military, and we stole a ship."

"The hell you say," grunted Innes.

"It's true," nodded Reginald. "Regretful, but true."

"In these times of lawlessness, it's hard to blame a man for turnin' pirate," George Innes winked. He had hit extraordinarily close to the mark without realizing it.

"Quite," the major commented and sipped.

"And how about you, soldier?" the old man asked of Elias Mulhaney, who blinked in surprise.

"Um, well… how did you know I used to be a soldier?" he responded.

"It's obvious," Innes answered gruffly. "You've had a hell of a time of things, too, it looks like," he indicated the sagging flesh on the man's right side with his hand.

It was crude and overly direct to mention such a thing, but the man was too old to care. They were all becoming used to the man's gruff way of communication.

"Yes, my implant has malfunctioned," Elias explained patiently. "It sent my adrenaline levels extremely high one day and I suffered a stroke."

"Do you think the effects are permanent?"

"I don't think so," Mulhaney explained. "Everything's been coming back slowly."

"Jesus," Innes commented. "That must have been hell. I'm happy I never got one of those damn things. Is that your unit tattoo? What is that?" The old man squinted and leaned closer to Mulhaney.

"Eighty-second Airborne Division, sir," Elias explained as he brought the arm closer to the old man.

"That's the devil of the five-oh-four."

The old man cackled and sat back, smiling and quite amused. "So, on my right I have a knight, on my left is a devil and 'cross from me's an Angel!" Innes slapped the table and laughed heartily until he coughed and his face turned red.

"I say, old man. Are you all right?" Mattersly said as his smile faltered. He did not like the sound of the cough. It was deep and watery.

"Yes, yes, son," George explained. "This has just been the most enjoyable of days. Reno doesn't have a chance in hell!" he declared and guffawed airily once again, finishing in another round of painful coughs. "Pardon the noise, kids," he said once he had calmed and caught his breath. "Just an old man gettin' older."

"How old are you, Mister Innes?" Angel asked just before taking a bite of trout.

"Don't know," he answered, "and I don't wanna know. So, you two wit' your implants that keep track 'a time jus' keep that to ye'sef. I've had no use for time since my wife, Nelly, passed. She used to make calendars for us, 'n' keep our birthdays 'n' holidays straight. Now, I don't give a damn what day it is. Any day I'm a' livin' without my Nelly is no day a'tall. So, I'm beggin' y'all not to tell me the date. Don't wanna know the year, either."

"We won't," Angel answered through a sad smile for the man.

She had no implant and she knew that Elias's was not functioning, but she knew the date from following calendars back in Lovelock, so she kept it to herself. Reginald and Elias nodded in agreement.

The evening in the old home passed none-too-quickly for one. Angel fell asleep on George's couch as soon as the sun fell and left them to candlelight. Innes explained that he saved the home's solar generator for the fans on the first and second floor to maintain a livable temperature. When it became even too hot for them to keep up, George would spend the day in the cellar.

"In any case, I maintain a certain level of comfort," he droned on as the other two men listened with interest dulled by exhaustion. "I have some electric lights, but I tend not to use them. Got used to it, I guess. Don't want to advertise my presence to most passersby, anyhow."

"Yes, about that," Mattersly took up, "I do apologize for our stalking the place and our unannounced arrival."

"Nonsense!" Innes called. "I don't consider you three in that group. I'm talkin' 'bout some a' Gillespie's roamers. They wanna be called 'rangers', but that's bullshit. They jus' roam about 'n' raid Lovelock or travelers."

"Say," Mulhaney spoke up, "one of them wouldn't be going by the name, Momo, would he?"

"Yep!" George exclaimed and pointed excitedly at Elias. "That's the son-of-a-bitch! Him and coupla' his boys drop by here unannounced. Raid my food. I tolerate 'em, but, damn if I was younger 'n' lil' faster..." he trailed, but his hands indicated a fatal revenge.

"You won't have to worry about Momo no mo'," Elias chuckled at his pun. "You're looking at the man who killed him," he finished with a point toward the major.

"Holy hell!" Innes shouted and slapped his knee. Angel stirred, so he continued more quietly. "Son, is there anyone that I hate that you haven't killed, yet?"

"Just one, I hope," Mattersly answered sincerely.

He did not feel pride over the deeds he had done, but the killings of late had been necessary.

As conversation went on, the cool evening air put a comfortable chill in the house, enough so that the droning of the fans became quieter as their blades slowed.

In a matter of a couple of hours, George Innes became fatigued, though it was clear that he was enjoying his guests. He had convinced the men that Angel would be more comfortable in a bedroom upstairs, so by the dim electric light of the staircase, Mattersly made his way up with Angel draped across his arms. As she was semi-conscious, she wrapped hers around his neck and thanked the major for his kindness. The heat of the day had not been wrung from the small woman's frame, so she asked him to leave the windows open, which he did.

The major was not comfortable leaving their weapons on the ground floor and Innes agreed. The men dragged their belongings up the stairs next and were directed to other rooms. As the building lacked traditional running water, George showed the men the upstairs bathroom, which had been rigged with an electrical pump with a manual handle for a backup. Here, they were able to wash themselves before collapsing into bed.

Like Angel, Mattersly had not received enough of the cool air to cleanse him of the day's heat. He opened both windows of his room, which the bed had been set between and sat in a cushioned chair to remove his boots.

The windows faced the north and, therefore, the interstate. The roadway had been busy today, George had said. Reginald smiled. 'Busy' with three armored personnel carriers heading one way and two trucks on a round trip. He recalled a memory of London traffic back from when he was a lad. The streets back then were constantly crowded with cars, trucks, and buses. The danger from being run over by something, even a courier riding a motorbike or even a bicycle was quite real.

Now, as he stared out into the night, lit by a partial moon, there was nothing but a pair of gray snakes stretching from west to east. Closer to the home was the pond, where here, the silver light smacked the water to a light green with white ripples. The croaking of frogs and the howl of a wolf far away accompanied the occasional swish or splatter of the water. Upon hearing these sounds, the major's eyes snapped open, but finding nothing other than the traces of fish in the water, he relaxed.

Mattersly dozed in the large chair for a time before he switched to the bed. It was a soft mattress, but not too giving. Its age was evident in the musty aroma, but even this was minimal. Innes had maintained his home rather well, despite the world around him. After but a few moments, the major slept.

Elias had been set up in the room on the northwest corner and his experience was similar. He had gone straight to the bed and within a few minutes had drifted to sleep.

As with all things electronic and even more so, driven by software, they are inherently haunted by gremlins. Such was the case with Mulhaney/Bartel's implant. Unwanted, it activated and randomly played a scene from an episode of his favorite satellite show, *Mulhaney.*

Upon closed lids, the program was projected and, therefore, inescapable. The sounds of heavy rain and thunder sounded off in the man's audio implants, which at first, encouraged him to remain asleep, but not as deeply as before the monstrosity within his brain had launched its will upon his psyche. Between the beating of galloping hooves, thunder rolled. David's eyes were first aware that something was amiss, for they followed the action before the man's mind was awake enough to acknowledge it.

A mighty crackling of a nearby thunder strike awoke Bartel with violence. He uttered a howl of surprise that morphed into a grunt of pain, for the malfunctioning implant provided that, too. His eyes were opened, but it mattered not as the scene remained unchanged and for a time, a matter of seconds, the scene was reality. His heart pounded as his horse ran madly along with another to his left. With every set of steps, David gave a cry of surprise and anxiety, and it was several long seconds more, an eternity, before he realized what was truly happening, for the camera angle of the scene had changed. He was no longer on top of the horse but on the ground, watching a pair of horses with riders go by him at a mad, ground shivering pace.

David cussed the darkness and his circumstances, but all he could think of to do for the moment was witness the antique snippet of entertainment as it unfolded upon his lenses and audio implants.

The pair of riders was pursued by another group of riders that outnumbered them, and they were close. The group of five or six was shown in short, quick scenes that did not feature the riders' faces. The storm was a great hindrance, but of some help to Mulhaney and his companion, as it kept the pair from being easily spotted in the wet, but intermittent darkness.

Bartel became cognitive enough to think the 'shut down' command, but the implant was not in a cooperative mood. The scene continued to play out and David had no choice but to witness it. Even through the painful pounding in his temples that accompanied these random implant 'attacks' as he thought of them, he had learned to take heed of the message.

In another instant, the pair found a town and rode into it at great speed. Not being familiar with it, Elias Mulhaney guided his partner to a lit saloon at the far end of the main street. The group of men chasing them bore down quickly, not even allowing the pair time to tie their rides to the post in front.

Gunfire quickly outperformed the thunderous night, sending Bartel to jump and shiver. Mulhaney pulled his riding partner inside the saloon and returned fire with one shot before ducking into the establishment.

"*Everyone get down or get out!*" Elias shouted. "*Terrell Yager 'n' his men 'r' on our tails! Anyone that don't wanna help, get outta here!*"

The Elias Mulhaney of the little 'big' screen got down behind the bar just in time to duck a volley of gunfire that shattered the saloon's front windows. In a flash, Mulhaney and the recurring character, Little Larry, were alone in the bar.

"*Well, that figures, Elias,*" the older man drawled as he nervously scratched his beard with the barrel of one of his big Dragoon pistols.

Elias nodded, saw movement at the saloons swinging doors, and fired twice into the wet night.

"*We may not make it out of this one!*" he shouted.

Mercifully, the errant implant acquiesced to Bartel's request for 'shut down'. The scene, the gunfire, the thunderstorm all ended. What remained was the pounding of his heart and the ache at his temples. Without a second passing, a knock came to his door. It opened before he had a chance to speak.

"I say, old man," came the familiar voice of the major, which brought a smile to Mulhaney's face. "Is everything all right?"

He nodded, knowing Mattersly's night vision would be active on his fully-functional devices.

"Dare I ask?"

"No, sir. Please don't," replied Elias as he lay flat and positioned himself on the bed as if he would sleep.

"I see," Reginald said with a regretful whisper. "Good night, then, Mister Mulhaney."

"Good night, sir."

The door closed with a light creak and a metallic snap from the latch, but Elias heard no receding footfalls. It was many minutes before he decided that the man was just that stealthy.

In time, sleep came to him, but the mood of contentment was shattered by the appearance of a scene from the *Mulhaney* series finale.

***

The light of dawn awakened Mulhaney from a sleep fragmented by naturally generated dreams. Angel, Mattersly, and Innes seemed quite rested and energetic when he appeared on the first floor, the last one to do so. The aroma of the home was a diversity of coffee, fish, and what the ex-paratrooper hoped was bacon.

"Good morning," he greeted and it was returned, though he noted the major's lingering gaze. He did not return it, but sat at the table and laid his walking stick down at his feet.

Elias thanked Innes for the breakfast, placed some food upon his plate, and coffee into the cup. He was well into the breakfast when he noted that there was almost no conversation until the major spoke up.

"You'll be happy to hear, Mister Mulhaney, that our host has an ace up his sleeve that will speed us along on our quest," Reginald oozed in his proper English manner.

"Oh? What might that be?" he grunted.

"I've got a truck in the garage. Runs on traditional petroleum-based gasoline. I'm gonna drive you three right into Reno!" Innes declared gleefully and banged a fist on the table.

"You don't say," Mulhaney declared with heavy doubt. A flurry of nods came from Angel, seated to his right, while the major simply folded his hands out in front of him and smiled. "You've seen it?"

From the expressions on his companion's faces, they had. Angel's smile was priceless and not to be doubted, neither was Mattersly's silent lucidity. He turned his amazed gaze to Innes, at his left.

"I use it regularly to visit merchants in town," George said. "My showing up more than a week early might raise an eyebrow or two, but when I show the fuel merchant an empty barrel, I'll appear legit as always," the old man explained with a giddy, almost wild expression. "See, there's a trail that I use that Angel here walked along the last time she went into town. I just wished I'da knowed, young lady," he addressed her.

"I told you, George," she responded, apparently not for the first time on the subject, "there's no way in the world you could have known."

"Why didn't you mention this last night?" Mulhaney blurted the question to Innes.

"How would I have known whether or not I could trust you three to not just steal it?"

"Really?" Elias asked, flabbergasted.

"He has a point, Mister Mulhaney," the major put in. "That vehicle is this man's lifeline to provisions. We are, after all, strangers."

"True," Elias conceded.

"The Major traced the route on his implant's map," Angel took up. "I showed them the roadmap and it's the same neighborhood I walked into and out of."

"It's only about thirty kilometers out," Mattersly added, "which means we could be there in less than two hours."

"You bet your ass, young fella!" George agreed exuberantly.

The morning's news dispelled much of the bad feelings Elias had incurred from the previous night's implant malfunction and strange dreams. A shortcut like this was not in the plan and to get to the objective so quickly to evaluate whether or not any of it was even possible was a great gift.

"Do I have time to pack?" Elias kidded with a

smirk.

Chapter Ten

Morning came to Lovelock several hours before Jazz could bring herself to leave her bed. She was still exhausted from her excursion to Fernley and, no matter how much water she ingested, her thirst would not be quenched. Her arms and legs ached terribly. She was not sure she could even walk, so she decided to postpone another attempt.

To lessen the harsh morning light upon her face, she turned her head to the opposite wall, where her tired eyes found her calendar. It was the twelfth of July, a Wednesday. She had met Reginald Mattersly and Elias Mulhaney less than a week ago, and yet, their arrival had changed so much. She hoped and prayed that the men and Angel were well, even if their attempt to infiltrate Reno had failed. Her heart ached when she pondered their fate, especially that of her niece and Reggie. She may very well have led her small town into a war by sending them, but something had to be done.

"Should have gone to Gillespie," she whispered to herself as she envisioned life in Reno with that maniac.

Eventually, she would have had to kill him to get her and Nora away from there. Hernandez shook the thought away and realized the futility of it. She wondered when the armored personnel carriers were coming.

Jazz forced herself to sit up to retrieve her nearly empty glass of water from the nightstand. The pitcher was low, too, so she knew she would have to get all the way out of bed to refill it. She finished the water and stood up, groaning with the displeasure that ran throughout her body.

"Ow, ow, ow," she mumbled as she shuffled across the wood floor.

She drew more water from the bathroom sink and returned to bed. After a few moments, a knock startled her out of a doze.

"Whaaaaat?" she called grumpily and covered herself with a blanket.

She did not wish to be seen in a nightgown by anyone except Reggie.

"It's Marco," he called from the other side of the door.

"Come in," she answered.

Her bodyguard stepped into the room with a rarely seen smile.

"Good morning," he greeted and stood to the side as Gigi entered the room, carrying a breakfast tray.

"Good morning, you guys," Jazz beamed as she accepted the tray and a hug from Gigi. "I appreciate that, Gigi. Thank you," she called after her friend and employee.

"Just happy you're still with us," she returned with a wink. She exited Jazz's chambers and quietly closed the door.

Hernandez had no idea how hungry she was until she smelled the scrambled eggs and toast. She dug in and looked to Marco, who simply stood by with his hands crossed in front of him.

"Thank you for my rescue yesterday."

"What else could I have done?" he returned with an edge to his voice that made it clear he was still upset by the incident.

"I know I should have told you," she said in between bites of breakfast. "I won't do it again."

"I hope not. How do you feel?"

"Everything hurts."

"Good."

"Hey!" Jazz protested.

"I simply meant that you won't be trying anything like that again."

"Well," she muttered as she took another bite, "I

have been thinking about heading into Reno myself and surrendering to Gillespie."

Marco blinked. "You can't be serious. We've talked about this."

"Marco, we can't be sure that Mattersly and his two remaining people will be effective in any way," she explained.

"So?"

"So, I think that if I can go talk to Gillespie and surrender to him, he might leave Lovelock alone."

"He'll kill you," Marco stated plainly. "That's what he's been trying to do since you shot him down last time."

"It may be different face-to-face," she shrugged as she ate her toast. "I think I need to do it for Nora, too."

Marco's expression turned dark as he thought of the young girl. He had hoped beyond hope ever since she had been taken that she had been treated well. The longer that Gillespie had her, however, the less likely that was. He was beginning to think that Jazz was right about an in-person meeting. The question in his mind was, 'would Jazz be forced to surrender her life for the sake of the town *and* her niece?' Boldly, he sat on the bed at her feet, frustrated and heartbreakingly confused by his ponderings.

Jazz said nothing over the odd behavior, understanding that she had made the loyal friend and employee worry with her stunt. She watched him as she ate her breakfast and could tell that he was trying to put together a thought.

"When you figure out what you wish to do, Jazz," the big man said lowly as he stared at her bathroom door, "tell me what I can do to help. I'll even drive you into Reno if that's what you want."

Hernandez could not think of anything to say. She tilted her head to one side and nodded. The shaking of the mattress from her movement called for him to look over at her. He nodded back to her, got up and quietly left.

Jazz watched the door close and wished that things had worked out between them so long ago, but they were two very different people then and truthfully, still were. They had remained friends and she kept him on as her bodyguard after the breakup. All through her time with Gillespie, Marco had warned her about his bad feelings about the man. Because of her past with the bodyguard, she dismissed it as jealousy, but it turned out that Marco had been quite correct.

Now, it seemed her heart belonged to Reggie. That straight-laced, former elite soldier that melted her heart whenever he spoke in that wonderful accent had haunted her mind since the night before he left for Reno. Her eyes teared over having not found the rest of the team, but she had faith that Mattersly, Mulhaney, and Angel were all right. Probably going through hell on her behalf, but she had to believe they were doing well.

***

"Not... liking... *thiiiiis!!*" Angel screamed over the howling engine as George Innes drove the antique, but quite rugged truck over an embankment to get to a trail south of the interstate.

After the front wheels regained contact with the ground with frame-shuddering force, she cussed and grunted with relief that they had not been thrown clear. Her arms remained solidly wrapped around the 'roll bar', a term that stirred her anxiety when Innes had spoken of it.

"Easy there, young miss," Innes shouted over his shoulder. "We're on the main trail now. It's a lot less bumpy from here on out."

This, she doubted immensely as she rolled her eyes at Reginald, in the front passenger seat, and Elias to her right. She had walked the very trail that this old man was driving along and if he kept this pace, bumpy it would remain.

The truck was large and had an open four-seated cabin with an enclosed cargo bed built behind them that had all of their things, except personal weapons, inside. Its wheels and tires were large, its suspension lifted high, and had all-wheel-drive for the terrain. George told them all that the he had built the machine himself nearly forty years prior, a fact which was made evident by the rusting body parts and worn seats. The engine itself sounded well-tuned and maintained, however, this was a fact that its creator was forced to admit was due to a mechanics' shop in Reno.

Innes might have become too old to do much work on the vehicle, but he knew how to drive it. Mattersly was impressed as he watched the old man's arms work quickly and firmly upon the steering wheel to keep the mighty truck on course over the trails of loose soil and stones.

The Truckee River lay to their left while the interstate remained all-too-close on their right for a good number of miles. After the trail, highway, river, and railway all turned directly south, Mattersly spoke up.

"Mister Innes, how much further until we get to this trail that takes us away from the main road?"

"Not much longer, Major," Innes returned with a strained voice. The growling of the engine drowned much of him out. "We're gonna have to slow down a bit and get this thing onta' the railroad tracks. There's a bridge that takes us over the river. From there, we'll find some paved roads to take. We'll be using them to swing south and get us some distance from the highway."

Reginald turned to look at Angel, who had leaned between the men to hear the conversation. She nodded at the major to confirm what the old man said.

True to his promise, Innes slowed down to guide his truck carefully over the rusted railway trestle. The old machine bounced and tilted, convincing Angel that either the narrow bridge would break or the vehicle would topple.

Neither did. Beyond the little bridge, George angled the vehicle to the right and drove it through some thick brush to find another trail, and then turned westward again. After a few minutes, George did find pavement and drove onto it. All around them were abandoned buildings of light industry and Innes wound through them, sticking to the decaying streets. They approached a four lane roadway that appeared to be very similar to I-80, but the map on Mattersly's implant indicated that it was not. The truck was only on that route for a short time, however. George guided the truck from it onto yet another paved road, passed a gigantic structure that had once been a bustling factory and finally, turned the truck onto a dirt path which appeared to lead directly into a mountain.

In a matter of minutes, the truck had wound its way over the path and climbed in altitude, leaving all traces of abandoned civilization behind them. The heat of the day was building with the help of a cloudless sky. Whenever George needed to slow the vehicle for a turn or sharp incline, the lack of breeze was instantly felt. This heat impacted Angel the most, as she was fair skinned and slight of figure. Noticing her discomfort, Mulhaney gave her an extra handkerchief, which he tied upon her head in an identical fashion as his own.

The truck bounced and bounded along the trail and for a long period, the drive continued uphill. Several times along the path, the truck passed underneath phone lines suspended by aged and rotting wooden posts strewn throughout the mountainous area. The drive was difficult, as the trail was well-established over the course of many years, but now was rarely traveled. The result was an occasional tricky spot, where George had to slow the vehicle to almost nothing to squeeze between large rocks, sometimes rolling the gel-filled puncture-proof tires over some of the smaller ones.

The trail wound in truly every direction over the low mountain range, certainly adding a great distance to the thirty-or-so kilometers that Innes had estimated. Fuel consumption was not a problem, the old man had claimed, and so far, he was right. The ride was rough, however, more so than anyone but Innes had anticipated. The old man knew what he was doing, and despite his fragile and stooped appearance, he handled the great hand-made vehicle triumphantly.

In just over two hours of this spine-shattering, buffeting ride, the low mountains settled to hillsides, and the hillsides smoothed down to foothills and even a few valleys. Innes found pavement once again. This led directly into a labyrinth of curvy streets which were interweaved between rows of luxurious homes. Many of them were not in very good shape, but some appeared at least to have been recently lived in, as they showed signs of upkeep and maintenance.

“I say, George,” Reginald spoke up as he watched the surrounding residential structures with high scrutiny, as did the other two. “We are not exactly approaching town in a clandestine manner.”

“Yeah,” Elias quipped, “some of these homes look occupied.”

“Not to worry,” Innes called back over his shoulder as he took a westerly turn onto a four lane road. “This is just the outskirts of town. Those people don’t want anything more to do with Gillespie and his little government than you guys do.”

Rounding another curve, Innes steered the truck northward onto another street.

Considering how sun-bleached and neglected the streets were in the area, the major decided that Innes was right. What resources Gillespie’s government possessed as far as street repair was obviously kept for the roadways of the inner city.

Innes allowed the truck to slow to a crawl. His left arm stretched toward the windshield as he indicated a northwesterly direction.

"You'll have to let me know when we get closer to where you want to be dropped. Up ahead a couple miles is the airport. Beyond that is downtown, where Gillespie's hotels are and such."

A thought occurred to Mattersly and he could not believe that he had not spoken of it, yet. "Are there any telephone systems linking the area together?"

"Sure is. But it's all local."

"Local is good enough," Reginald nodded and turned to Angel and Elias, who went to the edge of their seats to listen. "Perhaps if we are allowed to speak to this ruler of the land, he may be willing to negotiate for Nora's release."

"Maybe," Mulhaney emphasized with a smile.

The four were quiet for a while as Innes drove his vehicle closer to the interior of Reno. Mattersly kept the assault weapon in hand, but low as his eyes searched the surrounding area for signs of life or anything else hostile.

Elias, for his part, was doing the same and for the first time since the ambush where he met the Brit, he felt a rise of his natural adrenaline. This was not brought on by his faulty *CTL-Link*, which was something he hoped to never reoccur, but by the fact that they were in enemy territory and in plain sight. He grabbed onto the assault weapon and roll bar next to his head and pulled himself up to give a look behind them.

There was nothing following.

He sat down and kept his eyes sweeping the land as he saw Angel and Reginald doing. He could not help but recall last night's implant malfunction and the vision it had brought upon him, but he refused to dwell on it.

If this is my last ride, so be it.

***

Ricky Desmond left the elevator and entered the communications room. He had rested pretty well the previous night, receiving nearly six hours of sleep. He wore his light grey tweed sport coat, royal blue shirt, and black trousers. He even conjured up a smile when he saw his friend, Bill Atwood, on duty at his radio so early. They greeted each other with brief 'Good mornings' and slipped into the conversation at hand.

"*Necromancer* and *Lancelot* checked in thirty minutes ago," Atwood began. "Still in Fernley as ordered and no enemy contact," he said as he opened an envelope that he picked from his desk. "These came in over the imager."

Desmond accepted the prints from his friend's hand and looked them over as a grimace immediately took hold of his clean-shaven face. "Awk! That's awful."

"Yeah, that's what a smattering of fifty-cal does."

"Uh-huh," Ricky agreed. "Well, that's Antonio, all right. Lovelock's sheriff or whatever he wanted to be called."

Bill Atwood remained silent as he watched his friend and superior officer's face. He wondered if Ricky would see what he had found and comment on it. Desmond took a couple of the five-by-seven inch pictures, one in each hand and scrutinized them both with dancing eyes.

"Hey, he didn't have any of his boys open these doors, did he?" the appointed general asked.

"He didn't say, Rick."

"Get him on the radio for me."

"*Necromancer*, this is *Almighty Oz*," he called into the microphone, waited a moment then repeated it.

"*Almighty Oz*, this is *Necromancer*," Holsbeck

himself answered. "Go ahead, over."

Ricky took over the microphone. "Sam, this is *Straight Flush*. Acknowledge. Over."

"Roger that, *Straight Flush*. Acknowledged. Over."

"We've received your pictures of the destroyed vehicle, your location. I need to verify something. Did you or any of your group open the doors of the cruiser? Over."

"*Straight Flush. Necromancer*. That's a negative, sir. Those passenger doors were open when we came on scene. If you look close, you should see hits on driver's side rear door. Angle indicates they hit while the door was open. Over."

Ricky Desmond studied that print once again and noted what *Necromancer*'s commander meant. "Roger that, *Necromancer*. I see it and concur. Over."

Desmond released the microphone and stepped back with the one print in hand. It was a foregone conclusion that the car had not been empty when it arrived in Fernley, but the debate in his mind had been over who had taken out the *Ranger* team after the car had been destroyed. Seeing something in the print made him think of one of the other pictures. Ricky stepped to the pile on the desk and sifted through them.

"There," Desmond huffed and planted a finger on the print.

Bill leaned forward and looked over the picture for the hundredth time. "It's the trunk. So?"

The appointed general smacked the 'call' button on the microphone. "*Straight Flush* to *Necromancer*. Please advise as to what was found in the trunk of the vehicle. Over."

"*Necromancer* here, *Straight Flush*. Negative on contents of the trunk. My driver pried it open himself. Over."

Ricky nodded as he held the print to Atwood.

"Here's a picture of the rear seat. Full of bullet holes and pulled forward."

"Uh-huh," the radio operator agreed.

Desmond found another picture taken prior to the trunk becoming pried open. "No exit holes in the trunk lid."

"Shit," Atwood muttered and slapped the desk.

"The survivors pulled their belongings from the trunk after *Ranger* was destroyed. There are people on the ground, most likely elite ex-military on the way *here*."

"I agree, sir."

Desmond made a quick decision. A decision that he should have consulted Gillespie about, but he felt there was no time.

"*Necromancer*, *Lancelot*, this is *Straight Flush*. Acknowledge, the both 'a' ya."

Both commanders answered and the air silenced.

"This is a recall order. Fall back to your previous guard positions immediately. On the double or whatever you want to call it. Make it snappy! Over!"

The Stryker commanders acknowledged the order and all parties signed off. Desmond picked up the phone and made a call to the guardhouse located on the airport's premises.

"Hello, this is *Straight Flush*. I'm ordering full alert status as of right now. Sound it!" Ricky listened for a moment. "Sure, I'll hold," he replied and rolled his eyes and covered the mouthpiece. "I'm starting to think you were right all along, old buddy."

"About what?" Bill said in a near whisper.

"About getting the hell outta this town and making our luck in Cali," he said to his friend as he continued to hold.

"Ricky, man, any time you want to split, let me know," Atwood assured him.

"Gillespie is nuts if he thinks this Hernandez girl is

this important," he hissed and turned his attention back to the voice on the phone. "Good, crank it up! We're looking for a small elite force that may already be in town. Yeah. Call up everyone. Thanks," he finished and replaced the receiver. "I don't know where Lovelock got the talent, but I think we have some bad company comin'. I have to go brief 'his lordship'," Desmond declared as he opened the door. "Hold down the fort. Call Gillespie's penthouse if you need me."

"You got it, boss," Bill Atwood called cheerily.

For a few moments, he stared at the door. He watched Desmond step into the elevator and the doors close. He immediately picked up the phone and dialed.

"Hi. Atwood," he said into the mouthpiece. "We have a problem with Desmond, sir, just as you predicted."

***

The truck sped along an exceptionally nice strip of roadway when the sirens began. Without being told, George Innes stopped his behemoth and shut down the motor. The four of them listened and all looked to the major, who stood up in the seat and watched the western horizon. All that could be seen were mountains and blue sky.

The loudest of them all was a high-powered klaxon, generally used for military installations. Mattersly was certain that it was coming from the airport, which was to their west approximately three and a half kilometers away. The other two were identical to each other in tone and pitch, but were slightly out of sync. These were civilian defense types and possessed the long, low to high pitched cry.

"Well, there's no tornado," Elias joked but kept his eyes searching for trouble. "Think they're onto us?"

"We must react as if they are, Mister Mulhaney," replied Reginald. "Mister Innes, I'm afraid we may have put you at risk. I recommend that we depart and allow you to return home."

"Nonsense!" Innes replied and reactivated his truck's engine. He slipped the transmission into gear and accelerated, seating Mattersly down with the sudden force.

"Mister Innes!" Reginald protested as he held onto the roll cage.

"Just let me get you somewhere off the streets," he called as he turned the truck to the left at the next intersection.

Innes had been holding back on the power the entire trip, but now the truck launched forward as its engine's choppy drone changed to a howl. The wind tore through the open cabin, picking up any dust that had settled into the thin carpet at their feet.

"Lookout, George!" Elias shouted from the rear seat.

The old man had no chance to slow down for the next turn. Directly in their path were abandoned homes of a cul-de-sac littered with bushes and stones.

"It's all right…shortcut!" he replied as he braked all too lightly for everyone's taste.

He gave the steering wheel a twitch left then right, aiming the truck perfectly for a driveway instead of allowing the truck to bound up the curb.

"What's the hurry, Mister Innes?!" the major called over the truck's noise and the sirens just as the driver guided it quickly, but carefully between two homes.

"When this place goes on alert, all the militia people and volunteers… ooop… hold on!" he began to explain as he steered around a ditch which ran along the side of the next street. Utilizing a driveway, Innes was able to cross it and make a hard right turn onto the road. "Everyone comes outside to look around and see what's happenin'. Besides, I don't know where all their armored carriers are! They tend to head back to a guard position during this time!"

"They fall back to organize before patrolling the areas," Mulhaney concluded.

"Yes!" George called and made a hard left onto a large, winding driveway. "I'm taking a chance that no one's residing at this rec-center here. There weren't any last time I saw the place."

The klaxon and air raid sirens continued as the truck barreled toward a long and multi-faceted structure. Innes brought the truck to a stop underneath the main entrance's canopy, which was cocked at an angle due to an incident of inclement weather, but was otherwise intact. Immediately, the group cooled as the shade washed over their bodies. The old man shut down the engine and slid out.

"Get your stuff and bring it on into the lobby area," he started with as he circled his vehicle and peered out into the sunlit landscape from which they had just taken refuge. "Now, they generally don't worry about this part 'a' town. There's just not a lot of point for people to live too far from the main nugget of the city. There's no shortage of homes anywhere, but there are those individuals that the militia puts out on a kinda perimeter patrol. One 'r two men will head out to homes like these and camp out a few days." He talked as he followed the three younger people inside the vast facility.

"So, do they recall them when there is a general alert?" Elias asked as he pedaled along on his walking stick.

"No, they typically stay and report of any suspicious activity," George explained as he took the lead and motioned for them to follow. "They also serve as the eyes and ears for the artillery guns."

Mattersly's eyes widened and his head snapped around to find Angel. She was clearly shocked by this and shrugged helplessly.

"Bloody hell. How many guns are there and where are they located, Mister Innes?"

"Just three or four, Major," Innes said over his shoulder as he led them up a flight of stairs. "They're generally kept at the airport in a hangar."

The foursome stepped into a large game room and bar area, which overlooked a first-floor level pool outside to the south. Innes stepped around a wind-tattered wall and entered an even larger room that must have once been a restaurant, considering the scattered tables and chairs throughout the place. It seemed like the entire resort, club or whatever one wished to call it seemed utterly devoid of windows, for the summer breeze had its way, whistling through empty window frames and around corners of interior walls. The growling klaxon and the howling sirens echoed throughout the place, adding to its eerie emptiness.

Innes brushed off a chair and sat upon it backward, facing the three he had brought here. His right arm outstretched westward as a gnarled finger pointed through the glassless windows.

"Out there is the airport. That's where you'll find the hangar where you said they're assembling that second chopper, though I hope your wrong about that. To get there, you'll have to cross all that overgrowth you see, Elias."

Mulhaney had approached the outer edge of the room and took in the sight of the land beyond. "What *was* this place?"

"Used to be a golf course," George explained. "With no one around to take care of it, it just looks like hell. Y'all will have ta be careful going through that if you choose to. There are snakes 'n' some nasty mosquitoes 'n' such."

"Following the roads will prove to be much more dangerous," Major Mattersly said quietly. He had joined Mulhaney at the windows.

"I agree, but what are we hitting first, Major?" Elias asked quietly enough to let his voice be drowned out by Reno's sirens. Only Mattersly heard his question.

"I think we should wait out the day here and rest," Reginald answered, but addressed everyone as he turned from the sunny landscape. When he turned, the sirens faded away. "As it stands, with the entire town's militia on alert, I do believe it wise for we three to hide here. Mister Innes, I implore you to please return home. There's nothing more you can do for us and you have been most gracious. It's too dangerous for you here."

"I've been thinking about that and I'm beginning to agree with you," George replied with a smile and stood from the musty seat. "I'm going to meet my friend at his shop to buy fuel so my visit seems routine. Then I'm going to hit the road and get home before nightfall."

"Excellent idea," the major concurred and reached out to take the old man's hand. "Thank you, sir."

Mulhaney and Angel approached and bid Innes goodbye with another handshake and a hug respectively. Innes stepped to the restaurant's main door and turned back to the trio for one last look and word.

"I'm sure I said this before, but keep somethin' in mind for me while you go 'bout all this," he saw that he had their sincere attention and continued. "The people, the citizens of Reno, are good people. Every bit as good as those in Lovelock. Do what you need to do to rescue this girl and depose Gillespie, but take it easy on the civilians, will ya?"

"We shall endeavor to do just that, Mister Innes," Mattersly promised.

With that, Innes thanked them all and departed. A few minutes later, the trio heard the faint traces of the big truck's motor start up, rumble, and fade away once again.

"Tonight, my friends," Major Mattersly said as he

clasped his hands behind his back, "we move out. We need to reconnoiter that airport."

***

Ricky had heard the news that Miguel Costa, the man that had kidnapped the child, Nora and had killed her mother, had been allowed to die in Gillespie's penthouse, and that the body had been removed the previous night. This did nothing for the smell of the penthouse foyer, however. As soon as the elevator doors slid open, Desmond was struck by a wave of stench that was a mixture of death, excrement, and a chemical lemon fighting for supremacy. The lemon, so far, was not faring well.

He covered his mouth and nose with a white handkerchief and mumbled curses to himself as he quickly stepped through the suite's open front door. Ricky looked all over the floor and walls, expecting to see blood and entrails, but there was nothing. Everything appeared pristine.

During Ricky's trip up the elevator, the alert klaxons and sirens had silenced. He knew that as soon as *Necromancer* and *Lancelot* returned with their crews, the full complement of Strykers, save for the one destroyed, would be home and doing their jobs of protecting the inner city. Despite these facts, he had a nagging feeling that the cards would not be going his way. As a life-long gambler, he was attuned to his instincts and made decisions based on them, even when logic or the odds said differently. Listening to his gut and knowing the game made him more often than not a winner. This was no card game, however. He was in too deep as the appointed 'General' of the militia. Gillespie and his delusions of grandeur had been spiraling out of control for a few months. Ricky knew that it was a matter of time before his regime tumbled, possibly taking himself and his friend, Atwood, with him.

Stepping into the penthouse made the smell all the

more potent. Immediately, he was set upon by the 'armed Chihuahua', Harry Clima.

"What the hell happened in here?" Desmond demanded as he tried not to gag.

"Just a little clean up job, Desmond," Clima replied through the benefit of a biohazard mask which covered his nose and mouth, which gave his normally irritating voice a comically nasal tone. "What's the big idea with the alert?"

Ricky ignored the bodyguard's question and looked past him. Three men were cleaning the area where Costa was interrogated and eventually killed. They were wearing identical masks and coveralls that were once white. 'King' Gillespie was in his usual place upon his throne and also wearing one of the masks. Despite the instinct to regurgitate, Ricky Desmond smiled at the humorous sight.

"What's so damn funny, Ricky?" Harry sneered and came within inches of Desmond. The little bodyguard's face was upturned so that he may stare into the taller man's eyes.

Later on, Ricky would contemplate what happened next and chalk it up to a defense mechanism. Surrounded by filth and gore, unrealistic pressures from an employer that thought of himself as royalty, and being confronted by Harry, a demure, stupid, unscrupulous weasel who would have had to stand up on a chair to throw a punch to his jaw, Ricky Desmond broke into laughter. This was not just laughter as one would reward a well-told joke, this reaction was much more than that. Soon, Desmond was doubled over with one arm across his belly while the other was outstretched as he held an angry Harry Clima at bay with his palm on the little man's chest.

"Get your damn hand off me!" Clima shouted and swatted at Desmond's arm, never giving a thought to the fact that he could have simply taken a step backward.

This only refueled Ricky's gale of laughter. By this

time, all eyes in the room were on the general, even Gillespie's.

After a moment, Desmond realized that everyone but Clima had gone completely silent. All eyes were on him, however. He cleared his throat and stood to his full height. "Harry! *Harry*!"

Clima stopped struggling against the general's big hand long enough to realize that he was not being held in place. He slapped at the Desmond's hand, hard, but it remained.

Ricky's humor failed him at that point. Staring into the bodyguard's face, he clenched his teeth. "Harrrrry," he growled in warning.

Clima set his jaw and stared back, but slapped at the hand once more as he stepped to the side in one desperate act of defiance.

"Go on, then," he ordered in a shaky voice.

Desmond took his eyes from Clima and strode past the mess that was being cleaned. He watched Gillespie rotate his makeshift throne toward him as he approached.

"Quite a scene, General," the King of Reno granted. "Are you *trying* to get demoted to bodyguard?"

"No, sir," Desmond replied through his handkerchief. His head swam from the strength of the mixed odors in the room. "I'm here with a report. Figured you'd rather hear it from me than just over the phone."

"Oh, *do tell*, General," Gillespie oozed in a strange manner.

"Considering the extra element in the room, sir, I'd like to link," Ricky said and indicated the cleaning crew behind him.

"Continue," Gillespie granted and accepted Desmond's implant-to-implant communication.

"*Based on the pictures taken in Fernley, I believe a highly skilled group with elite military training is on the way here*," Ricky sent in text along with the pictures he had scanned into his implant's memory. He further explained the short exchange with someone from Lovelock in what he thought was Hernandez's personal vehicle, where another militiaman was killed and two others wounded. Desmond added that the city's militia was now on full alert and that he had ordered the two Stryker squads positioned in Fernley to return home.

The entire conversation was, of course, silent, but there was something in Gillespie's eyes that Desmond did not like at all. The mask on his face did nothing but make the hard gaze appear even more sinister. Ricky's gambler instincts told him that the dealer had one up his sleeve and was ahead of him, but he could not figure out how or why. Despite the bad feeling he had, he continued his report, though he kept an eye on Clima. If Gillespie was going to do something to him, it would be by the two-gunned bodyguard, and Harry was eyeing him steadily, hatefully.

"*We're thinking it's going to be a four or five man team*," Desmond continued in text, "*Since they didn't take out the Stryker at the outset with anti-tank rockets, I'd say they're limited to carrying the explosives that it took to destroy it after they killed the crew*."

"*Secure the usual places, General*," Gillespie sent in response as he sat back into his throne and looked down his nose upon Desmond. "*Are they on foot, this team of men?*"

"*As best as we can tell, sir*," Ricky described. "*The ambulance and escort vehicle that did the medical evac saw no other vehicles on the interstate*."

"*It sounds as if they could be here any time*," Gillespie opined and stroked his chin in thought. "*That helicopter had better be ready tomorrow, General*."

"*They tell me it should be ready by test flight time, Thirteen hundred hours*." This was a lie, of course.

The head of the engineering team had told Desmond that they were having a hard time getting the made-from-scratch instruments installed and working, just like the first one, and that they'd be lucky to get that done by tomorrow afternoon.

"*Good. I plan on being there to watch it go up,*" Gillespie announced.

"*I think that's a bad idea, sir,*" Ricky replied. "*It would be unsafe for you there. What if this enemy squad has the new helo as a target? If you showed up, you'd be one, too.*"

Gillespie seemed to think about this for a few moments, as the dark eyes continued to drill into his own. After a few too many extra seconds, Gillespie agreed. This was a relief to Desmond as he knew that there was no way for the people outside of Reno to know about the next helicopter. They had been discreet, moving the parts from the factory to the airport at night. Ricky agreed, though only because he had made a crucial decision. He was going to try to leave Reno that night.

"*I had better be able to see that Cobra from the windows of this suite, General,*" Gillespie sent in an audible message for dramatic effect.

Ricky Desmond agreed happily, anxious to leave the noxious fumes far behind him, get home, and pack.

Gillespie dismissed him abruptly by waving him away. As Ricky headed for the door, he pulled out a cigarette and lit it, desperate to add a pleasant odor to the smells of blood and death. With barely a look in Clima's direction, Desmond blew his first puff as he passed him.

"That's it," Clima seethed as he paced behind the appointed general, "you and me outside, pal."

"Aw, come on," Desmond returned, not slowing his gait. "Can't you do better than that?"

Harry sped on ahead of Ricky, opened the door for

the man, and eyed him as he went out. Clima slammed the door behind them and gave the bigger man a two-handed shove toward the elevators. He tore off his mask and immediately went after the general.

Desmond had expected the move and had allowed himself to go along with it, using the elevator doors to bounce from and meet his enemy sooner than he had expected. Before Clima understood what happened, a fist met him and he was sent to the floor on his back and seeing black. Blood flowed from his smashed nose.

Ricky had not so much as bent his cigarette in the exchange. He looked down at the semi-conscious bodyguard and allowed a smile.

"You know, Harry, I'd roll over if you don't want to choke on your own blood."

Clima did not respond, though his forearms remained bent at the elbow, stretching into the air as if he were still fighting. His unmoving eyes were crossed and the lids were barely open. Gurgling noises emitted from his throat as blood ran into it from his stricken sinuses.

Ricky struck the elevator call button as he watched the man on the floor. He knew that the security cameras would show Gillespie what happened, so he could tell for himself that he did not start the altercation. However, Desmond thought about his plan of departing the city that night and wanted nothing to stop him, not even a late night disciplinary chat about Clima.

As the doors opened behind him, Ricky bent and rolled the small angry man onto his side. Clima gagged and coughed blood onto the carpet, and in seconds, his breathing cleared.

"It's a good thing the cleaning crew's already here," Ricky said as he backed into the elevator.

The doors closed and immediately, the air quality around Desmond greatly improved. He breathed in deeply as he pressed the button for the floor he wanted.

***

It was approaching sundown when Mattersly led his two companions outside the old abandoned club. The grasses had grown nearly as tall as a man, but they were not green. The blades were brown and coarse, almost sharp to the skin as they passed through the brush on their way north. Occasionally, the grasses gave way to weathered and broken panels of concrete that had once served as a walking path which zig-zagged its way through the property.

After a few cautious moments, they stepped out into a small pond. Its surface was covered in green algae and moss. It was here that the insects grew to be annoying. They buzzed and landed, bit and harassed. The two military men wished they had insect repellent, but neither had seen any in years. Angel and Elias slapped at each one that landed. They got loud enough that the major had to halt them, turn around, and place his finger to his lips.

“Shhh,” he hissed gently.

The bugs were annoying him as well as the others, but he wiped them away with quiet fingertips, not slaps.

Elias and Angel nodded and adopted the quieter technique. The trio waded around the edge of the pond and entered another tall growth of brown grasses. Dozens of lizards and other creatures dispersed upon their entering this thatch. It was not very deep however, as the next thing they found was the back end of a cul-de-sac, bracketed by a gaggle of once expensive luxury homes.

Mattersly took a knee and signaled everyone else to be silent. The sun was in their faces at this point, so the major knew that they were vulnerable if anyone was watching for them. After a few moments, the SRR officer led them through the brush and around the empty space that was the street. Once they had the cover of the supposedly abandoned homes, Reginald moved from one to the next. In this manner, they passed from one neighborhood, into another valley of growth and insects, across a creek, which was not wide but was deep enough to soak Angel to her hips, and into yet another neighborhood.

More than an hour of this cautious travel was endured before Reginald heard a motor vehicle. It was now nighttime, but that offered little solace when it came to infrared technology. They still had to stay aloof and away from any suspected Renoite vehicles or militia members.

The three of them crouched alongside a structure while the major listened. It was a large motor, most likely diesel, like the Strykers, but perhaps lighter. Mattersly peered around the corner of the empty abode and could see a large street ahead of them. According to his implant's map, they were not far from the airport.

The sound of the motor faded, so the major continued around the corner and went ahead, motioning for Mulhaney and Angel to follow. Another small field was crossed and yet another neighborhood was discovered beyond that. This one was more diverse than the others from a construction standpoint. While all the structures were put together using the same materials, they differed in layout. They needed to turn northward at this point and head for the commercial/industrial district immediately east of the airport. Here, they could observe the airport and remain concealed.

They were now close enough to the airport that the lights of the airfield and some of the surrounding hangars gave the streets an ambience which could make it easier for them to be spotted out in the open.

After passing through the residential section, things got trickier. There was another creek to cross before they could reach the large commercial buildings beyond it, bracketed by somewhat steep embankments of soil and brush. Reginald stopped his companions near a group of trees and signaled them to sit.

"I shall cross first," he whispered, "Angel, you're second. Mister Mulhaney, please bring up the rear."

With that, he turned and silently descended the dirt embankment and entered the water slowly. Even with a heavy pack, a Dragunov on his shoulder, and an assault rifle in his hands, Angel and Elias had to strain to hear the man's movements. Only the dim light from the airport, the stars and the cloud-covered, partial moon above let them see that he was moving at all. The water was thigh deep and was crossed in a passel of steps. Through a break in the brush on the opposite bank, Mattersly scaled the incline and stood absolutely still for nearly two minutes as he watched and listened for signs of movement anywhere. Finally, he turned and waved his arm, which was barely visible in the gloom of night.

Angel went next, cringing at every sound she made as she trampled sticks and brush on her way down to the water, where she splashed like a wounded trout in comparison to the SRR trained Mattersly. As she was shorter, the water level settled above her hips, but she traced Reginald's steps perfectly. She crawled in the dirt to keep quiet and low, eventually joining the major at the top of the embankment.

He waved for Mulhaney.

"Sorry, Major," Angel offered in whisper. "I sounded like a bison crossing the rapids."

"You did fine," he replied, but placed a finger over his lips.

Mulhaney managed to cross nearly as quietly as Reginald, but his walking stick and awkwardness with the right leg made him the slowest of them.

From that point, the three moved from shadow to shadow along the rear of the first building, an abandoned trucking depot. Led by Major Mattersly, they disturbed nothing but the occasional lizard and a feral cat as they stepped slowly and silently along in the near darkness.

The building was long and, like many industrial or commercial structures, bore a high ceiling. The east side of it was lined with large garage doors that accommodated the extinct, over-the-road tractor/trailer vehicles, and many of them were fully opened. Each time they passed one, the wind whistled over the metal surfaces of the immense doorjambs. With his night vision set at maximum, Mattersly could see for a distance inside. There were scatterings of crates and bits of discarded junk all throughout the inside of the structure. The vast ceiling was supported with rows of white posts that were set in a regular and orderly spacing. There were even the remains of a few of the mighty tractor/trailers. None appeared functional, of course, certainly having been scavenged for parts.

After some minutes, they arrived at the building's northeastern corner. Mattersly peered around it to the west and saw nothing. He was expecting as such, as his map indicated that a runway lie in the distance. Ahead of them to the north was a large parking lot, scattered with the remnants of vehicles. There were cars, trucks, trailers, and even a few aircraft. The largest of which appeared to be a commercial airliner with its landing gear up. Thusly, the airplane's fuselage was flush with the ground. The engine-laden wings had succumbed to gravity, leaving the massive propulsion plants to lie almost as flat as the body.

"Our next destination is a building on the other side of this lot," Reginald briefed. "It appears we have much cover in case we're spotted, but let's move quietly. Shall we?"

"Lead on, Major," Mulhaney whispered.

To Mattersly's gratification, the former paratrooper sounded unfettered by their travels and quite upbeat.

Reginald walked into the darkness, heading for the cover of one abandoned vehicle after the other. With his head and eyes constantly moving, he led his companions across the graveyard of man's creations.

It was not until he came within sixty meters of the large airliner that he realized the fire damage to the craft. The plane was not simply discarded and allowed to decay, it had crash landed there.

Just another in a million stories of the aftermath of the 'Great Exodus', he supposed.

Silently, they all passed it, each staring at the once-great machine in awe. The youngest of them, Angel, had never seen one fly. As they came closer, she took in the sight of it, trying to catch all the details in the dim light, but it was not possible given her human vision.

The wind stirred up the junk in the parking lot. Something in the distance to their east sounded a bit like the wind chimes that Elias's grandmother used to have hanging in her backyard. He thought of her briefly as he shuffled along, tempted to activate his damaged *CTL-Link* to view some of his family photos. A shiver ran through his sweat-covered body when he thought about the consequences. He did not wish to put his companions in danger if the implant were to malfunction, as his body could react in seizure-like fashion. These occasions were rare, but something to fear.

Mattersly took a knee once he reached the last piece of cover on the parking lot. It was a tipped over cargo trailer. Ahead of them was the structure Reginald sought. It was a two-story office building across an empty four-lane highway. It was missing several windows and its entry was agape as if something had crashed through it. Magnifying his view, Reginald confirmed that an automobile had been driven inside the structure, taking out the entrance way.

"Does everyone see that building across this

roadway?" he whispered behind him. He received affirmative answers. "The entrance is at its far left. One at a time as before, I shall meet you there."

Elias and Angel nodded, so Reginald stood, checked the area all around them, and proceeded forward at a near jog. His footfalls were extremely light and inaudible after some meters of travel. Even the items on his person, the loudest of which were the metal rings on the Dragunov's strap, could no longer be heard once he made it to the center of the road.

A minute went by and Angel realized that it was too dark to see the major, even if he waved to them as he disappeared into shadow.

"All right, I'm just gonna go for it," she announced and stood. A rumbling noise pierced the quiet night and froze her in fear. A chill shot through her tired frame. "Oh, shit," she squeaked.

"Shhhh," Mulhaney urged as he patted her on the shoulder.

He looked everywhere, but could not find the source of the sound. The low-toned drone was hauntingly, freshly familiar to him. After a moment, it became louder as the machine began to move. As he could not see it, he assumed that the vehicle was to the west, toward the airport. Elias grasped Angel by her tunic's collar and leaned forward to whisper in her ear.

"Listen to me. We're going to back up. Come on. That's it, Angel."

The young lady swung her head in every direction, trying to pick out which direction the sound was coming from.

"Where is it?" she half-whispered, half-shrieked.

"Shhhh," Mulhaney insisted as he pulled her with him. "We're going inside this container here and let them pass. Okay?"

"Great," she agreed and turned around to see where she was being led. "I need a place to change my pants. I just shit myself."

"Nice. Come on!" he hissed and rounded the corner of the tipped-over container, stepping upon the door which had been laid flat on the ground. The inside was pitch black and it had the aroma of mildew and decaying aluminum, but it would keep them out of sight of anything passing on the street.

The two crouched in the darkness, listening to their breath echoing off the metal walls as the diesel engine droned on and on, increasing in volume by the second, and sending acute vibrations throughout the trailer via the concrete ground it lay upon.

From across the street, Mattersly watched his companions retreat just as the street began to be set aglow with blue-white light. He had made it within the broken entranceway and had crouched against the western-most wall when the engine of what he assumed was a Stryker kicked on. He could hear the machine rolling toward their location and looked about for a place to hide. He knew that the machines had night vision and infrared, therefore, he had to become as concealed as his companions across the way.

Quickly, Reginald slipped along the wall and went to the crushed nose of the vehicle, which had bounced back from its collision with an interior wall. Moving through this gap, he crawled behind the broken reception counter and removed a couple of items from his backpack, which he laid on the floor along with his Dragunov. If Mulhaney and Angel were discovered, he would have to strike fast. Almost from instinct, he thought the command to shut down his implant in case the enemy attempted a 'pinging' tactic. On his knees and crouched forward toward the street, Reginald held a C-4 charge in one hand and thought through his method of attack if the machine discovered them.

***

"I'm not seeing anything, now," the commander said lowly into his helmet microphone as he traversed the periscope from left to right and back.

"I'm telling ya, Chief, it was a wolf or somethin'," the driver repeated.

"Maybe," the young soldier in command of the vehicle mumbled.

He thought that the heat signature he had seen on the monitor was more upright than that of an animal, but now, finding nothing, he was no longer sure.

"Stop here a minute," he ordered and trained the machine gun turret to the left, aiming the fifty-caliber machine guns on the second floor windows of the building they were approaching.

The driver pulled the machine out of gear and let it coast a moment before applying the brakes. He peered through his driver's window, saw nothing, and then turned his eyes back to the monitor.

"Who wants to get out and have a look?" the commander turned to his six-man squad. Normally, off alert, his machine would only be assigned three, but it was a full house tonight.

"Aw, come on, Terry," the oldest militiaman chided, "you see a dog and we're supposed to go chase it for ya?"

At twenty-three, the disgruntled mercenary was known to be a complainer, which was the reason for his low rank. He was a large man, however, and somewhat intimidating.

The nineteen-year-old commander sighed heavily through his nose as he pondered the cost of bowing to the opinion of an underling. His periscope lit the night with a lime green sky and as it passed over a dirty white cargo trailer on their right, the monitor went bright with reflected infrared beams. He quickly traversed it in the other direction and made a decision.

"All right. Tell you guys what," he began and turned to face his detractor and the other five infantrymen, "We'll go around the block a couple of times. The report said to look for a squad of men, which that definitely wasn't." He turned to his driver, "Okay let's go for a ride."

***

Mulhaney stared into the dark depths of the trailer, turning his useless eyes toward the sound of the machine beyond. Angel's breathing came and went in small hitches. Her mind seemed clear, however, as she kept her weapon pointed to the open doors in the opposite direction. Elias turned toward her and could see the barrel of the weapon in the meager ambient light that graced the entryway. His heart pounded heavily in his chest as he listened to the idling mechanical monster outside. He slipped the sniper rifle from his shoulder and quietly set it upon the trailer wall, which was now the floor. Even though he knew the machine gun of the personnel carrier outside could tear right through the trailer, there was no reason not to back Angel, at least morally. It was conceivable that the machine had released a squad of infantry for a search. He pointed his M27 to the opening and waited with her.

Mattersly dared not sneak a look around the desk at what was happening, for to do so was to risk being picked up as a bright red and orange heat signature. It was bad enough that he was probably lightening the room a few shades of blue from his body heat. He gripped the C-4 charge in his hand and remained coiled and ready to spring into action if the men in the carrier made a move or opened fire. He wished he was closer to the door, for it was about forty-five meters to his target.

The machine lurched forward with a heart-pounding surge of its diesel plant. The tiled floor beneath the major's knees rumbled faintly as the eight-wheeled vehicle accelerated away. Despite his calm appearance, had anyone been able to see him at all, droplets of sweat left Reginald's face and fell to the floor as he resumed his normal breathing.

He remained still, however. Even though he had not heard the tailgate of the machine open, it did not mean that boots were not on the ground. The major took several more breaths as he quietly replaced the C-4 charge in his pack, took the assault weapon into his hands, and lifted his aching body from the floor just high enough to peek over the top of the upturned desk.

His eyes centered on a tree that grew amongst the brown brush on the island which divided the lanes. Beyond that was the trailer, unmolested as the ambient light of the night glowed from its dirty white surface. Quickly, Reginald gathered his backpack and Dragunov as he reinitiated his implant. In a crouch, he made his way toward the front of the broken building, leaving the cover of the wrecked automobile and daring a quick peek around the wall up the street. The Stryker was gone, but he could still hear the engine. It had rounded the corner and was heading north. There was no sign of any soldiers on foot.

As he stretched his spine under the weight of the backpack, Elias's identification flashed on his implant's display and was followed by a message. Mulhaney had dared activate his ailing unit to contact the major.

"*Is it clear?*" it read.

"*For the moment, yes. Send Angel. I have you covered,*" Reginald sent, though the promise of cover was a weak one considering the metal predator that they hid from.

Angel emerged from the trailer and ran at her best speed toward the major. In the dark, she nearly tripped over the brush in the center island, but recovered enough to keep her feet. She arrived nearly out of breath. Elias was on his way next before she could speak.

"Where... is... that damn... thing?" she managed from her knees.

"Keep your voice down," the major warned as he watched the night for the enemy.

Mulhaney was taking a painfully long time to cross in comparison to Angel and the personnel carrier's engine was becoming louder.

"I believe it's circling the area. I'm afraid that the commander caught a glimpse of me as I skipped across."

"That's just great," she went on after catching more of her breath. "I never came this far west, Major. We're too close to the militia posts."

"My dear, Angel," the major said, suddenly irritated, "perhaps you've forgotten the bloody point of this mission. Of course we're close to the militia guard posts and patrols or whatever the bloody hell it is that they wish to call them."

"Hey, guys..." Elias broke in as he entered.

"I intend on getting a hell of a lot closer," the major finished.

"...I think we better stay put for a few," finished Mulhaney.

"We're not staying put for a bloody moment," the major pressed hotly. "I need to get closer to the airport to determine the location of that Cobra, if there even is one."

"I think that Stryker crew may have something to say about that, Major," Elias whispered as he took a knee within the shadows of the building. "It's coming back."

"I can hear it, Mister Mulhaney," Mattersly agreed. "Come on, there must be an exit on the north wall somewhere," he declared and strode back into the dark depths of the structure.

The diesel engine's call was increasing in volume, confirming what Elias had said. As the major looked about the wreckage that was once a reception room, Mattersly found a recess in a wall and within it, a door. It opened freely and a small room lay beyond it. The windows facing that direction were cracked and shattered, keeping the area from becoming pitch black. The wall on the right was solid and windowless.

"Get in here, quickly," the major said loudly enough to be heard over the approaching vehicle's engine.

He knew that Angel could not see very well, so he reached out and took her hand to guide her inside. Elias followed slowly, but flawlessly. He seemed to have kept the implants on, at least for the moment. The man shut the door behind them as the Renoite vehicle rolled on by them.

"Right," Mattersly said as he stared northward into the night, "it's twenty-two hundred hours and I understand that you're both tired, but we must remember how much further we are along thanks to Mister Innes."

"True," Angel conceded and continued to catch her breath.

"As you have all seen, several buildings at the airport are well-lit," the major went on. "It is my plan to get you two to a safe position where you may sack out for the night."

"Wait, so then what are you going to do?" Mulhaney asked.

"I am going to determine whether or not there is a Cobra helicopter," Reginald explained flatly. "If I find it, I shall place a C-4 charge upon it and destroy it."

"Great, and we're supposed to just let you do that on your own?" Angel protested.

"You will both just slow me down," Mattersly said frankly. "I should like to get this girl rescued and out of here and as soon as possible. Destroying the helo may give

Gillespie the proper motivation to negotiate."

Elias and Angel looked to one another in the silvery gloom. They both knew he was right.

"Okay, Major," she said, "let's go."

A back door was soon located and the trio again stepped out into the night. There was no report of the diesel motor and, in contrast, the night had become ominously silent. Mattersly led his two companions between buildings at a pace that allowed him to be stealthy and cautious. They marched in a northwesterly direction, passing from block to block with no sign of life anywhere.

The trio marched through the maze of abandoned industrial and commercial structures for nearly a kilometer when the sound of a vehicle pierced the stillness. He froze and his followers did the same, looking to their leader as they listened intently. Reginald quickly pondered their situation and decided that no matter what building housed the supposed aircraft, it would be nearby.

"Right," he whispered to them, "we are heading to that building there," he pointed northward and strode off at a fast walking pace. Eerily silent were his steps as he led them.

Mulhaney followed as quickly as he could manage, but the other two left him in the darkness as they passed into the shadows of the next warehouse. His own steps were quiet in the extreme, however ruined by the rhythmic, but muted tapping of his walking stick. He cursed to himself as he struggled to catch up. Arriving in the utter blackness that his companions had stepped into, he found the need to tap the wall of the structure at his left to keep from straying from it. Looking up, he found that the overhang of the roof was keeping the three of them from the dim starlight. He contemplated restarting the *CTL-Link*, but refrained.

"Elias," Angel called out in a high whisper.

Her voice sounded close, so Mulhaney slowed. "Here," he replied in kind.

"The Major wants us to follow him across the street," she passed on. "As soon as I head out, count twenty before you start."

Elias could see the major scampering across the street, lit again by the night sky and the sliver of moon. In another few yards, he was indistinguishable from the trees which grew wildly along a strip of dirt embedded into the concrete, which had, at one time, served as a divider between properties. Beyond that was their destination.

"Got it," he whispered.

Angel looked about the area before exposing herself to the clearing then broke into a jog, which set her belongings into a soft jingling. Noting this, she slowed to a brisk walk, which helped to limit the noise.

Elias counted twenty just as she disappeared into the trees before setting off. When he came to the line of trees, he stopped and leaned upon one of them to catch his breath. He stared at the building across the empty parking lot and noted the side door, which appeared to be wide open, though he could have been mistaken as it was shaded by a tall and long-ungroomed tree.

In moments, he arrived at the shadowed doorway and stepped through blindly, but without obstruction.

"We're here, Mister Mulhaney," Reginald said quietly, to which Elias let out a breath of relief.

"I want you two to stay here and find a place to sack out for the night," he continued as he let his pack settle to the dusty floor.

"What are you going to do?" Angel asked from the darkness.

"I am going for a quick reconnoiter of the area," he announced quietly, "and attempt to reach an antennae tower that I saw on the way in here. It is directly to our west."

"Seeking a higher vantage point, Major?" Elias asked as he let go of his heavy pack as well. "Doesn't that put you at risk of being picked up on thermal?"

"It does, indeed," the major agreed as he fumbled through his pack. The swishes of coarse fabric could be heard as the major changed his clothing. "If you two would be so kind as to secure my pack and assault weapon, I shall be off."

"I'd argue with you, but I trust that you're right about moving faster alone at this point," Mulhaney felt obligated to admit.

He was exhausted and he could see in the dim light, which set the small office aglow, that Angel was, too. She lay on the floor with her torso relaxed against her pack, which was pressed into the wall.

"Seek an interior office to hide in for the night," Reginald advised as he set the assault rifle upon his discarded backpack. "I will be back as soon as I can. Mister Mulhaney, I have to ask you to at least try to access your implant to monitor for messages if I am unable to return by dawn, though I am hopeful that I shall return before that."

"I understand," Elias replied.

"Stay hidden and rest," the major directed as he shook Elias's hand and that of Angel's.

"Good luck," Mulhaney wished.

"Thank you, sir," Reginald responded as he approached the open door.

"Hurry back," Angel called after, not knowing what else to say.

"I shall," the major said over his shoulder just before disappearing into the night as if he had been nothing but black smoke.

"I sure as hell hope he knows what he's doing," she murmured as she struggled to regain her feet.

"I have no doubt that he does," Mulhaney added. "I

feel sorry for the bastards that get in his way."

"You have a lot of faith in that man," she commented as she picked up Reginald's assault weapon.

"I've been similarly trained," Elias answered as he followed the young woman around a counter and toward an open interior door. "Let's just say I understand him and would be helping him if I were able."

"I understand," she whispered. "I didn't mean any offense."

"I didn't take any," he replied as he set his weapons and backpack on the floor next to her things.

She had settled into a hallway that remained in the gloom. To have ventured any further was to step inside utter darkness.

Without another word, the two stretched out upon the hard floor, having cushioned it as best they could with the thin bedrolls they had been lugging around. In moments, both were dozing soundly, despite their worry about Mattersly and their mission.

Chapter Eleven

As much as Reginald Mattersly enjoyed the company of his two companions, he was glad to be rid of them for the moment. Although his doubts about Mulhaney's ability had been unfounded other than the man's speed and his faith in Angel's knowledge of the area made her invaluable, he was glad to handle this part of the mission alone.

He was able to move quickly in the darkness, free of the weight of his backpack. Reginald even found himself running from cover to cover instead of walking or jogging. The cool night air felt great on his sweat-covered skin and for the first time since they had abandoned the destroyed police car, he felt confident about their mission.

As he came closer to the antenna tower, the resonating sounds of engines became clearer. None sounded like the diesel plants that powered the personnel carriers, but they certainly represented large vehicles.

He stepped silently along the wall of yet another low, one story commercial building and set his Dragunov across his back, rather than upon his shoulder to keep it in place. If he were to discover Renoite guards at this point, he would have to dispatch them at close range and as quietly as possible. For that, he possessed other tools besides his firearms.

Reginald stepped past the long-unused satellite dishes that lay next to the gray building and peered around the southwest corner. It was here that the antenna tower had been built. He deduced that the structure had at one time, and perhaps still was, a radio or television broadcasting station.

Wasting no time, he located the tower's ladder and propelled himself into the air, step by stealthy step. Mulhaney's warning about being picked up by thermal imagers had been quite real, but he was gambling that the Strykers and other militia personnel in the area were concentrating on the ground, not in the air. Before he realized it, Mattersly had crawled nearly to the top, some forty to forty-five meters above the ground. From here, he found he could see everything in the lit airport grounds within four hundred meters to the west.

He sat upon a flat surface just a short distance from the very top of the antenna and utilized the scope on his rifle to search the few buildings of the airport. He looked at the grouping of warehouse-type structures in front of him. They were unlit, but benefited from the lights coming from a building and a series of light poles closer to the runway. Among these buildings, there seemed to be no activity. There was no light emanating from within them and no vehicles were parked nearby.

The building directly to his west seemed the most likely candidate for the purposes of assembling and storing an aircraft such as a Cobra. Recalling the intelligence map that Jazz had made from her spies' debriefings, it could very well have been the one hand-drawn rectangle that Angel had identified as the machine's hangar. In his estimation, it was probably a hangar once owned by a corporation, as it was nearly three stories tall at its peak and featured a large parking lot that faced the road between himself and it. As he scanned the well-lit property, he found two vehicles in the parking lot. Obviously, they were quite old as none had been commercially produced on Earth for more than thirty years, but both appeared to be well-maintained and functional. One was a rather large sedan and the other, a two-seater with a high stance, intended, perhaps for off-road travel.

What Mattersly saw next froze him solid. Two men in black and dark gray militia garb rounded the southeastern corner of the building. Through his scope, he could see that they were talking as they walked. Both were armed with rifles that hung onto their shoulders. One lit a cigarette, halted his walk, and leaned against the building. The other stopped and stood facing the smoker, with his back toward Mattersly.

Reginald held his rifle on the two men, took his eyes from the scope to check his surroundings, and then scrutinized them all over again. They appeared to be young men, having rather immature body language as they spoke. Both men were too animated and lively to be experienced soldiers. Neither seemed concerned that they were to be on the lookout for intruders.

He wondered if George Innes could have been wrong about the meaning of the sirens.

If so, had he been intentionally misleading? Was he setting a trap for us? Certainly not.

Reginald decided that the man could have easily turned the three of them in and they would never have gotten as far into Reno as they had.

Just as the major had decided which building was the most likely candidate for housing the Cobra, an approaching vehicle confirmed his deduction. From the north, a rather large truck slowly rolled along the well-cared-for street and turned into the parking lot. As it did, the open bed revealed a gaggle of darkly colored crates that lay in the back. Reginald focused on them as the truck stopped for two guards that he never saw until that moment. They had been seated around some trees that decorated the parking lot, possibly even taking a nap.

Fortunately, the truck stopped underneath a light. The driver spoke to one of the sleepy sentries while the other looked underneath the vehicle with a flashlight and quickly scanned the contents in the truck's bed. Upon one crate, the major read: "Hydra 70," amongst other information stamped in white. Checking his *UnitCom*'s encyclopedia of weapons, he discovered that a Hydra was an unguided, air-to-ground rocket originally created in the twentieth century. It made sense, as the AH-1 itself was originally designed in the 1960's.

Reginald had to give Gillespie some credit. Reno's weapons were simple to build, simple to maintain, and required no computer software or high-tech sensors. Anything more sophisticated would require a mind that was now probably trying to design computer or satellite networks on the colony planet.

"Blimey," he mumbled as he watched the truck drive into the large hangar in front of him. He secured the Dragunov to his back and turned to descend the tower.

He had found his target.

***

"Hey, let me have one of those, will ya?" the younger of the two sentries said to the other. "I can't stay awake here."

"Sure," said the other one, "but you owe me two, now."

"I'll remember," the first one replied over the sound of the departing truck engine. "Are they finally done? That's the third delivery truck tonight," he commented as he bent to light the tobacco.

"I don't know," the first one said. He was clearly unconcerned, though he watched the old truck drive away into the night.

Behind them and a mere handful of meters away, a dark figure passed. It made no sound as it went from tree to tree and shadow to shadow. Neither sentry had a chance to notice anything, as the figure was long gone before either of them passed their eyes over the space that it had briefly occupied.

The figure quickly approached the great white structure and its body adapted in color while crouching ever lower to the ground. Leaving the dirt surface, the intruder slithered along the pavement as it passed a closed garage door along the building's east wall. Just meters away was a door meant for human use. A darkly colored hand reached up to the knob and gave it a turn.

The sounds of voices wafted through the air over the sounds of approaching footsteps. The conversation was loud, considering what the mercenaries were supposed to be guarding and what their orders had directed.

The door opened and closed without a sound other than the gentle clicking of the lock in the knob. The sentries strode by without notice, never varying the level of their voices during their inane conversation.

Mattersly kept his ear to the door as he listened to their steps go quiet. His eyes scanned the room in night vision mode, as light could only be seen at the far end of the hallway in either direction. There were a few offices with glass windows across from him, but all were quiet and dark.

The reactive camouflage in Mattersly's tunic and trousers went a matte black and gray as it sensed the light levels of the room. Looking both ways, he noted no security cameras, though the walls at the far ends were marked with holes as if some large ones had once been present. Still, this was no guarantee that his presence was not in some way being monitored. For several seconds, he remained still before moving on. He chose to walk, heavily stooped, toward the large garage door at his left and crossed to the opposite wall as he approached the corner. At shin-level, he peered around it.

As if given a gift from a god, Reginald was rewarded with a view of the tail end of the Cobra. He smiled, though he was careful even here, not to display his teeth, which would have shown a brilliant white against the camouflaged makeup upon his face and neck. His boonie hat left the whites of his eyes in shadow. The hangar was active with people. He could hear them walking about on the pristine cement floor and speaking to each other in hushed tones. Many crates similar to those that had just been delivered lined the wall to his left, though many were set flush against it, preventing him from moving forward for a better look.

The sudden presence of a man in tan coveralls forced Reginald to retreat into the shadows, though he was able to keep him in sight for a second. The worker was short, sweaty, and obviously tired, giving the impression that he had been working on the Cobra for a long period of time. This made sense to Mattersly, for surely the Renoites needed to get this new aircraft in the air to replace the one he had shot down.

The major retreated and silently made his way down the hallway in the other direction. He encountered more unused offices and a main reception foyer, all in the dark and devoid of human life.

Dust on the floor indicated that the area was still at least occasionally used, as it collected near the walls, not in the high traffic areas. Counters and desks with chairs appeared to have more on their surfaces, telling the major that the foyer was seldom used for anything but a passageway. In short order, he found another, shorter hallway that led further into the building. His heart pounded with anticipation and alertness as he ventured into its dark depths.

Reginald checked the time on his implant's chronometer. It was just past midnight. He was not surprised, as a stealthy approach required much patience and time. He linked with his uniform's computer and noted its high power consumption, and shut it down. As it depended on solar energy for its aged nano-lithium cells, he knew that it would not be getting a recharge anytime soon and he would be depending on its color-adaptive technology to escape.

Additionally, the *UnitCom* itself only had only thirty-seven percent of its battery life remaining and the night vision he was employing was eating it up at a good rate. At the moment, there was nothing he could do about it.

Mattersly then found a sign upon a wall. "Conference Room" it read along with an arrow that pointed upward and to his left. Here, he found a set of stairs and decided to utilize them. As he ascended, he became grateful that the building had been built to a high standard. Not a single step creaked as he went upward and soon, he found the conference room and a wall made of glass. The room was dark, so Reginald ventured a glance. There, below him lay the nearly assembled AH-1 Cobra copy.

The mechanics and technicians swarmed about the flying machine, installing cockpit instruments and the rocket pods onto the hardpoints. Everything else about the helo appeared to be finished, including the twin fifty-caliber machine gun turret on its chin.

Reginald nodded to himself as he thought of the unfortunate pilot of the Cobra he had brought down. With her last breaths, she had told him the truth.

Now, all I have to do is figure out how to destroy this damn thing without being discovered, he thought.

He sat upon the dusty conference table and visually inspected the structure of the hangar. The major smiled when he saw the catwalks that ran along the north and south walls and it broadened when his eyes fell upon the maintenance crane mounted in the ceiling's steel beams.

The time on his implant's display read 00:33. It would be dawn in less than five hours.

***

A pleasant dream turned foul and awakened Elias

Mulhaney. It had become slightly brighter in the hallway in which he and Angel were stretched out, making him think that dawn was approaching. Without thinking, he sat up and began to stretch. In the blink of his eyes, the room went dark again and the floor rumbled.

"Shit," he breathed, as the rhythmic chuffing of an engine filled the air and shook the walls.

Elias watched as the glow of a spotlight reflected from surface to surface of their hideout's interior walls and furniture. He blinked the sleep from his eyes and struggled to his feet, the assault weapon was already in his hands as he pondered what to do.

"What the hell?" Angel whispered from her place on the floor.

"Get up," he ordered as he disengaged the safety of his weapon. "Take your stuff and find an empty room up the hallway. *Now*."

Angel scampered to pick up her own weapon and backpack. In the dark, her belongings were the only ones she could locate. She took one step backward and promptly fell over Mattersly's pack, which she had forgotten was there. Her M27 hit the tiled floor with a clatter and, though her fall was broken by her own pack, her breath was forced from her in a pained, guttural oration.

Elias winced, for he knew that if anyone was outside the building, Angel's error would have been heard. Against his trepidations over an implant malfunction, Mulhaney thought the activation command. Flawlessly, it responded and began its boot-up process.

The sound of voices erupted in response to Angel's fall and the reception area of the building lit up. In a blink, a Renoite militiaman appeared with his weapon up. Elias depressed the trigger of his M27 and dropped him in with a three-round burst. His ears were protected from the powerful sounds by the implant's audio receptors, but it was still loud in the close quarters of the narrow hallway.

Mulhaney turned to Angel and shouted, "*Move! Now!*"

Retreating into the darkness with his weapon trained forward, he adjusted his vision just as the twin machine guns of the Stryker opened up. Dust, bits of counter, and furniture filled the air as the rounds ripped the room apart.

Then, the turret began to rotate and rounds came through the wall ahead of him. He turned as he stepped backward unevenly and found a door. He reached for the knob and it opened for him. He understood that Angel could not see it, so he grabbed her by the shirt and brought her inside with him.

"*Get flat!*" he screamed over the rapid firing monstrosity and flung himself over a long-unused metal and wood desk.

He flipped it onto its side and dragged the young woman behind it right as the wall and door they had just passed through began to be torn up by the hail of bullets. He fell to the floor and got as flat as he could.

***

"Man down! We have a man down!" the driver of the Stryker known as *Wolfhunter* called out in his young screechy voice.

His gunner was experienced and was able to aim carefully as the driver turned the machine in a tight circle to put more distance between it and the infiltrated building.

"*Almighty Oz*, this is *Wolfhunter*. Repeating! We are under fire and I have a man down!"

The driver put another twenty meters between his vehicle and the building and stopped. Covering the microphone of his helmet, he turned to the remaining two men in his assigned squad.

"Get out there, join Anton and get Volpe the hell

out of that building. We'll cover!"

One of his squad smacked the button that opened the ramp at the rear of the vehicle. Both men jumped out and began a sprint to toward the assaulted building even before it was completely lowered.

In the gloom of predawn, the quicker of the two militiamen found Anton crouching at the doorway to the office building that the Stryker was reducing to dust with its machine guns. He changed his direction slightly to meet his fellow soldier and poured on the speed just as something struck him from behind and sent him to the pavement, lifeless.

The militiaman behind the stricken soldier dropped to the ground immediately and searched westward from where the round must have come from. It was a logical deduction as his colleague was struck on his left side and sent sprawling to the ground with utter finality. He could see no one, even with his night vision. There were trees lining the strip of dirt that separated the parking lot from the street.

"*Christ!*" screeched *Wolfhunter*'s driver when he saw his second man drop. "We're taking fire from the west," he proclaimed as he traversed his periscope in that direction.

"On it," answered the gunner as he swung the turret that way.

Even though he saw no one, he opened up on the building that lay in that direction, spraying the windows with rounds.

The militiaman named Anton could see what was happening and decided to take cover inside the building that his friend Volpe had been investigating when he had been taken down. On the chance that the shot that felled his second squad member had come from inside the torn up building, Anton covered the hallway with his weapon and charged inside.

"*Almighty Oz*! This is *Wolfhunter*! Over!" the Stryker's driver tried again.

"*Wolfhunter*, *Almighty* here. Go ahead. Over," came the lazy voice of the militia's night shift radio operator.

"Wake the fuck up over there and get us some help! I've got two men down!" he shouted then turned his attention to the vehicle status on his monitor.

He then realized that he had left the ramp open and stabbed the square on the screen to close it. As it lifted from the pavement, a metallic object tumbled inside.

"What the hell?" he had time to say before the world went white and his ears became painfully deaf.

***

"*Wolfhunter*... *Wolfhunter*! *Almighty Oz* here. Report. Over!" the young trooper called into the microphone for the tenth time. He cussed harshly, picked up the phone, and dialed for help. "Mister Atwood. Apologies, sir, but we have a Stryker that was just engaged by enemy fire and now he's off the air."

"Where?" Bill Atwood asked as he hopped out of bed just two floors below.

"They never got a chance to tell me, sir, but it's *Wolfhunter*. It was assigned to the airfield."

"Alert the airport guardhouse and call General Desmond," Atwood directed. "I'm on my way up."

He hung up the phone, finished dressing, and hoped that Ricky had not split town like he had alluded to doing. He was fairly sure he had not, for Atwood was still convinced that Desmond had full confidence in his old friend and would not have left him behind. That sentimentality would lead to his demise.

Atwood slammed the door to his suite and bolted for the elevator.

***

Wolfhunter's driver regained enough of his senses to realize that someone had entered the vehicle from an overhead hatch and a struggle was going on near him. He still could not see, though the quality of the whiteness had changed. His ears screeched more than rang and a tremendous pain, dizziness, and nausea enveloped him. He tried to speak, but managed only to cough each time he inhaled. It mattered not a bit as he realized that his helmet with the microphone had gone.

The body of his gunner fell to the floor. His eyesight returned to make out that much under the dim cabin lights. The man's face was purple and grotesquely swollen with eyes nearly out of their sockets. The driver tried to yell, but could not. When he reached for his hatch to escape, a kick to his ribs stopped him and he was dragged out of his seat and onto the floor of the vehicle. The whiteness turned to darkness. Only his struggle for air let him know that he was still living.

"What's your name, son?" a voice said to him.

The accent was strange and it was hard to hear given the ringing and pressure in his ears. At the moment, he had no recourse than to answer the question put to him.

"Jim," he managed and followed with a cough.

He looked into his attacker's face and found it to be heavily camouflaged. In the smoky and dim cabin, he could not even determine the man's hair or eye color.

"Jim, I need your help."

The driver turned to see the face of his dead gunner and nodded quickly. He realized at that moment that the camouflaged man was holding him in place with a knee across his pelvis and a stiff arm to his chest. It was difficult for him to breathe and almost impossible to move. He had a feeling that if he had chosen to swing upon his attacker, it would have little effect. Jim nodded in acquiescence.

"I need you to get your commanding officer on the

radio," the strange man explained calmly. Gunshots erupted from outside the vehicle, drawing the attention of the man that had just captured the Stryker to the gun monitor. "Ah, it would seem that my team has disposed of your remaining men."

Jim's eyes bulged in surprise, anger, and fright. Still, he remained quiet for the moment.

"You see, I need to talk to your town's leader, Gillespie," the captor went on. "He has a little girl in his possession that he needs to return to her aunt."

"Who are you?" Jim coughed out.

"You'll find out shortly if you make that radio call."

Jim nodded.

"Good man," the captor said and picked him up from the floor with tremendous ease and set him in the commander's seat. Jim received his helmet and was forcibly turned forward. "Now, you will watch what you say, young man or I shall have to put a bullet in your brain."

"Yes, sir."

"What is your commander's name?"

"General Desmond," the young soldier answered.

"A general? Really."

Jim nodded.

"Right, well, put this conversation on speaker."

Jim nodded stupidly again and pressed a key. A speaker popped and crackled.

"Very good. Now, get the general on the radio," the man urged with a pistol in his hand.

"*Straight Flush*, this is..." Jim coughed and went on, "...*Wolfhunter*. Over."

"This is *Almighty Oz*, *Wolfhunter*," the regular radio operator answered. "What is your situation and location? Over."

"Uh-uh," the camouflaged man warned with a

brilliantly white smile. "None of that, now. Tell him you're being held captive and the leader of the group from Lovelock needs to speak to Desmond."

Jim nodded and relayed the demand.

"Roger, *Wolfhunter*. Understand," came the reply. "*Straight Flush* is on the way here now. Over."

***

Elias had managed to take another Renoite by surprise, having shot him in the hallway while the man began to sift through the backpacks that had remained. A third was found lying on the pavement in front of the Stryker with his attention to a building to the west for whatever reason. For him, Mulhaney had used the big revolver. The machine gun on the personnel carrier had gone silent, but the reason had not become clear until a message arrived over his implant.

"*Mister Mulhaney, I have secured the Stryker and am inside, conducting a conversation with the commander. Please approach the rear ramp of the machine and knock five times slowly.*"

"Hot damn!" Elias shouted.

"What?" a very nervous, but determined and alert Angel answered from the depth of darkness.

"The major's captured the Stryker outside."

"Really?" she blurted incredulously. "Are you sure it's him?"

Elias nodded, having checked the identification a third time. "It's him. Come on."

***

The five knocks came within moments, startling the driver of *Wolfhunter*. His eyes traveled between the pistol pointed in his direction and the ramp.

"That will be a couple more from my team. Open it."

The ramp descended and Mulhaney entered

unabashedly. Angel hung back with her eyes locked on the dead man on the floor next to the major.

"I take it everything's going well, Major," Elias said with a smile.

He deactivated his implant and was happy that it had not malfunctioned. For the first time, he saw the man's adaptive camouflage outfit. He had not seen one of its like for many years.

"Nice outfit," he commented genuinely.

"Quite," Mattersly replied. "Be a good fellow and retrieve my garrote from this brave man's neck then remove him for Angel's sake."

"Yes, sir," Elias agreed.

With that done, Mattersly ordered Jim to drive the Stryker northward while Elias sat in the gunner's seat and familiarized himself with the controls. A few minutes later, Reginald's implant registered contact with his C-4 charges, which he had set for six hours. He now accessed them all and armed them for detonation on command. It was at this precise time that *Wolfhunter*'s radio chirped and the man that the major had called for spoke.

"*Wolfhunter*, this is *Straight Flush*," the general said.

"Stop here, James," Mattersly ordered the captured driver.

The machine was just blocks from the hangar. He realized that they would be in danger if they stayed too long, for surely, this General Desmond had alerted other forces. Reginald placed the deceased gunner's helmet upon his head and answered.

"Hello there," the major said into the microphone, deliberately avoiding proper radio procedure to show contempt for the enemy. "I say, is this Desmond?"

"It is," the man replied, ditching the rules as quickly as Mattersly had voided them.

"Very good. I am Major Reginald Mattersly of the British Army's Special Reconnaissance Regiment. I am in command of the forces that have infiltrated Reno. We are a combined force with elements of the eighty-second airborne of your American army."

"Okay," Desmond returned, sounding unimpressed, but in truth was unenlightened. "What do you want?"

"Your Mayor Gillespie, or whatever he calls himself these days, is holding the young niece of a friend of ours. Do you know of this matter?"

"I do."

"We are here to reclaim her and to apprehend her kidnapper," the major added, "a Mister Miguel Costa."

The radio was quiet for a few heartbeats. "I'm afraid Costa is no longer with us," said Desmond.

Something in the man's tone told Mattersly everything he needed to know. "The girl is in good health, I trust?"

"That, she is."

"Very well, Mister Desmond, I think it may be about time to let your boss know why we're here."

"I'll patch him in," Ricky responded and the radio went silent.

"Any signs of company, Mister Mulhaney?" Reginald asked over his shoulder.

"None," Elias answered, "but I think we'd better keep moving. It's not good to sit still like this."

"I understand," replied the major. "We'll be moving on shortly."

A few more minutes went by before Desmond's voice returned to the radio. "Major, I have Lord Gillespie patched in. Go ahead. Over."

Elias chuckled as he studied the gunnery monitor. "Lord Gillespie. Ha!"

"Thank you, Mister Desmond," said Reginald,

careful to avoid mentioning the man's given rank. "Do I have the pleasure of speaking to Mister Gillespie, mayor of Reno?"

"That you do, whoever you are. I suggest you surrender immediately," Gillespie thundered, making the speaker distort. "My Stryker force is tracking you as we speak."

"Interesting," Mattersly replied. "I would call them off if I were you."

"Why the hell would I do that for murderers of my men and invaders of my good city?"

"Because, my team and I are prepared to level this town of yours, *Mister* Gillespie."

"What a load of nonsense!" the leader of Reno screeched into the microphone.

"Now, listen here," drilled Mattersly, "I have team members spread throughout your city. They are experts in demolition and have key targets located and they are prepared to bring them down one by one. You will deliver Miss Nora Hernandez to us and stand down as the mayor of this city, or we will reduce it…and *you, sir*, to rubble."

As Gillespie laughed, Mattersly set the C-4 charges to twenty seconds.

"Major Mattersly, if that is indeed who you really are," Gillespie drawled, "I will have you and any surviving members of your team brought to me on your knees!"

"As a gesture of our sincerity," the major said with deliberation, "you may say your farewells to your helicopter…and its hangar."

Perfectly timed with his words, six successive explosions sounded off in the distance. They were barely more than short tremors by the time their kinetic energy met with the armored personnel carrier, but they were distinct.

"What the hell did you do?" the young driver

mumbled as he turned to his captor.

"Exactly as I have described," the major explained plainly just as secondary explosions spewed debris into the dawn sky.

Fuel and munitions detonated in the heat of the collapsed hangar fire. Crate after crate and barrel upon barrel went up in succession.

"Now, then, James," Reginald said as the ground shook, "drive us eastward to McCarren Boulevard. I take it you know where that is."

"Yes, sir," the nervous driver answered.

"Good, then drive us to the corner of McCarren and Nugget," he ordered and the vehicle began to roll.

Through the periscope, Mulhaney could see debris raining down from the decimated hangar to their west. A few pieces rang off the machine's armored roof.

Gillespie must have seen the black smoke from his hotel suite, for he howled, screamed, and cussed into the radio at such a volume he was barely understandable.

"Be a sport and shut him off, won't you, James?" the major said to the driver, then turned to Elias. "Do not open fire on anyone that isn't firing at us, Mister Mulhaney. I want the Renoite militia to think we're still one of theirs."

"Very well, sir."

***

Harry Clima stumbled into Gillespie's living quarters to witness a one-sided screaming match. His beloved leader was insanely angry as he bellowed into the telephone threats of revenge and promises of utter destruction. A trembling floor had shaken the little bodyguard awake, but it took the voice of his leader to roust him from the bed.

Clima was still strapping his forty-five's to his body when Gillespie caught a glimpse of him and struck out a finger to the southeast. Harry followed it with his eyes and found the tower of black smoke besmirching the early morning sky.

"Son of a bitch!" Harry grunted, wide-eyed. This explained the shifting floor that had awakened him.

"Atwood!" Gillespie shouted into the phone. "*Atwood!*"

Clima touched his bandaged nose, which had been broken by Ricky Desmond. Whatever had happened, he hoped the general was going to pay for it. Harry was tired of being made to look like a fool and needed payback.

"Atwood," Gillespie said again in a calmer voice as he sat upon his throne. He had swiveled it to look at his burning hangar through the window. "Where is Desmond?"

He listened to the response with eyes ablaze with hate, anger and perhaps a little fear.

Clima stared at the fire nearly five kilometers away and wondered what kind of force they were dealing with. Even to a dullard like Harry, he understood that someone must have known of the whereabouts of the helicopter beforehand.

"It's time you carried out what we discussed," Gillespie murmured and put the receiver down. He turned his attention to his faulty bodyguard. "You there, Pagliacci," he called drawling anger as he stared into the colorfully bruised face of Clima.

Not even the borrowed moniker of the famous clown brought a smile to Gillespie's face, which chilled the two-gunned protector down to his toes.

"Bring that little Hernandez bitch up here and try not to let her beat the shit out of you again."

Clima fumed at that, but knew there was nothing he could do about it at the moment.

"Yes, sir," he grumbled, foregoing the 'Lord Gillespie', turned and quickly left the penthouse floor.

***

Ricky Desmond sprang out of bed the second he heard the explosions. Before he even looked out the window, he *knew* that it had come from the Cobra's hangar as he had predicted. What he did not know was exactly how it occurred even after he had doubled the guard and told the airport security team what to look for. Ricky stared at his packed belongings and wished that he had mustered the courage to go through with his evacuation of the city. He had perseverated throughout the previous evening over when and how to exit the building, but in the end had decided to postpone the attempt. Now, with the enemy clearly in town, he knew it was too late.

He picked up the phone to call the radio room upstairs, but the line was busy. Dropping the receiver back into place, he dashed for the shower and took the quickest one in his forty-seven years of life. During this, he listened for the phone call that never came. This alone drew his suspicions that something other than just the airport bomb had occurred.

As he buttoned his lucky red shirt, he watched the black smoke from the burning hangar proliferate. He slipped on his black slacks, fastened the belt, and glanced at the silent phone. After putting on his favorite gray tweed sport jacket and pair of shoes, he picked up the receiver and dialed the radio room. The line was still busy.

Ricky then activated his implant as he lit a cigarette and went to the window. Magnifying his vision, he could see a few emergency vehicles had arrived. They were backlit by the fire and the rising sun, but their flashing red and yellow lights marked their place.

"*What the hell is going on, Bill?*" he sent in an audible message to Atwood, who was a mere two floors above him. He stepped to his nightstand and retrieved his revolver, stuffing it in his belt as he exited his room.

"*You better come up when you can, Ricky,*" came

Atwood's reply in text form.

"No friggin' kidding," he mumbled and remained vigilant as he walked the hallway to the elevator.

A bad feeling ran throughout his body, giving him a chill along his spine. Ricky had not experienced such anxiety since the time he was thrown out of a casino in Vegas and beaten for winning at Black Jack. They had accused him of counting cards and proclaiming his innocence had not saved him from the violence. He had been a young man then and quick to heal with the help of medical sciences that were no longer available.

As he pressed the 'up' button, the bad feeling deepened in his chest, shortening his breath. Besides which, ever since clocking Clima, Desmond had been expecting an ambush in retaliation. He had heard through the rumor mill, via Bill Atwood, that he had broken the little guy's nose and that his entire face had sprouted into a spectacular black and blue pattern. Ricky assumed that the man would wait until he could see straight to try anything, but his father had taught him about what happened to people that assumed things.

Before the elevator doors slid open, Desmond's revolver was in his hand, kept tightly at his side to keep out of the view of the cameras. He pressed the button for the top floor and waited.

By the time they opened again, Desmond had leaned against the control panel of the car. His eyes darted up and down the hallway and saw no one. Knowing that he was on camera even here, he kept his hesitation to a minimum and strode quickly to the radio room. In the back of his mind, he registered the fact that the curtains were drawn, which was highly unusual.

As he was about to knock on the door, as was customary, curtains or not, he was met by roaring gunshots that erupted from the other side of it. Wooden splinters filled the air, sending Desmond to his knees as he rolled out of the way. He popped up onto the balls of his feet and held the snub-nosed thirty-eight to the bullet-torn portal. Pushing off from the opposite wall, Desmond flung a foot to the radio room door and kicked it open.

Another flurry of gunshots filled the doorway, forcing Ricky to again drop to the floor and roll away. He had no idea if he had been hit or not, for the adrenaline boost he felt clouded his mind. He quickly thought the command to stem the flow and his implant obeyed immediately. Ricky's gun hand steadied and he was able to think things through.

The shooter within the radio room was most likely Bill Atwood. The gun firing at him was not one of Clima's semi-autos, as the rate of fire was too slow. It was more like his own revolver. Atwood had a revolver, a short-barreled three-fifty-seven Magnum for which ammunition was rarer than a dinosaur bone, therefore, it was usually loaded with thirty-eights, like his own. The rounds that had just been launched at him were certainly not thirty-eights. All six rounds had shredded the door and the wall too horrifically, they had to be Magnums.

Ricky discontinued his hearing protection and stilled himself. From inside the room, he could hear the clicking or tapping of metal. It was a familiar flurry of sounds one made when reloading a revolver.

Quickly, Desmond stepped into the doorway and held his thirty-eight outright, with its barrel pointed at his former friend's face. Bill Atwood's expression was that of fear and desperation, for he had nearly reloaded the larger handgun.

Atwood froze when he saw Desmond.

"I missed you with *all six*?!" he shouted incredulously as he looked over his now ex-friend.

Despite his heartbreak over the betrayal, Ricky

smiled. "Looks like it. Face it, Bill, we were never gunslingers or soldiers. That kind of work is for thugs and brave men, not gamblers like us."

Atwood nodded as his eyes darted to the mostly reloaded pistol in his hand. "I don't suppose you'd let me walk outta here for old times' sake?" he asked and gave the slightest hint of a smile. His eyes showed a glimmer of hope, but there was something else, too.

"Tell me 'why' first," Desmond replied as he gave the appearance of relaxing his stance in the slightest.

"I believed in Gillespie," Bill answered with a regretful shrug.

"You know the man's a loon, right?"

"I do. That revelation came too late, Ricky."

"No, Bill. Right up until you ambushed me, there was nothing too late about it!"

In a flash, Atwood dropped the bullet that was halfway into the chamber and snapped his right wrist, locking the cylinder into place. Though he had only partially reloaded, one shot would have been enough.

Ricky Desmond squeezed the thirty-eight's trigger six times, emptying them all into Bill Atwood before his old friend had a chance to aim.

In a matter of seconds, a friendship that lasted almost twenty years was over.

Desmond stared at the corpse for what felt like several minutes. Once the fog cleared, he realized that he was in no pain. Until that moment, he had not been completely convinced that Atwood had missed.

Ricky knew he had to find out what was happening and quickly. He removed the Magnum from Atwood's hand and shoved the body, office chair and all, into the hallway, and slammed the door. Placing the radio operator's headphones on his head, he listened to the chatter on the militia channel.

He could decipher only a little of what was happening, but it was clear that all checkpoints into the city, including the bewildered airport security group had no idea where the enemy were. General Desmond had a card up his sleeve, as he usually did.

"*Necromancer*, this is *Straight Flush*. Acknowledge," he called, silencing the rest of the mindless chatter.

"*Straight Flush*. *Necromancer*. Over."

"Switch to alternate channel for orders. Over."

"Roger," answered Sam, *Necromancer*'s commander.

The alternate channel was not simply one of the many frequencies preset and published for the other militia men, but a full ten gigahertz above that range. This required a separate radio set altogether that only the Stryker commanders of *Ranger* and *Necromancer* had been supplied with. Since Pop of the *Ranger* was gone, that left Sam.

Ricky plugged the headset and microphone into the higher frequency transmitter and turned it on. He quickly yanked the cord toward the window, pulling the curtains wide. He reloaded his thirty-eight while he watched the hallway through the suite's unobstructed windows. He suspected that Gillespie had ordered his assassination and most likely just heard his voice on the radio set in his living quarters. Certainly somebody, hopefully Clima, was on their way to him.

"*Straight Flush*, this is *Necromancer*. Over," called Sam Holsbeck.

"*Necromancer*. *Straight Flush*. Give me your location. Over."

"We've been pulled back to blockade I-80 at the Center Street exit. Direct orders from *Royal Flush*. Over."

"Damn it!" Desmond exclaimed off the air as he

hammered the desk with a fist.

He did not blame the opposing force for the mess, for it was Gillespie who was leading his men and the city of Reno to ruin over this fascination with the Hernandez woman. It had driven a lifelong friend to attempt to kill him and now his command over the militia was circumvented.

Ricky lit a cigarette as he keyed the microphone. "Sam, *Almighty Oz* is permanently off the air. He tried to kill me. I'm afraid I have to initiate our contingency plan. Over."

"Understood. My squad is with you, Desmond. I can't speak for the other crews. Over."

From the corner of his eye, Ricky saw from both elevator floor indicators that they were on their way up.

"Sam, I think I better get the hell out of here. I've got people on the way up. Over." He stood and stuffed his revolver in his belt and kept Atwood's in his hand.

"I'm on the way. I'll pick you up at the kitchen entrance. Can you get there?" Sam said quickly.

"Meet you there! Out!" he shouted and yanked the microphone from the special transmitter just before he burst through the door. He quickly searched for, and found a handful of Magnum rounds from his dead friend's pockets before heading for the stairwell. He jerked the door open and listened for the sound of footsteps below. Shutting the door silently, Desmond descended the stairs as quietly as he could manage.

He made it five floors before he heard a rush of men below him. The hotel was mostly empty, especially desolate were the upper floors, making it quite easy to hear his pursuers. Ricky went through the door, leaving the stairwell to take a chance on the elevators. The indicators showed that they had both gone to the penthouse. He pressed the 'down' button and looked about him for a place to hide. Surrounded by empty, locked hotel rooms, the only way into any of them would be to kick a door and possibly announce his presence.

Desmond froze with the burning cigarette dangling between his lips as he heard a flurry of footsteps just beyond the stairwell door. There was no place to hide.

The bell of the arriving elevator car startled the cigarette right out of Desmond's mouth. Absently, he stamped it into the carpet as he held the Magnum out in front of him in case the car was not empty. It was. He lunged inside and pressed '5'. It would be foolish to think that the lobby would not have Gillespie-loyal militia trolling the place for him.

***

The hijacked Stryker bounded over the bridge as it approached Nugget Avenue. Mattersly had instructed James to drive in a casual fashion and not at top speed, which would gather attention and, so far, he had done a wonderful job. They had cruised through a checkpoint several blocks back without being stopped. The militia that waved them on had apparently not been informed that a Stryker had been stolen.

The corner of McCarren and Nugget was littered with armed militia and barricades. In the parking lot of the building on the northwest corner, another Stryker was parked.

"Angel, would you identify this building as the one with the fabrication equipment inside?" Mattersly asked as he leaned back to give the lady a look at the monitor.

"Yes, Major. That's it," she said and retook her seat.

"Very well, thank you," Reginald granted, and then turned to the driver. "Now, then, James, I want you to make a left turn onto Nugget."

"Yes, sir," the nervous driver replied.

None of the militiamen gave the Stryker much

scrutiny as it rolled by them. Two young soldiers even moved a barricade out of the way for them and waved them through. James made the left turn as Mattersly followed the action with his periscope. It was 05:25 and the sky was lightening quickly. Reginald knew there was little time to waste.

"James, drive around this building coming up on your left. I want you to approach the fabrication facility from behind," Mattersly ordered. "I trust you know how to do that."

"Uh... yes, sir," the captive militiaman said with a nod. "There's an alleyway between two buildings that leads right up to it."

"Excellent, get us there," the major pressed.

"I have to tell you, though," Jim went on, "you don't have a lot of chance of getting in there. You saw all the men on the street."

"I understand, that is why I'm going to have a lend of your jacket," Mattersly explained as he unbuttoned his color-morphing tunic, "and Mister Mulhaney will engage in diversionary tactics."

"I am?" Mulhaney asked with a smirk.

"Indeed," Reginald replied in kind.

Chapter Twelve

A garbled transmission mottled by background gunfire went out over the main channel and was heard by all militia units and every Stryker. This included the new *Almighty Oz*, a captain in the militia in command of the squads that were conducting a search of the hotel for the deposed General Desmond.

"This is *Almighty Oz* to whoever sent that message," the captain spoke urgently, "repeat and give your location. Over."

"Just outside airport… Peckham Lane," the speaker repeated with a scratchy, muffled voice. The gunfire made it more difficult to hear.

"Peckham Lane?" the operator's adjutant pondered and regarded the giant map of Reno on the wall. "That's just west of the airport."

"We've run into…large number of men…green camo…everywhere!" the unknown voice transmitted.

Before the operator could reply, a Stryker team broke in. "*Valkyrie* here! There's an enemy force trying to attack the fab plant! Another Stryker team is here with us. We're moving to engage! Over."

"Almighty Oz, this is *Demon*," another broke in, "we're heading to Peckham Lane right now to assist, but we have no enemy contact at this point. Over."

"Roger, *Valkyrie* and roger, *Demon*," the captain said quickly then turned to his lieutenant, "Get Gillespie on the phone."

"Yes, sir."

***

The deposed general of the militia stepped lightly but quickly into the basement level and left the stairwell. He passed through the musty and unlit laundry room and adjusted his vision for the dark. He exited and slipped into the hallway that separated it from the kitchens and turned left. Through the window of the exit door at the end of the hallway, he could see the fading stars amidst the medium blue sky.

As he approached the door, he could hear and feel the rumble of a Stryker's diesel engine. With Atwood's revolver in his hand, he peered through the window. To the right was Sam Holsbeck's machine. His men were deployed and watching the windows of the hotel while Sam himself stood in the open gunner's hatch.

Ricky opened the door partway and called out, "Sam!"

"Quick! Get in!" Sam replied and waved him toward the open rear of the carrier. As he ran, the squad of six infantry made way for him and covered the windows. Once Desmond was inside, the soldiers followed him, shut the ramp, and they were off.

"Thanks, Sam," Desmond said gratefully as he shook the captain's hand.

"You bet, General," Captain Holsbeck replied. "Where to?"

"Get me to Gillespie's place," Desmond answered. "We have to take him down and give these people the Hernandez girl. He's crazy enough to kill her even if he's cornered."

"Yes, sir," Captain Holsbeck answered. "You should know there's been chatter on the radio that two groups of Major Mattersly's infantry have engaged us west of the airport and near the fabrication plant."

"Jesus," spat Desmond. He knew that if he was still in charge, he would order his militia to stand down as he tried to negotiate with Mattersly, but as it was, he was with the only group that trusted him.

As if to punctuate his dire straits, a voice on the

radio made it clear.

"All units, this is *Almighty Oz*. Per *Royal Flush*, *Straight Flush* is to be regarded as a traitor to the city-state of Reno. *Straight Flush*, a.k.a. General Ricky Desmond is no longer in command of the militia and is to be arrested immediately."

"Well, shit," Ricky exuded and placed his head in his hands. He could not help but wonder if the declaration would turn any of the soldiers that he sat amongst.

"All Stryker units and checkpoints acknowledge this order," the new radio operator commanded. One after another, the militia units called in.

"*Necromancer*. Roger that, *Almighty*," Sam Holsbeck transmitted. He then turned to look over his squad and then to Desmond. The two shared a long look and until Sam shook his head and smiled. "I don't think there's anyone here that doesn't want to see Gillespie removed."

"Gentlemen," Desmond said, addressing the eight men around him, "I thank you."

***

Mulhaney fired another few bursts of fifty-caliber from the Stryker's twin guns into the empty building to their right as the major ran to the rear door of the fabrication plant. In between bursts, he put out the fake calls on the radio.

James, the kidnapped militiaman, shook his head and bit his lip as he wondered what to do. The handgun that Angel held on him convinced him that it would be nothing for the moment.

Through the gunner's periscope, Elias saw the door that the major was heading to burst open seconds before he had a chance to get there. The major was met by a Renoite militiaman.

"Oh… shit," Mulhaney murmured and fired another

burst into the abandoned building to help sell the part. "Angel, stick your rifle out the rear hatch and fire it."

"Got it," she answered.

"And, Jimmy-boy," Elias added as he pointed his giant revolver toward the driver. "No funny business up there."

***

"What the hell's going on out here?" the militiaman shouted at the man running toward him.

"We've got a group a' them infiltrators inside that building," Reginald replied in an adopted American accent. "My squad's in there, holdin' them up. I saw two come in here, Sergeant!" he lied, having taken note of the rank on the man's sleeve."

"No way," the younger man said in reply as he cycled the action on his assault weapon. "How the hell did they get past me?" he said and retreated inside.

Major Mattersly smiled and followed. "Dull green camouflage with green berets," he added to the mix as the two of them jogged through the building, passing empty offices and into a larger room where stockpiles of metals, plastics, and fibers were kept.

Keeping up appearances, Reginald swept the barrel of his assault weapon from side to side, just as the Renoite sergeant was doing.

"They could be anywhere if they made it this far in," the fooled militiaman said over his shoulder.

"We'd better check the control room," Mattersly suggested.

"Good idea," the sergeant said and took off in a run.

Reginald followed and fished through a pocket for one of his C-4 charges. As they passed the main steel processing chamber of the building-sized fabrication machine, he activated it and flung it in the air. It landed on the machine's steel roof with a ringing thump.

The militiaman stopped and took a knee. “What was that?” he whispered as he looked around.

“It came from up ahead,” Mattersly bluffed once again and took the lead. “Come on.” As he rounded the corner of the building-within-a-building, he startled another militiaman who was stationed at the main computer console, a large, upright component with three computer monitors, and a holographic projector. This machine oversaw the entire fabrication process from design to finished product.

“What the hell…?” the surprised private called and stepped back.

“Did you see ‘em come through here?” Mattersly shouted.

“Who?” answered the young, surprised soldier.

“Enemy infiltrators,” supplied the sergeant, “green camo and berets.”

“No one came through here,” the private insisted.

“Shit,” Reginald spat as he walked behind the main computer, attached another charge, and came out the other side. “They must have double-backed, somewheres. Sergeant, you and your man stay vigilant. I’m gettin’ back to my men.”

“Yes, sir!”

With that, Reginald ran back up the narrow and dim hallway.

***

Wolfhunter’s activity in the alley was drawing attention. A handful of militiamen appeared and took cover near the stolen Stryker. A few of them peered into the building through broken windows and, seeing nothing, shrugged and looked at one another in confusion.

“Back us off, Jimmy,” Elias ordered in a nervous sing-song.

To his immediate delight, he saw Mattersly burst

through the door that he had disappeared into. He sprinted toward the Stryker, appearing to yell orders to the Renoite militia.

The captive driver put the vehicle in reverse and guided the machine slowly back up the alley. He had gone about twenty meters when Mulhaney ordered him to stop. Once done, Elias dropped the ramp to let Mattersly enter.

As Reginald ran toward the Stryker, he accessed the two charges he had planted and detonated the first one. From behind him, the roof and western wall were turned to dust and debris with a barely muffled explosion.

He gritted his teeth as he shouted to the Renoite soldiers that went flat to the cement for cover, "They've got RPG's! Fall back!"

As he approached the Stryker, he thought the command for the second charge. He heard the report as he flung himself inside and slapped the button to close the ramp.

"Get us out of here, Jimmy," Elias ordered as he pressed a button that launched smoke grenades ahead of the vehicle. Very soon, nothing forward of their previous position could be seen.

"Nice work, Major," Elias granted as the Brit took a seat and worked to catch his breath.

"Thank you, Mister Mulhaney," he replied as he removed the driver's uniform. "James, I trust you know where your Mayor Gillespie resides. Its precise location, that is."

The driver sighed before answering. "I do."

"Head west, please," Reginald requested and took the seat behind the driver. "Where might that be, James?"

"He lives in the penthouse of the old Platinum Reata," James explained as he guided the vehicle through a field of fuel tanks belonging to an old refinery. "I don't think we'll be able to get past the blockades there.

Everything is checked before it goes through. There are a couple of other old hotels that are attached to the Reata. You could get to one of those without too much suspicion, but you'd have to find your way through the area. "

"Why, James, I do believe you're becoming accustomed to our company," Angel drawled sweetly.

"It just beats getting shot, ma'am."

Mattersly addressed the driver in between sips of water. His olive drab undershirt was soaked with sweat as he panted for breath.

"If it means anything to you, young man, we're here to rescue a young girl from your Mayor Gillespie and return her to Lovelock. We've just achieved two of our three objectives."

"Well, you've killed quite a number of my friends doing it," the Renoite grumbled angrily.

"That, unfortunately, is the cost of war, James," the major spoke gently. "It gives me no pleasure to do such things. But the people of Lovelock were being killed and maimed for no reason other than your Mister Gillespie wished it so."

After a moment, the young militia sergeant shrugged. "I never did understand the reasons for harassing Lovelock."

"We are simply trying to end it with as few casualties as possible," Reginald explained. "I have no interest in seeing civilians hurt or killed."

"I understand," James stated glumly.

He knew the major was correct, but he had seen his squad killed by these people. As he thought about it, only two of them were truly his friends and even they were not close to him. He thought of his mother and father who lived in the north of town and decided that for their sake, he would trust Major Mattersly, at least for the time being.

***

"Just listen to that chatter," Captain Sam Holsbeck of *Necromancer* marveled. "It sounds like Mattersly's forces are everywhere. Now the fabrication building's been hit."

"I wonder if we can call a cease fire," Desmond thought aloud.

"Sir, at this point, I believe that getting you on the air would give us away," Sam insisted. "With only six Strykers left to the militia, our approach to Gillespie's place would be compromised."

"Right," Desmond said and sighed.

"And, if you don't mind me sayin' so, sir," the commander went on, "about your attire. At a distance, a Gillespie-loyal militiaman would take you out on sight."

"Good point," Ricky agreed. "Would anyone have anything I can borrow?"

***

"Major, that building dead ahead is the Platinum Reata," Angel said excitedly as she pointed to the monitor.

"Ah! Very good! Pull into that alleyway to the left, James," Reginald directed.

The sergeant did not understand the reason for the order, but he obeyed without question.

Once the Stryker had passed between two single-story commercial structures, Mattersly ordered the driver to stop.

"Now, young man, I'm offering you the opportunity to get away."

"What?" protested Elias.

"Major, we need him," Angel put in.

James did not know what to say. As he studied Reginald's face, he could find no trace of deception. As if to test the man's word, he reached up and popped open the driver's hatch. The interior of the Stryker came alive with orange morning sunlight as the driver looked about for signs of life. The alley was empty save for some long unused garbage bins. He unbuckled his seatbelt and lifted himself through the hatch. When he got out, he turned back to look inside.

"What if I go and rejoin my militia and tell them about your plan?" James asked.

He suddenly felt stupid for asking the question. They were letting him go and now he was pushing his luck.

"That's the chance that I'm prepared to take, James," Mattersly answered as he slipped into the driver's seat.

"Well, good luck, Major, Elias, Miss Angel," he said to each with a nod and slid off the vehicle.

Reginald pulled the hatch closed and watched the young Renoite walk up the alley through the driver's window. At the next abandoned building, James rounded the corner heading south and disappeared.

"I'm not sure that was wise, Major," said Angel from the seat behind him.

"Wise or not, I've done it," replied Reginald as he reversed the Stryker out of the alley and back onto the street. He had been watching James more carefully than the others had suspected. "As I saw it, he was conflicted and eventually, would have become a liability. Besides, I liked him and didn't want to have to shoot him."

"I understand you," Mulhaney stated. "So what's the plan?"

Reginald made a left at the next block and pulled the vehicle alongside another building. They were in plain view of the civilian population, which appeared to be sparse thus far, but they received no undue attention. It was certain that some of the citizens of Reno had heard some of the commotion, but the few that wandered the streets so early in the morning did so as if it were routine.

"Well, now," the major began as he took out the

roadmap from a pants pocket. "We are here on Lake Street. I propose we approach from a back street from the south. I'm sure we shall encounter the blockade and other Strykers, so we will have to be quick."

"If we make a right here," Angel pointed to the map, "which is just after this building we're next to, we can do exactly that."

"Smashing," Mattersly commented. "My plan, Mister Mulhaney, is to drop Angel here and…"

"*What?!*" she shrieked.

"…have you lay down suppressing fire at the blockade sites while I drive this vehicle at a respectable speed. We shall make a go around this facility, including the Reata and come right 'round again."

"I'm not going!" Angel shouted.

"I'm afraid we've gone too far into enemy territory to see you back home," the major quickly added, "so, as the coast is now clear, you will get out of the vehicle and blend in with the civilian populace as best you can."

"Major! I'm not leaving you two!" Angel insisted hotly.

"Angel, you promised," Mattersly reminded her sternly.

"It's not right," she said more quietly.

"My intentions will be clearer once you hear my next radio broadcast to Mister Gillespie," Reginald said to her as he held her stare.

***

Desmond crossed his fingers as *Necromancer* approached the rear of the Platinum Reata. Now wearing a medium-gray uniform and a combat helmet, he would be harder to recognize among the regular militiamen. Unfortunately, there had been no spare boots, so the deposed general was forced to stay with his black loafers.

He could see on the monitor that the men of the

blockade ahead paid them little attention. *Necromancer* appeared to be just another squad sent to reinforce the inner part of the city. Further, he noted civilian workers had begun to report to work at the hotels and restaurants that served the most influential citizens of Reno, who also lived in suites and hotel rooms within the complex. Desmond hoped that none would get caught up in the crossfire, for it was to their benefit that he and the brave men with him were attempting to remove Gillespie from power.

"All right, drive in through the exit," Sam Holsbeck ordered the driver.

This part of the Platinum Reata was the parking garage. Mostly unused as there was a minimum of vehicles among the populace, the squad could access the hotel from the rear and work their way up. Holsbeck ordered one of the men to poke their head through the infantry hatch and check behind them, for driving a Stryker into the parking garage might have gathered attention.

As the large eight-wheeled vehicle wound its way up the floors, the soldier reported that they were not being followed.

"Captain, the clearance has run out," the driver proclaimed and brought the machine to a halt.

"Yes, I see," Sam answered. "Okay, General. This is as far as we go with the machine."

"It'll do," Desmond said with a nod. He turned to the squad and continued. "We're going to head right up to Gillespie's. If we encounter resistance, let's try to bluff our way through. Our last resort is to get engaged in a firefight. Our fellow Renoite militiamen have not ceased to be that just because their loyalty is to Gillespie. Is that understood?"

"Yes, sir!" the group, including Captain Holsbeck answered.

"Okay, then. Driver drop the ramp and close this

thing up tight when we leave. Turn it around and wait for further orders," Ricky commanded.

"Yes, sir," the driver, a young, thin sergeant replied.

The rear door clanged with an echo as it struck the pavement. All eight men quickly made their way to the elevators and stairwell. Once they were clear, the ramp was raised, and the Stryker's diesel growled as the driver maneuvered it around.

Ricky Desmond was first to the stairwell. He went to the door that led into the third floor hallway and peered through the small rectangular window. He was not surprised to see a pair of militiamen guarding the door.

"All right, Gillespie's got the building on a security lockdown," he explained to the group. "I expected this. We won't be able to access the elevators from the outside and every door to every floor will be locked tight."

"How many floors are there, sir?" one of the recruits, a corporal, asked.

"Thirty-two, but that's not the worst of it," Desmond explained. "The penthouse floor is accessible only from a central bank of elevators in the lobby. All we can do is break into one of these floors and locate the stairwell that leads to the thirty-second. Let's go."

Ricky stepped through his group and led them up the stairs to the next floor. He dared another look through that door and found it guarded as well. He and his squad kept ascending as Ricky thought through a possible bluff.

***

The argument over whether or not Angel would remain with Mattersly and Mulhaney for the duration ended with the young lady sitting steadfast on one of the infantry seats at the rear with her arms and legs crossed. For the moment, she refused to speak. Mattersly acquiesced, as there was simply no more time to argue about it.

With regards to the route, Reginald found that

Angel had been correct. Around the next corner, he turned right and drove alongside a building with a large overhang and a bank of lowered railroad tracks on their left. He stopped the Stryker upon reaching the next cross street to check both directions. A few pedestrians hung about the area, but it was clear of Renoite militia. He accelerated and joined the street that led them westward.

"Here's where I shake them up a bit," Mattersly said to his companions as he brought the vehicle to a stop next to the Silver Sierra Hotel. He switched the radio frequency to the main combat channel and listened for a moment.

The Stryker with call sign, *Demon* was reporting that it had discovered no enemy soldiers west of the airport. The ruse had been uncovered. The radio operator, *Almighty Oz*, was directing the show, sending troops and a couple of Strykers from one place to another. The destruction of the fabrication equipment was also causing great confusion, as no enemy combatants had been found in that area, either.

Mattersly decided to interrupt. "*Almighty Oz*, this is Major Reginald Mattersly, commanding the SRR force and elements of the Eighty-Second Airborne of your former United States Army. Acknowledge."

The chatter silenced immediately. Nonetheless, *Almighty Oz* ordered all units to stay clear of the channel momentarily.

"What is it that you want from us, Major?" the radio officer asked in a barely restrained anger.

"As Mister Gillespie can plainly see, we have the advantage and have destroyed his fabrication factory. All he need do now is surrender the Hernandez girl to us, unharmed."

The radio was quiet for nearly half a minute. It was Gillespie himself that broke the silence. "Mattersly is it? Lord Gillespie here. I have the Hernandez girl that you want so much."

"Put her on," the major directed.

"Child, say 'hello' to your rescuers," Gillespie said with his mouth away from the microphone as the line clicked and a scuffle ensued in the background.

The child yelped in pain before blurting, "Hello?"

"Hello, there," the major greeted. "What is your name?" While it was certain that the voice was that of a small child, Mattersly wished to confirm her identity and listen for hesitations, which were signs of coaching by the others.

"Nora Hernandez," she answered clearly and immediately.

"Very good to speak to you, miss," he said with a smile. Before he could continue the conversation, she was removed from it.

"Well, Major," Gillespie oozed obstinately, "you and your little group have been a pain in my ass!"

"I am quite aware of that, Mister Gillespie," Mattersly answered, saying it with a smile, "and unless we receive the child from you unharmed, our attacks will continue. Other targets have been identified by my forces and your militia seems unable to do anything about us. Surrender the girl and we shall retreat in peace."

"I don't think so, Major," Gillespie retorted with a smile in his voice. "I think I will just dispose of the child and let my militia decimate you. See, I don't think there are as many of you as you're pretending to be."

The major looked over his shoulder at Mulhaney, who wiped his mouth with his hand. His eyebrows were furled and he appeared deep in thought. Mattersly tried to transmit, but Gillespie was not finished.

"I think I'll shoot this little bitch, find you, and then level Lovelock once and for all!"

Reginald waited for a few heartbeats before

answering, "Very well, Mister Gillespie. Have it your way."

The radio remained silent. The three of them waited for a few minutes before Reginald turned off the transmitter. The talking was indeed over.

"I say, old man," the major spoke calmly as he rolled the vehicle slowly forward. "Are you quite ready on the guns?"

Elias took hold of the turret control and took a deep breath. He spoke as he let it out. "Yes, sir, Major."

He rotated the turret to the right side of the vehicle and released the safety.

"Very well. We're driving alongside the southernmost hotel in the complex at this moment. I will come to a brief halt in the intersection long enough for you to acquire targets and fire."

"Okay," Elias mumbled nervously. He knew that he was not to fire at anyone directly, only stir them up.

However, in his mind, he realized that the Stryker's armor was not impenetrable, so he decided that any militiaman that had a weapon capable of damaging the vehicle would eat fifty-caliber rounds for breakfast.

Their stolen Stryker rolled onto Sierra Avenue and Reginald brought it to a stop. Mulhaney could see another such machine parked across the street with a collection of infantrymen lingering alongside it and upon the street and sidewalk. He counted about twenty men before he depressed the trigger and opened fire.

The first few rounds raked the other Stryker's gun mount. Sparks and bits of metal showered the militiamen standing nearest the machine. They ducked and ran from it while their fellow mercenaries returned fire from whatever they had on them. Bullets rang against the outer hull of the vehicle or thudded heavily into the bulletproof tires.

Mulhaney fired over the heads of some of the

enemy to cease their fire, but one man jogged toward them as he prepared to throw something. Elias took him down with a short burst from the twin guns. Above the now disarmed enemy Stryker was an enclosed walkway which joined the Silver Sierra Hotel with the parking garage across the street. Elias aimed for the tinted glass windows that lined its side and shattered them, bringing the shards to the street in showers of glittering fragments. Mulhaney was about to recommend that they get moving when the major had beat him to it. The Stryker lurched forward and accelerated up the narrow path, putting the parking garage between them and the Renoite guardians of Sierra Street.

Throughout this exchange, Angel was silent. Whether her lack of speech was the result of the exchange of fire or anger over the major's plan to drop her off, she could not say. Dutifully, she popped her head through a rear hatch and saw nothing but an uninhabited street behind them before ducking back inside.

***

Desmond and his group went from floor to floor with Ricky checking through each window before moving on. Fortunately, he had not been seen leering through the tiny rectangular windows and Holsbeck's squad was impressively quiet.

It was on the tenth floor that Ricky found no one in the hallway. He tried the knob and was not surprised to find it locked.

Sam Holsbeck pulled a long combat knife from a leg sheath and approached. "Excuse me, General," he warned and struck the blade into the gap between door and doorjamb. Pulling it downward, he forced the latch to release and the door came free.

Desmond smiled and gave a wink as Holsbeck gestured for the man behind him to follow him into the hallway. They were no sooner inside when a voice called out in surprise at their immediate right. Holsbeck struck quickly with the knife as it was still in hand. Blood flowed with great intensity as he let the victim drop to the floor, face down and quite dead.

"Damn it," Sam Holsbeck grunted.

Hopes of pulling this mission off without spilling fellow Renoite blood were destroyed. He bent down and removed a small radio from the body, and tucked it into a tunic pocket.

"Let's move, Captain," Desmond pressed.

He was careful not to look at the dead body. Ricky knew he was no soldier and was worried that his stomach would turn.

From behind them, the corporal who carried the handheld radio approached the two men in charge.

"Excuse me, sirs," he whispered, "Sergeant Schamski reports that this Mattersly guy got on the main channel again and pushed Gillespie for that girl and Gillespie says he's gonna just go and kill her."

"Damn fool," Ricky Desmond muttered.

The corporal nodded and continued, "The Brit says other targets are already identified and will be destroyed," he finished just as muffled gunfire erupted.

From what direction, they could not tell, but it was definitely from outside.

"Let's hurry up and take Gillespie out before the bastard gets us all killed," Ricky ordered as he jogged passed a bank of elevators. "Those won't get us far, we need to get to this other set around the corner and down the hall," he whispered as loud as he dared to the group.

Holsbeck took a quick peek around the corner and saw no one. Past a line of doors that were most likely empty suites, he could see the elevators that Desmond indicated.

"Come on," Sam ordered and led the way.

In short order, the squad stuffed themselves into two of the four cars and went straight to the twenty-fourth floor. Both sets of doors opened almost simultaneously and the eight of them poured out, taking the two guards on that floor completely by surprise.

The pair of them were disarmed, tied, and gagged. Left to lie on their stomachs, their radios were removed as well as their weapons.

Desmond found the door to the stairwell. "Everyone ready? Just eight flights more," he said with a grin, which earned him a few groans from the squad that were offered in jest.

"Okay, knock that off," Captain Holsbeck ordered with a crooked grin that quickly disappeared. "Let's move before that girl pays for us being slow."

With that, the squad slipped into the stairwell and set out to make their best speed upward.

***

Reginald turned the machine around the next corner and pushed the diesel plant for all the speed he could get out of it. Elias fired a quick burst eastward as they rolled through the next intersection. Renoite militiamen scattered and had no time to return fire. The stolen Stryker flew behind the western side of the Platinum Reata and disappeared.

Mattersly hit the brakes as they approached the next intersection. It was blocked with orange and white striped barricades of wood and manned by a number of militiamen.

"Mister Mulhaney," the major called, "we have trouble dead ahead."

"On it," Elias answered and swiveled the turret forward and fired over the heads of the men he saw.

One man stood and took careful aim of the approaching vehicle's driver's window. Just for a moment, Reginald was convinced that the man could see him, though he knew it was impossible.

The man fired just as Mulhaney's machine guns took him down. Amongst the symphony of gunfire, Mattersly could swear that he heard the militiaman's bullet hit just above the slim rectangular window.

"Turning right!" the major announced as the machine burst through the barricades.

Militiamen scattered and fired back with whatever they had on them. Rounds sang off the armored flanks of the Stryker, though Angel still gave a little shriek and went flat on the floor.

"Another Stryker's behind us!" Mulhaney shouted over the noise.

The machine had been parked to the left of the intersection and had been out of sight until they had turned. Elias punched the touchscreen to send off a couple of rounds of smoke grenades just as the enemy vehicle's twin fifties opened up. The much heavier rounds struck *Wolfhunter*'s rear ramp with such ferocity that Mattersly as well as Mulhaney knew that it was doing damage.

The world behind them went white and Reginald swerved to dodge the incoming rounds. Mulhaney laid down suppressive fire into the smoke, not knowing if he was hitting the enemy machine or not. Before he knew it, his vehicle swung to the right and they had entered a building.

"What the hell?" he muttered in confusion.

"This is the Platinum Reata's parking garage," Mattersly announced. "I think it's time to depart and take the fight indoors."

Reginald had driven the vehicle into the taller of the building's pathways, which appeared to be the exit ramp. He wound around the structure with the intent of rising to the highest floor possible. In seconds, however, he found it to be impossible.

"Bloody hell!" he shouted and braked hard.

"What now?!" Mulhaney bellowed.

"Have a look, mate," Reginald directed and pointed his finger forward.

Elias gave the turret and camera forward and quickly found the problem. A Stryker had been laying a trap for them.

But how the hell did they know we were coming in through here?

Mulhaney was in the process of taking aim of the enemy machine's turret when the other Stryker did the unthinkable.

Instead of opening fire, or even moving its own turret to take aim, the driver flashed its headlights in quick succession.

"Hold fire!" Mattersly ordered.

"What's he up to?" Elias wondered aloud.

***

"Son-of-a-*bitch*!" Necromancer's Sergeant Schamski proclaimed as the other Stryker flew around the corner and came to a shuddering stop, just meters from his own.

Unfortunately, he had not been able to sit still for very long and had left the gunner's station. All he could think to do was jump into the driver's seat and flash his lights.

"Corporal Gifford! I've been discovered! Another Stryker just showed up!"

Gifford told the sergeant to stand by as he relayed the message to Holsbeck and Desmond.

"Shit," Ricky mumbled. After a moment's thought he said, "Tell the young man to save himself and surrender."

"Sir?" Captain Holsbeck questioned.

"Sam, we're what a poker player would call, 'all

in’,” Ricky said in hushed tones as he looked his friend in the eye.

The captain nodded and turned to Corporal Gifford. “Tell him.”

Sergeant Schamski saw no alternative and was quite relieved, in fact, when Gifford relayed the order. He acknowledged it and wasted no time opening the commander’s hatch. He showed his palms and slowly rose up out of the hole. He could feel and hear his heart pound when the turret of the other personnel carrier swept over him and then moved away again.

“I’m surrendering!” he shouted. “I’m alone here. The rest… took off!”

The driver’s hatch of the Stryker facing him swung upward, revealing an older man he did not recognize. He thought he had met all of the other crews from training missions.

“Do not move, young man,” the driver called in a freshly familiar accent. “I’ve no wish to harm you.”

The identity of the man flashed on him like a grenade going off. “You’re him!” he shouted. “You’re Major… Mattersly! Right?”

“That’s correct.”

As quickly as he could speak, Schamski explained what General Desmond and the Stryker’s entire squad were attempting to do.

“Outstanding!” Mattersly proclaimed. “Give me their radio frequency so that I may verify.”

Schamski explained how to tune it as Angel popped her head out of a rear hatch of *Wolfhunter*. She needed fresh air, but was also quite anxious to see if they had been followed. She quickly discovered that they had.

“Major!” she called once she dropped back in to retrieve her weapon. “We’ve got company!”

In a heartbeat, she stuck the assault weapon through

the hatch and fired at the first man she saw. He quickly ducked away amidst the dust and bits of asphalt that her rounds had dug up.

"Damn," Mattersly grumbled and put the vehicle in gear and performed a tight U-turn. He dropped the driver's hatch and spoke into the microphone. "Help us fend off these men!"

Schamski dropped the commander's hatch and shifted over to the gunner's seat as he called out for Corporal Gifford. It was Captain Holsbeck who answered. As Schamski traversed the turret back and forth over the graded pavement, he explained the situation.

Holsbeck's reply was marred with gunfire and incomprehensible.

***

Desmond and the rest of the squad were four floors below the penthouse level when a hand grenade dropped onto the steps one floor beneath them.

"Grenaaaade!" someone at the rear of the squad screamed just prior to an immense explosion, made all the more nerve-shattering in the close quarters of the concrete stairwell.

Automatic gunfire ensued immediately as Holsbeck and his men leaned over the railings and fired upward. Their rounds ricocheted from the walls and steps and clanged off the metal railings above them.

Ricky felt a hand yank him to his feet. It was Holsbeck, who had just pocketed the radio that Gifford had brought to him.

"Let's go!" he howled and bolted up the stairs.

Without thinking, Desmond followed, as did the men behind him.

Captain Holsbeck saw another grenade fall past him. He halted and bellowed its arrival. His men all fell as flat as they could against the stairs. Fortunately for all, this one, too, was overthrown and exploded on the steps one floor below them.

A militiaman appeared from above them, taking aim at Holsbeck, who was quicker. With a burst of fire from his rifle, he brought the man down.

"Keep going!" Sam shouted behind him and took to his feet once again.

***

"We've got men coming up the stairs, Sire!" Clima shouted and pulled both his pistols.

"What? Already?" Gillespie answered incredulously just as the first grenade exploded some floors below.

His face went pale as he began to realize the military power of this Major Mattersly. As the man had alluded to, other Renoite targets had been chosen, but he had failed to appreciate the man's intelligence and his force's mobility.

Automatic gunfire thrummed through the floor and a second grenade explosion let Gillespie know how truly close the enemy had come. He stared upon the face of the Hernandez child with great fury, but he knew that even she could see the fear behind it.

"Do they not understand that I'll just kill you?" he shrieked at the girl. He gave her no time for one of her flippant retorts as he snatched up the phone. "*OZ*! I need reinforcements sent here immediately! Mattersly's men are in the stairwell!"

He listened to the new radio operator's answer.

"I don't care what you have to do to destroy the captured Strykers, but get some backup over here! NOW!" he bellowed into the receiver before slamming it down.

***

Between *Necromancer* and *Wolfhunter*, the hail of fifty-caliber machine gun rounds kept the enemy from rising up to their floor. Another Stryker had even attempted to round the corner, but due to its odd, uphill angle could not get sufficient firepower onto either of the captured machines, so it reversed out of sight.

Mattersly listened anxiously for acknowledgement from the Renoite general that was supposedly trying to overthrow Gillespie. He kept in mind that it all could be a ruse, but he had to hope.

The machine guns of both vehicles went silent. Renoite militia had begged off for the moment.

"I have to reload here," Mulhaney said. "Both belts are about out."

"Do it. Quickly," Reginald replied.

Just as he finished speaking, an explosion rocked the parking garage.

"What the hell was that?" Elias wondered aloud and froze. "Artillery?"

"Just reload, now!" Reginald ordered.

Seeing no one beyond his driver's window, the major dared open his driver's hatch to listen.

Another explosion rocked the building, this time more violently. Angel opened the infantry hatch and took a look behind them. Bits of concrete and dust filled the air around the two machines. Just as she was ducking back inside, a third explosion struck the building, directly above them. The outer hull was struck with falling concrete from the ceiling.

"Mortars!" Reginald shouted into the microphone for the benefit of their new ally, Sergeant Schamski.

He slammed the driver's hatch, locked it, and extracted himself from the seat, leaving the helmet behind.

"Angel, get into the driver's position and move if I tell you. We are being shelled!"

With that order given, the major snatched up his Dragunov and lowered the rear ramp.

"Major, I don't know how to drive this thing!" she

protested.

"Just do it! Shut the door when I get clear!" he shouted as the next mortar round struck against the side of the parking structure, this time on their floor.

Mattersly was shielded by flying bits of concrete by *Necromancer*, which was immediately covered in dust.

Reginald used the dust as cover for his run to the southwest corner of the building. He had judged from the trajectory of the first three rounds that whoever was launching the mortars would be found in that direction. He crouched low as he met with the wall, pulled his beret from his tunic's breast pocket, and placed it on his head. The action was more out of necessity than pride, for the gray surface of the cap would not reflect the sunlight.

Another mortar round struck nearly the same place as before, only one floor below. Wasting no time, he took a peek over the top of the waist-high wall, where his eyes found another large hotel across the street. Having adjusted his eyes for distance, he immediately located the mortar crew, who had taken a room on a floor slightly below the level of the garage on which *Necromancer* and *Wolfhunter* were trapped.

He quickly reset his eyesight to normal and brought up his Dragunov, being careful to remain in the shadows. Reginald watched as the crew fired a sixth round. In seconds, it was clear that this one was going to be rather close. He lay flat and covered his head as the round struck just left of his position, taking out the short wall and the leading edge of the pavement. Mattersly felt several bits of concrete strike him and was covered by dust.

His ears rang despite the audio devices' cancellation attempts and his eyes burned from the dust. Reginald noted that *Necromancer* had again opened fire on targets trying to come up to their level. Without further thought, the major rose upon one knee, lifted his rifle to his shoulder and located a target. It was the mercenary attending or perhaps firing the mortar.

Reginald squeezed the trigger and dropped him. Training told him to move to another location, but he had found Renoite militia to be undertrained and inexperienced. He found a second target. This one was another militiaman which came to the aid of the man Reginald had just brought down. With another squeeze of the trigger, the second man was felled.

This time, Mattersly did drop to the floor to crawl to another location. It was none too soon, as the place where he had just fired from was struck with a smattering of assault weapon rounds, returned from the militiamen supporting the mortar. As the two Stryker's fired at targets that he could not see, the major lifted his body onto his knee and prepared to take another look. Just then, the seventh round struck the parking garage, close enough to knock him flat.

***

Ricky Desmond tried desperately in between exchanged gunfire to reason with the Renoites protecting Gillespie's penthouse. Nothing he said worked. As soon as one gun emptied, another took over and soon, two of Holsbeck's men were wounded while another two of the opposition had at least been badly hurt.

"*We'd better get this over with fast, General,*" Sam Holsbeck sent over the implant in text, "*I'm sure that we'll have people out flanking us from below soon.*"

"Agreed," Desmond spoke aloud.

He was glad to have someone like Captain Holsbeck around, as he had not even considered reinforcements arriving to back up Gillespie's security force. He was not sure if there were three or four men above them, but they were careful about exposing themselves to fire.

Ricky leaned forward, shaking off the hand that tried to hold him in place for his protection. Now was not the time to be careful. The old gambler could see that all the men above them could hit were the railings and the leading edges of the staircase. The railings were dangerous, because they were causing fragments of the bullets to ricochet, which had wounded both of Holsbeck's men.

"*Keep two men back and have them fire up the steps in intervals*," Ricky Desmond ordered in a text message to Captain Holsbeck. "*You, me, and the corporal are charging up, keeping as close to the walls as possible on the way.*"

Sam Holsbeck nodded and moved off to tell the men in person. They were too young to have implants and needed to be told in verbally or with hand signals. Ricky Desmond and the corporal flattened themselves against the outer wall, pressing their hips against the mounted handrail.

In a moment, Holsbeck returned and went to take his place at the head of the line when Ricky held him back. The captain had no chance to protest as the older man simply started taking the stairs two at a time. The men at the rear fired upward as commanded, keeping Gillespie's men back.

***

Mattersly scraped himself up from the ruined asphalt and was aware of a deep pain in his left side. He had been struck by a flying piece of concrete. He ignored it and lifted himself onto one knee. Putting himself at risk of being seen, the major moved forward and rested his Dragunov upon the half-wall. Reacquiring his target, he fired and killed the militiaman that had taken over the mortar. With his next round, he rendered the mortar itself useless by placing a substantial dent into the firing tube. Others with that fallen militiaman returned small arms fire, but their accuracy paled in comparison to Mattersly and his Russian-made sniper rifle. Every one of them that approached a window was taken down by at least one seven-point-six-two millimeter round.

Reginald emptied one magazine, retreated into the shadows to reload and popped back up on the other side of the concrete divider. Looking through his scope, he found two targets remaining and he quickly dropped them both.

Behind him, the two Strykers held their positions. Both fired at the persistent Renoite militiamen that were trying to ascend to their level of the parking garage. Mattersly sat for a moment with his back to the wall, placing his empty magazine into a pocket. Movement out of the corner of his eye caught his attention.

Militiamen poured into the parking garage from the third floor access door. Reginald scrambled to his feet and bolted for the cover of the personnel carrier to his left as the Renoites filled the air with lead rounds. The major slid to a halt and crouched behind the rear tire of *Necromancer*, trying to figure out where to go next.

From inside *Wolfhunter*, Elias was made immediately aware of gunfire from his extreme right and swung the turret to return it. His first volley sent three men to the floor in bloodied masses. The third one had just thrown something in the air. Mulhaney cussed to himself, expecting a grenade.

Amongst the gunfire that filled the third floor of the parking garage, a piece of shrapnel was heard striking the floor and then the wall to Reginald's right. The major gave it a cursory glance and threw his body around to the front of the rear tire, hiding his entire self behind the hunk of rubber just as the hand grenade exploded, filling the air with shrapnel, much of which struck the tire and the vehicle.

Major Mattersly crawled out from behind the life-saving tire and went flat onto his stomach, bringing the Dragunov to a firing position as he searched for targets that had entered through the door. Even with his implants' hearing protection, his ears rang, so he knew that he would have to keep his eyes moving to compensate. As he swept his eyes left, an unbelievable sight came to him. Somehow, a militiaman with an anti-tank rocket had made it to the northwest corner of the garage and was partially concealed by shadow. In the dimmed and dust-filled air, he had made it without being discovered and was now aiming his shoulder-held weapon at *Necromancer*.

With speed that would later prove to have pulled a series of muscles, Major Mattersly swiveled his body to bring his rifle to bear. In lightning-quick succession, two rounds felled the mercenary, but not before the rocket had launched.

***

Desmond rushed up the stairs as his squad fired from below. As the first of the guards came into view, Ricky squeezed the trigger on the assault weapon and took his target to the ground in a mass of lead and blood. Still running, the second target was taken by surprise and had no chance to raise his weapon before suffering the same fate.

The third man had caught onto the trick by this time and spun on the general, who dove onto the landing with a spent magazine. The third guard's rounds went high, spreading chips of cinderblock into the air. Holsbeck, who was right behind Desmond, took this man down with a flurry of lead.

The fourth man slipped out of sight behind the door to the penthouse level and locked it behind him.

***

The anti-tank rocket was sent high as the launcher of the weapon was killed. The missile screamed toward *Necromancer*, struck the angled armor on the vehicle's nose and was redirected into the ceiling, where it detonated. Concrete and steel was ripped apart and sent crashing to the floor, partially covering the two armored vehicles and obscuring the vision of anyone trying to conduct combat for several long seconds.

Dust filled Mattersly's lungs and the area around him went gray. He could not see more than a few feet in any direction. At that moment, Mulhaney contacted him via the implant.

"*Where are you? Are you all right?*" the man sent.

"*I believe I am, yes,*" Reginald answered.

"*What the hell was that?*"

"*Anti-tank rocket. Someone made it to the northwest corner before I took him down,*" Mattersly explained.

"*Necromancer was reloading. I doubt he saw him,*" Elias composed and sent as he fired at movement in front of them. More militiamen were trying to crawl up to their level. "*Get back in here, Major. Please!*"

"*On the way,*" Reginald answered as the guns of *Necromancer* resumed. He knew they would have to get out of here soon, whether General Desmond was able to retrieve the girl or not.

Angel dropped the ramp of their stolen vehicle and she hopped out, spraying the area near the door with suppressing fire as the twin fifties on the quickly swiveling turret seemed to drill holes in everything it saw.

As Reginald ran to enter the vehicle, he counted at least nine bodies of men that had come through that side door. Whether or not they were all dead, he could not tell. He jumped inside, tugging Angel's sleeve to bring her with him and slapped the button to lift the ramp.

"Holy shit, Major," Angel exclaimed. It was obvious that her ears were ringing quite loudly. "You look like the building fell on you."

"It did," he answered loudly enough for her to have heard. "The mortar fire should stop, at least for a while."

"Best news I've heard all morning," Mulhaney said

from his gunner's chair. "We've got to get the hell out of here, Major."

"I know," Reginald answered as he pocketed his dirty beret and put the helmet back on.

He was about to contact the driver of *Necromancer* when the young man's voice cut him off.

"I've got infantry in the parking garage across the street… dead ahead," he called shrilly as he fired.

Reginald verified it. Directly to the north of them was another parking garage for the massive three-hotel complex. Men in gray and black uniforms were moving about, taking cover once their positions were sprayed with fifty-caliber rounds. He knew that the odds were good that a few of them held anti-tank weapons. Fortunately, the structure appeared too narrow to accommodate other Strykers.

"He's quite correct, Mister Mulhaney," the major stated.

"That's great, Major, but I've got guys trying to come up from below."

"There's still a few of them trying to come in from that side door!" Angel shouted. She had opened one of the infantry hatches at the rear of the vehicle and was busy suppressing entry from there.

"I say, Sergeant Schamski, do you read?" Mattersly called.

"Yes, sir!" the young man answered while keeping his gun busy.

"Have you heard from General Desmond?"

"Not yet, sir!" the young soldier answered.

"Major, I've got a problem here," Mulhaney put in. "I think the barrels are gettin' hot. The accuracy just went to shit."

"Slow your rate of fire, Mister Mulhaney. You, too, Sergeant," the major ordered. "We're overheating the barrels. They'll seize up entirely quite soon."

Both men acknowledged the order and became picky, but the major knew that it was simply a matter of time.

"Shit!" Angel called as she ducked inside. She had emptied her magazine just as a militiaman with a special weapon appeared. "EMP!"

"Where?!" Elias growled just as the Stryker's power failed and the engine coughed to a stop. "Crap."

"He came in through the side door! He's hiding near one of the pillars! Southwest corner!" Angel shouted as she slapped another magazine in place.

Mulhaney pulled his revolver from his belt and threw the gunner's hatch out of his way. As his eyes scanned the area, he promptly found targets and fired, filling the open concrete structure with its thunderous reports. Each one brought down a militiaman. The fifth one held the electromagnetic pulse weapon that had robbed his vehicle of power. With the handgun empty, Elias dropped back down inside and went about reloading as fast as he could.

"Angel! Cover fire!" he yelled.

The girl straightened and popped up through the hatch. In seconds, her M27 peppered the area.

Mulhaney watched the major as he reloaded his weapon, one cylinder at a time as was the limitations of the gun's design. Mattersly was frantically going through the Stryker's fuse box, as he tried to determine which fuses had been destroyed by the electromagnetic pulse.

"I hope you brought down that blighter, Mister Mulhaney," Reginald called over his shoulder.

"I did, sir," Elias replied just as his fifth round was replaced.

Without another word, he emerged from the gunner's hatch and proceeded to return fire.

"Ah!" the major shouted as he located a decimated fuse and replaced it.

When the lights in the cabin did not return, he continued his search. The very next one he found had also been destroyed, so he replaced that one as well. He was rewarded with ambient lights and a low hum.

"Ha!" he exuded as he reached over to the driver's position and ignited the engine.

Instantly, the vehicle's computers began their reboot process. It would be minutes before they would find out if the systems had taken any damage.

Mattersly propped open the commander's hatch and put his Dragunov to work, searching primarily for infantrymen with anti-tank weaponry. He found targets across the street and engaged them as Mulhaney and Angel both shouted that they were reloading. To their left, the major could hear *Necromancer* was still firing, swinging the twin guns from the ramping entrance to the third floor and the militiamen gathering across the street.

In moments, Reginald needed to reload his rifle and took cover inside the Stryker. Seeing Mulhaney reloading his handgun, he ordered, "Try the fifties, man!"

Elias glanced at the computer monitor and noticed that they were ready for firing.

"Back in business, Major!" he called and slipped into the seat, slamming the gunner's hatch shut.

Mattersly made the decision at that moment that he would attempt an escape of the premises. He was certain that Desmond and his men had failed.

***

The entire squad, including the two wounded men, made it to the penthouse's stairwell door. They were tired and shaken, but angry and determined to finish the job.

"Brooks," Captain Holsbeck said to the largest man on the squad. "Door."

The big man said nothing as he took three brisk steps toward the metal portal, removing it from their path with a kick on the fourth step. He followed through and stepped into the foyer. Stupidly, the guard inside the penthouse panicked and fired through the doorway. Brooks jumped out of the way and returned fire, both combatants tearing huge gaps in the apartment's front door. Holsbeck jumped into the foyer to back up his man. Inside, he could see that furniture had been rearranged around the door in a roughly 'U' shape.

"Smoke," he muttered to Brooks.

Both men took the smoke grenades from their pockets and pulled the pins. Nodding to each other, they threw them inside simultaneously.

Desmond and two others moved into the foyer.

"I've been up here a million times, Captain. Follow my lead."

To this, Holsbeck did not object. He knew the gambler-turned-general was correct. He nodded and tightened his grip upon his weapon.

Ricky shot a slanted grin to the men behind him and burst into the room with all his speed. In the smoke, he could not see the body of the last of Gillespie's militia guard and promptly tripped over it. However, as he knew that the majority of the living quarters lay to his left, Ricky bounded back onto his feet and faced that direction.

Immediately, he was fired upon by Clima's twin forty-fives. With the room full of smoke, Ricky was afraid to hit the Hernandez girl, so he dropped flat to the floor. In the thick haze created by the smoke grenades, Harry's slugs were wild and aimless, much like the man himself.

"Whoever you are… I have reinforcements coming!" Gillespie screamed shrilly from somewhere ahead.

Ricky could see that Holsbeck, Brooks and two of

the other squad members were inside the penthouse and taking cover. However, they, too, could not see the shooter and did not return fire.

In another moment, Ricky counted fourteen shots. Harry was empty. From directly ahead of his position, Desmond could hear the little twerp attempting to reload. Without further thought, he lunged into the slightly clearing air. On his third sprinting step, he was able to see Gillespie's bodyguard. With all his weight, Desmond rushed the littler man and struck out with the butt of the assault weapon. The impact destroyed much of what Clima had left for teeth and sent him to the luxurious carpet like a sack of beans. Desmond landed on his unconscious body and heard several distinctive snaps. Whether they were of bones, ligaments or both, the deposed general could care not.

Ricky sprung back upon his feet and found Gillespie on his throne, holding his prized revolver to Nora Hernandez's head. Desmond took aim of the insane mayor's face.

As the smoke continued to clear, Gillespie recognized his former ally.

"Desmond!" he howled with passionate frustration. "How the hell are you not dead?! God damn it!"

With the smoke clearing, the cornered leader of Reno began to count the men in the room, all pointing their weapons on him, save the one at the rear who was watching the door. All were wearing the familiar gray and black of the Reno Militia.

"How dare you point those weapons at me." Gillespie spoke deliberately and sadly. To Desmond, the man looked as if he were going to weep. "You are my subjects, and I, your king."

"Let the Hernandez girl go, my Lord," Desmond attempted.

"Betrayed," Gillespie said forlornly. "You betrayed my trust, General Desmond."

Ricky was not about to get into an argument. Instead he sent a message to Holsbeck. "*Does anyone have an EMP?*" he asked.

An electromagnetic pulse could be used to knock the handgun from Gillespie's grip. He transmitted this idea to the captain, who agreed.

Holsbeck lowered his assault weapon and stepped to the rear of Corporal Gifford. He fished through the young soldier's pocket and retrieved the low-powered device. "*It's only a handgun, sir,*" he transmitted by text. "*It's good for one, maybe two non-lethal shots.*"

"*That's all right, Captain,*" Desmond composed and replied. "*Focus on his handgun and get ready to give it a shot.*"

Gillespie looked to each man in the room with desperation. "All I ever wanted was to rule this land with a queen by my side. Was that too much for a ruler to expect?"

"It's over and done with, Gillespie," Desmond said plainly. "There's nowhere to go. You've overplayed your hand."

"Have I?" the self-proclaimed King of Reno said and smiled sadly as his eyes turned to the child wrapped in his arms.

His thumb moved to the hammer of the revolver.

"Don't do it," Ricky warned. "You won't get out of this room alive if you kill the child."

"You've all come here to finish me, anyway, Desmond!" he called out in sudden fury.

"No, Sire, we need you," Ricky said in the most sincere manner possible.

Gillespie blinked. In his surprise, the thumb rested on the hammer.

"What?" he nearly whispered.

"We need you to give the order to our forces," Desmond said. "All the enemy wants is the little girl. That's all."

"My militia is… defeated?"

"Not yet, sir," the deposed general explained. "We can rebuild and live to get back at them another day. It was a dirty surprise attack, Sire. They just have us at a disadvantage."

"Live to fight another day?" Gillespie murmured absently.

"That's right, sir. *If* we give them the Hernandez girl."

A devilish grin appeared on the King of Reno's face. Desmond knew that his ploy was only working halfway. He was mad and was going to kill her.

"They can have the little bitch," Gillespie seethed, "*in a body bag!*"

Holsbeck took the chance and fired the EMP pistol. With a report which resembled static electricity and a baseball bat striking a pillow, the pulse hit Gillespie's gun hand, forcing it off target. The girl took the opportunity to wrestle away from her tormentor and mostly made it, for Gillespie's left hand let her slip, but he was quick enough to grasp a handful of hair.

As Gillespie recovered himself, Desmond's finger tightened on the trigger of his weapon, as did those of the rest of the squad. Sam Holsbeck followed up with another EMP blast, which struck the King of Reno on the temple, knocking him off his throne, unconscious.

Nora Hernandez escaped, but not knowing where to go, dropped to her knees, and fell to sobs.

"Captain, call *Almighty Oz* and see what you can do to get this mess halted," Desmond ordered and went to the girl.

"Yes, sir," Holsbeck acknowledged.

As he passed Gillespie, he removed the giant revolver from the injured man's hand before getting on the phone.

"It's all right," Ricky said to the young girl as he set down the assault weapon and discarded his borrowed combat helmet. "You're okay, Nora. You're going home."

She said nothing through her hysterical sobs as Desmond swept the child into his arms.

***

The activity in the parking garage was not improving for the two Stryker crews. While militiamen had stopped trying to enter the floor through the side door, the incoming fire from across the street had increased.

"I have to reload!" Schamski called over the radio.

"Very well, Sergeant," Mattersly acknowledged. "I suggest you be expedient. These boys are not giving up."

"He better do it quick," Mulhaney stated, "I'm almost out, too."

Mattersly dropped inside the vehicle and shut the hatch above him. He scrambled to reload his Dragunov's magazine when he realized that he did not have enough rounds left to fill one. "Hell and blast!"

"Same here, Major," Angel chimed in as she shook an empty magazine before dropping it to the floor.

Elias fired a few more rounds of the twin fifties and then stopped. He traversed the turret back and forth quickly, but found no targets. "What the hell?"

"What's happened?" Reginald asked from his side.

"Major Mattersly! Get on Tac channel one!" Schamski called.

Quickly, the Major did so and activated the main speakers. The voice of Gillespie filled the vehicle.

"I say again: All Renoite forces are to cease hostilities immediately," the man said.

To Mattersly, the man sounded exhausted and beaten. He hoped that his depleted state would not insert doubt into the minds of his most devoted soldiers.

"We are surrendering, for the moment, to Major Mattersly's SRR and Eighty-Second Airborne forces."

"Nice," Mulhaney said, grinning.

"Further, I am handing control of the city of Reno to General Ricky Desmond," Gillespie went on, "whose arrest order I hereby rescind. As I am in need of recuperation, you, the militia of Reno, will carry out his orders as you would mine. All hostilities are to immediately *cease*. That is all."

"Hot damn," Angel mumbled before collapsing along the seats of the carrier.

"Well, let's hope that his men carry out those orders," Mattersly said with some skepticism.

"This is General Desmond," Ricky's voice floated over the radio. "To Major Mattersly, I ask that he and his forces remain where they are. I will be presenting Miss Hernandez to you personally in a few moments. To all Renoite Militia, I reiterate that hostilities are concluded. No reprisals against members of the SRR or Eighty-Second Airborne will be tolerated. Desmond out."

"Well, I'll be damned," said the major.

Through his commander's periscope, he could find no trace of Renoite militia and in a few minutes, Sergeant Schamski knocked on the back door of *Wolfhunter*.

Angel and Elias looked at the major before lifting a finger.

"Go ahead and open it, please, Angel," he granted.

She pressed the button by the door and the ramp dropped, clanging on the pavement.

"General Desmond's on his way down with the girl," Schamski announced with a smile. "He kindly asks that you don't shoot him," he chuckled.

"I think there's been plenty of that today," the major replied.

There was no trace of a smile on his face as he looked over the casualties on the monitor. He had hoped that Gillespie would have surrendered the girl after he had destroyed the Cobra and the fabrication building.

In a few moments, Elias could see a man and a young girl emerge from the ruined door. The girl, upon seeing the dead militiamen, halted and began to cry. Desmond bent and picked her up, pressing her face against his shoulder to keep her from seeing any more.

"Here they come, sir," Mulhaney said quietly.

Reginald stood and stepped out of the vehicle, slapping dust from his beret before placing it on his head. He tried not to react to the pain in his ribs. He was sure that the bits of concrete had delivered some bruising. Upon seeing the approaching pair, he stood erect and saluted.

Awkwardly, Desmond returned the gesture and set Nora onto the floor in front of him.

"Major," he greeted.

"General Desmond," he returned and introduced Angel and Mulhaney, who had stepped out to join the others.

With little prodding, Nora stepped toward her rescuers, naturally gravitating to Angel, who scooped her up and held her tight.

"Well, I'm glad this is over," Ricky said and stuck out his hand.

"Is it?" Mattersly inquired with a hint of doubt and withheld.

"Oh, yes," Desmond nodded and kept his hand out. "Gillespie will never regain power over Reno. We made him say it was a temporary handover to help keep the reprisals down."

"I see," Mattersly said and shook the gambler's

hand. “I sincerely hope that we can put this unpleasantness behind us.”

Ricky chuckled, “Unpleasantness? Major, your forces have taken Reno apart. Not that I blame you for any of this. Just so you know, I never wanted anything to do with this campaign against Lovelock. It was wasteful and stupid and I always advised against it.”

“And yet, you were the one in charge of the militia,” Reginald said with a hint of accusation.

“I never wanted the job, Major. Still don’t. I’ll be ditching the title as soon as I can.”

“Good to know.”

“I take it that your forces are withdrawing as we speak?” Ricky asked with hope.

Mulhaney chuckled. Angel smiled. Reginald grinned and tilted his head back slightly, looking down his nose upon his opponent.

“What’s funny?” General Desmond inquired and went white.

The thought occurred that Reno was now in the hands of a superior, occupying force.

“I have a feeling that I can trust you, Desmond,” said Mattersly. “You see, I *am* Major Reginald Mattersly of the SRR and this *is* Elias Mulhaney, formerly of the Eighty-Second Airborne.”

Mulhaney turned and displayed the tattoo on his bicep. “Five hundred and fourth parachute regiment, to be exact.”

Desmond’s mouth dropped as he looked to the short-haired blond woman.

“I’m just a lil’ ol’ spy. Helpin’ out,” Angel said with a wink.

“Are you tellin’ me that’s all of ya?” Ricky Desmond leaned forward, incredulous.

He glanced at Sergeant Schamski, who shrugged.

"Before you become too angry, General, just remember that you got what you wanted. Gillespie's been removed from power," Mattersly added.

Desmond shook his head and began to laugh. He and the entire Renoite militia had been bluffed out of a game of high stakes, and he had helped them do it. As his laughter leaned toward the hysterical, he took a deep breath and brought himself under control.

"You'd better get the hell out of town before anyone else finds out," Ricky said through an amused grin that would not quit. "Sergeant, tell the captain it's clear to join his rig."

"Yes, sir," Schamski agreed and stepped inside *Necromancer* to make the radio call.

"We'll escort you out of town. Take this thing with you, you've earned it," Desmond granted.

"Very well, General," Mattersly said as he urged his companions and the child aboard, "I hope next time we meet, it will be under peaceful circumstances."

"Me, too, Major. But you can bet it won't be another game of poker," Ricky chuckled.

"Quite," Reginald grinned and gave a casual salute as he boarded and shut the ramp behind him.

***

With the Platinum Reata's exit secured, the two Strykers drove off without incident, other than a few bottles and rocks thrown at them as they drove by Gillespie sympathizers that disappeared quickly. As the blocks rolled by, however, the speeding vehicles barely warranted a look from either Renoite citizens or militiamen on the street.

Necromancer led Mattersly and his companions of *Wolfhunter* to I-80 and pulled over just beyond the checkpoint at the Greg Street overpass.

"Mattersly, Desmond here," called the new mayor of Reno. "Give our regards to Miss Hernandez once you get home and let her know that I intend to fix our relations."

"I will, Mister Desmond," Reginald replied into the helmet microphone as he steered around them. "Thank you for your help today."

"No problem. Desmond out."

Mattersly turned the transmitter off and turned to talk to Angel. "Make sure nothing's following us for a bit, would you, love?"

"Sure," she answered and popped the infantry hatch. The sun was nearly in her eyes as it was nearing 09:30 hours. She shielded them with her hand and watched *Necromancer* turn around and head back through the checkpoint.

"They're headin' away, Major!" she called.

"Smashing," Reginald mumbled as he accelerated to a speed somewhere between expedient and safe.

Twenty-two minutes later, the diesel plant, which had been running rough since being struck by the EMP, coughed and died. The machine rolled to a stop. Reginald tried a few times to restart the engine, but all power in the vehicle failed, leaving no turret movement and no radio.

"Major, I recommend we evacuate," Mulhaney said somewhat nervously.

"Agreed," Mattersly uttered as he tossed the helmet off and extracted himself from the driver's seat.

Angel found the emergency release for the ramp and it dropped to the pavement with a gong-like thrumming. In seconds, everyone had removed themselves from the vehicle and started walking along the road. Even Nora Hernandez did not seem to mind, as long as they were heading home.

"Where are we?" Angel asked after a time.

She had been watching Major Mattersly stare at the ancient roadmap in his hands, no doubt comparing it with the map in his implant.

"I dare say this is McCarren," he said with an arm passing over the assumedly abandoned buildings in the distance, which lie on both sides of the interstate.

"We've got what? Five hours to sunset?" Mulhaney asked as he trudged along on his walking stick.

He, as well as the others, had left the M27's in the broken vehicle. There was almost no ammo for them left. Even so, with only Momo's sniper rifle, his revolver, and a small nine-millimeter pistol, Elias walked along as if he was twice his own age. The heat and the unabashed sunlight would make the travel that much harder.

"That's about right, Mister Mulhaney," replied the major.

His pack felt extremely light as well. Almost all of his Dragunov's ammo was gone as were most of his C-4 charges. While he could have hoped for no better outcome of the mission, he worried about the immediate future, for though the river was nearby, they had very little food on them.

"I'm hungry," Nora said a few minutes later.

Angel slipped her some salted pork, which the girl did not like, but ate anyway.

Nearly forty minutes later, an engine could be heard. It hummed along with the easterly breeze for a time, fading in and out, before becoming constant. Whatever it was, it was traveling quite fast given the terrain. A few minutes later and the dust it raised could be seen in the sky above the interstate.

"All right, everyone," Mattersly addressed the group as he looked about for cover, "fan out and take cover wherever you can."

Angel took Nora to the center of the road and crouched down near a tumbleweed that had gotten caught on the guardrail at the center of the highway. Elias moved as quickly as he could in the other direction, lying flat in a dip in the sandy grit and brown brush.

Seeing his friends had been properly hidden, Mattersly saw no other alternative. He assumed that a Stryker was coming after them, and whether or not it was manned by Desmond's squad or some Gillespie faithful, he no longer cared. Mattersly jogged the way they had come and fished through his backpack. He retrieved two C-4 charges and linked his implant to them.

Reginald dropped the pack at the side of the road and shouldered his rifle, keeping the two armed charges in his hands. In a moment, the vehicle became visible among the heat waves rising from the pavement.

"Right then, you blighters," he whispered as he adjusted his beret, "let's finish this."

The droning of the approaching vehicle's motor was different than that of the diesel armored personnel carriers that had drilled their way into his head for the past couple of days. It was somehow still familiar. In a few more moments, the major was able to magnify his vision and he realized the reason.

The oncoming vehicle was George Innes's truck.

"Thank fucking Christ," Mattersly spat and smiled as he disarmed the charges.

They had been returned to his backpack by the time George braked to a halt next to him.

"Hello there, Major," the old man called down. "I just couldn't go back home last night. I needed to know how it would turn out, so I stayed in town. Where's the rest of your group?"

"Just up ahead, Mister Innes," said Reginald with a childlike smile. "Hiding."

"I take it from all the radio chatter that you boys and the young lady were successful," presumed George.

"We were indeed, sir."

"Then hop on up, young man, and let's get you all home to Lovelock!"

Chapter Thirteen/Epilogue

Jazz heard a loud rapping upon the door to her living quarters. Despite her instructions and the loud celebrations on the floor below, someone felt it necessary to go against her wishes. She ignored the knocking at first, hoping that it was a drunk, lost on his way to the washroom.

The knock came again, more urgently this time. To Jazz, it sounded like Marco's hand, though he above all should know better.

"What?" she grumbled.

"Jazz," Marco said through the door, "you should come down. We have visitors."

Her eyes rolled, though a feeling in her heart gave her a twinge of anxiety.

"Who?" she asked, imagining a trio of Renoite armored vehicles and squads of armed men.

"Please, just come see," he nearly pleaded.

His tone forced her to jump from her bed. She stared at the closed door as she dropped her nightgown and gathered the first clothing she put a hand to within her closet. Marco's voice contradicted her assumption as it sounded almost joyous.

Jazz's heart pounded as she sped through the process of dressing. She checked her hair. Sprayed a short burst of perfume onto her neck, and corked the aged bottle of Rye that she planned on attacking once the sun fell.

There's no way. No way they pulled it off. No chance that they're here.

Her mind raced a million miles per second and her hand closed on the doorknob to her room when she heard boisterous conversation from downstairs.

She opened the door and saw no one, though the

voices became louder. Jazz Hernandez, Mayor of the embattled town of Lovelock ran like a child to the stairwell and plummeted recklessly down them, for she had not bothered with shoes.

Jazz threw herself into the crowd of citizens, who were all too happy to make way for her to pass. The cacophony of voices confused her mind, and she could not tune in on a single word spoken to her.

The people of her town saw her approach and backed off further for her to see who had come to her place that afternoon. Firstly, her eyes found her beautiful niece, Nora. She looked very thin with her eyes sunken into their sockets and bruises upon her dirty face, but she was still beautiful. Her body was cradled into the arms of a ruggedly lean fellow with an emerald gray beret and blue eyes that pierced her very soul. He was covered in desert from head to toe, making his smile ever the more sparkling white.

Beside him was the tall and equally sandy Elias Mulhaney, leaning on a walking stick, wearing a filthy olive drab sleeveless shirt and camouflaged trousers. He looked strange without his big black hat, but she was thrilled to see him, nonetheless.

Then there was Angel. Dirty, tired but every bit as lovely as she ever was, the most famous spy of Lovelock smiled then laughed aloud when Jazz shrieked with joy upon gathering the vision before her.

Reginald set young Nora upon the floor and let her run to her aunt, only to have her aunt scoop her right back up again and pirouette several times, shouting and crying with joy. The next thing she knew, she practically fell into Reggie's arms, strong and tight they immediately became as he gathered the two remaining Hernandez women within them.

"What took you so damn long?!" Jazz shouted between kisses and happy sobs.

"Tank trouble," Mattersly replied with a smile as he accepted her welcome.

News of the returned heroes and Gillespie's fall from power spread quickly throughout the town and people from all over dropped by the club to greet and thank them.

Amidst the adulations, Jazz took Reginald to the side. As she again embraced him and stared her pleading black eyes into his blue ones, she asked lowly, "Will you be sticking around, Reggie?"

"I can't imagine a place on Earth I rather be," he answered truthfully. "The house on the ocean front can wait."

That night, Jazz's club swelled with patrons who celebrated the night away as the band played on, long after the exhausted ones had been cleaned up, fed, made drunk and had been tucked in bed.

About the Author:

Frederick was born in Chicago in 1970 and now lives in Villa Park with his wife, Rae and their three dachshunds. He began by writing fictional works all through high school, earned an Associate Degree of Applied Science in Electronics in 1994 and the Bachelor of Science in Technical Management from DeVry University in 2005.

In 2009, Frederick began writing his first novel, *The Dregs of Exodus*, which was self-published in late 2010. This was followed up with another novel, *The Pirates of Exodus* in 2012.

Throughout that year and early 2013, he continued writing and published four short stories in eBook form for Kindle. All of these stories share the same premise, but all are independent from one another, though the short eBook, *Campanelli: The Ping Tom Affair* and his third novel, published by Solstice Publishing, *Campanelli: Sentinel*, share the same main characters.
Minuteman Merlin was released for the Kindle by Solstice Publishing in March of 2015 and followed up by *Of Knight & Devil* that September.

Social Media Links:

Website: http://frederickcrook.wix.com/crooksbooks

Facebook Page: https://www.facebook.com/home.php

Twitter: https://twitter.com/FrederickHCrook

Pinterest: https://www.pinterest.com/frederick_crook/

Amazon Author Page: http://www.amazon.com/Frederick-H.-Crook/e/B00P83FW02/ref=ntt_athr_dp_pel_1

YouTube Channel:
https://www.youtube.com/channel/UCIiKxKPL6iaEmKqOLfoYbqQ